"Sweeping history, deep emotions and lyrical storytelling animate this tender love story that illuminates the inner lives of neglected legendary heroines. I loved it."
    –Michelle Gallen, Author of *Big Girl, Small Town* and *Factory Girls*

"*As a Lover* is that rare and precious thing, an historical novel whose concerns are every bit as urgent now as they were then. A story of real power, told by a writer of consummate skill. Read it. Do."
    –Glenn Patterson, Award-winning novelist and screenwriter

"We're gripped immediately by this novel, hooked into the impeccably researched history of the publication of *The Well of Loneliness*, which acts as backdrop to the coming out experience of Maggie our firefighter, whom we can do nothing but love, as she learns about herself and her world."
    –Evelyn Conlon, Novelist, short story writer and anthologist

"*As a Lover* vividly imagines the world of 1920s London, of lives riven with desire, intrigue, and ambition, with fascinating glimpses of lesbian life, full of glorious details and moving encounters. It's a riveting and immersive novel that makes wonderful links between past and present."
    –Ger Moane, Author of *Keeper of Stones*

AS A
LOVER

Hilary McCollum

Other Bella Books by Hilary McCollum

Golddigger

About the Author

Hilary McCollum is an Irish writer and creative activist on lesbian visibility, violence against women and girls, and the environment. Her first novel, *Golddigger*, won the 2016 Golden Crown Literary Society prize for historical fiction. In 2021, she completed a PhD in Creative Writing at Queen's University Belfast, which focused on lesbian historical fiction. She has written four plays, including *Life & Love: Lesbian Style*, which was shortlisted for best new writing at the International Dublin Gay Theatre Festival. Her memoir, *Funny Peculiar* (Brandon, 2008), was published under the name Constance McCullagh. She lives by the sea in Ireland with her partner, cat and two dogs.

AS A
LOVER

Hilary McCollum

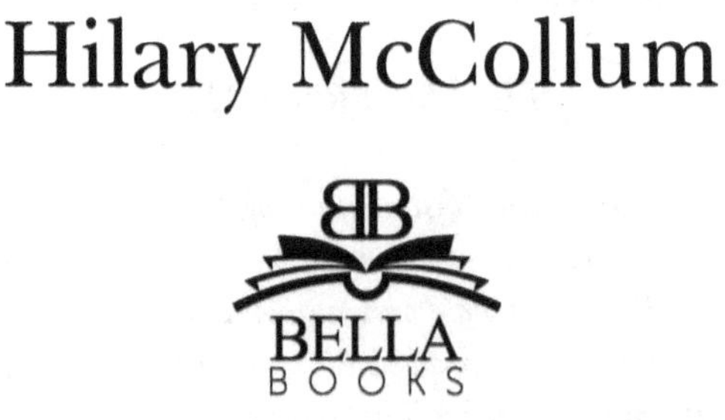

Bella Books, Inc.
P.O. Box 10543
Tallahassee, FL 32302

This is a work of fiction. Names, characters, businesses, places, events and incidents are either the products of the author's imagination or used in a fictitious manner. Any resemblance to actual persons, living or dead, or actual events is purely coincidental. The publisher does not have any control over and does not assume any responsibility for author or third-party websites or their content.

First Edition - 2026

Editor: Cath Walker
Cover Designer: Kelly Welch

ISBN: 978-1-64247-723-8

PUBLISHER'S NOTE

Acknowledgments

This novel began as the creative component of a creative writing PhD at the Seamus Heaney Centre, Queen's University Belfast. I acknowledge with gratitude the support of the Arts & Humanities Research Council, which funded my PhD via the Northern Bridge Doctoral Training Partnership. It enabled me to carry out the research that underpins the novel. I would like to extend my heartfelt thanks to my creative supervisor, Prof. Glenn Patterson, for his insightful supervision throughout my PhD and his support since. I would also like to thank Dr. Edel Lamb and Prof. Moyra Haslett for their kindness and encouragement.

The support and advice of Evelyn Conlon and Michelle Gallen has been invaluable in the process of developing this novel for publication. I've also appreciated the support of friends including Alyson Campbell, Claire Dooher, Davina James-Hanman, Dawn Watson, Fiona O'Rourke, Jo Egan, Sue Divin and Suzie Taggart. I am indebted to Dinah Cox and Rachel Wingfield for discussions about racism and trauma respectively and for their feedback on the emerging novel. Most of all, I would like to thank my partner, Darlene Corry, whose endless store of patience, kindness and encouragement has sustained me every step of the way.

Special thanks to my mum, Marian McCollum, who gave me a love of stories as a young child that has stayed with me all my life, and my "second mum," Anne Wingfield, who has always encouraged my writing.

It has been a pleasure to work with Bella Books in readying *As a Lover* for publication. I am especially grateful to my editor, Cath Walker, for her valuable insights, suggestions and feedback.

I would like to acknowledge the kindness of: Keith Knight, who lent me the biography of his great, great grandparents, *Courage: an account of the lives of Eliza Adelaide Knight and Donald Adolphus Brown* (2007) by Winifred Langton and Fay Jacobsen; the Worshipful Company of Launderers, who sent me a copy of Roy Brazier's research on Achille Serre Ltd.; Lynne Walsh and Rosalind Hardie for their help in tracking down working-class history; the Contracts and Advice Team at the

Society of Authors for informal discussions about Radclyffe Hall's contractual position; and McCall Gilfillan and Paul Maddern for providing nourishing writing retreats at Downhill Beachhouse and the River Mill respectively.

I am grateful to the staff of a number of libraries, museums and archives where I undertook research: the British Library, the UK National Archives, Waltham Forest Archives, the Working Class Movement Library, the People's History Museum and Greater Manchester Fire Service Museum. I am also grateful to the Irish Writers Centre and the National Lottery through the Arts Council of Northern Ireland for supporting my writing over the years, including funding mentoring support with Michelle Gallen and Jan Carson respectively.

Finally, I would like to thank John Radclyffe Hall and the women of the Achille Serre Ltd. fire brigade for inspiring this novel.

Dedication

To my mum, Marian McCollum, and my "second mum," Anne Wingfield

To women everywhere, past and present, who have stood up to repression and tyranny and fought for freedom, justice and a better world.

"I prefer, where truth is important, to write fiction."
–Virginia Woolf

CHAPTER ONE

I read somewhere that life works in seven-year cycles. Maybe it's true. I was born in July 1907. When I was seven, my father took himself away to war and I learned how to breathe. At fourteen, I started work at the mill and I saw my father with the blood of a dead man on his hands. I'll be twenty-one in five days' time. I won't celebrate it. It's the day I killed my mother. That's what my father always says, anyway. He'll say it this Friday, but I won't be there to hear him. I'm far away across the sea. I've been in London for six months now.

I open the front door of 65 Dunlace Road. The house is fragrant from Sibyl's cooking. "It's only me," I call, "Maggie." I feel the need to announce myself even though I've been living here a week already. Baby Girl, a mostly black terrier with splashy white paws, gallops along the hallway, greeting me like the prodigal returned.

"We're in the kitchen," Sibyl says. Her voice is upper-crust. There's a story as to why she's living in a terraced house in Hackney and not some country mansion but I don't know it.

Sibyl's the reason I'm here. She put a notice in a shop advertising a room. She'd drawn a wee picture of it, the bed and the wardrobe and the window looking onto the garden. I could hardly believe my luck when she said I could have it. A room to myself at last and an inside bathroom and everything. Her friend Tilda lives here too. I'd guess they're both somewhere in their thirties, close to my Auntie Ruth. She was thirty-six when she died.

The pair of them are sat at the kitchen table drinking tea from fancy porcelain cups.

"Did you buy anything at the market?" Sibyl says.

"Cherries." I put the bag on the table.

"I love cherries." Tilda helps herself before I've the chance to offer her one.

"Can you swim?" Sibyl asks me.

"Aye, I can swim."

"We're taking a picnic to the Women's Pond if you'd care to join us."

I left Belfast in the clothes I stood up in, taking the boat train the day after my Auntie Ruth's funeral. I've not got as far as buying a new bathing suit. Sibyl has a spare costume I can borrow. Soon we're on the train to Hampstead Heath, London passing by outside the window.

I've not been to the Heath before. The sunshine's brought the crowds out but the tree-lined track that leads to the Women's Pond has an air of tranquillity. A wooden sign reads:

Welcome to Kenwood Ladies Pond.
No men allowed beyond this point.
WOMEN ONLY

I follow Sibyl and Tilda towards a wooden platform facing a small lake. A sloping lawn to our right is strewn with towels and blankets.

"We should have got here earlier," Tilda says.

"There's plenty of room." Sibyl leads the way across the lawn to an empty patch of green. She lays out our tartan blanket.

I look around. A hundred women or more are spread out across the grass, talking in groups, or lying alone, reading or sleeping. Shrieks erupt from the lake below. I can feel the energy of the place, a buzz like a hive. My heart quickens.

"Swim first, picnic after?" Tilda says.

The changing rooms sit behind the platform. Women are in all states of undress and I don't know where to put my eyes. Auntie Ruth brought me up to keep myself private. I try not to notice the soft breasts and bristling curls. The ribbed silk of my borrowed costume is night and day from the mohair one I left behind in Belfast. I slip off my stockings and knickers and pull it up as far as I can before removing my skirt. Off with my blouse and up with the black silk over my brassiere. I unhook it discreetly and slide it out before quickly slipping my arms into the costume.

"Are you ready?" Tilda says. She's as lean and lithe as a whippet in her navy swimsuit, hard muscles visible on her arms and legs. Sibyl's more womanly curves.

I follow them out of the changing rooms. A rowing boat sits in the water next to the platform and two lifeguards are on duty. I won't be needing them. Swimming is the only thing I've ever been really good at.

You're your mummy's double. It's the mermaid in you.

Those were my Granny Palmer's first words to me. My father had kept me from my mummy's people, but the summer after he went to war my Auntie Ruth took me to Portmuck where Granny Palmer lived. I was eight years old.

"M-mermaid?" I used to stammer in them days.

"Aye, my granny, which mean's your granny's granny, was a mermaid by the name of Julie. One day, back in 1816, she was swimming in the sea off Portmuck when a fella by the name of William McClelland captured her in a net. He brought her ashore and put her on display in a salt-water bath. It was in the newspapers so it must be true." She opened a cupboard in the wall and fetched out a frail cutting, kept safe between the leaves of a book. She wanted me to have it. Auntie Ruth said no. She was feared my father would come back from the war and know she'd brought me to my granny against his wishes. I say wishes, but really it was orders, orders that were never spoken, that you had to work out for yourself and then follow to the exact letter.

The war years were a holiday. I'd visit my granny as often as I could. She'd tell me stories of elf-stones and broonies and wee-folk and witches. Granny Palmer was sunshine in a person. I met my mummy through her. Now she whispers to me in my dreams.

Tilda makes her way over to the ladder. Gingerly she backs down the steps into the pond. Sibyl tucks her fair hair into a bathing hat, ready to follow her.

"Is it deep enough to dive?" I ask.

Sibyl nods. The green-brown water waits beneath me as I stand on the edge of the platform. I hesitate for a moment then plunge in. Cold embraces me. This is my first swim since I moved to London. The freedom electrifies me. I flash through the water, racing past Tilda and the next woman and the next. I turn at the marker and speed back towards the platform. Up and down I go, up and down, needing to burn off the excess of energy that's bursting out of me. Up and down, up and down. At last, my pace slows. Treading water, I look around me. The pond is edged with dense foliage, protection from prying eyes. Back on the platform, women continue to get in and out.

"Enjoying yourself?" The woman's hair is sleek as a seal. She treads water next to me. "I was watching you from the platform. You're a fast one. You should be in the Olympic Games."

Heat rushes to my face.

"Your first time?" she says.

"It is."

"Thought as much. I'd've noticed you. I'm here every weekend. Janet Vause."

"Maggie Dillon."

Treading water, we shake hands awkwardly across the surface of the lake.

"You here on your own?"

"No. I came with my landlady and her friend." I look around for Sibyl and Tilda. "I should be getting back to them."

"Well, nice meeting you, Maggie Dillon. See you around." She winks before diving under the surface. Her head pops up a couple of yards away and then she's into a smooth breaststroke. Every weekend, I think, as I swim in the opposite direction, back to the platform. I could come every weekend.

Gathering my clothes, I hurry across the lawn. I feel ridiculous in my dripping costume when I catch sight of Tilda and Sibyl on the blanket, fully clothed. Worse still, they're not alone. An impish-faced woman sits cross-legged on a striped blanket that abuts our red tartan. An older woman lounges by her side, her long legs stretched out onto the grass. I wonder if I should go back and get changed. Before I can, Tilda looks up. "Ah, Maggie. At last."

"I'm sorry for keeping you."

"Not at all. You looked like you were enjoying yourself," Sibyl says. "These are our friends, Rachel Barrett—"

"Pleased to meet you," the older woman says, sitting up.

"And Ida Wylie."

"My friends usually call me Uncle," the imp says. I don't know whether this is a joke, a dig at Sibyl, or an instruction as to how to address her, so I just nod as if she's made a perfectly reasonable statement.

"This is our new lodger, Maggie Dillon."

"Shall we eat?" Tilda says.

I help unpack the picnic hamper—mushroom and leek tart, tomato salad, cucumber sandwiches, a flask of tea and bottles of ginger beer. I set the dishes on the tablecloth Tilda has laid out next to the blankets.

"We brought a few things, too." Uncle removes a cloth from her wicker basket to reveal bread, crackers and several cheeses.

With Auntie Ruth, a picnic was a doorstep butty at the top of Cave Hill. I hardly know where to begin with the feast in front of me.

"Tuck in," Sibyl says.

I start with the tart. The pastry is crisp and light, the filling rich and creamy.

"Mmm, the salad's excellent," Uncle says. "What's in the dressing?"

"Mayonnaise, red wine vinegar, a little parsley, mustard and a touch of garlic," Sibyl answers.

"Garlic, indeed," Uncle says. "Most English women would run a mile."

"Sibyl isn't most English women." Tilda looks at her friend fondly.

"Have you taken in any productions since you got back from America?" Sibyl says.

"No, I've been rather a homebody," Uncle replies. "Anything you would recommend?"

"We went to see *Show Boat* at Drury Lane last week. It was rather good."

"I saw it when it opened on Broadway. Have you read the book?"

"I didn't know there was a book."

"Yes. Edna Ferber," Uncle says. "Our sort of woman, I'd say. I think you'd enjoy it. Oh, and you're going to love Radclyffe Hall's new one. It's even got your old ambulance unit in it. I'm reviewing it for *The Sunday Times*. If I'm not mistaken, it's going to make rather a splash."

"How are you finding London?" Rachel asks me, her voice a singsongy Welsh.

"I like it, so I do. What I know of it so far."

"Have you found yourself a job?"

I don't waste words on the laundry where I've been working till now. Tomorrow my new life begins. "I'm training to be a firefighter."

"Firefighter!" Uncle exclaims. She smirks at Tilda.

"At the Achille Serre Dry Cleaning Factory." They must have heard of Achille Serre. It's the biggest dry cleaning company in England. They've shops all over London.

"I've never known a fire*fighter* before. Have you Tilda?" Uncle says.

"I can't say that I have. Would you pass the stilton?"

The conversation subsides and we return to eating. Surely firefighter is a job to impress anyone. It's no reason for smirking. I'm not sure I like Uncle. Perhaps if I'd told the woman in the pond I'd've got a different reaction. What was her name? Janet Something.

Vause. Janet Vause. She comes here every weekend.

CHAPTER TWO

For years I was roused at half past five by the tap, tap, tap of the knocker-upper. Out of bed and into my clothes, empty the overnight pot into the privy, a wash of the hands at the scullery sink and away to join the flood of women down North Queen Street to the mill. There's no knocker-upper in Hackney. Sibyl lent me her alarm clock but I'm awake long before it's due to go off.

I'm too excited to get back to sleep. My Auntie Ruth used to say even if you're not sleeping, you're resting. I force myself to stay in bed until half past six when I get up and go to the bathroom. I'd a bath last night but I lather soap thick on my hands and face to be extra sure I look clean. Back in my bedroom I step into my new fire brigade tunic with the shiny gold buttons that run up the front. I tie my hair into a neat bun and put on my navy cap, adjusting the angle several times before I'm satisfied I look the part.

Tilda's in the kitchen making a pot of coffee. "Ready for the big day?"

"I think so."

"Are you nervous?"

"A bit."

"I'm sure you'll be fine."

At least no one will be shooting at me, I don't say. I started at the mill during the riots of 1921. Mobs ready to rip the throat from anyone of the wrong religion, snipers to the left and right, hundreds killed. Terrible days they were.

The coffee pot is bubbling. Tilda takes it from the heat and pours two cups, one for herself and one for Sibyl, still in bed upstairs. She leaves the kitchen door ajar when she departs. I stand still, not wanting to miss anything. I know I shouldn't be listening but I can't help myself. Her tread is soft on the stairs and along the landing. She never knocks on Sibyl's door, not like I have to. Sometimes I hear them in there, laughing together. Today only a murmur reaches me before the door closes. There's no point lingering now. I hurry a slice of bread into me before setting off.

The walk to Achille Serre takes twenty-five minutes, through streets busy with the tramp, tramp, tramp of thousands of people on their way to work. When I arrive at White Post Lane, workers are already streaming into Achille Serre, a big brick building with the company name painted in fancy letters on the side. I carry on to the personnel department in the offices across the road. A wooden counter separates me from a middle-aged woman who's flicking through papers in one of the many filing cabinets that line the room.

I clear my throat. "Excuse me, I'm supposed to be starting work today."

The woman looks up and puts on a practised smile. "Welcome to Achille Serre. That's A-sheel Sair. Not A-killy Serry. Not A-kill Sir."

She comes over to the counter and hands me a card entitled Employee Record Form. While I'm filling in my details, she tells me that national insurance contributions will be deducted from my wages. "Should you wish, we can also make deductions for the holiday fund, sick club and Dr. Barnardo's Homes."

She hands me a booklet, *About Your Firm*. I go to open it. "Read it in your own time. Captain Johnston will be expecting you."

I follow her directions to the fire station, a single-storey building facing onto the yard at the rear of the Achille Serre factory. I've been imagining a big red fire engine haring through the streets, me hanging on the back ringing the bell while people jump out of the way. What I find is a black motorcycle, attached to an expanded sidecar stocked with hoses, fire extinguishers, ropes and axes. Golden-yellow letters spell out the company name. A pair of feet and the lower half of stockinged legs stick out from underneath it.

"Excuse me."

No response. I count to thirty. "Excuse me." Louder than before. "I'm looking for Captain Johnston."

"Coming," a muffled voice says.

After another minute, a woman slides out from under the motorcycle appliance on a gurney. "Yes?"

"Sorry to bother you. You wouldn't know where I might find Captain Johnston?"

The woman gets to her feet. She's taller than me, touching six foot. A patch of puckered skin disfigures the left side of her face.

"You're late."

"I didn't…I had to go to person—"

"This way."

Is this Captain Johnston? I've no chance to ask as the woman marches over to the station and through its open doors. I hurry in her wake. Wheeled fire escapes and another motorcycle appliance are parked in the large apparatus bay that lies beyond the doors. I want to stop for a closer look but she carries on to a room built into the back wall of the station. A sign on the door says Common Room. Inside there are a couple of sofas, a table and half a dozen lockers. The woman stops in front of a metal cabinet in the corner. She turns to me. "Any experience of fighting fires?"

"Not yet."

She sighs in irritation. "Not yet, *Captain.*"

"Not yet, Captain. But I'm a quick learner. Captain."

"You'll need to be. I won't stand for a weak link in my team." She unlocks the cabinet and takes out a ring binder labelled *Achille Serre Ltd. Firefighting Manual.* "Homework. Learn it or leave. Fires are dangerous. Fires in dry cleaning factories are especially dangerous. What do you know about benzene?"

"Eh, benzene. Is it…it's inflammable, isn't it?"

"Exactly, Dillon. It wants to catch fire. This factory uses heated benzene to clean everything from carpets to bow ties. A million pairs of gloves last year, 700,000 dresses, 150,000 hats…Put together a ton of fabric, temperamental machines and inflammable liquids at high temperatures and what you've got is a recipe for fires. Ones that'll spread quickly if you let them.

"Our first priority is to prevent fires from starting. Our second, to extinguish them as rapidly as we can." She removes a metal helmet and a leather-shielded hatchet from the cabinet. "Put these on."

I replace my cap with the helmet and attach the axe to my belt.

"Let's see what you're made of. Twenty press-ups."

"Sorry, Captain, what are press-ups?"

She sighs again. Dropping to the ground, she takes her weight on her palms and toes and pushes herself up and down.

I follow her example. I'm on the seventh press-up when the door opens. Two uniformed women enter. I pause at the top of the push to gawp at them.

"Keep going," Johnston says. "Eight. Nine." The others watch on as she counts me through to twenty. I do them as fast as I can. When I've finished, I get back to my feet as if the effort's cost me nothing.

"This is Dillon," Johnston says.

A plain girl my own age gives me a brief handshake. "Josie Clarke."

The other woman mutters something that I don't catch as she steps forward. I've barely ever seen a black person before let alone touched one. "P-pleased to meet you," I say. She scowls.

"Dillon knows nothing," Johnston says, letting them know that I'm a weak link. "It's up to us to make her into a firefighter." She turns to me. "What's our job?"

"Er, to, to p-prevent fires and put them out. Captain."

"We'll start with a ladder drill. I'll need you too, Seven."

Seven? Is that even a name? Johnston strides from the common room into the apparatus bay. We follow her to a metal ladder mounted on the wall. "Firefighting is all about teamwork. When I say, *prepare to lift*, get a hold of the top stile with one hand, the bottom stile with the other. When I say, *lift*, get it onto your shoulder. Ready?"

I wish I didn't have to ask which bit's the stile.

"The long side. Ready?"

I tuck my chin in, determined to do this right.

"Prepare to lift."

I grip the top stile with my left hand, my right hand on the bottom stile.

"On three. One, two, three, lift."

The ladder is heavy but manageably so. We carry it the fifty yards to the factory wall. Under Johnston's instruction, I lower my end to the ground and Seven walks it into an upright position. Johnston pulls on a rope running down the middle of the ladder. First one section and then a second extend out. The ladder towers above us. I help position it against the wall.

"Have you ever been up a ladder?"

"Yes, Captain," I say. Only once, I don't add, the day I took the tests that landed me this job.

"And do you know what a leg lock is?"

I shake my head.

"Demonstrate, please."

Seven shimmies up the first half a dozen steps, hooks an ankle round one of the rungs for a few seconds, then descends without a word.

It's my turn. I stop at the sixth rung, ready to leg lock.

"Not there. Get to the top."

Seven, eight, nine, ten, eleven, past the first-storey window and the sight of row upon row of huge machines, workers scuttling around them. The ladder bounces as I climb and the sweet aroma of benzene saturates my nostrils. Up and up, past the second-storey window, and the third. I'm a few rungs from the top when Johnston bellows for me to stop.

"Right, lock your legs."

I play Seven's movements back through my head before sticking my left leg through the space above one rung. I hook my foot around the rung below, bracing it against the stile.

"Lean back."

I tighten my grip and lean back, taking in the view of the factories that litter White Post Lane.

"I said lean back," Johnston yells. "No hands."

What? There'd been no *no hands* with Seven. When I started at the mill I was sent in search of a bucket of blue steam and everyone laughed when I couldn't find it. Maybe *no hands* is a practical joke. I look down towards Johnston, fifty feet below.

"Lean back," she barks.

I don't think she's joking. The ground looks unforgiving. Surely Johnston wouldn't try to kill me on my first day? I take a deep breath and let go. The ladder clicks and cracks against the wall but I don't fall.

"Further," Johnston commands. "Arms out. Further."

I spread my arms like a star, flying free in the London sunshine.

"Lean forward."

I pull myself towards the wall.

"And back."

A boat is docking at the canal. *Land ahoy*, I shout in my head.

Johnston calls me to the ground. Down I go, taking my pleasure with me. "Firefighting isn't a game, Dillon," Johnston says, quelling my smile. "People's lives will be in your hands."

"No, Captain. Sorry, Captain."

We return to the station where Clarke is polishing one of the appliances. While Seven and I hang the ladder back on the wall, Johnston retreats to the common room. She returns with a rubber mask with the eyes blacked out. "This way."

A low wooden structure draped in black tarpaulin lurks behind the fire station. "Smoke is the biggest enemy of any firefighter. Not only can it kill you outright, it can disorientate you. Let's see how you manage the tunnel."

I put the mask on and the lights go out. Some people are terrified of the dark. It doesn't bother me. My father used to lock me in the cupboard under the stairs. He didn't know that while he was at work, I would play hide-and-seek with Auntie Ruth. Long before he ever dragged me by the hair from the table and thrust me into that dingy cupboard, she'd made it my favourite hiding place, somewhere to sit between the coats and the coal bucket and listen to spiders, spinning me stories.

I enter the tunnel on hands and knees, crawling forward, right hand, right knee, left hand, left knee, right hand, right knee, left—My hand knocks against a wooden wall. I feel for the turn, where the tunnel bends. I shuffle right and crawl again. Hand, knee, hand, knee. A sharp turn left and another right and I'm out into fresh air. My hands reach up for the mask. I'm glad to escape its chemical taint. I blink into the sun.

I've barely time to take a breath before Johnston leads me to the front of the fire station. Seven lounges against the wall. A rudimentary dummy with only the vaguest resemblance to a person slumps next to her.

Johnston takes a whistle and stopwatch from her tunic pocket. "You've got sixty seconds to carry Charlie here to the factory and back."

I lean down to pick up Charlie.

"No, no, no. No touching till I blow," Johnston says.

I straighten up.

"On your marks, get set..." The whistle shrills and I'm down almost to my knees, hauling the dead weight over my shoulder. The dummy's lolling head thumps into my back as I force myself upright. It must be as heavy as a full-grown man, far heavier than anything I've lifted before. I half-stagger forward as quickly as I can.

Seven lopes easily beside me. "Hurry up," she shouts.

I try to break into a run. My legs are having none of it.

"Are you a woman or a worm?"

I reach the factory and turn. Can I make it back in time? Sweat's breaking on my brow, my shoulders throb.

"Come on, Dobbin."

I try again for the run but my trembling legs refuse.

"Faster, Maggot."

Half-crouching I stumble on, keep going, almost there, keep going. The ground swims, nausea threatens. I drop Charlie at the finishing point and collapse on top of him, panting.

Seven thrusts a flask into my hand. "Drink."

I ignore her. "Did I…make it? Captain?"

"No," Johnston snarls. "You did not."

No? I've always been fast. Quickest worker at the linen mill. Winner of the girls' sprint on Sunday School outings to Bangor.

"That was a plodding sixty-one-point-eight seconds."

Is Johnston going to throw me out on my first day? I look up at her stern face. "Please, Captain. I'm very quick usually. Honestly, I am. I hadn't realised how heavy…But I'll do better next time. Please, Captain. Please, give me another chance."

She looks at me for a long moment. "One chance."

I lie in bed that night remembering that moment. *One chance.* I should be sleeping. I've never had as tiring a day in my life. Johnston is relentless. All day she's had me up and down ladders, running out fire hose, lugging extinguishers around. I'm exhausted already and it's only Monday. She's testing me with Charlie again on Friday. I wish it was any other day. The twenty-seventh of July. The day I came into the world, the day I killed my mother.

CHAPTER THREE

The callus on John's middle finger was throbbing long before she got to the final box of books. Radclyffe Hall. Radclyffe Hall. A little discomfort was nothing. Radclyffe Hall. Radclyffe Hall. Signed copies boosted sales. Radclyffe Hall. And there was a certain satisfaction in the mindless monotony. Carefully she packed away the last batch of signed books. Soon they'd be on their way to Hatchards, Harrods and the Times bookshop. Let them find a welcome wherever they landed.

An unsigned copy remained on her desk. Plain ivory dust jacket, sombre black lettering.

THE
WELL OF LONELINESS
A Novel
By Radclyffe Hall
Author of 'Adam's Breed'

The design was perfect. A serious book by a serious author. She opened it at the title page.

My dearest Squig,
Without you The Well of Loneliness *would never have been written. Thank you for your never-ending patience and support.*
Your John

Would *Una* have been better on this occasion than *Squig*? Too late now. She placed the book in the top drawer of her desk. She'd give it to Una later. She checked her list of things to do for the day. Against *Sign Books* she added a tick. *Pray* was next. She called her chauffeur. "Be ready in five minutes."

John settled into the soft leather of the Daimler's rear seats. "Brompton Oratory." Absent-mindedly she sucked the callus. After the struggles to find a publisher, everything was under control. The press adverts were booked, reviews secured. She'd done everything she could. Hadn't she? She pushed away the lingering fear that she'd missed something. First-night nerves. She was always jittery on publication eve, emotions blurring like the colours on a child's spinning top. Fear, hope, excitement, hope, excitement, fear. Excitement. *The Well of Loneliness* would change the world.

The chauffeur eased the Daimler to a halt outside the Oratory. The Italianate church would not have looked out of place in Florence or Rome, a lavishly decorated symbol of the glory of God. John had first fallen under its spell twenty years earlier. She hadn't been a believer then. Attending Mass was an opportunity to spend an extra hour or two with Mabel Batten—Ladye—John's married lover.

Dearest Ladye, the most beautiful woman she'd ever met. And the kindest. Being in Ladye's presence had been sufficient blessing for John at the time. Her earliest memories of the Oratory were sneaked glimpses of her beloved knelt in prayer, or stood, head back, mid-hymn, her rich soprano blending with the choir. It had been Ladye's church then. It became Ladye and John's. Now it was John and Una's. Our Three Selves.

"I'll be half an hour," John said.

Entering the body of the church, John blessed herself with holy water. The nave stretched ahead of her, the high altar at its apex. The church was almost deserted, only a few souls lost in their own prayers. Soon the faithful would begin to arrive for confession before the six o'clock service. John would be gone before then.

Her footsteps echoed in the silence as she made her way to the Chapel of the Sacred Heart. The statue of Saint Anthony of Padua glowed behind a stand of blazing candles. She had taken Anthony as her saint when she'd been accepted into the faith. Anthony the miracle worker, patron of the lost and disadvantaged, the saint who could deal with any problem.

She bowed her head, calming her mind, focusing the strength of her faith. Carefully she lit her chosen candle, then kneeled in supplication before the statue. "Oh, Saint Anthony, hear my prayer. Please, please, please let my book fly."

* * *

It started with Pippin, singing in his cage, joyful, innocent. A shadow stole into the room. John tried to call out, "Fly away." But she had no voice. Shadow became flesh, Alberto Visetti growing larger and larger. His huge hand reached into the cage and grabbed Pippin. He began to squeeze, crushing the life out of the poor fluttering bird. As John watched, she became the bird, the fingers tightening round her throat. She felt Visetti's hardness, inhaled the male stink of him. Hair oil, sweat and lozenges. The last thing she would ever smell. Visetti smiled. "I'm going to kill you, Marguerite."

John woke in terror, a scream in her throat. Where was Visetti? She scrambled for the switch on her bedside lamp. Light flooded the room, driving him back into the walls.

Next to her, Una stirred. "Are you all right?" She sat up and switched on her own lamp.

John's hand shook as she lit a cigarette. She sucked smoke deep into her lungs. Her stepfather was dead. Sitting up in bed in the lamplight, she knew he was dead.

"What is it?" Una said.

"I thought…He tried to…Visetti. A dream. A nightmare. He tried to kill me."

"My poor darling."

"You're dead." John said it aloud, a reminder. "You're dead."

"There, there," Una soothed.

"It was so real." She touched her neck where Visetti's hands had been. "Why did he have to die now? Why now, when my book's about to come out?"

"It'll be all right, darling. I promise."

"My most important work and he's found a way to spoil it." John sucked hard on her cigarette.

"We won't let him spoil it. It's a brilliant book."

She exhaled slowly. "Are you sure, Squiggie?"

"It's the best thing you've written."

"Better than *Adam's Breed*?"

"Even better than *Adam's Breed*."

"But will people like Stephen?" Stephen Gordon, the greatest character John had ever written. How was she to bear it if the world turned from her hero?

"The pettiest of petty bigots cannot fail to be impressed by Stephen. Her name will live on for generations. So will yours."

The first cigarette had brought the edge of nausea. John lit the second anyway. "This book could ruin my reputation."

"It will seal it. You're a pioneer, darling."

"It won't win me any awards."

"You don't know that."

"I do. Newman Flower wouldn't touch it, despite all the money I've made him." Her voice took on a nasal drone. "'It would do a lot of harm to our other books.' Spineless toad. The prize-givers will be the same. They'll run scared."

"There's a bigger prize to be won. Your bravery will change the world."

"I don't feel very brave."

"You're the bravest person I've ever met."

John ground her cigarette into the heavy ashtray until it was almost in shreds. She swung her legs out of bed. "Sleep's gone for me. I'll leave you in peace."

Una's hand on her arm stayed her. "Please, darling, don't go. You need to rest."

But John knew if she were to lie down and close her eyes for more than a few seconds, she would feel again the pressure of Visetti's fingers round her throat, smell again his loathsome reek. *I'm going to kill you, Marguerite.* The hated name of the hated child. "I can't."

"Shall I read to you? Would you like that?" Una leaned over to her bedside table to retrieve Frank Harris's biography of Oscar Wilde.

"You should sleep. It's still early."

"I know, darling. But I'm always happy to read to you."

"Maybe later. I have to be up." John went over to the window and opened the edge of the curtain. St. Mary Abbott's church glowed in the early-morning sunlight. "I'm going to walk the dog."

Dogs had been part of the fabric of John's life for as long as she could remember. The light in the darkness of childhood, the comfort in the uncertainties of adulthood. A home was hollow without a dog.

It was a passion she shared with Una. They'd turned the drawing room of their first proper home together, a mock castle in Hadley Wood, into kennels for John's aging collie, their six breeding Brabançons, two French bulldogs, three dachshunds and Olaf the Great Dane. *Only twelve miles from Marble Arch*, they'd told their friends. It proved twelve miles too far. On their return to life in central London, John had established off-site kennels for their show dogs. Only Una's favourite, Mitsou, lived at Holland Street with them. The dog's short tail whizzed into action at the sight of John.

"Good morning to you, too." John stooped to fondle Mitsou's velvet ears before attaching the lead to her collar. Less than ten minutes later they were in Kensington Gardens. At this early hour few people were out walking. John was glad of the quiet. The park would restore her far more than an hour of troubled sleep.

As a child, she'd often come here with Granny Diehl, their arms hooked together, chattering as they strolled along the paths. When John came into her inheritance at twenty-one, her first home had been close to Kensington Gardens. She'd galloped away from her mother and stepfather as quickly as she could, taking Granny Diehl with her. In all conscience she could not have left the older woman to face the Visettis alone.

John wished her granny had lived to see her success as a novelist. Granny would be proud of her. It was one of life's mysteries that Granny Diehl could have given birth to John's monstrous mother. Marie Visetti was a bully. She bullied John. She bullied the servants. She bullied Granny Diehl. Visetti was even worse. He took a sadist's pleasure in tormenting John from his earliest days in their household. It was intolerable that he could reach out from beyond the grave to shake her life up again now.

Without planning it, John found herself on the path towards the Serpentine. In Granny's day, they'd always stop to feed the ducks and swans. Today John had nothing to give them. She paused instead to light a cigarette before heading north to the Italian Gardens where she took a seat on an empty bench. Mitsou gazed intently at her.

"I suppose you want up."

With her dark eyes and silky black fur, she was the handsomest French bulldog John had ever seen, and she had the champions' rosettes to prove it. John reached down and lifted the dog up beside her. Mitsou turned round twice on the bench before lying down, her head resting in John's lap. The dog's warmth and solidity were a comfort. Moments later, a slight snore signalled that Mitsou was already asleep. John closed her eyes, listening to the music of the water flowing through the fountains. In the distance she could hear a woman's voice calling. She blotted it out, tuning her mind to the heaviness of Mitsou's head and the soothing sound of the water. There was no need to worry about Visetti here, no need to worry about her book, no need to worry about anything. She had the company of the dog and the fountains and for now that was all she needed.

Suddenly Mitsou sat up. Reluctantly John opened her eyes. A fawn pug was bundling towards them. Mitsou eyed the newcomer from the stronghold of the bench.

The woman's voice came again, closer now. "Bertie."

"Are you Bertie?" John said to the pug.

He bounded closer, then dropped onto his front legs, his ample bottom thrust in the air. *Come play*. Mitsou jumped down and a festival of sniffing followed.

"Bertie."

John looked over her shoulder towards the source of the voice. The woman was young, perhaps in her early twenties. A becoming flush had risen on her cheeks.

"Have you lost a pug?" John called to her.

"Have you seen him?"

"He's here."

"Oh, please, get a hold of him, before he runs off again."

John put one hand on the pug's collar and scooped him onto her lap with the other.

"Thank you," the young woman said, arriving at the bench. "He's had me all over the park."

"It would be wise to keep him on a lead if he can't be relied upon to return."

"Do you hear that, Bertie? I think this gentleman may be right. Lead time for you."

John made a point of wearing skirts. She did not wish to deceive anyone. It did not prevent people mistaking her for a man. As the young woman bent to attach the lead to Bertie's collar, she noticed for the first time John's skirt. Her eyes flicked to John's cropped hair, then back to the skirt, then up the torso, taking in the shirt, the tie, the mannish jacket that did not hide the swell of John's breasts. The flush on the woman's face deepened.

"Come along, Bertie."

The pug remained where he was, tongue curled like a pink wave, hot breath coming in quick pants.

The woman tugged on the lead. "Bertie, come." At last he hopped down, claws briefly digging into John's thighs. The woman hurried off,

Bertie trailing behind her. John walked away in the opposite direction, Mitsou trotting at her heels.

CHAPTER FOUR

At home, what I still call home in spite of myself, I used to take myself up Cave Hill on my birthday, her deathday, and imagine the mother I never knew living in the city spread below me. If only I'd come out right, what kind of life would we have had?

Hackney has no hills. On Friday, I make do with a detour to St. John's Church on the way to work. The graveyard's quiet. I walk beneath the trees, stopping to look at the inscriptions on the headstones. In loving memory, in loving memory, in loving memory. I have no memory. I wander on among the graves of people I don't know and don't care about. Whatever it is I need, I won't find it here. My dead mother is hundreds of miles away. My father's probably at her graveside now. He always went on the anniversary of her death. He'd always go alone. Before he set off he'd remind me that I killed her.

In Loving Memory of
ELIZABETH DILLON
Beloved wife of Samuel
Who died on 27th July 1907
In her 23rd year

I've been to my mother's grave only once, the day of Auntie Ruth's funeral. It was a brutal day of wind and hailstones. My father didn't want me there. He said it wasn't seemly for a woman to be at the graveside. He'd never wanted me near my mother's grave, which was where Auntie Ruth was to be buried. I didn't care what he wanted.

We'd already rowed that day after I found him crying over Auntie Ruth's coffin. "Away with your crocodile tears," I said to him. "You never showed her a moment's kindness when she was living."

It shocked us both, me speaking up like that. He turned to face me and I thought he was going to say something in his defence. But then he whacked me hard across the face with the back of his hand. He still wears his wedding ring. It caught me on the cheek, cutting it open. If the minister hadn't arrived, I don't know what would have happened.

My Auntie Ruth's death hits me afresh, an iron punch to the heart. It was her that raired me, that loved and encouraged me. I'll never see her again or hear her call my name.

I learned long ago to swallow grief like gristle. On Armistice Day, when people were celebrating the end of the war, my Granny Palmer told me I wouldn't be able to visit her again.

"Why?"

"You know why."

And I did. He'd be coming back.

She sent me letters every week after that. Not to our house in Lilliput Street where he might find them but to a friend of my granny's on the Limestone Road. For years he never knew that I was getting secret letters from her, secret letters that kept me going. One day I turned up and there was no letter. My granny had passed. She was buried already. I went home and never let on I even knew.

I walk out of the graveyard into the busy Hackney street. It's another day of sunshine but I feel dark. I don't belong in this world.

Johnston's sitting at the common room table making notes when I arrive at Achille Serre. Seven is stretched out on one of the sofas drinking a cup of tea. "There's tea in the pot," she says.

I half-nod.

"Everything all right?" The most words she's spoken to me. It's been all insults and orders till now. Tears choke my throat. I swallow them down. The locker provides an excuse to turn away. I take my time depositing my cap and retrieving my helmet and hatchet. It gives me the chance to get a grip of myself. This is no place for weakness. Was there ever one?

Seven puts her cup down. "Shall I take Dillon on inspection with me, Captain?"

It's the first time I've been invited to take part in the daily check of the factory.

"Take the stopwatch," Johnston says, without looking up.

"Stair sprint?" Seven says.

Johnston nods.

Seven looks so strong and confident as she walks across the yard that separates the fire station from the factory. Shoulders back, head up, arms loose, hips dipping. That's how I want to look. I don't have the swagger to pull it off. And if I don't pass the Charlie test I'll be out of a job by the end of the day.

"What's a stair sprint?"

"A run to the top of the factory and back down. Five flights up, five down."

We pause at the door to the factory. "How long have I got?"

"No more than forty seconds. But if you want to impress Johnston, aim for less. Ready? Go."

Off I pelt, my feet thumping against the stone stairs. The first couple of flights are easy but my legs are burning and I'm gasping by the top. Round I turn and clatter my way downstairs, nearly knocking down a woman coming the opposite way.

"Sorry," I shout over my shoulder.

"Thirty-one, thirty-two…" I can hear Seven's voice calling out the seconds as I scamper down the last two flights. I reach her at thirty-seven.

"Well done, Maggot."

After I recover my breath, we make our way up to the top of the factory where a well-lit room is filled with rows and rows of long tables. Women and men are already at work.

"These are the spotters," Seven says. "Most important job in the factory. After us."

A woman nearby picks up a glass bottle from a tray in front of her and dabs the clear liquid onto the dress she's examining. She holds it up to the light, nodding to herself.

"Got it sorted?" Seven says to her.

"Of course. Black ink. Isopropyl alcohol. It'll need another couple of applications." She puts the dress down and nods towards me. "Who's your friend?"

"This is Dillon. Started on Monday."

"Pleased to meet you, Dillon. You have a first name?"

"Maggie," I say.

"How are you enjoying working with this reprobate?" Her laugh's a throaty wheeze, redolent of Capstans. She looks at Seven expectantly. There's a pause. "I see I'll have to make my own introductions. This one's got no manners. I'm Wilma, the best spotter in the business." She picks up a man's dress shirt from the rail next to her. A label's pinned to it. "Chewing gum, left cuff." She manoeuvres the cuff towards me. I see the mangled mess of gum on it. "It's my job to get that off. That's what my chemistry set here's for." She indicates the glass bottles in front of her. "This'll need hot vinegar. Once I'm done it gets a final clean and then back to the customer quicketty-quick."

She hangs the shirt back on the rail. "Best in the business, don't forget it." She bows towards me. I've only ever been taught to curtsey but it feels too frilly for Wilma who has the shortest hair of any woman I've ever seen. I do my best with a stiff duck of my head towards her, making her laugh. "I'll look forward to seeing you around. And don't take no nonsense from this one."

Seven and I carry on through the spotters' floor, checking that fire extinguishers are in place and that exit routes are clear. We zigzag down the building using the staircases at either end of each floor. Big cylindrical machines on stubby metal legs dominate the steamy third and fourth floors where the clothes are cleaned.

"The mill was hot like this," I say. "Hotter even."

"What kind of mill?"

"Linen. In Belfast. I was a doffer."

"And what's a doffer when she's at home?"

"Someone who fixes breaks in the yarn and replaces the bobbins whenever they're filled. You'd be on the run all day, barefoot to keep from ruining your shoes. It was a terrible place to work. The only good thing about it was singing with the other doffers to make the time pass."

"Can you imagine Johnston singing?"

> *I will not stand*
> *For a weak link.*

She laughs.

I don't.

"Are you worried about the Charlie test?" Seven asks.

I nod.

"You don't need to be. You won't fail."

"Easy for you to say."

"Easy for you to do. You just need to hold Charlie right. Get him across your shoulders, not down your back."

Johnston and Clarke are waiting outside the front of the fire station when we return from our inspection. Charlie's propped against the wall.

"Ready?"

I won't fail. I won't fail.

Johnston blows the whistle. Down I go.

I won't fail.

I heave Charlie across my shoulders and I'm off.

"Come on," Seven shouts.

It's not quite a run but it's better than a walk. Sweat beads my face as I reach the factory and turn. It looks a long way back.

"Come on."

Clarke is on my other side. "You can do it."

My shoulders ache. My legs begin to tremble.

Don't fail. Don't fail.

"Nearly there."

I'm tiring fast. Ten yards to go.

"Keep going."

My legs are trembling as I drop Charlie at the finishing point. I rest my hands on my knees, gasping in deep breaths.

"Did she do it?" Seven asks.

Johnston doesn't answer. She puts the stopwatch in front of me.

I beam wide as the Lagan Valley. Fifty-nine-point-one seconds.

Clarke and Seven pat me on the back and tell me well done. Even Johnston allows herself a momentary smile. When my breathing's back to normal, she asks, "What's our job?"

"Preventing fires and putting them out, Captain."

"What's the number one priority in responding to a fire?"

"Getting people out safely, Captain."

"How do you put out a fire?"

"Remove one of the elements of the fire triangle, Captain."

"Which are?"

"Oxygen, fuel, and heat, Captain."

"You've been studying the manual. Well done. I think you've just about earned your first fire, Dillon."

"Really?" I say, excitement bubbling through me.

"Get yourself an extinguisher."

I've been practising using extinguishers all week but there's never been a fire before. I choose a foam dispenser from the rack. Seven and Clarke each fetch one too.

At the rear of the station, Johnston pauses by a metal trough mounted on casters. It's maybe four feet by four feet and eighteen inches deep. Several steel jerry cans sit in the middle of it. "Give me a hand, Dillon."

I put my extinguisher in the trough and help Johnston haul it away from the wall and into the middle of the space between the rear of the fire station and the works canteen.

"This'll do."

I pick up my extinguisher, my heart pounding.

Johnston loosens the jerry-can lids, one by one, and pours the contents into the trough. The heady scent of petroleum soaks the air. "Right," she says to me. "I'm about to set this ablaze. How do you think we should approach it?"

"Direct attack, Captain."

"Why that method?"

"Because we have a clear line of sight to the fire."

"Good. Into positions."

Seven, Clarke, Johnston and I each take a side of the trough, standing a couple of yards back.

"Ready?" Johnston lights a match and tosses it towards the trough. Time slows as it arcs through the air, tumbling forward, bright end gleaming, a tiny flame flickering through infinity. And then it lands and the whole trough is ablaze.

"On three, engage. One."

I remove the clip from my extinguisher.

"Two."

I point the nozzle in the direction of the flames.

"Three."

I squeeze on the lever and out streams the foam. For a moment I'm caught in the beauty of the flame.

"Keep moving," Johnston says.

I step sideways, following Seven and Clarke in a circle round the fire, playing the foam from side to side, our jets battling the flames, subduing them, extinguishing them. It's out all too quickly but I know my life has changed forever. I'm not a weak link. I'm a firefighter.

CHAPTER FIVE

Hatchards on Piccadilly was not only the oldest but the best booksellers in London. Lord Byron, George Eliot and Charles Dickens had all shopped here. Pride surged through John at the sight of her book prominently displayed in the window. Twenty years earlier, she'd had to pay to publish her first poetry collection. Now she was a writer of note. Her book in Hatchards' window proved it.

"Shall we go in?" Una said.

The Well of Loneliness shared a table close to the entrance with Storm Jameson's *Farewell to Youth* and John Galsworthy's *Swan Song*. John was acquainted with both writers through the PEN Club, the international organisation of poets, essayists and novelists. She'd rather have had the table to herself but at least her book was in decent company.

John and Una positioned themselves at a display of travel books, close enough to observe any prospective buyers. Before long, a young woman picked up *The Well of Loneliness*.

"I hope this is as good as *Adam's Breed*. I devoured it in one sitting," she told her companion.

John felt a moment of uncertainty. What if it wasn't? What if the woman came knocking on Hatchards' door demanding her money back?

Not that you could do that with a book. It wasn't like returning a badly stitched coat. But still.

Una squeezed John's hand. "It's every bit as good," she whispered.

A lady with a large-brimmed hat was next to take an interest. She opened a copy with care to read the inside flyleaf, then skipped over Havelock Ellis's appreciation to the first page of the novel. Her eyes moved rapidly across the text. The woman closed the book decisively. Tucking it under her arm, she scrutinised first the Galsworthy, then the Jameson. *Swan Song* joined *The Well of Loneliness* under the woman's arm. *Farewell to Youth* was discarded.

"It's rather thrilling, isn't it, watching people buying your book?" Una said to her.

It was, but first-day interest didn't guarantee success. John took a last look at the table. She'd done everything she could. Now it was time for the public and the critics to decide.

As they emerged onto Piccadilly, Una slipped her arm into John's. "I'm so proud of you, darling."

"We've not had a single review yet," John said.

"You have mine. *The Well of Loneliness* will change everything. I'd like to get you something to mark its publication. Let's go to Bond Street."

Bond Street: the best of life's luxuries in the space of a few hundred yards. When John had first inherited her fortune, she'd taken herself on a trip to the acclaimed shopping street and bought everything that took her fancy—crocodile-skin shoes, a ruby brooch, a cashmere dressing gown for Granny. In *The Well of Loneliness*, she'd had Stephen Gordon walk the length and breadth of Bond Street in her quest for a ring for the woman she loved. Poor awkward Stephen, discomfited by the strangers who stared as she searched for that perfect pearl ring.

John knew all about the stares. Whispered comments had been part of her life for years. *Is that a man or a woman?* It had not always been so. On her first trip to Bond Street, she'd looked like any other debutante. Her hair had been long, her clothing feminine. She'd still been working herself out then. Only women excited her passions, that had long been clear to her. She'd been lucky enough to have her own money and no need for a husband. But she didn't yet know how to be comfortable in herself.

The dresses were first to go, discarded in favour of shirts and skirts. Neckties and cravats replaced sashes and ribbons, bold simple jewellery instead of anything fussy. Lastly, her long curls were shorn and tamed, the Eton crop her final liberation. Let people whisper. She'd rather put up with the stares and the comments than go back to dressing against her nature.

Una squeezed John's arm. "Say yes. You deserve a present after all your hard work. And I deserve the chance to buy it for you."

John looked at Una's eager face. How could she say no? "Only if you let me get something for you."

"But this is your day," Una protested.

"That's my condition," John said, smiling. "Go on, Squig. You deserve a present every bit as much as I do."

It was Una's turn to smile. "Where shall we go first?"

* * *

John tried to slide her new cufflink into place, but the bottom edge of the cuff slipped out of her grasp.

"Squiggie. I need help."

There was no reply.

John tried again but succeeded only in dropping the cufflink. "Damn and blast. Una! Now!"

"Have you lost something?" Una said, arriving in the dressing room to find John with her nose almost to the floor, peering under the chest of drawers.

"Yes, dammit. My cufflink." She looked up. The blue dress looked even better on Una now than it had in the shop that morning. "I've always loved you in blue."

"And I've always loved you in a bow tie." Una rang the bell with one hand and encouraged John up with the other. "No point having servants and grovelling on the floor oneself." She kissed John lightly on the cheek.

A minute later the maid had the diamond cufflink blinking in her palm. "Will that be all?"

"Yes, thank you, Cartwright." Una placed the cufflink deftly through the crisp white cuff.

"You've spoilt me." John looked at the cufflinks appreciatively. The onyx and gold setting contrasted beautifully with the bright white shirt, the diamond sparkling in the centre.

"You deserve it."

John opened the wardrobe and removed her dinner jacket.

Una took it from her. "Let me." After helping John into the jacket, she stood next to her, looking at their reflection in the wardrobe mirror. "You're as handsome as the first time ever I saw you."

"The second," John reminded her. "You barely noticed me the first time."

"The second then." She kissed John on the lips. "I thank God for you every day. I thank God to be so lucky."

They looked at each other for a moment.

"Shall we go down to The Drey?" John said.

Since John had finished *The Well of Loneliness*, they'd spent time redecorating Una's sitting room on the ground floor, creating a comfortable den. The fireplace had been retiled, a new carpet laid, an antique bookcase and two leather armchairs purchased. Una's statuette of Adeline Genée graced the mantlepiece. When they'd first met, Una had still been sculpting. They'd had more than one assignation in her little studio in Kensington, snatched moments in the hours while Una's daughter had been out with the nanny. Those days were long gone. Una had given up sculpting in favour of supporting John's literary career. And hadn't it turned out well for them both? Money and prizes had poured in. As Una herself said, it's a rare marriage that can survive two artists.

The scent of flowers filled the room. Bouquets had been arriving all day, filling every vase in the house. Purple delphiniums and pale freesias adorned one end of the bookcase. A crystal vase of red roses from Tallulah Bankhead sat on a walnut side table. A silver ice bucket held a bottle of champagne. They were only occasional drinkers but today was a day to celebrate.

"Can I tempt you to a glass, darling?"

"Just a small one," Una said.

John eased the cork out of the bottle and half-filled two glasses. They settled together on the divan opposite the French windows, looking onto the garden. Outside a nightingale sang.

"This really is a lovely room," John said.

"I thought the house was perfect before The Drey. It truly is now."

John removed a cigarette from the silver case and lit it. "How long have we got till they arrive?"

"About forty minutes."

"Would you mind reading to me?"

"Shall I fetch Oscar?" Una said. "He's upstairs."

"Actually, I'm rather in the mood for poetry."

Una fixed her monocle into her eye. After a quick perusal of the bookshelf, she chose Elizabeth Barrett Browning, opening it at a favourite.

> *"If thou must love me, let it be for nought*
> *Except for love's sake only—"*

The telephone rang. They ignored it.

"Do not say
'I love her for her smile—her look—her way
Of speaking gently,—for a trick of thought
That falls in well with mine—"

The housekeeper interrupted. "Excuse me, madam. I'm afraid your mother insists on speaking with you."

"I've told you before," John said, "I do not wish to speak with her."

"She says it's an emergency."

"It'll be another hoax," Una said, but John got to her feet.

"I won't be long."

She took the call in her study. "What do you want?"

"Oh, that's a fine way to greet the woman who brought you into this world. Never forget, you'd be nothing without me."

John sighed as she sat down.

"Don't you go sighing at me. You've no respect. Publishing today when he's only in his grave a fortnight. You're—"

"Is this your emergency?"

"I'm dying, but what do you care? You're the most hateful, ungrateful child—"

"What's wrong with you this time?"

"That nurse you hired is trying to poison me."

"I am quite sure she is not."

"That's what you're paying her for, isn't it? To murder me. And then—"

"You're being ridiculous."

"Evil child to turn on its mother—" Her mother was shouting by now. John raised her own voice in response.

"I have to go—"

"Don't you dare—"

John hung up the receiver. She sat for a moment, her head resting against the heel of her hand. What had she ever done to deserve such a mother? The phone began to ring again. She walked away from it.

Back in The Drey, she discovered that her agent, Audrey Heath, had arrived. What had started as a professional relationship had soon developed into friendship. She was their sort of woman—clever, literary, and an invert. There was something quietly attractive about Audrey, with her delicate features and hazel eyes. Her young assistant, Patience Ross, sat next to her on the sofa, sipping champagne.

Audrey got to her feet, smiling. "Sorry to be early. We thought you'd—are you all right?"

John shook her head. "It's nothing. Just my beastly mother."

"What did she want? Money, I suppose," Una said.

"She thinks I'm paying the nurse to poison her."

"Good grief," Audrey said.

"She really is the limit," Una said. "We mustn't let her spoil your day."

"Any word on reviews?" John asked Audrey.

"Tomorrow for *The Saturday Review*. *Sunday Times* next weekend. *The Nation & Athenaeum* and *Evening Standard* will both be the week after next."

"I've been following up a few others," Patience said. "No timescale for *The Telegraph* but they'll definitely review it. So too, the *New Statesman* and *Time and Tide*."

John asked about *The Observer*. She had written personally to James Garvin asking him to support her book. He was not only the paper's editor, he was also Una's brother-in-law.

"No plans as yet," Patience said. "I'll try them again on Monday."

"I suspect you'll be wasting your time." John tried to keep the bitterness out of her voice. Una's family had never approved of their relationship. Her mother had been appalled when Una left her marriage to Admiral Troubridge, horrified that her daughter would trade a respectable life as the wife of a naval hero for an unnatural union with a notorious deviant. Even Una's supposedly liberal sister questioned the decision. Twelve years on, John was still barely tolerated let alone accepted, despite everything she had achieved and how well she provided for Una.

"And how about sales?" Una said, eager to move the conversation on.

"I've been ringing round the bookshops. We're selling briskly," Patience said.

Her use of "we" was unexpectedly endearing. Una's family may not be on board, but John had her own team. She had taken a liking to the young woman who'd so efficiently organised interviews and photographs after John's prize-winning feats with *Adam's Breed* two years earlier.

"I told you." Una beamed.

"It's going to be a success," Audrey said.

"Let's drink to that," Una said.

John clinked her glass with the others but she couldn't quite let go of her fears. Nothing was guaranteed, not yet.

Later, in the midst of her friends, she forgot to worry. Una had been right to insist on a launch-day party. The drawing room was abuzz, conversation flowing as easily as the champagne. Waitresses glided among the guests, filling glasses and offering canapés.

Ida Wylie came over to congratulate her. "It's a tremendous book. I've given it five stars for *The Sunday Times*."

"That means a great deal, coming from you."

"I knew when I sent you to Audrey that you'd be a hit."

"I'll never forget how nervous I was climbing the steps to her office, *The Unlit Lamp* clamped to my chest. It's such a peculiar thing, don't you think, that simultaneous belief in the brilliance and banality of one's work?"

"Oh, goodness, I've never considered my work brilliant. I leave that to the highfalutins. My aim is to tell a good story as well as I can."

"How's Hollywood?" John asked.

"I've settled to it. I hadn't a clue the first time. I knew my book backwards but nothing about making movies. They didn't seem to mind. Paid me money and did what they liked. Now I'm rather more involved."

Toupie Lowther, looking suave in black tie, joined them. In her twenties, Toupie had been an international tennis champion and a jujutsu expert. Now in her mid-fifties, she still lifted weights every day and fenced three times a week. "I'm loving your book, Johnnie."

"How far have you got?" Ida said.

"Stephen's just kissed Angela on the lips 'as a lover.' I could hardly tear myself away."

"I'm very gratified," John said.

"Vere and Budge send their apologies," Toupie said.

John shifted guiltily. Vere had been one of her closest friends. She couldn't remember the last time she'd visited her. "How is Vere?"

"More good days than bad at the moment."

"Vere Hutchinson?" Ida said. "I didn't realise she was still ill."

"She's better than she was," Toupie said.

"Some terrible infection, wasn't it?" Ida said. "It must be two years now."

"Nearly four," Toupie said.

"Goodness. How awful."

"She's lucky to have Budge," Toupie said. "Do you know her, Budge Burroughes?"

"Not well," Ida replied. "Artist, isn't she?"

"Do you remember those monkey posters for the London Underground? That was Budge," Toupie said, as proudly as if she'd painted them herself.

"What an impressive couple. I thought Vere's latest collection of short stories was tremendous. Have you read it, John?"

"Oh, no. Not yet. I only read trash when I'm writing myself." John made a mental note to track the book down. And to visit her friends.

A few feet away Una clapped her hands together. "Attention," she called over the hum of voices. "Attention." Eyes turned towards her. Conversation lulled.

"Thank you everyone for joining us on this propitious evening. In a moment we will have the pleasure of hearing from John. But first, can we raise a glass to this genius amongst us. To John, may she get the success that she deserves."

John felt her old shyness return as heads turned to her expectantly. She wished she'd not let Una pressure her into speaking. These were her friends in the mood to party not earnest readers assembled for a lecture on the state of the English novel. She cleared her throat.

"I am grateful to every one of you for coming here tonight to celebrate the publication of *The Well of Loneliness*. I've taken up my pen in defence of the most misunderstood and vilified people in the world. It's my hope that my book will usher in a new era of tolerance and acceptance. I'm grateful to those of you who've already read it and for the kind words of support you have offered me. To the rest of you I say, the bookshops open at nine tomorrow morning."

Laughter rippled around the room. John waited for it to die out.

"I would like to thank Una for her never-failing belief in me, and my agent, Audrey, and everyone else at A.M. Heath, for their help in bringing my words to the world. And finally, I would like to raise my own toast. To Stephen Gordon and all who support her."

Women raised their glasses. "To Stephen Gordon." John allowed herself a moment of pleasure. This was her creation, recognised and praised.

"And now it's time for dancing." She nodded to Una, who'd made her way to the gramophone. It sprang to life with "Yes Sir, That's My Baby." Couples formed and began to dance the Charleston. John loved women dancing together. The drawing room was the perfect place. The scent of freak may linger in the clubs but here at home they could be themselves with no concern as to who was watching. She sashayed across to Una. "May I have this dance?"

CHAPTER SIX

My face is like a baked beetroot by the time I set off for home at the end of the Saturday morning shift. After the thrill of yesterday's fire, Johnston exercised me harder than ever this morning. It's raining. I turn my face towards it, enjoying the coolness.

Sibyl offers me a bowl of soup when I get home but I've no time to tarry. I'm only in the house long enough to take off my uniform, throw on my ordinary clothes and grab my bag. I make the train with a couple of minutes to spare. Forty minutes later I'm at the Pond. There's only a smattering of women today instead of the hundreds of last Sunday. No one's sitting on the grassy bank. Those that are here are already in the water. Other than a stout woman heaving her way into her costume, the changing rooms are deserted. Battle finally won, she leaves me in peace.

I hum under my breath as I change. It's a song Tilda and Sibyl were playing on the gramophone last night. "It's me, Maggie," I called when I got in the door but they never heard me over the music. They were in the front room, dancing, kicking their feet and swinging each other back and forth. My father would have called it abomination. He was against anything enjoyable on principle. The pair of them were laughing, looking into each other's faces and laughing. There was a shine about them that warmed and scared me. But then they saw me and stopped. The music carried on playing and I said don't mind me and I went into the kitchen even though I wanted to stay and stare but I knew I shouldn't.

It's damp underfoot on the platform outside the changing rooms. I'm careful as I make my way to the edge. I don't want to slip and make a fool of myself. I try to see who's already here without looking like I'm looking but from a distance all swimmers look the same. Once I'm in, I quickly gain on the stout woman with her sedate breaststroke. The next woman is paddling along like a three-legged dog. Someone wants to teach her how to swim properly. Next is a slow back crawler and then another breaststroker, head held high out of the water. The final woman is making good speed with a determined front crawl. It takes me nearly half the length of the pond to catch her. And that's the lot. None of them is Janet Vause. Not that I came here looking for her. I'm here to swim, plain and simple.

The changing room's empty when I finally relinquish the water after an hour. I dress quickly while it's still private. I'm famished. I stand in the doorway looking out onto the pond, eating a cheese and pickle sandwich. It isn't the feast of last Sunday, but it fills a hole, as Auntie Ruth would say. I gather up my towel and wet costume and make for the exit. Three young women arrive as I'm leaving, all talk and laughter. I walk away quickly before loneliness swamps me.

The rain is taking a break as I make my way back across the heath. People are out with dogs and prams. Up on Parliament Hill children fly kites. Even on a grey day like this you can see London sprawled in front of you. There's so much of it. I'll never fit it all in my head the way I did Belfast. I'd planned to walk home but I feel suddenly tired. I make my way back to Hampstead Heath station. I'm in the queue for a ticket when Janet Vause hails me from the street. She looks better than I remember. Her hair's cut in a short bob like an American film star. Mine hangs below my shoulders, still wet.

"Are you going to the Pond?" Janet says.

"No, I'm away home."

"Come for a swim."

"I've been already."

"Come again." Her face is bright and expectant.

"Now?"

"No better time."

"My costume's wet."

"So what? It'll get wet anyway once you're in."

She's right but there's something queasy about putting on a wet costume.

"Can I help you?" The ticket man brings me back to the queue.

"Oh, eh…"

"Go on. It'll be fun."

"Do you want a ticket or not?"

"No, sorry." I step out of the queue.

Janet beams. She hooks her arm into mine. "You won't regret it."

My costume is cold and damp. I put it on the bench next to me, not ready to face it. Janet's already out of her skirt and stockings. Her nearby semi-nakedness is unsettling.

"Hurry up." She turns towards me, blouse half-unbuttoned. Her breasts strain against a firm white brassiere.

"I'll follow you in," I say, making for the WC. I contemplate hiding in the stall till she's finished, scared of seeing more of Janet Vause than I'm prepared for and horrified that she might see any of me.

"You all right in there?" It's her.

"I'll be out in a minute. Go on in."

"I'll wait for you. It's more fun together."

I've no choice but to come out. She's sitting on the bench in a scarlet costume, towel loosely draped around her shoulders. I need to get on with it. She won't bite.

"I won't bite," she says, seemingly reading my mind. "Unless you want me to."

My face could rival her costume. I huddle behind my towel and begin to undress.

"I hoped I'd see you again."

I'm in the middle of removing my knickers and nearly drop my towel in surprise. I grab at it in panic. "Did you?"

She laughs. "Of course."

I slither the damp costume on. It clings to me like cold porridge as we walk out to the wooden platform.

"Do you breaststroke?" Janet asks.

I half-imagine a pause in the middle of the final word. It sounds rude. I've never thought about that word with a pause before. It makes me laugh.

"What?" she says but I don't answer.

"Race you to the final tyre and back?" she says. "On your marks, get set—"

There's no "go," only the splash of her hitting the water. It gives her a head start. I plunge in too. She's a good swimmer but I'm not long in catching her. The question is not whether I'm going to win but by how much. I keep it close until the last ten yards but then I let myself surge home beating her by two or three strokes.

"You was holding back, wasn't you?" she says to me an hour later. "During the race."

We're sitting in Frankel's, a fancy-pants café with gold-framed paintings on the walls and patterned tiles on the floor. Best of all are the cakes behind the glass counter that runs the length of the place. Sponges and pastries and tarts with cream and buttercream and custard and all manner of flavours and decorations. "I've seen a lot of swimmers in that pond and you're the fastest by a mile." Janet leans forward. "What else are you good at?"

I drop my head. "Oh, I don't know. Nothing really."

"Nothing? There must be something. Sport or dancing maybe."

Dancing. I'd love to be good at dancing, whirling around like Tilda and Sibyl. "I don't know."

She smiles. "You don't know much, do you?"

I smile back. "I suppose not."

The waitress arrives with our order.

"Look at that," I say. It was her choice, layer upon layer of sponge sandwiched together with chocolate buttercream and topped with caramel.

"Wait till you taste it."

I hold back so she can go first.

"After you," she says. "It was you won the race."

I raise a forkful of cake to my lips. It tastes so good that for a moment I close my eyes so I can give all my attention to it. "Oh, that's the best thing I've ever put in my mouth."

She laughs and cuts a piece off. "I told you it would be good." Now it's her turn to close her eyes. It changes the look of her—pure pleasure mixed with an innocence I've not seen before. I feel like I've strayed into her private world. I pick up my cup of tea and take a sip. It's too hot and I wish I'd blown on it.

Her eyes open, looking at me. "You should blow on that."

Our forks collide as we both make for the cake. I pull mine back but again she says, "You first."

"No, no, it was your idea."

"So what do you think of Frankel's?"

"I love it."

"Correct answer. Budapest's loss is Swain's Lane's gain. That's harder to say than you'd think. I live round the corner." She reaches over and touches my cheek. "You'll have to come visit me sometime."

CHAPTER SEVEN

"It's good to get out of London," John said.

"Let's hope you're still of that opinion when we get there. This Miss Elsner's 'little period cottage' could turn out to be a hovel."

"Of course it won't be."

"You barely know Anne Elsner. I really wish you'd consulted me before agreeing to drop everything to run down to the south coast."

"I told you, you didn't have to come." John slid her right hand into her inside pocket while continuing to steer with her left.

"Of course I had to come. How could I not?"

"By staying in bed." John flipped the silver case open and, with only the hint of a swerve, extracted a cigarette. Lighting it would be easier with Una's assistance but she was damned if she was going to ask for it. "Really, Una, you'd think I'd signed you up for an army camp on the Romney marshes. It's a Tudor cottage and we're only staying one night."

"It's you I'm worried about. I don't want you getting ill, not with our holiday coming up."

"I'm perfectly fine."

"You should be resting."

"I have been resting."

"Only when I insist. Otherwise, you're always on the go."

"And who arranged the lunches and dinners and people to tea and first nights to attend that fill up our time? I think you'll find, my dearest, that it was you." With a lurch of the car she retrieved her lighter.

"Let me help," Una said, taking the lighter from John's hand and the cigarette from her mouth. She passed the lit cigarette back. John sucked gratefully. Una lit one for herself. "I didn't mean to overload you. But Norman Haire's going to be the next big thing in sexology and I'd been putting Gabrielle off for weeks and we couldn't miss Richard's first night and Jimmy's been such a darling and we haven't even got to Vere and Budge—"

"I know, Squiggie, I know. We've a lot of people to catch up with. I'm sorry I'm such a beast when I've a book to write. It must be lonely for you."

"You are a beast. A perfect beast." Una took another drag of her cigarette. "You're lucky I love you anyway."

"I'm glad of that." John reached over and fondled Una's silky leg with one hand.

"Keep your eyes on the road," Una said, but she placed her hand on top of John's.

They'd set off early to avoid London's snarling traffic. Now the roads opened before them. It was the perfect English summer's day—gentle sunshine, blue sky, puffs of white cloud. They motored on past ripening crops and thatched villages. The tiredness that had dogged John for weeks began to slip away. The countryside had always been a balm. At Sandhurst they stopped for petrol. A road sign soon after signalled *Rye 11 miles*. Una fished Anne's directions out of her bag and read through them.

"Do you think I'll like her?" Una said.

"Anne? She's been very pleasant company the few times I've met her." She'd become acquainted with Anne Elsner through the PEN Club. They were both regular attendees at the monthly dinners held by the writers' organisation.

"Have you read any of her work? Travel, isn't it?"

"Yes, but I've not read any of them."

"Most travel writing's rather a bore."

"The only travel guide I've ever used was on my first trip to Teneriffe with Ladye."

"Was it any good?"

"Not really, no. The concierge in the hotel at Orotava told us all the best places to visit."

"If I can't discover a place myself, I'd rather see it through the eyes of a proper writer than some travel hack. Your Orotava is one of the most appealing places on Earth. If I had better sea legs I'd adore going to Teneriffe."

But John would never take her. Orotava was the place where she and Ladye had been happiest together, before Una had insinuated herself between them. Giving it to Stephen and Mary was one thing, to Una quite another. Poor Ladye. She'd deserved John's loyalty. John had intended to give it. She wasn't a philanderer, not like her father. More an occasional strayer. Ladye had readily forgiven a previous indiscretion. A full-blown affair with Una was quite another matter. It had broken Ladye's heart. John knew it as she did it, but somehow she could not quite resist Una's persistent charm.

"Have you ever been to Rye?" John said.

"I don't believe so. One of the Cinque Ports. I was in Dover and Hastings with the admiral but never to Rye."

"Sink ports?"

"First line of defence against the French and all that. Notorious for smuggling, of course. 'If you wake at midnight, and hear a horse's feet, Don't go drawing back the blind, or looking in the street.' Kipling. I read it to the Cub when she was an infant."

"Better hold on to our jewels." John smiled to cover her resentment. They'd managed to ship Una's daughter off to guide camp, her father's relatives and granny but soon she'd be back home, demanding her mother's attention. It was another of life's injustices. John had always wanted a child of her own, a son to raise to manhood. Instead she'd had more than a decade of the unsatisfactory stepness of Una's unsatisfactory daughter. She'd tried her best, God knew. In the early days she'd spent endless hours playing dominoes with the child and taking her for walks with the dogs. She'd bought Andrea her first bicycle, paid for her expensive education. The child wanted for nothing but always wanted something.

"How delightful," Una said, as they edged through the arch of Landgate, its thick walls still ready to repel the enemy. Old buildings were stacked on either side of the street.

"What are we looking for?" John said.

"East Street. It should be somewhere along—Oh, look at the ships."

A gap where buildings gave way to railings afforded views down the river to the tall ships in the harbour. John had the briefest of glances before returning her eyes to the road.

"East Street. Left here. And right at the top," Una said, consulting the directions. "Then left. Here. Left." The car juddered over cobblestones down the road past the church. "She says to park wherever we can around Church Square."

"It's too narrow here," John complained.

"I'm just telling you what she says."

The bottom side of the square was fractionally wider than the one they'd just come along. John nestled the Daimler against the curb and switched off the engine. The cries of gulls filled the air as she stepped out of the car. She stretched and looked around. The centuries-old parish church dominated the centre of the square, flanked by a pleasing mix of timber-framed and red-brick houses. Una was still seated in the car. John went round and opened her door with a half-bow. "My lady. Sorry if I was short."

"You know how I hate directing you," Una said, getting out.

"You did very well." John smiled. "Lead on, Friday."

Mollified, Una returned to the directions. "She says to look for an archway opposite the south side of the church."

They missed it the first time and had to retrace their steps, looking and looking for the entrance to Hucksteps Row. "Ah, here it is," Una said. It wasn't so much an archway as a doorway without a door, so low that both women felt obliged to duck as they walked through it into a narrow passageway. Cottages crowded in on both sides but then the path kinked to the right, opening up views of sunlit countryside. Journey's End was the final cottage. The white paint was peeling and the criss-crossing timbers a faded black, a hard-times version of the Tudor dwelling John had imagined. But there was something inviting about the overgrown garden and the bell hanging beside the porch. She pushed open the wooden gate.

Anne Elsner was out of the cottage with handshakes of welcome before they'd even rung the bell. "Come in, come in," she said, bluebell eyes smiling warmth.

They followed her into a low room with a beamed ceiling. "It was let furnished," Anne said, noticing Una looking round at the jumble of furniture. "But it's the perfect bolthole for me between trips abroad. Shall I show you to your room?"

They climbed the warped staircase to the next floor.

"How old's the house?" John asked.

"Sixteenth century, I believe, though a lot of the interior's been vandalised. If I owned it, I'd rip out the fake wooden panels and bring it back to itself. Anyway, here you are. I'll leave you to freshen up before luncheon."

John gazed out at the river snaking across the marsh to the lighthouse and lurking sea. "Look at the view. Not bad for a hovel."

"Don't tease," Una said.

"It wants old oak furniture and the outside repainting. Can you imagine what fun it would be to do up a house like this."

"Don't go getting any ideas. We've only just finished The Drey."

"Ideas? I don't know what you're talking about." John laughed. "Shall we go down?"

The dining room was furnished with an ugly table and mismatching chairs, but the sublime views made up for the decor. Luncheon was served by a sturdy woman in a pristine apron. The crab soufflé was as good as John had eaten in restaurants in Paris. It was followed by a platter of salmon mousse and a tureen of minted potatoes.

"You've certainly got yourself an excellent cook," John said.

"I don't know what I'd do without Mabel. She's five servants in one. I'm always glad to get back to her care."

"I suppose you must travel a great deal," Una said.

"I was in Morocco in the spring but I may stay home now until Christmas. Except perhaps a trip to Paris. I thought I'd tired of its charms but *The Well of Loneliness* has made me long to return."

"We're off there ourselves in a couple of weeks' time," John said. "It's actually where I started writing the book."

"Really? Well that decides it."

"It was plain old *Stephen*, then, before Una came up with a better title. She's named all of my novels, as a matter of fact. Quite the knack for it, haven't you, darling?"

"I know people always ask novelists where they get their inspiration from, but I always want to know the answer."

John paused. "Usually, I start with the principal characters and their circumstances. With *The Unlit Lamp*, for example, Joan Ogden came to me in the dining room of the Lynton Cottage Hotel, watching a vampire mother and her put-upon daughter. I never met either of them, but they provided the spark. With *The Well of Loneliness*, however, it was the theme first. I wanted to break the great conspiracy of silence that surrounds female inversion."

"Well break it you certainly have."

"I wouldn't have done it without Una's blessing."

The day after John had won the James Tait Black Memorial Prize for *Adam's Breed*, she'd sat Una down to tell her of her intention to write a novel about women like them. "I think I'm well enough established now for such a novel to be taken seriously. It's a risk, of course. It could shipwreck my entire career." She'd looked into Una's grey eyes. "The one sacrifice I'm not prepared to make is your peace of mind. If you do not wish me to write it, it will remain unwritten."

The answer was immediate. "Write what's in your heart."

She wondered now at her Henny Penny fears. The reviews had been overwhelmingly positive. Only Leonard Woolf had sounded a negative note, but his quibbles were with style not content. The sky had not fallen in.

"I understand that you're planning to introduce Colette to the British public, Lady Troubridge," Anne said.

"Una has quite the talent for translation," John said.

"It's a real skill. I've read the originals but I shall look forward to reading them again in English. Have you met her?"

"Colette? Yes. She's an enchanting person. Scandalous, of course, but enchanting," Una said.

They took their coffee in the parlour. Anne retrieved *The Well of Loneliness* from the bookcase. "Would you mind signing my copy?"

"Is there anything in particular you'd like me to say?" John found book signing requests both a tremendous boost and a terrible pressure. She always felt that more was expected than her scrawled Radclyffe Hall. Colette was a woman who knew how to do dedications, always something witty to say. It was not a gift John shared. She squirmed, trying to grab a thought before it ran away from her but couldn't get hold of a single interesting word. Aware of her hostess's eyes upon her, she scribbled,

To Anne
With all best wishes
Radclyffe Hall

Anne read the words aloud with the reverence of prayer. "I will treasure this. Thank you."

* * *

They'd left the curtains open the night before, delighted by the rhythm of the lighthouse, sending its beam across land and sea. John eased gently from sleep, a slight smile on her face.

"Ah, you're awake." Una put her book aside.

John yawned and stretched. "What time is it?"

"Almost half past eight." On cue, the church clock chimed the half hour.

"You should have woken me."

"And curtailed the first decent night's sleep you've had in weeks? It's good to see you rest."

"And no bad dreams. Perhaps it's the sea air." John yawned again and sat up. "I do like it here. The beach yesterday and pottering around these quaint little streets. It's been good for me. You, too. You've a better colour in your cheeks."

"Is that a compliment or are you saying I usually look peaky?"

"You're never less than gorgeous. With the sea air, doubly gorgeous. I'm sure it can't be good for us cooped up in the city all the time."

"I know what you're after."

"After?"

"I suppose you want to start looking today."

John laughed. "No time like the present."

The auctioneer, a balding man with bad breath, took them first to a house more than a mile out of town. "This has just become available. A delightful option. Four bedrooms—"

John refused to go inside. "I'm looking for a property with character."

"It's bursting with character, madam. Tiled floors, beautiful bathroom, views—"

"It's modern. I'm looking for a period property, preferably Tudor, Georgian at a pinch."

"They're very difficult to heat, those old properties. A lot of them don't have electricity or running water. This by contrast—"

Una, sensitive to the shortness of John's temper, intervened. "My friend has set her heart on a period cottage. Perhaps you would be so kind as to show us what you have in the area of the Citadel itself."

There were three on offer. "This is more like it," John said, as they drew up at the first one, a cottage on the west side of Church Square. The promising beamed exterior gave way to an inside that was dank with mildew. John's asthma would never tolerate it. The next property was another letdown. Two bedrooms and no garden was too tight a squeeze. Their last chance was a substantial eighteenth-century house on the High Street, with bay windows, a marble bathroom and a study looking out onto the garden. John walked from room to room, excitement growing as she imagined living there.

"How much is this one?" she said casually.

"The reserve is eighteen hundred pounds."

"Eighteen hundred pounds." It was a great deal of money for a house outside London, more than double what she'd had in mind. She liked the house, but eighteen hundred pounds?

"You're getting a lot of property for that. The drawing room, the library, the study, five bedrooms. A good-sized garden…"

John sighed, letting the house go. "That's part of the trouble. In truth, it's rather larger than I require. It won't be my primary residence. I'm looking for a retreat, a bolthole. Three bedrooms should be more than sufficient. And a garden."

The estate agent puffed out his cheeks and a gust of foul breath engulfed them. "I've nothing else in the Citadel. If you're interested, I could show you somewhere a couple of minutes outside Landgate."

"Is it old?" Una said.

"Mid-nineteenth century."

"What do you think?" Una said.

John shrugged. "We might as well, now we're here."

She was glad she hadn't got her hopes up for what turned out to be a drab terrace. "Well, you have my number if anything else becomes available in the Citadel."

They made their way back up to the town via steps set into the cliff. Una hooked her arm through John's. "Try not to be too disappointed, darling."

John pulled away. "No doubt you're relieved."

"Of course not."

John grunted in response. At the top of the steps, she stopped to light a cigarette. Una came to stand next to her, looking out across the lower part of the town to the fields beyond. "I'd have thought you'd have known by now that if you set your heart on something, there my heart goes also."

It was true, and John knew it.

Fifty yards along Watchbell Street they discovered a small Italianate church set back from the cobbled street. The door stood slightly ajar, inviting them in. A sharp tang filled the air inside the church. Two men in overalls stood atop a scaffold in the nave, applying varnish to the wooden buttresses holding up the roof. A fat priest sat in a pew making notes in a book.

John exchanged a glance with Una, unsure whether they should depart or introduce themselves.

The priest caught sight of them before they reached a decision. He got to his feet. "Welcome to Saint Anthony of Padua, ladies." His voice was a pleasing bass, his English spoken with a Mediterranean accent that John couldn't place. He introduced himself as Father Bonaventura. John immediately renamed him Father Bony in her mind. "Are you of the faith?" he said.

Una confirmed that they were. "I converted when I was twenty while staying with relatives in Florence."

"My dear friend, Mrs. Batten, God rest her, was first to introduce me to the faith," John said. Despite Ladye's devotion to the church, for several years John was by no means a believer. Her Damascan moment had come at a performance of *The Miracle* at the Olympia Exhibition Centre. The cavernous exhibition hall had been transformed into a Gothic cathedral. Two thousand actors and a choir of five hundred brought to life Reinhardt's story of a nun who'd strayed from the Lord's path. In the final act, she repented. Sitting in the audience, John had felt as though God was speaking directly to her. She'd been confirmed at Westminster Cathedral the following month. It had healed an ache in John's soul. She was part of God's plan.

"We travelled to Rome together to meet Pope Pius the Tenth," John continued.

"You met the Peasant Pope?"

John nodded. She didn't add that she'd been too shy to say a word and had genuflected so excessively that one of his aides had hauled her to her feet.

"I defy any Anglican to live in Italy for six months and not choose the one true faith," Una said.

"You may be right, but my mission when I came to England twenty years ago was to bring the Catholic faith back to the people of this country. By the grace of God, my congregation here has grown to the point that we have needed to build this new church to house us."

John looked around. The plain white walls and high vaulted ceiling made the building seem larger than it was, a miniature cathedral rather than a parish church. At the far end, steps led up to an ornate marble altar and pulpit.

"The stained glass windows will be installed next week. You will have to come back and visit us."

"We usually attend Brompton Oratory in London," Una said.

"A fine church," the priest said, "with such wonderful music."

"There is a beauty here that I feel in my heart." John pressed her hand to her bosom to emphasise the point.

"I want my church to uplift the souls of my parishioners."

"I took Saint Anthony as my name-saint when I converted," John said.

"In that case, my child, I have a gift for you." The priest reached into the pocket of his habit and removed a silver gilt medal. He handed it to John. The medal featured a haloed monk holding the infant Jesus in his arms. *Saint Anthony Pray for Us* was inscribed around the edge. "Keep it with you and know that you will never be truly lost while God is by your side."

CHAPTER EIGHT

There's still no sign of Janet. I've been here an hour, not wanting to risk being late. The queue's building up behind me. The doors will be opening soon and then I'll not know whether to go in and buy tickets or wait out here for her. I catch sight of my reflection in the long window of the door. I don't look normal. I thought a bit of lipstick and rouge would be the thing, but I know less than nothing about makeup. If Sibyl had been home, she would have helped me. Except I wouldn't have asked her. *What makeup should I wear to go to the cinema with my friend Janet?* I couldn't have said that. It would have made a thing of it as if there is a thing and even if there was I wouldn't know what to be doing about it.

A young woman goes past who looks like I want to look, blush-pink cheeks, red lips, dark eyes, free and easy in her green beaded dress. My face is that of a clown. The doors open and the crowd surges in. I decide to follow so I can go to the ladies and wash this mess off but then Janet arrives. She smiles and I know it's at the ridiculous look of me.

"I'm taking it off as soon as I can," I say.

"What off?"

"The makeup. I can see you don't like it."

The crowd buffets past us, eager for tickets and the best seats.

"You look lovely. Let's go in."

The lobby's hot and I feel the perspiration breaking under the thick foundation. I hope she doesn't notice. It's a relief when we're finally in our seats and the lights go down. I can hide here in the semidarkness. The main feature's a film about the war through the eyes of a German family. As the first son lies dying on the western front, I can't help but think of my father. Why did he survive to come home? My whole life would be different if he'd died. I'd have had years more of visiting Granny Palmer. And Auntie Ruth might still be alive. Not that he killed her. It was a motor accident. But she was out buying thread to darn his socks when it happened. Why was there no bullet for him?

I'm distracted from these thoughts by Janet who casually strokes my hand then leaves her fingers resting over mine. A new wave of heat floods my face. I lose the run of the film for the distraction she's causing me. What does she want with my hand? I flick a glance towards her and away, and back and away. She gazes serenely at the screen.

The credits roll and I focus forward, like I've been concentrating the whole time. I'd have missed it otherwise. "I.A.R. Wylie."

"What?" She's still holding my hand even though the lights will be up in a moment. Not that that should worry me. Nothing unusual in two women holding hands.

"Adapted from a story by I.A.R. Wylie, it said. I know her. She was at the Pond the day I first met you."

"Shouldn't she be living in Hollywood? If it is a she. I.A.R. That's a man."

"No, it's her. She's a writer. Her name's Ida, but she calls herself…"

"Calls herself what?" I notice she's let go of my hand but I don't know when.

"Oh, emm…She does live in America, some of the time anyway. I remember her saying she wasn't long back."

"I'll take your word for it." Though it sounds like she doesn't. We're outside now. "You ever been to the Cave of Harmony? There's a load of writers hang out there."

"No, I haven't." I've never even heard of it.

"It's for theatre types and intellectuals and all that, but my friend Beryl's a dresser at the St. James's so I've gone with her a few times. It's a great place to dance. Do you like dancing?"

"I don't know."

"Do you want to find out?"

"At the Cave of Harmony?"

"Nah, it doesn't get going till late. Friends of mine are having a party if you fancy it."

The party's in a flat above a fishmonger. Janet rings the doorbell. A young man with slicked back hair answers. "Janet. Glad you could make it."

"Wouldn't miss one of your dos for all the tea. Bobby, this is Maggie. Maggie, Bobby."

"Come in, come in."

"How are you settling in?"

"Yeah, all right. Jean's good at playing wife. I'm glad to be out of that dump of a bedsit." He laughs. "Though we did have some fun times there."

The wallpaper's hanging off the wall in the staircase and the smell of fish follows us up. I pull my thin jacket closer against the damp. Muffled music greets us as we climb. Bobby points out the door to the lavatory shared with the first floor flat before carrying on up another flight of stairs. He opens the door at the top. A dark-haired woman is pounding out some fast beat on an upright piano in the corner of the sitting room. The furniture's been pushed back against the walls to make space for dancing. Two of the couples involve a man and a woman but it's the three pairings of women that take my eye. Their feet are moving back and forth and they're in and out of each other's arms every few seconds. I don't know what the steps are but I know I want to learn them.

"Here, let me take your jacket," Janet says, helping me out of it. "Would you like a drink?"

"Emm…"

"There'll be plenty of time for dancing," she says with her disconcerting knack for reading my mind. "Anyway, this one's too difficult for a beginner. I'll get Gert to play a waltz after we've had some refreshments. Punch all right?" She doesn't wait for an answer, taking herself off across the hallway. A wave of noise bursts out from the door she opens, voices laughing and talking. I wonder should I follow her. I don't know much about parties and how you're supposed to behave.

But then one of the men that's been dancing turns and I see his face and it's not a man. It's Wilma, the spotter from Achille Serre, in a bow tie and fancy waistcoat. I notice the curve of the breast of the other male dancer and know he's a woman too.

And I feel confused but I don't even know what I'm confused about because from the moment I entered the room and saw the women dancing together I felt a great yearning in my heart. A yearning bigger than the sea and the stars. *Let that be me. I want that. Let me have that.* And I don't know why thinking that some of the dancing couples were a man and a woman made a difference, made it feel safer, because it was in a woman's arms that I wanted to be dancing. But now that I know that everyone here is a woman, even Bobby who brushes past me with two tall glasses in her small hands, I'm scared. And the music stops and some of the couples break apart but two of the women lean closer together and kiss and I stare. I can't help but stare. In the background a voice calls, "Any requests?" And someone shouts "*The Blue Danube*," and the shouting voice is Janet's and she takes hold of one of my hands and she puts her other arm around me and my skin quivers under her touch, even through my blouse. And she's smiling and she says follow me and I do but my clumsy feet are stiff and she says relax, you're doing fine, step left, right, left, step right, left, right. And the music enters my body, weaving through me, loosening my legs, and I'm able to move my feet and this is the happiest I've ever felt and I sway in her arms and the music stops and two women kiss and one of them is me and Janet's lips are softer than I could ever have imagined in my hard life and they mould to mine and mine mould to hers and there are small explosions all over my body and it's a kind of heaven, perhaps the closest I'll ever get because I know now for certain that I'm an abomination—

"Excuse me." I flee down the stairs to the lavatory but there's someone in there so I just keep on going past the dank wallpaper and I hear "Maggie," but I ignore it and run out into the night.

CHAPTER NINE

I'm glad of the busyness of work. Checking for fire hazards and hauling Charlie about gives me something to do that's not spiralling round the same confused thoughts about Janet. Yesterday was an endless day to be filled. I even made the mistake of going to church, the first time I've been since landing in London. I was brought up in religion—Sabbath School, morning worship, evening worship, prayers before meals, prayers before bed. I was taught that God would forgive us our sins if only we asked Him, that salvation was at hand through the Lord Jesus Christ who died to save our souls. I never thought He would save mine.

St. John at Hackney is a short stroll from Dunlace Road. I know nothing of Anglican habits so I hurried instead to the Presbyterian Church at Covent Garden yesterday morning. The preacher took Matthew Chapter Four as his reading. "Then was Jesus led up of the Spirit into the Wilderness, to be tempted of the Devil." It was a prelude to his real interest—"What is Sin?"—a short question with a long answer involving the Devil, human weakness and the fall from grace. I'd stopped listening to him long before the end. There is no saving knowledge of Christ for me. I don't know why I thought that I'd find something in the church in Covent Garden that I couldn't find in years and years with Auntie Ruth at Newington Presbyterian.

The sun was hiding as I stepped out onto Russell Street. I wasn't ready to go home to Tilda's questions and Sibyl's kindness. I drifted along till I found myself by the Thames. Memories of the previous night pulsed in my mind. Peeling wallpaper, women dancing, Janet kissing me, the cinema's half-light, the girl in the green beaded dress, Janet kissing me, the bus to Finsbury Park, Janet kissing me. Janet kissing me. I let it linger, my body clenching as I recalled the Palmolive smell of her, the cotton of her dress, the soft warmth of her lips on mine. People strolled across Westminster Bridge. Could they tell my thoughts from the look of me? Unclean. I am forever unclean.

"Are you listening to me?"

I blink at Johnston. "Pardon?"

"Press-ups," she says. "Forever."

I'm beginning to think she means it as I carry on through thirty and thirty-five and forty. She calls me to a halt at fifty.

Clarke and Seven have been polishing the motorcycle appliances but when Johnston and I make our way to the common room, they take a break too.

Clarke settles on one of the sofas. "Only five more days till we're off. Any plans?" She takes a bite of her biscuit, awaiting a response.

The factory's closing on Saturday for the annual summer holiday. My idea of swimming at the Women's Pond every day hasn't survived Saturday night. How am I ever to face Janet again?

"A whole week off. You have to do something," Clarke says.

Seven shrugs. She never mentions a word of what she gets up to outside work.

"I'm going to Southend," Clarke says.

"That's at the seaside, isn't it?" I say.

"Southend-on-Sea. Of course it's at the seaside," Clarke says.

I grew up with the sea. From I was no age my Auntie Ruth would take me on the train to Bangor. Winter and summer we'd go, to walk or paddle on Ballyholme Beach. We'd have an ice cream on the way home or a portion of chips if we were hungry.

My father never came with us. He'd be off at one of his meetings, ranting and raving about Home Rule and Papists or away drilling with the Ulster Volunteers, preparing for Ulster to fight and Ulster to be right.

I was glad he didn't come. He'd never have let me splish-splash in and out of the sea. And he'd have had a fit if he'd seen Auntie Ruth taking off her stockings and holding up her skirt to let the water wash over her feet.

"It's the perfect place for a holiday," Clarke says. "The pier and the pleasure palace, deckchairs on the beach—"

"Don't be going soft on your week off. I want you back as fit as you are now." Johnston's eyes lock onto mine. "Fitter in your case, Dillon."

At the end of the tea break, Johnston announces that it's time for a competition. They have become a regular occurrence in my working day—who's best at coupling and uncoupling hose, who can carry a sandbag to the wall and back quickest. Today it's an escape ladder race—Johnston and Clarke against me and Seven. I never knew there were so many types of ladder till I joined the fire brigade—the double extension, the single extension, the Ajax, the hook. The escape ladders are our longest, able to reach the top of the factory when they're fully extended. Each one is mounted on a carriage. We wheel them to the front of the apparatus bay.

"On your marks. Get set. Go."

Our feet pound as we speed towards the factory. Seven and I pull up a couple of yards from the wall. While she puts blocks in front of the wheels to keep the carriage in place, I turn the crank and the ladder rises above us. Up Seven goes, fast as a cat. I glance to my right where Johnston's also started to climb.

"Come on, Seven," I shout.

Johnston's fast but Seven's faster. She touches the top of the ladder first and begins to make her way down. I get out of her way so she can dismount and then it's my turn. Up I go, arms and legs like pistons, driving me on.

At the top I see Wilma through the window of the spotters' floor. She looks up from the stain she's working on. *I've got your jacket*, she mouths. And again, *I've got your jacket*. I knew what she was saying the first time. Lip reading's one of the first things you learn in the thunder of the linen mill. Now she's pointing at the rail next to her and giving the thumbs-up, while I stare on. My jacket, left behind when I fled the party as if my very life was at risk, hangs next to her. *Your jacket*. She thumbs-up and points again and I am pure mortified. Why oh why did someone from work have to be at that party? I'd written the jacket off in a *let that be a lesson to you* way. Now I'll have to reclaim it from Wilma and maybe it'll be Janet who's given her it and there'll be a message and I'll have to work out how to respond, or maybe there won't be a message and that definitely feels worse though I know it shouldn't.

"Hurry up," Seven shouts.

I stumble as I take a step down and I have to get a hold of myself for I'm high, high above hard ground with no time to be thinking of jackets or Janet or messages. Clarke has made up my lead while I've dithered at the top and I rush down half a dozen rungs determined not to let Seven down.

A flash of orange changes the game. A second later the alarm bell's ringing. I'm down the ladder as fast as I dare. Johnston and Seven are already disappearing into the factory by the time I reach the ground. Clarke and I sprint across the yard. Workers emerge through the door, lining up in orderly groups on the far side of the drill yard. Smoke leeches out of a gap around the frame of one of the second-floor windows. The alarm bell continues to ring.

I grab a fire extinguisher from the bay at the bottom of the factory staircase and hurtle up the staircase to the second floor. Workers from the upper floors file calmly down the opposite side of the stairs, as if it's just another drill.

I burst through the doors onto the drying floor, Clarke close behind me. Johnston and Seven are already battling the flames emerging from one of the dryers. We join them in a march around the blaze, playing the foam from side to side. It's just like our practices behind the fire station. And nothing like it, the heat more intense here in the enclosed space, the glow of the flames more unearthly, the smoke thicker. The danger's greater, too. In the yard, there's nothing nearby for the flames to jump to. Here we're surrounded by drying machines, all full of the same benzene fumes that made this one catch light. I keep moving, directing the foam, containing the threat, subduing the fire, putting it out as quickly as possible.

"Well done," Johnston says, when the fire is extinguished.

Two words—well done—make me feel like I've conquered the world.

CHAPTER TEN

"Darling, we were unexpectedly detained." Una hurried over to her offspring, who sat reading in The Drey in the late afternoon sun. She had a habit of overcompensating when she felt guilty about her daughter, offering explanations and excuses where John felt none were required.

It wasn't even that late, for goodness' sake. Barely six o'clock. Andrea was almost eighteen, she could manage an hour or two at home on her own. Not that she looked like a young woman on the brink of adulthood. More like an overgrown twelve-year-old. She stood for her mother's enveloping embrace.

"So good to see you, sweetie."

After a final squeeze, Una relinquished her grip. "Rye's the most darling place. We might buy a cottage there, mightn't we, John?"

"You'd leave London?" Andrea said.

Una laughed. "Oh no, of course not. It would be a second home. Wouldn't it be fun to have a house near the sea?"

"I'd like that."

"How was Granny's?"

"Very pleasant. She sends her regards."

To Una, maybe. Not to John.

"Uncle James bought her a wireless. We had such fun listening to it."

Typical of James Garvin to be ingratiating himself with his mother-in-law. He still hadn't bothered to commission a review of *The Well of Loneliness* for *The Observer*.

"Mummy with a wireless. How unlikely."

"She loved it. The concerts, the news, the gardening tips."

John wasn't in the mood for Andrea's prattling. "I might go to bed."

Una turned to John. "Are you all right, darling?"

John rubbed her forehead. "I think I've a headache coming on."

"We should have had the chauffeur drive us."

"I'm perfectly capable of driving my own car."

"I know you are, darling. Perhaps you need a day in bed tomorrow. We have been frightfully busy."

"I'm visiting Vere and Budge in the afternoon. It's been too long already."

"Oh yes, of course. Well, an early night then. How about I bring you up a cup of cocoa?"

John trudged upstairs to the bedroom. The lightness that she'd felt in Rye was ebbing away. She reminded herself that she'd be in France in a fortnight. A proper holiday. How she needed it.

She was drifting towards sleep when Una arrived with the cocoa and a copy of the *Evening Standard*.

"It's yesterday's edition. Andrea saved it. Arnold Bennett's reviewed you at last."

John sat up, eager to discover what the *Standard*'s influential book reviewer had to say. "Will you read it to me?"

Una settled herself on the bed next to John. Bennett started out by querying celebrity endorsements of books before acknowledging that the inclusion of Havelock Ellis's commentary had attracted him to *The Well of Loneliness* in the first place.

"'Havelock Ellis stands by it. He praises it for its fictional quality, its notable psychological and sociological significance, and its complete absence of offence. I cannot disagree with him.'"

John's assiduous courting of the world-renowned sexologist had paid off.

"'This novel is in the main fine.'" Una paused to look at John before continuing slowly, "'It is honest, convincing, and extremely courageous.' Oh darling, you must be thrilled."

John brought her hands to her lips, eyes closed, savouring the moment. She doubted she would ever tire of hearing her work praised but having it understood meant even more to her. She lay back on the pillows, registering the warmth of happiness radiating through her.

"I'm going to start a scrapbook. I've got all your reviews. You can look at it on the days when you forget how brilliant you are," Una said.

"Sorry I was short before. I know I can be a monster to live with."

Una kissed her on the forehead. "No apology needed."

* * *

"Ready?" Una said.

John nodded, steeling herself.

Una rang the doorbell. A dog barked.

"Quiet, Teddy." A command from inside the house, silencing the dog.

John and Una waited. Twenty seconds passed. Thirty. A minute.

"Shall I ring again?"

"Not yet."

The door opened.

"Thanks for coming," Budge said. Even at forty-five, she retained a boyish charm, but tight lines now marked the downturned corners of her mouth.

"How is she today?" Una said.

"Tell them to go away," Vere shouted from a nearby room.

"It's not been one of her better days."

"Shall I go in to see her?" Una offered.

Budge grimaced, deepening the lines. "Best not. Why don't you two go out into the garden? I'll be with you as soon as I can."

They followed the corridor down to Budge's studio at the back of the house. Light flooded in through patio doors. Half-finished sketches littered the desk.

"I don't know how she's getting any work done," Una muttered.

The doors opened onto a cottage-style garden, colour and scent spilling out of borders, pots and baskets. A brick path led them to a table and chairs under an apple tree. John pulled out one of the chairs, inviting Una to sit.

"Thank you, darling."

Before sitting down herself, John took off her jacket and hung it on the back of her chair. Her temperature was all over the place these days.

"I wonder if she knows it's us," John said.

"She's completely herself a lot of the time. More so than she was."

They fell silent, each wondering how they'd have managed if one of them had been struck down by a devastating illness, if one of them had been called upon to look after a shadow of the woman she'd fallen in love with.

Una declined an offered cigarette. John lit one for herself. Smoke filled her lungs, bringing relief. She fetched an old flower saucer to use as an ashtray.

"Maybe we should come back another day," Una said.

"When? We've a hundred things to do before Paris as it is."

"There's no need to bite my head off."

"Let's give them a little longer."

Una got to her feet. "I think I should make tea."

"They won't want you interfering."

Una turned to John long enough to say, "I'm helping," before carrying on down the path. She'd only taken half a dozen steps when the patio doors opened. Budge backed out of them, pulling a wheeled chair. Carefully she swung it round, then pushed it up the path towards the tree. Teddy, the West Highland terrier who'd been riding on Vere's lap, jumped down. He ran up to John and planted his front feet on her leg, tail wagging, demanding attention. John obliged, fondling the back of his head.

"Welcome, darlings," Vere said. "How lovely to see you." Her delicate face drooped on the left and glasses had replaced the dashing monocle she used to wear. Her voice, however, remained as melodious as it had been when John first met her. It had been at a tea party six years earlier, the room full to overflowing with women writers and artists. John had felt like a fraud when Ida Wylie had introduced her as a wonderful writer who was going to do great things. She'd still been thrashing around trying to finish her first novel at the time, whereas Vere Hutchinson, thirteen years her junior, had already published her debut to much acclaim.

"I'll look forward to reading you," Vere had said, a smile lighting up her face.

It had been the start of one of those happy friendships set to last a lifetime. For two years, they'd lunched and dined and walked and talked together, celebrating each other's successes, delighting in each other's company. And then, out of nowhere, Vere got sick. Intense fatigue punctuated by bouts of paralysis and psychosis. Doctors debated the nature of the illness which had laid waste to Vere's mind, lungs and limbs. The only thing they could agree on was that there was no cure.

In the first weeks after Vere fell ill, John had prayed every day for her friend to be cured. She still prayed for Vere, though not so often and not so fervently. The miracle hadn't happened. It seemed there was nothing to do but watch her friend's decline.

"Would you like tea?" Budge said. "Or lemonade?"

"Budge makes the most perfect pink lemonade," Vere said.

"Lemonade it is," John said.

"Let me help." Una followed Budge back to the house.

John got out her cigarette case, went to offer one to Vere, remembered the state of her friend's lungs, and pulled her hand back. "Sorry." She put the case away, defying the voice in her head demanding a cigarette.

"No need to deprive yourself on my account."

"Are you sure you don't mind? They help my asthma." John lit the cigarette with a mixture of guilt and relief. She sat smoking, trying to think of something to say. Small talk had always been beyond her. With Vere she hadn't needed it. Now the illness sat between John and her friend. She wondered how long Budge and Una would be.

"I read your *Evening Standard* review," Vere said. "What was it? 'Honest, convincing, and extremely courageous.' You must have been pleased." Her smile was tight.

John had brought the review with her to show to her friend but decided it should stay in the pocket of her jacket. "Oh well, yes, I suppose I was. Not that reviews are everything…"

Vere snorted. "You're talking to me, Johnnie. I know how much they matter to you because that's how much they matter to me." She looked away. "Teddy," she called. The terrier came bounding over from the corner of the garden where he'd been surreptitiously digging. His mistress tapped her lap and he jumped on board. She fondled his ears, staring off into the distance.

"I'm so glad that you're writing again. I'm taking *The Other Gate* on holiday with me."

"You're taking…*The Other Gate*?" Tears formed behind the horn-rimmed glasses.

"I've heard very good things about it from Uncle."

"From Uncle," Vere echoed. Tears slid down her face.

John wondered if she should pass her handkerchief. "Ida Wylie. You remember? She was there the first day I met you. She's back from America."

The clinking of glasses drew John's attention down the garden. A large jug took up more than its share of the small tray that Una was carrying, leaving the glasses to jostle for what little space was left. Budge followed with a cake and plates.

"Let me help," John said, getting to her feet. She removed the jug, almost causing Una to drop the tray, and brought it to the table. Vere was still crying.

"What's wrong, darling?" Budge knelt down next to her lover. Teddy, offended, jumped off.

"From Uncle," Vere said.

"What's from Uncle?"

"I was just telling Vere what good things Ida Wylie was saying about her short story collection."

Budge glared at John.

"I didn't mean to upset her," John said.

"It's all right, darling," Budge said.

John removed the handkerchief from her pocket and handed it to Budge who took it without a word. Gently she dabbed at Vere's face.

"How can we help?" Una said.

"Help? Can you imagine what it's been like for her?"

"Stop," Vere said, mopping her own tears.

But Budge had held her tongue for too long with too many people. "Two years she was barely able to write a word. Two years. Imagine that."

John was haunted by the terror of not being able to write. Sometimes she'd manage to get the latest book published before the fear began to build about the next one but often it started within weeks of finishing the final draft.

She had no talent.

She had no ideas.

Whatever talent she'd had was used up.

Whatever ideas she'd had were gone.

This was the last book. She'd never write again.

Una would comfort. "You're tired, you need a rest, you've plenty more books inside you." John would turn from her in despair. Until eventually Una would cajole her into starting work again. John would scratch away at some weak thought like a hen on dry dirt, dragging out worthless words that never went near her agent but saw her through until better days and real work.

"Stop," Vere said again.

"Finally, a new collection of short stories, brilliant stories I might add, and not a word of congratulation or even acknowledgment from you, John. I never expected you to be another fair-weather." Words sharp as slaps. A flush had risen on Budge's throat and her eyes gleamed with fury. "The day your first novel came out we took you out to dinner. I can't count the times we've celebrated your success since then. But when *The Other Gate* was published, you couldn't even be bothered to send a card."

"John's had a lot—" Una began.

John shushed her. She turned to Budge. "You're right," she said, quietly. Shame bubbled up like bile. Friendship and loyalty and trust and decency, the things she held dear. Just words. She searched for a way to explain herself. "When I'm working, I get so…" She shook her head. "It's no excuse."

Vere's leg stiffened and kicked against the table, dislodging a glass which hit a chair and smashed to pieces. Teddy barked and John dropped to her haunches to gather the glass to protect the dog's feet, but another kick knocked the table over, plates and cake and glasses flying as Vere thrashed and writhed, her face contorting, foam gathering at the corners of her mouth, John staring, not moving, as the wheelchair looked set to topple until Budge's cry of help brought her to her senses and she grabbed hold of one side while Budge grabbed the other, holding tight against the storm.

* * *

"You should eat something, darling," Una said later, over dinner at home.

"I should have done more," John said.

"Please eat. You've had hardly a thing all day. I don't want you getting ill before our holiday."

"I'm fine." John pushed away her plate. "All this money I have but it was Toupie Lowther who thought to take care of their rent. I should have known they'd never manage on what Budge is able to earn in the hours she can fit around looking after Vere."

Una put down her knife and fork. "You offered them money. Don't you remember? When Vere first fell ill. They refused."

"I should have made them take it. Toupie got them to take the house."

"You paid for her to see that infectiologist, or whatever they're called. Though, as you know, I've always thought it was syphilis. Her father was crippled with—"

"It's not syphilis."

"I wouldn't have thought I'd need to remind you how widespread that vile disease is among military men." She pushed away her own plate.

"Don't, Una."

"Don't what?"

"When was I ever anything but sympathetic about your own misfortune with the admiral?"

"It can be passed on during pregnancy. I was terrified when I was expecting the Cub."

John sighed. Once onto syphilis, it could take a long time to get Una off the subject, and the iniquity of the admiral marrying her when he knew he was riddled with it.

"What?" Una said.

"Nothing."

"You're sighing."

"I'm too tired for this."

"I don't know why you have to torture yourself about Vere. It's not like you were idling your thumbs when her book came out. The contract issues with Cape, and trying to find an American publisher, and—"

"I still found time to go shopping with you for The Drey."

"So I'm to blame?"

"You know that's not what I'm saying."

"I hardly had any time with you for months. You know what you're like when you're working."

"I can't help the way I work. When it's coming, I have to let it."

"And I organise everything around you to make that possible. The servants, the meals, the house, the typists you insist on firing, keeping friends away, occupying Andrea when she's home from school, looking at drafts and redrafts and redrafts—"

"I had no idea what a burden I was to you."

"You know I support your work. You know it. Don't you dare to suggest otherwise." She turned her chair sideways, not wanting to look at John. Silence prickled between them.

John took out her cigarette case. She fidgeted it back and forth on the table but didn't take one out. It had been a bloody day. Her back ached, her leg was bruised and her heart was choked with gloom. The whole world felt heavy.

"Why are we arguing?" John said quietly.

Una didn't reply.

"Can we be friends?" She hesitated. "Please, Una."

Una moved her chair a fraction back towards John, just enough to signal her agreement.

CHAPTER ELEVEN

Mrs. Smith set the breakfast tray down on the table in the corner of Una and John's bedroom. Quietly and efficiently, she laid the table—vase of flowers in the centre, silver rack of hot crumpets next to it. Dishes of butter, marmalade and seedless raspberry jam. Pot of tea, jug of milk, bowl of sugar cubes. Cups, plates, cutlery. Finally, a copy of *The Daily Telegraph* on one side of the table, the *Daily Mail* on the other.

In their ten years of living together, Una and John had started almost every morning with breakfast in their room. It was a time to peruse the newspapers and contemplate the day ahead.

John stretched, feeling it through every joint in her body. She'd turned forty-eight the week before. Fifty lurked around the corner. To most people, it wasn't old. John's dilettante father had died at fifty-two. Dear Ladye at fifty-nine. She mustn't take time for granted.

"Anything else, ma'am?"

"That'll be all for now," John replied. She got out of bed, put on her silk dressing gown and took her place at the table.

"Sweet pea. My favourite." Una bent to inhale the scent.

"Happy anniversary."

Una kissed John on the cheek. "Happy anniversary, darling."

They marked three dates—the day they'd made their private vows after Una's divorce, the first time they'd made love, and today's, their first kiss. Eighteenth August 1915. They'd both been married at the time, Una to the admiral, John to Ladye. It hadn't stopped them.

Una settled herself on the opposite side of the table and began to butter a crumpet while John poured the tea. "Do you know it's five years today since you started writing *A Saturday Life*?"

"Is it?"

"Yes. I remember thinking we were going to have an anniversary dinner together. Instead, you shut yourself up in your study for the evening."

"How very rude of me."

It had been her third novel, started before she had a publisher for the first two. What she did have was an agent who believed in her work and a wife who repeatedly told her she was a literary genius. The following month Arrowsmith had offered on *The Forge*. Then *The Unlit Lamp* found a home with Cassells, the eleventh publisher Audrey had approached. They'd given John a foothold. *Adam's Breed* had taken her to the mountaintop. Now she was changing the public view of inverts with *The Well of Loneliness*. Yesterday, *The Daily Telegraph* had called it truly remarkable.

John had published five novels in four and a half years. But a writer was only as good as the book she was currently working on. She wasn't writing. She knew she should be starting something new. If only she could find an idea… "I'd like a quiet day, today. There's been so much socialising recently. And more to come in Paris."

"Of course, darling. A quiet day will do us the world of good."

The doorbell rang.

"Perhaps we could have lunch out? Just us."

John had been hoping for a day to go through previous short story ideas she'd not got round to writing. "Where had you in mind?"

"How about the Ritz Grill? We've not been there for a while."

The housekeeper knocked on the door. "Excuse me, madam. Miss Heath wondered if you could spare a moment?"

"Audrey?"

"Yes, madam."

"Show her into The Drey." John stood up. "Finish your breakfast, darling."

"You weren't expecting her, were you?" Una said.

"No. Perhaps she has news of the German translation. She was hoping I might be able to sign before we go on holiday."

"On a Saturday morning?"

Audrey stood in the middle of The Drey, flicking her fingernails against each other. She turned as John entered, followed by Una.

"To what do we owe this unexpected pleasure?" John said.

"I thought you'd rather hear the news in person. The *Daily Express* has attacked *The Well of Loneliness*."

"What do you mean?"

"Degrading, unspeakable, the end of civilisation as we know it." Audrey removed a copy of the newspaper from her soft leather briefcase and handed it to John.

Even without her glasses John could read the headline.

A BOOK THAT SHOULD BE SUPPRESSED

"The editor's calling for it to be banned."

John felt like she'd been hit in the stomach.

"Sit down, darling," Una said, putting her hand on John's arm.

John shrugged the hand off. "Who is this man?"

"James Douglas. He wants the government to do more to protect 'Christian values.'"

"I need my glasses." Striding to the bookcase, John removed her spare pair from their case and silently began to read.

I would rather give a healthy boy or a healthy girl a phial of prussic acid than this novel. Poison kills the body, but moral poison kills the soul. This book must at once be withdrawn... I appeal to the Home Secretary to set the law in motion.

A well-known woman writer has published an astounding new novel. It is the first English novel devoted to a particularly hideous aspect of life as it exists among us to-day.

It discusses frankly and vividly a subject so utterly degrading that decent people regard it as an unspeakable horror. Moreover, it attempts to defend and justify the degeneracy with which it deals.

VIGOROUS EXPOSURE

The Editor of the "Sunday Express," in a vigorous exposure of the book in to-morrow's "Sunday Express," demands that it be suppressed by the publisher, the circulating libraries, and if necessary, by the Public Prosecutor.

"It is no excuse," he writes, "to say that the novel possesses fine qualities or that its author is an accomplished artist.

The answer is that the adroitness and cleverness of the book intensifies its moral danger. If Christianity does not destroy the doctrine that this book preaches, then the doctrine will destroy Christianity together with the civilisation which it has built on the ruins of paganism.

John stared at the page. She'd been so careful in her drafting and redrafting. "Why doesn't he name me?"

"He's hooking them in," Audrey said. "Your name will be all over it tomorrow I'm afraid."

"We must stop this," Una said.

"I don't see that we can," Audrey said.

"We didn't even send them a review copy."

"Oh, this won't be a review. It'll be an editorial piece, all guns blazing."

"He can't really get my book banned, can he?" John said.

"No, I'm sure it won't come to that," Audrey said. "It's not like D. H. Lawrence. There's nothing explicit. Try not to worry. And at least you can have the pleasure of knowing that Douglas's vitriol has ensured *The Well of Loneliness* will be a huge bestseller now. There's nothing like the threat of a ban to get the reading public buying."

CHAPTER TWELVE

"Left a bit," Tilda says. "Left. Left."

"It won't go any further," I say.

"Damn it. Put it down then. Gently."

I ease the table to the floor. It's heavy as sin. You'd think it was made of lead not mahogany.

"How on earth did I get it out the last time?" Tilda says.

I don't know. I wasn't there. But it's not going out this time. Not at this angle. Not without taking the back door off. I wouldn't put it past her to do it so I don't suggest it for now. I've grazed my knuckles in the effort to go further left. I suck at the raised skin.

"You're killing us," Tilda shouts in the general direction of the kitchen.

There's a shouted "Uh uh-uh" in response but I can't decipher the words.

"Moaning indeed," Tilda says. "Easy for her to say." Despite her mutterings I know she's enjoying the challenge of moving the table from the dining room to the garden. Ida and Rachel are coming over. It was Sibyl's idea to have lunch outside—"I do adore eating in the sunshine, don't you?" Tilda suggested the picnic blanket, but Sibyl stood firm. It had to be the table. She gets her own way usually. Tilda likes to make a play of how the latest request is too difficult or not worth the bother, but she nearly always gives in. "Whatever your majesty wants." She stands back contemplating the table and the doorframe.

"There has to be a way. It's been out before."

"What if it was on its side? Then the legs could go out first, and we could—"

"Of course. You're smarter than you look."

Is that supposed to be a compliment?

"We won't be able to turn it here," Tilda says. "Back to the dining room. On three. One, two, three, lift."

It's the same drill as manoeuvring ladders at work. The factory closed yesterday for holiday week. Eight whole days to fill. There was no message from Janet when I collected my jacket, but Wilma had one of her own. "Janet Vause is bad news. Take my advice and steer well clear of her." I wanted to ask her more but someone was earholing nearby so I thanked her and went on my way.

Baby Girl whines and scrabbles with her paws at the double doors that divide the front room from the dining room.

"Stop it," Tilda says. "You'll have the door in matchsticks."

Slowly we make our way back down the hallway. I'm impressed at the strength of Tilda who doesn't do the physical training I do every day but is holding up her end no trouble.

"Aha," she says triumphantly as we get the table out through the door and into the garden. We carry it to the paved area at the far end, which is backed by a wall painted white. It's alive with sweet pea, honeysuckle, clematis and jasmine. The table wobbles slightly when we set it down but Tilda fixes it with a bit of cardboard wedged under one of the legs.

Sibyl emerges through the back door. I'm hoping for praise for a job well done but instead she stoops at the bed closest to the house to harvest a few fragrant leaves from her herb garden.

"How's the cooking coming along?" Tilda shouts.

Sibyl looks up. "I'm at a crucial stage." She notices the table next to us. "Where are the chairs?"

"Slave driver," Tilda says, grinning. "Do you want the table extended?"

"No, that'll be fine." She disappears back into the house.

Baby Girl is delighted to be released from the front room. She prances around us, getting in the way, as we ferry the chairs out to the garden. "Right, let's see what else her ladyship wants doing," Tilda says.

The kitchen is awash with steam and delicious smells. I'll enjoy the feast, if nothing else. No doubt Ida will have some mocking comment to make when she sees me but I helped put out a fire last week so I mustn't let it matter to me. It's not as if she isn't rather odd herself. Uncle indeed.

"You could lay the table," Sibyl says. "And put a tablecloth on."

Leaving Tilda rifling through the linen drawer, I carry out the plates. I can't be laying the table till the cloth is down so I sit enjoying the sunshine until Tilda arrives.

The tablecloth is white linen embroidered with the palest lavender silk. Tilda takes two corners and I take the other two and we lay it flat over the mahogany. "What do you think of my tablecloth?"

"Lovely quality. You can't beat Irish linen," I say, wondering if this cloth came from Belfast, maybe even from my old mill.

"I meant the decoration."

Now I take a closer look, I realise the lavender isn't an abstract design. The cloth is adorned with signatures.

"Whose are the names?"

"That's the question. Try the one in the middle."

I trace the letters with my finger. The first one's a flourishing *E*, then a full stop and a capital *P*. Next a small *a* and a *u* and a *k* and an *h* and a *u* and an *s* and an *l*. Paukhusl. That can't be right.

"I'll give you a clue. It's a woman and she's famous. Was famous."

Suddenly I see it. "Pankhurst. It is, isn't it? E. Pankhurst. Emmeline Pankhurst." I'm thrilled to be touching something the leader of the suffragette movement touched. "Did she embroider this?"

"No. When would she have had time for embroidery alongside changing the world? But it is her signature, copied onto the cloth. What about this one?" She points to a signature in the right-hand corner.

The first name is easy. Rachel. The surname begins with a *B*, small *a*, squiggle, two vertical strokes at the end. I don't want to say it in case I'm wrong.

"I'll make it easy. You've met her."

"Rachel Barrett. Oh, I've always wanted to meet a real suffragette."

Tilda laughs. "Meet one? You're living with one." She points to another signature.

The *T* is no-nonsense, *R* fat and firm, clear *a*, *v*, and *e*, determined *l* at the end. T. Ravel. "It's you, isn't it?"

"It's me."

"I never knew you were a suffragette."

"Oh, yes, and I've the Holloway brooch to prove it. Rachel was one of the leaders. Head of Information. She's the smartest woman I've ever met."

"What about Sibyl? Was she a suffragette?"

"In feeling, yes, but not quite in practice. She didn't come of age until the war had already broken out. But Uncle's on here." She shuffles the tablecloth round to show me Ida Wylie. "She was in the Bodyguard. And this one's Mary Leigh. She was in Ireland in 1913, nearly died in Mountjoy prison. And Annie Kenney. She started out a mill worker, same as you. Lilian Lenton, the elusive suffragette the press called her because the authorities could never keep a hold of her."

I want to have heard of these women. If only I'd been born twenty years earlier, maybe I could have been a suffragette and done daring deeds.

"I can't get over you being a suffragette. Were you one of the militants? I bet you were, if you're on this tablecloth."

"They're here," Sibyl calls from the doorway.

Tilda turns away without answering and makes her way down the garden. There's always been a confidence about her. I noticed it the first time I met her. I should have known she would have been a suffragette. To me they're as exciting as highwaymen or pirates, only better, because they're women. My father hated them. I remember him frothing like a mad dog after suffragettes burned down the mansion of some high-up in the Ulster Volunteer Force. If he'd got his hands on them, my father would have strung them up from a lamppost and flailed them till they were past begging for their lives. I'm glad I'm living with a suffragette. It's another strike against him.

The plates are still stacked on the chairs and I decide I may as well get on with laying the table.

"Hello again," Rachel says.

I almost curtsey because here in front of me is one of the leaders of the suffragette movement and I have to turn it into stooping to pat the dog who's not even anywhere near me.

"How's the firefighting going?" Ida says and I nod but don't say anything.

"She tackled her first proper fire this week, didn't you?" Tilda says, and there's almost a note of pride in her voice.

"Johnston and Seven got there first but Clarke and I weren't far behind and the four of us attacked the seat and got the job finished." I blurt it all out in a rush but now everyone's looking at me and I'm embarrassed so I take myself away to the kitchen to offer Sibyl a hand. She sets me to slicing an orange into a jug of water.

When I take the jug out to the garden, Tilda's looking at a newspaper, Ida and Rachel standing next to her.

"I didn't much like the book—misery, misery, all is misery. But this is abhorrent." Tilda folds the paper and hands it back to Ida.

"Keep it. Sibyl will want to see it."

Tilda nods and sets it on her chair.

I put the jug down on the table then return to the kitchen where Sibyl has dishes of olives and salted almonds for me to take out. I leave her going about her final touches and rejoin the others. They're examining the tablecloth.

"Dear Mrs. P." Rachel touches the signature. "I'm glad she lived long enough to know that equal voting was on its way."

I've been hovering in the background, not wanting to interrupt. Now I step forward and offer round the dishes Sibyl gave me. Ida helps herself to an olive. "Mmm, these are good. Moroccan, I'd wager. I must find out where she gets them."

I lurk by the table. These women have known each other for years. I don't want to be in the way but I don't want to miss anything either.

"Sibyl knows every good food supplier in London. Which is just as well as I'd have egg on toast every day otherwise," Tilda says. "She's teaching this one a few recipes. She considers it her duty to convert everyone she encounters to vegetarianism. You can sit down, you know," she says to me.

I slide into one of the seats facing the wall, opposite Rachel. She looks like she could be brainy. Threads of silver mark her temples and her lined face is serious. I mustn't say anything to let myself down.

"Tilda!" Sibyl calls from the kitchen door. "Can I borrow you for a minute?"

"Excuse me."

"Do you want me to go?" I say, half-rising from my chair.

"No, it's fine. You can stay and entertain our guests."

"Don't worry," Ida says. "We won't bite." She picks up another olive and snaps at the end of it, as if she's practising for a chomp at me.

"Leave the poor girl alone." Rachel looks at me encouragingly. "Don't pay any attention to her."

"Oh, but I rather want attention."

I take her at her word. "Tilda said you were in the Bodyguard."

"Oh, did she indeed? That, my dear, is top secret."

"I won't tell…What was the Bodyguard?"

"What was the Bodyguard? I'll have to write a memoir. Remind me to do that, Rachel. The Bodyguard, my young innocent, was a group of suffragettes trained in jujutsu to protect the leadership."

"Oh…What's jujutsu?"

"It's a Japanese martial art. Close combat. Great for dealing with the police. And obnoxious men in general. It's a skill every woman should learn. I'm sure Tilda would teach you the basics."

"Was she in the Bodyguard too?"

"No, she was—"

"In the Suffragette Self-Defence Club." Rachel exchanges a meaningful look with Ida. Meaningful for them. I've no clue what it's about. Before I've the chance to find out, Tilda and Sibyl emerge through the back door, each carrying several dishes. I get up to help them, ferrying bowls and plates laden with food from the kitchen out to the garden. Some are hot from the oven, others cool from the icebox. There's barely an inch left on the table by the time we've finished.

"Perhaps we should have extended the table after all," Sibyl says, a hint of frown between her eyebrows.

"What a spread," Tilda says. "I feel like I'm back in Spain."

"Tell us what everything is," Ida says.

"This one's white bean stew. Then we've got tortilla, piquillo peppers stuffed with goats' cheese, patatas bravas, spinach and cheese croquettes, pan con tomate and a green salad."

"You must have been up since dawn," Rachel says.

"I did a lot of the preparation yesterday. Anyway, tuck in. Oh, I forgot the drinks. Who'd like a glass of fino? Or lemonade?"

The others opt for fino but I suspect that it's some type of alcohol. I've never taken a drop and I'm too feared to try now with all this cleverness around me.

"I'll get it. You sit down." Tilda's hand lingers on Sibyl's shoulders for a moment before she sets off down the garden.

"Help yourselves. Tilda won't mind if we start without her."

There's not room on the plate for everything at once so I prioritise the potatoes and peppers in my first serving. Tilda's back shortly with the drinks. The newspaper falls off her chair as she sits back down.

"The *Sunday Express*?" Sibyl says, picking it up. It's not the sort of paper I've ever seen her reading.

"There's a tirade against Radclyffe Hall's new book," Ida says.

"You can read it later," Tilda says. "We're eating."

"It's absolutely vile," Rachel says. "The editor goes so far as to say he would rather kill a child than let them read a copy of *The Well of Loneliness*." She puts her knife and fork down to hide the tremble in her hands.

I focus my eyes on my plate, cutting into a potato, loading on a slice of pepper, raising my fork to my mouth.

"There isn't a shadow of offence in *The Well*," Ida says, "except to those who fear the truth."

"The world is full of people who fear the truth," Rachel says.

"I wish she'd told rather more of the truth," Tilda says.

"What on earth do you mean by that?" Ida says.

"Finally a writer steps out from the shadows and what does she give us? Heartbreak and misery. And don't get me started on inversion—"

"She's making a point," Ida says, "about society and—"

"Couldn't the point be that women can be happy together? Is that too much to ask?"

"I didn't have you down as the romantic type," Ida says.

"You'd be surprised," Tilda says.

"Do you think the *Sunday Express* would have liked it any better if she'd given us a happy ending?" Rachel says.

"Probably not," Tilda concedes.

I've continued eating while the talk has raged round me. My plate is almost empty. I don't want to draw attention to myself by getting another helping.

"No matter the plot, Radclyffe Hall has had the courage to put her head above the parapet. Now the right-wing press is shooting at her," Rachel says. "It's despicable."

"How's she taking it?" Sibyl says, softly. She's been as quiet as me till now.

"I haven't managed to speak to her yet," Ida says.

"Will you tell her that I loved the book?" Sibyl says.

"Of course," Ida says. "Of course I will."

CHAPTER THIRTEEN

The slight figure of Audrey Heath stood on the pavement outside the offices of A.M. Heath Ltd. on Golden Square. "Pull in here," John instructed the cabbie. She had the door open before the taxi had come to a halt. Audrey stepped lightly into the cab, graceful as a ballerina.

"Bedford Square," Audrey said to the driver.

"Did you manage to get a copy of the letter?" John said.

"I have it here." Audrey extracted a sheet of buff foolscap from her briefcase and handed it over. The letter, on Cape's headed paper, was addressed to the Home Secretary.

> *As you may know, Radclyffe Hall's new novel,* The Well of Loneliness, *has been subject to criticism in today's* Sunday Express. *I stand by my decision to publish it. If, however, you conclude that the best interests of the public will be served by withdrawing the book from circulation, we will be ready to do so and to accept the full consequences as publishers.*

John had to hold herself back from screwing the letter into a ball and setting it alight. Cape must know that the current Home Secretary was the most puritanical man ever to hold the office. His nickname, Jix, might sound jolly, but Sir William Joynson-Hicks was every bit as fanatical a moraliser as the *Express*'s James Douglas.

"How could he do this? And why on earth did he send a public letter to the *Express* telling them he's written to the Home Secretary? Douglas isn't going to let up now."

"Cape's either been very stupid or very cunning. He's made a profit on the sales to date. My fear is he's decided to quit while he's ahead rather than risk the costs of a legal battle."

"It's not up to him to make that decision without me. We share liability for any legal action."

"Morally, you're right, John. Legally is another matter."

"Surely he can't take it off the market without my say so?"

"In theory it would be breach of contract, but if he can argue it's at the behest of the Home Secretary…Well, we're in difficult waters."

"I may have to kill him."

"What number?" the cabbie said.

"Thirty. Anywhere here will do." Audrey reached into her briefcase for her purse.

"I'll get it." Pulling her wallet from the inside pocket of her jacket, John fished out a pound note. "Keep the change."

The publishing house of Jonathan Cape Ltd. occupied a substantial Georgian residence on the western side of Bedford Square. Before they entered, Audrey turned to John. "We need to try to stay calm."

"You mean I need to try to stay calm."

"Our best tactic is to start by giving him the chance to explain. Maybe we can find a way out."

Jonathan Cape's office occupied a grand room on the first floor overlooking the garden square. One wall was lined with bookcases housing titles Cape had published in the seven years he'd been in business. He rose from his desk as they entered. At more than six feet tall, he towered over both women. John stiffened her back and puffed out her chest, determined to look just as imposing. "Ladies," he said, a false smile on his handsome face. "Do sit down."

In no mood for a cosy chat, John preferred to stand. Audrey caught her eye with a look halfway between plea and instruction. Reluctantly she took a seat.

"Thank you for making the time to see us," Audrey began.

"Not at all. It's a delicate situation."

Delicate? He'd offered her book up to the most abominable bigot. Desperate would have been closer to the mark. Her book was in grave danger. John reached into her pocket for the gilt medal. *Saint Anthony Pray for Us*. Running her thumb round the inscribed words, she called down his help.

"I must say that both my client and I were shocked by your decision to write to the Home Secretary without consulting us," Audrey said. "We've been trying to reach you since the *Express* began its unwarranted attack on Saturday morning."

"The situation called for action," Cape replied.

"What did you hope to gain by your letter?"

"Well, obviously, to get the Home Secretary on our side."

John fingered the medal, seeking the calm Audrey had urged.

"And what makes you think he'll be on our side?" Audrey asked.

"Two reasons. Firstly, there is no obscenity for the Home Secretary to find. I would never have taken on such a highly dangerous book had there been any—"

John sat forward. "Highly dangerous. Whatever do you mean by that?"

"Simply the topic, the unusual topic. As you yourself told me, Miss Hall, other publishers had already turned it down for fear of the consequences."

John's face flooded with hot blood. When she'd signed with Cape, she'd thanked him for having the courage to publish that others had lacked. Now he was using her honesty against her. Audrey's hand on her arm urged silence. With a supreme effort, John hauled her emotions in.

"Ladies, what you need to understand is that James Douglas has made a grave error. On Sunday he went from attacking Miss Hall's book to demanding that the whole of the literary establishment put its house in order. The Home Secretary will not want to take on every author and publisher in the land."

"You are aware that Jix prides himself on upholding traditional values?" Audrey said. "And your letter doesn't mention the whole of literature. It refers solely to my client's book."

"I promise you, ladies, Jix is not going to ban *The Well of Loneliness*. There is nothing in it that could possibly justify banning it, which is exactly why I sent it to him."

"He doesn't have to ban it, though, does he? You've volunteered to withdraw it if he finds it offensive," Audrey said.

"He's not going to ban it," Cape said.

"Are you planning to withdraw it?" Audrey said.

"Of course not."

"And if the Home Secretary tells you that he finds parts of the book offensive—?"

"He won't."

"But if he does?"

"Jix will face down Douglas. I'll put my shirt on it. And that will be the end of it."

John looked at Cape, the flush on his face, the eyes that wouldn't quite meet hers. Who was this man that she'd entrusted her precious book to? For all Audrey's earlier warning, it would be as well now to tell the waves to be still. "Don't you know what these people are like? I don't suppose you do. You've never been an outcast. Any deaths that come from this will be on your head."

"There's no need for melodrama, madam."

John leaned across the desk. "You know nothing. Nothing. There are suicides every day. I wrote this book to give my fellow inverts courage. I thought you would defend it as it deserves to be defended. Instead you go offering to do the censor's dirty work for him. I didn't know I'd signed with a coward."

"Now listen here, Miss Hall—"

"No, you listen here. I will not have you throw away the chance to keep my book in print. You have a contract with me. I intend to see you fulfil it. If Jix tells you to withdraw you will have to defy him. Let him take us to court if he wants to ban *The Well of Loneliness*."

CHAPTER FOURTEEN

Hackney Central Library opens at nine o'clock. I'm waiting on the steps from half past eight, though I've no idea how I'll actually ask for the book when it comes to it. I hope whoever serves me doesn't read the *Sunday Express*.

I filched the newspaper during the tidy up after yesterday's lunch. The condemnation started on the front page, with the full offensive on page ten. *A Book That Must Be Suppressed.* It was all *nauseating* and *perverted* and *contaminating*. God was in there too, and the plague and lepers and evil and depravity and being damned for choosing to be damned.

I could hear my father's voice thundering the words out, even though your man that wrote the article is English and would sound nothing like my da. But it's the type of tirade he loved to launch into about anything he didn't like, be it dancing or drinking or priests or pacifists.

Abomination. Depraved. Words I've been saying against myself. But yesterday I was reading them knowing that Tilda and Rachel and Ida and even Sibyl had a different view about women loving each other. The article said that bookshops shouldn't be selling the book and libraries shouldn't be stocking it. That's what gave me the idea to come here today and get a copy, even though there's one at home but I'm not ready to be asking for it.

A picture of Radclyffe Hall accompanied the article. She'd have fitted right in at that party in Finsbury Park with her bow tie and smoking jacket. Her hair was swept back off her face like Rudolph Valentino and she held a cigarette in one hand. I wonder if I should buy a bow tie. Wilma had one, and Bobby, and now Radclyffe Hall.

When I started at Achille Serre, I knew nothing about firefighting, but I had Johnston training me and a firefighting manual to guide me. I'm hoping this *Well of Loneliness* will be like a manual for abominable women that'll teach me how to become one and then maybe I could venture back to the Women's Pond and see if Janet will give me another try.

A man arrives to wait outside the library. He leans against the opposite side of the entranceway, staring at me with eyes bulgy as a frog's. There's not a hint of him looking away when I catch him doing it. He runs his tongue over lips moist as raw liver. I look away. People wait at the bus stop along the street. A bus chugs to a halt beside them and they clamber on. Still the man watches me, his gaze like a hot poker on my flesh. I'm scared to look at him in case it encourages him, but I'm scared not knowing what he's doing. A flick of the eyes confirms he's still in the same place, one hand thrust into his trouser pocket. I look away again. To my relief, an older woman arrives on a bicycle. She freewheels to a halt on the pavement next to me before dismounting with elaborate care. Taking a rope from the basket on the front, she secures the bicycle to the railings with a constrictor knot.

"That'll keep the blighters off," she mutters.

Instead of worrying about Mr. Lewd, I should be practising my knots while I'm standing here. I retrieve a length of string from my pocket and make a loop. *Through the hole, round the tree, down the hole and off goes she.* I pull the knot free and begin again.

Three children and their harassed looking mother join the queue. The younger two are twins, identical down to the red bows in their hair and the sulks on their faces. An older boy lurks behind. A button's come undone on the woman's blouse revealing glimpses of the top of her breasts. I wonder should I mention it. I'd want to know if it was me but I don't want her thinking I've been looking at her bosoms. Mr. Lewd decides me. I can't have him leering at her cleavage.

"Excuse me," I say to the woman. "You've…" I look down at my own blouse hoping she'll follow my drift.

"*Milly-Molly-Mandy,*" one of the twins says.

"*Just So*," the other sings.

"I want *Milly-Molly*—"

"Shush," the mother says.

"*Just So*."

"Excuse me. Your button."

She looks away from her squabbling twins as if she's only noticing me for the first time.

"Your button," I say again.

Finally she catches on. She turns away and fumbles with her front.

The library doors open and we're in. A door on my left is marked Newspaper Room. I take the one on the right into the lending department. It takes a moment to orient myself, but then I see a sign for fiction and I'm tearing over the wooden floor, zooming past the A, B, C's. Mr. Lewd is on the same track and he's got a head start but he doesn't have weeks of speed and reaction training to call on. I'm almost running as I swerve past him to the H's, my eye dashing along the names and titles, looking and looking, and he's doing the same but here she is, Hall, and I get my hand to the copy of *The Well of Loneliness* first. I smirk into his face in triumph.

Before taking it to the issue desk I pause at D for Dickens. We read him at school. I pick out *Hard Times* because I've had a few of those myself. In the C's I grab an Agatha Christie and at A, I gather in Jane Austen's *Persuasion*. It'll look like I've got—what's that word Sibyl uses? Eclectic tastes. Pleased with myself, I make my way over to the desk and set the books down. A pinch-faced librarian looks over her glasses at me in a way that is far from friendly.

"Tickets, please."

I look at her.

"I need your library tickets. You are a member?"

"I don't..."

"Have you registered here before?"

"I haven't, no."

"You can't take any books out till you're registered. Do you live in Hackney?"

"Aye, I do."

She passes me an application form. I sit down at a nearby table and fill in my name, address, age and occupation. She's not given me any blotting paper. I stare at the ink, willing it to dry. A couple of people are at the issue desk when I return. The first is Mr. Lewd. The librarian stamps a date into his book and hands it over to him. It's *The Well of Loneliness*. I look at my pile still sitting on the issue desk.

"That's mine," I say. "He stole my book."

"Keep your voice down," the librarian hisses.

"Well it's mine now," the man says.

"You're a right sickener, aren't you?"

"I will have to ask you to leave the library if you can't be quiet," the librarian says.

"I'm sure your mother's very proud of you," I say to the man. I cast the librarian a hostile stare and stomp away out of the library, seething at the low tricks of Mr. Lewd and the connivance of the librarian. I needed that book. My whole plan for the day was reading it in Victoria Park. I stand for a moment outside the library, then turn right, heading for The Narrow Way.

I've never been in a bookshop before, not a proper one that doesn't sell newspapers and stationery as well. I enter to the sound of a clanging bell. It's dark and cool inside with a musty smell like damp earth. Bookcases crowd the aisles and walls, stacked with row upon row of books. A balding man browses in the far corner.

"Fiction in the middle, nonfiction on the left, secondhand on the right," a small man behind the counter says. He has some sort of accent, but I don't know it. London's like that, full of people from all over. I nod in acknowledgment and start on the fiction bookcases. My heart is loud as I reach the H's. Hall. There's *A Saturday Life* and two copies of *Adam's Breed.* No sign of *The Well of Loneliness.*

"Were you looking for something in particular?" the accent man says.

I hesitate. "Do you have Miss Hall's latest work?" The words come out in Sibyl's voice though I didn't plan it that way.

"*The Well of Loneliness?*"

"Yes, that's right."

"I'm afraid I sold my last copy the minute I opened this morning."

"When will you have it again?"

"That is the question. The trade counter at Jonathan Cape sold out on Saturday. Who knew so many booksellers read the *Express?* Collectors too, all fighting for the last copies in case it's banned."

He says I can leave my name and address and he'll contact me when it comes in again. I tell him no thanks and make my exit. Enough of these shenanigans. There's a copy of *The Well* in the house where I live. That's the one I'm destined to read.

I ease the front door open and enter without my customary, "It's only me, Maggie." From the splashing of water and the bursts of song, I can tell Sibyl's in the bath. If I can get in and out of the house quickly, she'll never know I've been. I know I'm being ridiculous as I creep into the front room. I could just ask to borrow the book but I don't want her thinking about why I want to read it. It's none of her business.

The alcoves on either side of the fireplace are shelved from floor to ceiling. I start with the books closest to the window. It's not like the library. There's no obvious fiction section and you'd wonder if whoever organised them has heard of the alphabet. If there's any kind of a system, I can't decipher it. The copy of *The Well of Loneliness* that I held in my hands for those brief minutes in the library wore a cream dust jacket lettered in black. I scan the shelves for cream and black but it's false alarm after false alarm. I cross to the other side of the fireplace and begin again. From upstairs I hear the sucking gurgle of the bath emptying. My eyes race faster, cantering over titles. Where is it?

The bathroom door opens. Sibyl pads to the bedroom above me, still singing in snatches. Drawers open and close. I hear her talking in that special voice reserved for Baby Girl. How long will it take her to dress? A couple of minutes? I've reached the bottom row of shelving. No *Well*. I must've missed it. I start again, words blurring in my panic though this is hardly a situation justifying panic. It's only Sibyl and what's she going to find if she comes down? Me looking for a book. Sure didn't she tell me when I moved in to feel free and what did I like to read and help yourself?

I go back to the window bookshelves but I know I won't find it. Maybe Tilda's given it away. A clip, clip, clip of nails on wooden floor announces my time is almost up.

"Slow down," Sibyl says to Baby Girl, who ignores her and plunges down the stairs. I sit down, ready for her arrival. She bursts in with her usual excess, cavorting over to me.

"Hello." I reach out to stroke her.

"Is that you, Tilda?" Sibyl calls from the staircase.

"It's me, Maggie."

Sibyl appears in the doorway, her hair hidden in a towel turban. "Would you like a cup of tea? I'm making a pot."

"No, you're grand, thanks."

"I thought you were going out for the day."

"Aye, I am. I only popped home to borrow a book. If that's all right."

"Of course. There's absolutely nothing better than a good book on holiday."

She departs for the kitchen and I begin again on the shelves, slowly this time, no need to rush. I look at every spine, regardless of colour. *Jane Eyre, Mrs Dalloway, Regiment of Women*, and hundreds more besides, titles upon titles filling my mind. *Dracula*, *Frankenstein*, *The War of the Worlds*, and on I go to the second set of shelves. Halfway down, Hall catches my eye. I stop. But it's Marguerite Radclyffe Hall, *A Sheaf of Verses*, not Radclyffe Hall, *The Well of Loneliness*. I crouch down to make sure I don't miss it as my eye follows along to the end of the bottom row and nothing.

"What did you decide on?" Sibyl says, returning with her tea.

"Oh. Emmm…"

"It can be hard to find the right book."

"I was…the paper yesterday…I thought you had…But it's not here."

"Oh. *The Well of Loneliness*. Is that what you're after?" She hesitates. "It's up in my studio."

I follow her up the stairs. The studio's directly above my bedroom but I've never been in it before. The sharp smell of paint greets me as I enter. The wooden floor is splashed with colour all around an easel set at an angle to the window. A huge painting is in process, a naked woman, all muscle and power, ready to leap off the canvas and into the room. I catch myself staring and look away. A desk is littered with sketches and notebooks. Above it, a bookshelf. I'm eager to find *The Well* at last but my gaze is arrested by a sculpture serving as a bookend. The squat female figure has her hands between her legs, holding everything private out on show. I don't know where to put myself.

"That's Sheela," Sibyl says. "Have you seen one in person?"

"No!" I say, shocked at the implication. My face burns sunset red. "I've not…No."

"Oh, I didn't mean…" It is Sibyl's turn to blush. "It's a Sheela na Gig. I heard you could find them all over Ireland. This one's in a church in Roscommon. I carved her from photographs."

"There's nothing like that in any church I've ever been in. It must be a Catholic thing."

"Pagan actually, or so it's believed, incorporated into Christianity. The sacred feminine. Anyway…" She reaches *The Well* down from the bookshelf. "Here you go."

CHAPTER FIFTEEN

Now I've got my hands on *The Well*, I can't wait to read it. Instead of going to the park as planned I get a deckchair and settle myself in the garden.

The Well of Loneliness by Radclyffe Hall
'*Dedicated To*
Our Three Selves'

I turn the next page to a commentary by someone called Havelock Ellis who says how good the book is and that it's about people who are different. I turn over again to an Author's Note saying it's all imaginary, even the women's ambulance unit, though there was one in real life. Over again, and at last I'm at the story, Book One, Chapter One. The setting is the Malvern Hills and Lady Anna Gordon comes to Morton Hall as a bride. She's from Ireland and I think she must be a Catholic on account of coming from County Clare and with a maiden name like Molloy but it doesn't say. Her husband's Sir Philip and he's tall and handsome and they're in love.

A whole ten years pass before Anna comes with child but because it's a book it only takes a couple of paragraphs. Sir Philip is sure they're having a boy and Lady Anna starts to think so too but when the child is born it's a girl. They call her Stephen, which is the name Sir Philip had picked out for his son. Lady Anna doesn't like the child and I feel for Stephen because my father didn't like me. Well, worse than that, he hated me. He used to say you were born wrong and you'll never be anything but wrong.

Lady Anna tries to love Stephen, but she can't, and Sir Philip tries to protect Stephen, but he can't. And Stephen has a crush on the maid, Collins, and throws a flowerpot at the footman for kissing her and Collins and the footman get sent away. When Stephen learns to ride, she sits astride not side-saddle, and if I had to ride a horse I'd definitely want a leg either side of it not perched up in the air courting a fall. And she learns to fence but all I learnt was to sew.

They hire a governess, Miss Puddleton, to teach Stephen her lessons and Puddle looks after her and loves her. I think of my Auntie Ruth who looked after me and loved me when my father sent for her to come and rair me after my mother died. Puddle disciplines Stephen's mind and Stephen disciplines her own body and she grows into a young woman and she makes a great friend, Martin Hallam, a young man from Canada. It's the first time she's had a friend because the local children don't like her. Martin loves the trees and the countryside as Stephen herself loves them but when he proposes to her the thought repels her. Her father knows the reason but leaves her in the dark.

Lady Anna got her hopes up when Martin came along. She feels cheated when he leaves and turns further against Stephen. Sir Philip sees it and they argue and bitterness grows between them. Then a big tree falls on Sir Philip, crushing his chest and he dies. I close the book for a moment to take it all in.

I'm still sitting thinking about it when Sibyl comes out to ask if I want lunch. I can't be having her doing it all herself so I get up and wipe the mushrooms while she chops the garlic and herbs. Soon everything's frying in a pan, the smells filling the kitchen. Sibyl serves the cooked mushrooms on toast thickly spread with butter.

"How are you enjoying *The Well of Loneliness*?" Sibyl asks.

"Poor Stephen. How's she going to cope now that Sir Philip's dead? If I were her I'd get away from Morton."

"I take it you don't like Lady Anna."

"Harsh as bleach. Do you think Radclyffe Hall really thinks she's a perfect woman?"

"Does she say that?"

"Aye, in the first chapter. She's going to do something horrible to Stephen, isn't she, now the father's dead?"

"You'll have to wait and see."

"But she is, isn't she?" I say, though I don't want her to tell me.

Sibyl laughs. "Wait and see."

I wash the dishes in record time and soon I'm back on the deckchair in the sunshine with my book. Johnston's expecting me to run at least three miles a day during holiday week. She couldn't care one jot that the Olympic Committee won't let women do anything longer than 800 metres. I plan to read for an hour and then go for a run. But Stephen falls in love with Angela Crossby, a married woman with a tedious husband. One more chapter, I keep saying to myself as I read on, just one more chapter. Stephen's love is pure but Angela uses and betrays her and Lady Anna disowns Stephen and sends her away from Morton.

I should stop and go for my run. Instead I follow Stephen to London where she becomes a writer and then on to Paris where her friend Jonathan Brockett with the pale feminine hands introduces her to Valérie Seymour, a glamorous salon hostess. I want them to fall in love and for Stephen to be happy with a woman worthy of her but they don't and then the war comes and Stephen joins an ambulance unit and goes to serve at the Front.

Sibyl interrupts me at five o'clock to tell me she's off to dinner and the theatre with Tilda. I look up long enough to say enjoy yourself, but my eyes are straight back to the page because Stephen has met a young woman in the ambulance unit called Mary Llewellyn and feelings are developing between them and I need to know what happens next. And Mary asks if Stephen will send her away at the end of the war, and Stephen says she won't, and I'm so excited I feel it's nearly happening to me.

The war ends and off they go to Stephen's house in Paris but Stephen keeps Mary at arm's length out of fear of the hate that Mary would face if they became lovers. And I could shake Stephen for it couldn't be clearer that Mary wants to come to her but that's the way Stephen is with her sense of honour even though it would drive you mad.

The sun has moved round, casting shade across the garden. I put away the deckchair and go inside and make myself a cup of tea. I help myself to a large slice of fruitcake and a couple of rounds of shortbread and take it all up to my room to carry on reading. Baby Girl comes too and curls up at the bottom of the bed.

Stephen thinks Mary needs a holiday to recover her strength and she takes her to Teneriffe, to a place called Orotava, and a villa on a hill looking over the sea with a garden full of flowers and trees. It's a magical setting but Stephen is still being noble and when Mary reaches for her she always moves away. At last Mary's had enough and decides she must leave and it gives Stephen the shake she needs and she kisses and kisses Mary and tells her she loves her. The words Mary wants to hear are hardly said before Stephen's warning her how the world will persecute and shun her. Mary doesn't care what the world will do and Stephen kisses her hands.

"And that night they were not divided," it says.

Blissful days they have now, blissful days of love and contentment. And their time in Orotava is beyond magical and I want to go there, I want to go there, I want to go there and be there with a woman, like Stephen goes with Mary. At last Stephen is happy, and she deserves it after all she's been through, and I can't decide whether I want to be her or I want to be loved by her and I think I want both. And then it's time to go back to Paris and that's the end of Book Four.

My tea's gone cold but I eat the cake and the shortbread. I put my bedside lamp on to be better able to read. I've never let a book take me over like this before. Even if I had thought of reading all day, it wouldn't have been permitted at Lilliput Street. And a book about women falling in love with each other would have been put on the fire and my father would have thrashed me for having it. I'm lucky to be living here with Sibyl and Tilda and that they have this book that they let me read and they don't agree with the *Express* about it being an abomination. And the suspicions I've had about them for weeks are so firm now I could sit on them but how do you go about asking that kind of thing?

It's time for Book Five. Stephen and Mary make Stephen's house in Paris their home. Mary finds a stray dog, an Irish water spaniel, and they take him in and name him David. And then Lady Anna asks Stephen to visit Morton but doesn't invite Mary and Stephen takes it as the slight it is, even though she'd never have taken Mary to be insulted in person.

Mary's left alone in Paris and when Stephen returns, she turns to her writing to protect their future but Mary has nothing to do. And I'm angry with Stephen for not explaining why she must work so hard and for leaving Mary bored and wasted instead of encouraging her to find an interest of her own. Jonathan Brockett intervenes and Stephen takes Mary to a party at Valérie's and they meet all sorts of artists and writers, all inverts marked as Cain, the same as Stephen. Barbara and Jamie become particular friends. Jamie's studying to be a composer and they've hardly a penny and Barbara develops a cough.

And I'm beginning to worry because Stephen and Mary's happiness is ebbing but then Stephen's book is a huge success. They holiday in Italy and make friends with Lady Massey who invites them for Christmas but withdraws the offer when she realizes that they're lovers. And it cuts

Mary to the quick and they turn back to their invert friends and Mary begins to drink, not a lot, just a little, and they go to grim bars where they can dance together. And Barbara's cough gets worse and worse and she dies and Jamie kills herself. And they weren't much older than me and I can't help but cry.

I put the book down and get a hankie and Baby Girl crawls up the bed and nuzzles her nose into my hand to make me feel better. I stroke her and stroke her and stroke her till I'm ready to read on.

Martin Hallam turns up in Paris and he falls in love with Mary. Stephen fights him for her, not with a gun or a sword, but with her heart and soul and love. Mary chooses Stephen but noble Stephen decides Mary would be better off with Martin and a normal life so she pretends to be unfaithful with Valérie Seymour and poor Mary leaves and Martin's waiting for her. Stephen sits at her desk, surrounded by the spirits of legions of tortured inverts, and she cries out to God to give them too the chance to live. I can hardly read the last lines for the tears are tripping me because I love Stephen and it's terrible that she can't have a happier life and I clutch the book to my heart, silently crying at the pure and utter heartbreak of it.

CHAPTER SIXTEEN

Even though I'm on holiday, I'm up at my usual time. Tilda's in the kitchen on coffee duty. "Have you finished the opus yet?" she says.

"The what?"

"Sibyl said you're reading *The Well of Loneliness*."

"Oh…Yes."

"What do you think of it?"

I don't want to answer. Although I don't have the odd look of Stephen, I'm sure I'm one of her legion. But on Sunday I heard Tilda saying she didn't like the book and I'm not ready to hear anything bad about it here and now when it's so fresh and raw for me. "It was interesting."

"Too much doom and gloom for my taste. Barbara and Jamie dead, poor Mary cast off to that bore Martin Hallam, Stephen martyred like her namesake. Now, to add to the despair, the publisher's as good as invited the Home Secretary to ban it."

She hands me the *Daily Herald*. A front-page article confirms that Jonathan Cape has placed the book's future in the Home Secretary's hands. There's a picture of Radclyffe Hall, elegant in a dark hat, and a quote from her saying that the truth is never a bad thing.

"What do you think's going to happen?" I ask.

"I've no doubt that Jix will demand it's withdrawn."

"But there's nothing…" After all the fuss in the *Express* I'd expected more detail than a kiss on the lips. I bet Mr. Lewd from the library was disappointed when he got it home.

She snorts. "That won't matter to Jix. Radclyffe Hall's plea for tolerance is one that someone as intolerant as our esteemed Home Secretary would never accept. Unless Cape can be persuaded to find himself a spine, *The Well of Loneliness* will be banned by the end of the week."

I give the newspaper back to Tilda. She tucks it under her arm along with *The Times* and departs upstairs. I fill a glass from the tap and take it to my room. *The Well of Loneliness* sits on my bedside table in its sober dust jacket. It doesn't deserve the bile coming its way. Neither does Radclyffe Hall. She looked so handsome in the newspaper. I want to look like that, stylish and dashing. I should get my hair cut.

The minute the thought comes in my head I know it's a great idea. I've had long hair all my life. When the other girls at the mill were getting theirs shingled or bobbed, I stuck with a dull bun or a plait, the same as Auntie Ruth. It's time for a change.

The hairdresser isn't open yet so I go for a run through Hackney and five times round Victoria Park to make up for not exercising at all yesterday. I stop every now and then to do press-ups, as Johnston would want. As I run, I feel the weight of my plait against my back. What will it be like to be free of it after all these years?

By the time I'm washed and breakfasted, it's after half past nine before I set off again. When Stephen Gordon had her long hair cut off, she went to a barber but I don't feel brave enough for that. I opt for Muriel's Ladies' Hairdressers round the corner on Chatsworth Road. A sign in the window says: *The Most Up-to-date Methods and Appliances.*

Inside, a young woman has her hair in big rollers. Electrical cables snake from her head to a metal contraption plugged into the wall. I'd be terrified of getting electrocuted but she sits there calmly flicking through a women's magazine. A poster on the wall announces *Bobbed Hair is Here to Stay.*

A dapper man approaches me. "Can I help you?" Before I have time to answer he says, "Indeed I can because that style, and I use the term loosely, is doing nothing for you."

I've worn it down to save the bother of undoing pins and bows. It's still damp from the bath. I squirm, mortified.

"Let's see how Terrence can help." He leads me over to a swivel chair in front of a mirror. My face is tinged pink with embarrassment.

"What were we thinking?" Terrence says, draping a cloak over me and tying it at the neck. "Something short? Am I right? It's 1928 after all, my love. Where have you been for the last decade?"

He runs his fingers through my hair. "Wonderfully strong hair. Lots of options. A shingle perhaps. Or how about a Marcel wave? We've got all the equipment."

His hands are pale and clean, nails buffed to a shine. I think of Jonathan Brockett with his soft women's hands. Maybe Terrence is one of Stephen's legion. It gives me confidence. I take the page from the *Sunday Express* out of my pocket. I've folded it and folded it to hide Douglas's tirade against *The Well*, leaving only the photograph of Radclyffe Hall on view.

"I want it like this."

He looks at the picture. "Eton Crop. How daring."

He stands back and looks at me. He comes close and looks at me. He touches all over my scalp with his fingers. "Lovely-shaped head." He lifts my hair up at the side. "Nice ears." He gazes into the reflection of my face in the mirror. "A crop will suit you. But it's a big step. You might find a bob easier to begin with."

"I want the crop."

He claps his hands excitedly and I notice the flash of a gold wedding ring on his third finger. So much for the legion. He's a married man, though not like any I've ever encountered before. "Marvellous, darling." He lifts a portion of my hair above my head, holding it straight up.

"Sure?" he says, looking again into my mirror eyes.

"Sure."

He picks up a pair of silver scissors from the counter below the mirror. They sparkle as he cuts a swathe of hair about three inches from my scalp. He lifts another portion of hair and cuts again. And another portion, and another. In a couple of minutes, a lifetime of long hair is gone. A different me looks back from the mirror, my face somehow finer and lighter, as if it's the hair that's been dragging me down all these years. Emotions bubble through me. I could laugh or cry or both.

"Beautiful neck," Terrence says, "if you don't mind me saying so."

I allow myself a small nod and a smile as a single tear slips down my face.

He picks up a double-handled device from the counter. "How short do we think? The clippers will take it to an eighth of an inch."

"All over?" I say, alarmed. Radclyffe Hall isn't practically bald.

"No, no, only at the back. The rest I'll shape with my scissors so you can sweep it from your face like in the photograph."

He works quickly, clipping and snipping, and with every cut I feel lighter and lighter till I could almost float from the seat. He finishes off with a touch of pomade.

"Happy with it?" he asks, when he's done.

I nod, because I've no words to tell him what he's given me, the burden he's taken from me. All it's cost is two and six. It's the bargain of my life.

When I get home Sibyl is all look at you, what a transformation, it really suits you. I beam at her in delight.

"What are your plans for the rest of the day?" she says.

"I'm going to walk into town. See a bit of London."

I told Sibyl it was a walk but really it's a pilgrimage. I plan to trace Stephen Gordon's steps across London, from Bond Street, where she searched for the flawless pearl ring for the treacherous Angela Crossby, to Chelsea embankment where she lived with the ever-loyal Puddle, writing her books and gazing out to the river, to Hyde Park where she rode her beloved Raftery until he went lame and had to be shot.

I've never been to Bond Street before. My eyes are agog at the finery, window after window of diamonds and rubies, silk pyjamas and fine leather shoes, glamorous dresses and smart dinner jackets. Wealthy people glide by, pausing now and again to contemplate the latest offering. A motorcar eases to a halt ahead of me. The chauffeur jumps out to open the door for a stick of a woman clutching a tiny dog in her arms. The driver may as well be invisible for all she acknowledges him before disappearing into a shop.

I wonder if it's one of the jewellers Stephen Gordon went into while people stared at her and muttered. I know in my head that Stephen only ever walked these streets in the pages of a book but I don't care. She feels more real to me than people I've met. And I bet Radclyffe Hall's been here, which is practically the same thing. Maybe she has white crepe de chine pyjamas and a man's dressing gown, the same as Stephen. It said in the newspaper that she lives in Kensington but it didn't say where. I might go there later and wander round on the off chance that I'll see her though I wouldn't know what to say if I did except thank you for your book and I hope it's not banned and it's really helped me and I don't feel so alone and I'm very grateful and you're a hero. Maybe I'll write to her. I could put, To Miss Radclyffe Hall, Author of *The Well of Loneliness*, Kensington, London, England, on the envelope. Surely that would get to her.

I pause outside a gentlemen's outfitters. In the window there's a dummy dressed in gentlemen's evening wear. What would I look like dressed in a shirt and tie, waistcoat and trousers? I can't imagine it. But crepe de chine pyjamas? They probably sell them in here. I don't dare go in to have a look. I wouldn't be able to afford them anyway, even if I saved up every week for a year.

I turn away and as I do a familiar figure emerges from the rotating door of a hotel up ahead. She's full of style in a dark suit, pale-blue shirt and striped tie.

"Hello," I say.

Wilma looks startled for a moment, like she's been caught out in something, but then she saunters over to me. "Love the hair. Very butchy. What's brought you up these parts? I didn't figure you for a West End girl."

"I'm just out for a dander."

"Dander?"

"A wee walk, stretch the legs. And yourself?"

"Visiting a friend."

"In this hotel?" I'm surprised that she has a friend that could afford somewhere like this. Unless it's one of the staff.

"This is where she stays when she's in London."

"Is it your friend from the party?" I say, my new haircut making me daring.

"No, not her. This is another…This one lives in Paris."

Imagine knowing someone from Paris. It seems there are a lot of women like me there, Valérie and Wanda, and poor Jamie and Barbara, and a load more at Alec's bar. If I can't sort things out with Janet maybe I could go to Paris and meet someone and maybe she wouldn't be tragic because surely all of them can't be, though things don't always end well there, especially not for Marie Antoinette who had her head chopped off.

"Have you ever been?" I ask.

"To Paris? Yes, that's where I met Scarlett."

"Where? In Alec's?"

"Alec's? No, I don't know it." She leans forward and I smell her musky perfume. Sotto voce—a fancy term for quietly I picked up from Sibyl—she says, "It was in Le Monocle." She raises an eyebrow for emphasis. "*The* Le Monocle. You have heard of it?"

I shake my head. She looks at me like she's deciding something. "Do you fancy a cup of tea?"

We pass several perfectly presentable establishments in the ten-minute walk to Berkeley Square. Gunter's Tea Shop is worth the wait. Chandeliers and fans are suspended from the high ceiling and tropical plants are interspersed among the white-clothed tables. They all look to be taken, but the waitress spies one coming free near the centre. We follow her over the tiled floor to take our seats. My eyes nearly fall out of my head when I see the prices. It's ten times what you'd pay at the café in Chatsworth market, though comparing the two establishments is like comparing Queen Mary to the woman who cleans her lavatory.

"Don't worry. We're only getting a pot of tea and a few biscuits." Wilma catches the waitress's eye and gives our order.

I look around. A gentleman in the corner plays the piano, a pleasant accompaniment to the babble of conversation and tinkling of teacups. The customers are nearly all women, but I suppose that's the way with cafés.

"Can I ask you something?" Wilma says. "What's the story with you and that Vause woman?"

"I thought you didn't like her."

"I don't. That's why I'm asking."

I shake my head. "There is no story."

"It didn't look that way at Bobby's party."

I stare at the pattern on the vase, a delicate freesia painted on a pale-cream background. A real freesia sits in the vase's slender neck.

I shake my head again. "I don't know what to say."

"Say what you like. There's no offending me. I'm just trying to look out for you."

I formulate sentences in my head. *I ruined it with her. Why don't you like her? Are you an invert? How can I get her to give me another chance?* None of them make it to my lips.

"There's nothing to know." I say it as if it doesn't matter to me.

"Take my advice and keep it that way. Janet Vause is a player, Maggie. And I should know, because I've been a bit of a player myself in the past."

The waitress arrives with our order. The biscuits are crunchy, flavoured with walnut and fig. I follow Wilma's lead by dipping them into my tea, even though I suspect it might be considered common in these parts.

"Can I ask you another question?" Wilma says.

I nod.

"You have to promise first you won't go all funny on me."

I wonder how I'll stop myself. I find going funny far too easy.

"Have you noticed the woman near the piano glad-eyeing you?"

I splutter out my tea and look wildly towards the piano and then away as a dark-haired, red-lipped woman catches my eye and smiles.

"Stop panicking."

"Who is she?"

"I don't know her. Could be a bored housewife up to town for the day. Could be someone vacationing in London. Either way, she's probably rich and certainly looking for company. If I wasn't here, she'd have sent the waitress over by now to ask if you'd like to join her."

"She never would."

Wilma laughs. "Course she would. It happens all the time in here."

"Does it?" I say, scandalized.

"All the time. Some of the best evenings of my life have started off in this place."

"It's not a bit like Alec's."

"What is this Alec's you keep mentioning?"

"It's a bar in Paris. I read about it in a book." I lean forward and whisper, "*The Well of Loneliness.*"

"I saw something about that in the *Daily Herald*. So do you like the look of her? Shall I take my leave?"

"No," I say, over loudly, then whisper again, "No."

CHAPTER SEVENTEEN

John always left it to the chauffeur to convey them to Mrs. Leonard's cottage. It left her free to prepare for the sitting. She'd first visited the celebrated medium after Ladye's death, twelve years earlier. In those early months of bereavement, she'd been consumed by guilt and grief, tortured with memories of Ladye's final days—the quarrel after John's late arrival back from a trip with Una, Ladye's accusations, John's evasions, building into a full-scale row.

"Do you care nothing for me? Leaving me endlessly alone while you go off gallivanting with her."

"You agreed, Ladye. You agreed that I could go to Maidenhead to get Una a puppy."

"I did not agree to you staying away with her overnight or spending all day—"

"We were delayed. I've already explained—"

"I've been worried sick, wondering would I see you alive again—"

"Why ever would you not?"

"There's no end of lunatic drivers on the road. And now the Zeppelin raids. It's damnable of you to leave me worrying when you know I'm not well. My blood pressure, the clot on my eye—"

"There was no need for you to worry."

"Maybe it's time for me to live on my own. Then I wouldn't…have to…worry."

"Is that a threat?"

A slow step towards John.

"I c—an't…st—aaan—d-it…John-nie." Words slurring, John staring. "I c—an't…" The stumble forward, hand reaching for the table, reaching and missing, Ladye crashing down.

John rushing to her. "Ladye, Ladye." Crouching over her lover, as the eyes flickered and the mouth slackened. Scrambling for the telephone, desperately calling for help. "You're going to be all right, darling. You're going to be all right." Praying it would be so.

Ladye had tried to speak several times in the days that followed the stroke. Words were beyond her. All she could do was draw John's hand to her lips. She'd slipped into unconsciousness with no word of forgiveness and from unconsciousness into death.

John's faith forbade suicide. If she'd been born a man, she would have volunteered for the front and an honourable death at the Somme. Instead, she was left to remember and remember the worst of herself. How could she have been so cruel? Ladye was the love of her life, the woman who'd shown her that love could be trusted. John had repaid her with betrayal.

She'd agonized over what Ladye had been trying to say in her final speechless days. Had they been words of condemnation or absolution? Her desperation had led her first to Mrs. Scales, who turned out to be an unhinged charlatan. Despair deepened. What kind of a person was she, to have killed her lover with her faithlessness and disloyalty?

And then John discovered Mrs. Leonard. Mrs. Leonard had the gift. Mrs. Leonard could open up a passageway to the dead. Through it, John had found Ladye. Ladye forgave her. She was waiting for John on the other side. They'd be reunited in the afterlife, in a house with a paddock and stables, dogs sleeping by the fireside. Till then she was watching over John on the earthly plane.

"Do you think Ladye will know what's happening with my book?" John said to Una, seated next to her in the Daimler.

"It's possible."

"More than possible. I've lost count of the times she's surprised us with the things she's known over the years."

"You're right, of course, darling. I'm sure she'll help if she can."

"She can. I know she can."

"I wasn't suggesting—"

"I should think not."

"I wasn't."

They drove on in silence, heading away from London's beating heart to the drowsy outskirts. John wished she'd come alone. Una had long taken her attendance for granted. It had not always been so. In the early days of Mrs. Leonard she'd had to earn the right to come. If she'd annoyed John, she'd be told she wasn't welcome. There had been a savage sweetness in hurting Una in those days, every cruel act proof of John's loyalty to Ladye. Two years of punishment had to be paid before John could allow herself and Una more than a few moments' pleasure at a time. Now John was being punished again. The Home Secretary had a lit match in one hand, her book in the other.

The car eased to a halt outside a pleasant two-storey cottage. John had bought it for Mrs. Leonard at the time of her own move to Hadley Wood. She had wanted the medium close to hand. It had been a convenient arrangement while it lasted but when John and Una moved back to Kensington, Mrs. Leonard had stayed put. She liked the quiet. It was good for the spirits.

Mr. Leonard opened the front door at their knock. Wordlessly he showed them into the front room where Gladys Leonard stood waiting. She was on the gaunt side of thin, with black hair coiled in unbecoming plaits. "Be seated," she said.

John sat down at the table in the centre of the room. Una settled herself in an armchair, monocle in place, notebook and pen at the ready. Mrs. Leonard closed the curtains. Silently she lit a small red lamp, throwing dark shadows onto her bony face. At last she assumed the seat opposite John and closed her eyes. The medium's breathing slowed and settled as she sank into a trance.

Suddenly Mrs. Leonard's face brightened. "Mrs. Twonnie, this is Feda." Her tone was high and girlish.

"Good morning, Feda." Over the long years and hundreds of sittings, John had become genuinely fond of the Indian girl who navigated the spirit world for Mrs. Leonard. She'd even grown accustomed to being called Mrs. Twonnie.

"I have with me a gentleman," Feda said.

"I have no interest in speaking with him. Please try to find Ladye."

Feda was silent for a moment, then put up a hand as if beckoning to someone. "Here's Ladye. Her face is sad today. She says she's been worried about you. She knows you are a worrier but you worry her. She says Mrs. Una needs to look after you."

"Tell Ladye not to worry. I'll look after Mrs. Twonnie," Una said.

"She says thank you. She knows it is a difficult job. A perfectly dreadful job sometimes."

"I need to talk to Ladye. I need her help," John said.

"Feda is trying…"

The pause lengthened.

"Feda?"

There was no response, only the sound of Mrs. Leonard breathing out a long and heavy breath. As the out-breath continued, the medium twitched. Her hand grabbed the air and grabbed again.

"Where are you?" The voice was low and quiet, quite unlike that of Feda or Mrs. Leonard.

"Is that you, Ladye?" John took hold of Mrs. Leonard's bony claw, so different from Ladye's elegant hand. Yet, the feeling of connection to her dead lover was unmistakeable. Ladye was here with her. "Thank you for coming through."

"You've placed yourself in grave danger."

"What have you seen?"

"You could lose everything. You must try to be careful."

"I've taken every care possible."

"I know it's not in your nature. Una must keep you safe."

"I'll do my best," Una said.

"I'm watching over you."

"Can you tell me what you've seen?"

"Bless you both." Ladye's customary parting message.

"No, stay. Please. Please, Ladye." John tried to keep hold of Mrs. Leonard's hand. The medium slowly withdrew it.

"Ladye's gone."

The medium's head slumped towards her chest. For a few moments she sat perfectly still while Una's pen scratched in the background, finishing the record of the sitting.

Mrs. Leonard opened her eyes. She shivered. A visit to the spirit world always gave her a chill. She got up and stoked the fire then stood with her back to it, warming herself. "How did it go?"

John discussed the session with Una on the drive home. *"You've put yourself in grave danger. As if it's my fault. She'd never have permitted me to write The Well of Loneliness. You know that, don't you? The risk of it inviting common gossip about our relationship would have been a torment to her."*

"She was a different generation, darling. And the danger she mentioned might not be your book. She's always been worried about your health. Maybe she senses how little rest you're getting."

Sleep had become impossible. Each night as John lay in bed trying to drift off, phrases from Douglas's tirades would force themselves to the front of her mind. *An intolerable outrage… Moral poison… Lepers… Must be withdrawn…* He'd attacked her every day for the last five days in a row. A loathing of the journalist had settled in her soul. She had no intention of taking it to confession. Confession would mean penance. How was she to be sorry for hating this man who wished to destroy her? Thinking about Douglas would lead her onto Cape and his cowardice and then she'd set to wondering how far Jix had got in reading her novel and when was he going to come to a decision. Powerless rage would swamp her, driving out any hope of rest.

"Doesn't she know I'd be resting if I could? That I long to rest." It was so unfair. Attacked by Douglas, let down by Cape, and now Ladye demanding that she rest when her book was in mortal peril. "Do you think she knows we had to cancel our holiday? Believe me, I'd love nothing more than to be off to France tomorrow. Damn Douglas to hell and back. I don't know how he can call himself a Christian. The man's a Pharisee to the core." She wondered should she go to church that afternoon to pray again for the deliverance of her book from this persecution. Her hand slid into her pocket, fingering the Saint Anthony's medal. Had it only been three weeks since Father Bony had given it to her? She'd left Rye full of hope for the future. Now she might lose everything.

What had Ladye meant, everything? Was everything more than her book? What else did she stand to lose? Next to her, Una continued to peruse her notes. How had John missed the pallor of her skin, the tightness round her mouth? For the first time, John realised that this nightmare wasn't happening to her alone.

John reached for Una's hand. "I know this situation with Douglas isn't easy for you, either. I'm snappy and irritable and impossible to live with but I couldn't bear to lose—"

"Oh no, John, never think that." Una gripped John's hand tightly. "You'll never lose me. Ever."

The rain was heavy by the time they reached Holland Street. Mrs. Smith held the front door open as John hurried Una into the house under the shelter of an umbrella.

"Miss Heath telephoned."

John's heart thumped hard. "Was there a message?"

"Only to call her as soon as possible."

Had Jix made a decision? Please, God, let it be good news. How could it be, given Jix's views? But there was nothing obscene in her book.

Surely Jix would have realised that? Please, God. What if he hadn't? Hope, dread, hope, dread, fighting it out. She made her way to the study, Una following close behind. Audrey answered on the first ring.

"Tell me."

"I'm afraid it's as we feared—Jix considers *The Well of Loneliness* obscene."

The pain came, relentless as an avalanche. Obscene. Her beautiful book branded obscene. John's hand tightened on the telephone, as if tightening her grip would help her control the unravelling fortunes of her poor book. "Is Cape going to defy him?"

"He's running scared, John. It seems Jix has threatened to prosecute if he doesn't withdraw."

The first hint of a challenge and Cape was cowering behind the sofa with his thumb in his mouth. "Damn and blast him. Damn and blast him." How could this be happening? No, she wasn't having it. "No, Audrey. He is *not* withdrawing. Do you hear me? He's not. We'll meet you at Cape's."

Jonathan Cape was pacing up and down his office when John and Una arrived at Bedford Square half an hour later.

"Miss Hall, Lady Troubridge. Please have a seat." Cape gestured towards the leather sofas near the fireplace. Una took a seat next to Audrey, who was reading the Home Secretary's letter. The head of Cape's publicity department, Norah "Jimmy" James, sat on the other sofa, worrying at her thumbnail. John nodded a brief acknowledgment but didn't take a seat.

"You are not withdrawing my book," she told Cape.

"I just need time to think." Cape resumed his pacing.

"There's nothing to think about. You need to face Jix down."

"That's easy for you to say, madam."

"You think this situation is easy for me? I told you Jix would never side with us."

"Yes, well, hindsight is the most marvellously useless gift," Cape replied.

"This isn't hindsight. If you'd consulted me at the weekend, I would have told you so before you made such a stupendous blunder as to send that letter to Jix." She fought the desire to kick Cape as he passed by on his latest lap of the room.

"Let's keep our tempers, shall we? We're all on the same side, after all."

"That remains to be seen," said John darkly.

Jimmy came over to her, offering words of sympathy. John had only met the young flapper in April. Since then, she'd become a regular visitor to Holland Street, bringing extracts of her first novel for John's expert opinion. Cape might pay her salary, but Jimmy was on John's team. John let herself be persuaded to the sofa.

Cape paced to the window, turned, paced back again.

"You're not obliged to withdraw *The Well of Loneliness*, Jonathan," Audrey said, her voice reasonable. "This letter has no power. Force Jix to take us to court. If he dares."

"We've got to consider the company's reputation."

"What about my reputation?" John said. "If you concede, you're as good as saying I've written an obscene book."

Cape paced on, back and forth. "I'm afraid it's too late."

"No, it's not. You can ignore his letter."

He paused near the window. "I've already written to *The Times* telling them we're withdrawing."

"You imbecile." John was back on her feet, hands clenched so tightly her knuckles shone through. How could she have trusted this gutless weasel? "Why do you insist on always doing the wrong thing? If you suspend publication, I'll sue."

"Don't threaten me, Miss Hall."

"It's not a threat. If you breach our contract, I fully intend to see you in court."

Cape was on the move again, but this time he stopped only inches from John. "And what good will that do you? The best you can hope for is that the court terminates our contract. They can't force me to keep you in print, as I'm sure Miss Heath will confirm." He turned towards Audrey with a supercilious smile.

"A breach of contract ruling will reflect very badly on your company, Jonathan. You must realise that. The opposite is true if you stand up to censorship."

"Here's how I see it. I have my business to protect. You have your client to protect. Miss Hall has her book to protect. I have a plan that can work for all of us. It gets me off the hook with Jix while keeping *The Well of Loneliness* in print. Perhaps you'll give me a moment to explain."

John folded her arms. Was this a trick? "Go on."

"My printers have the type. I'll get them to make moulds and we sublease the rights."

"Sublease? To whom?" Audrey said.

"I was thinking Pegasus. Do you know them? John Holroyd-Reece. Decent chap. Paris."

"How would that work?" Una said.

"Assuming Holroyd-Reece is agreeable, he'd use our moulds to produce a new edition of *The Well of Loneliness*. The inside pages would look exactly the same as our edition. The only difference would be the Pegasus cover. We'll send order forms to the bookshops and supply them from Paris."

"Oh no. No. I won't have it. The whole point of my book is to bring the subject of female inversion out of the shadows and into the light. I won't have this sneaking, underhand approach. You need to write a new letter to *The Times*. Defy Jix. Defend my book."

Cape still stood by the sofa. John stared at him, willing him to accept her argument.

"My dear Miss Hall, be reasonable. Having invited the Home Secretary to make a decision I can hardly defy him."

"This isn't only about John's book," Audrey said. "Douglas has called for the whole of literature to put its house in order. What topic will be beyond the pale next time?"

"We cannot allow petty bigots to decide what can and cannot be written, what can and cannot be read," John said.

Cape shook his head. "I gave the Home Secretary my word that I would withdraw the book if he objected. He has objected. I can do nothing but withdraw."

"So it's accept your devious methods or allow my book to die?"

"I prefer to consider it as a way that we both get what we want. I keep my reputation. You keep your book in circulation."

CHAPTER EIGHTEEN

I'm at the Women's Pond bright and early on Sunday morning. It's my last chance to see Janet before I go back to work tomorrow. Despite Wilma's warning I'm hoping I can fix things with her. For all I know Wilma's got it wrong. But even if Janet is a player, maybe I'm ready to be played. In the quiet of my room, I've been remembering that kiss at the party and the sensations that whirled through my body before abomination fears took over. I've been imagining what it might be like to be in bed with Janet and to feel her hands touching me and mine touching her. I want to go beyond imagination.

She told me she came here every weekend. I waited for her all day yesterday. She didn't come. It was hard not to be disappointed but here I am again and surely she'll come today. I've it all worked out. She'll see me, and smile, and say hello Maggie, it's good to see you, love the new hair. And I'll say I'm sorry about the party. I got scared. But I'm not scared now. (Though I am, a bit, but I won't tell her that for fear of putting her off.) And she'll say, how would you like to come with me to the Cave of Harmony next Saturday night and I'll say, I'd love to. We'll want to be kissing, there and then, but we'll have to hold ourselves in on account of the other women at the Pond. She'll invite me back to where she lives and the moment we're over the threshold she'll be kissing me and then it'll all happen and I'll feel fantastic like Mary and Stephen do on Orotava after they become lovers.

I glance at the women already at the Pond. None of them is Janet. It's only nine o'clock. There's still plenty of time.

I ran the six miles from Dunlace Avenue to the Heath, Tilda's old wartime rucksack bouncing on my back. I'm sweating. Time for a swim. One of the lifeguards smiles at me as I make my way to the edge of the platform. I think it's the hairdo that's getting me attention. I smile back before diving in.

I scan the lawns again after my swim. Janet hasn't arrived yet, but it's still early. I stake a claim on a patch of lawn with a good view of the path leading down to the changing rooms. If she comes, I'll see her.

I settle on my towel to dry in the sun. I'm rereading *The Well* at home but I didn't dare bring it here. I couldn't risk it being stolen. All of London wants a copy now that it's been banned. I retrieve *The Unpleasantness at the Bellona Club* by Dorothy L. Sayers from the rucksack. Sibyl said it was a good read but it takes me a while to get going with it on account of looking up every five seconds to see if Janet has arrived. I have to do a deal with myself that I'll check for Janet at the end of each chapter.

I spend the day reading and swimming and checking for Janet. She doesn't come. I should've taken her address. I could have called in to see her, though that sounds too bold a move for me. At least I could have sent her a note suggesting we go to the cinema or to tea at the Hungarian café. I think to myself, why not try there now? What have I got to lose? I take time in front of the changing room mirror smoothing my blouse and fixing my hair so I look my best.

The walk to Swain's Lane takes less than ten minutes. All the way I'm rehearsing variations of, *hello Janet, nice to see you, sorry about the other night, do you mind if I join you?* The second I open the door to the café I see her. She looks even better than I remembered, but worse, too, because she's with another woman. They're eating the same cake we ate and their forks are flirting like ours did and Janet reaches out and strokes the other woman's cheek and all I can do is stare. That's when Janet looks up, and she doesn't smile a warm smile like I've been imagining. It's a smirk and she leans across the table and whispers in the ear of her companion who turns and gawks at me and then she turns back to Janet and the pair of them laugh. A waiter asks me if I'd like a table and it brings me to my senses and I'm out the door as fast as I can, my cheeks scalding.

Sibyl's in the kitchen when I get home. She calls to me. I'd rather go straight to my room where I can die of shame in peace but I've no choice but to go in.

"How was the Pond?"

"It was a great day for swimming, so it was."

"And gardening. Though the moment I suggested we catch up with the weeding Tilda decided it was imperative she go to Speakers' Corner to defend *The Well* against government interference."

"To make a speech?"

"She's been speaking there on and off since her suffragette days."

"I thought she didn't like *The Well*."

"She doesn't. But she won't have the government deciding she can't read it."

"She's brave, isn't she, standing up in front of people and making a speech?" Whereas I couldn't say a single solitary word to Janet.

"She is rather. During the war she'd always be first to volunteer for anything dangerous." Sibyl turns back to the sink.

"Do you want a hand?"

She sets me to shelling broad beans. I run my finger down the seam of a pod and pop the fat beans into a dish. "Did you really serve in an ambulance unit at the Front?"

"I did."

"And that's where you met Tilda?"

"It was."

Like Stephen and Mary. I practise it in my head. "Like Stephen and Mary." I say it aloud, because they are like Stephen and Mary, but with a happy ending.

"I suppose so. I think it's part of why *The Well* annoys Tilda."

"She told me she didn't like all the misery."

"No. And she has no time for the pseudoscience of the sexologists that Radclyffe Hall draws on."

"Do you think Stephen and Mary could have been happy?"

"Plenty of women like them are. But that wasn't the point that Radclyffe Hall wanted to make. She wanted to challenge the stigma."

"What did you think of it?"

"*The Well*? I loved it, despite its flaws. And her bravery for writing it. How about you?" She's finished scrubbing the potatoes and turns to look at me.

"I…I loved it too."

"You seemed so eager to read it." She fills a pot with water.

"I'm reading it again. Is that all right? I should have asked."

She pauses in her work. "It seems to have made quite the impact on you."

I answer slowly. "It has. I think…I…" My courage fails me. "What do you want doing with these beans?"

"In the colander, please." Sibyl busies herself with getting the potatoes on to boil while I try to formulate the words to keep the conversation going.

I bend to stroke Baby Girl so I don't have to look Sibyl in the eye. "Were there women like Stephen in your ambulance unit?"

"Mannish women, do you mean?"

I meant inverts, women who love women, but I don't know how to say so.

"The Head of our Unit, Toupie Lowther, loved wearing trousers. She used to tell a funny story. Apparently she was arrested once at the Franco-Italian frontier for pretending to be a man. She wore a skirt on the way back and they arrested her for pretending to be a woman." She laughs. "When I read *The Well*, I wondered whether Toupie had inspired parts of the story. She's a friend of Radclyffe Hall's." She laughs again and says, more to herself than me, "I must remember that—a friend of Radclyffe Hall's."

"I thought Stephen was based on Radclyffe Hall."

"Well, I'm sure she is partly, but Radclyffe Hall didn't serve in the war, whereas Toupie did. Hall wasn't a champion fencer. Toupie was."

"Oh."

"I'm convinced Valérie Seymour is inspired by an American woman called Natalie Barney. Tilda and I went to one of her salons in Paris after the war. Valérie is just how I remember Natalie."

"You've been to Paris? Is Alec's a real place? My friend Wilma's never heard of it. All she talks about is Le Monocle."

"I've heard a lot of stories about Le Monocle. It wasn't open when I was last in Paris."

I start to get out plates and cutlery. Sibyl knows about Le Monocle and the type of place it is and she knows someone who's a friend of Radclyffe Hall's. "Was there someone like Mary in your unit?" I say, my back to her.

"Most women in the unit were like Mary. Ordinary women, there to do a job. I suppose I was in many ways."

"And did they…did any of them…with any of the other…"

"Fall in love, do you mean? Is that what you're asking?"

I look at the knives and forks. I'm being far nosier than is polite. But how else will I find out? I don't even know why it matters to me. I've already found Wilma. But I've lost Janet. I want to know about Tilda and Sibyl, for certain, not just guessing and hoping. I need to know there's a happy ending.

"Yes. Some did. I did." Her voice is soft. "Is that what you wanted to know?"

"With Tilda?" I whisper.

"Yes, with Tilda."

"And did she?"

"Yes, she did."

Tears fall like raindrops. A few become hundreds. I stand at the counter and weep.

CHAPTER NINETEEN

The Savoy Grill glittered with celebrities and aristocrats—dance sensation Adele Astaire in rapt conversation with the theatre impresario C.B. Cochran, the Prince and Princess Wiasemsky clinking cocktail glasses with Gordon Selfridge, easy smiles on their faces. John followed the waiter towards an empty table on the far side. She nodded here and there to acquaintances but saw no one she felt the need to talk to until she reached a bespectacled man, sitting on his own perusing the menu. The novelist Hugh Walpole had been one of the first to write offering his support after Douglas's attack.

"I hope you don't mind me disturbing you," she began.

Walpole immediately got to his feet to shake her hand. "My dear Miss Hall, how good to see you." His smile warmed her.

"I wanted to thank you for your letter."

"It was the least I could do. I've written to the Home Secretary and the Prime Minister, too, though in rather different terms. And to Cape. What on earth was he thinking?"

"I've been wondering that myself."

Walpole beckoned to someone behind John. "Arnold. Here."

John turned to see Arnold Bennett, the *Standard*'s literary critic, making his way towards them.

"I assume you know each other," Walpole said.

Bennett's pouchy eyes and droopy moustache gave him a mournful air but when he spoke his voice was animated. "Not in person, though we've corresponded. It's a pleasure to finally meet you, Miss Hall."

"And you, Mr. Bennett."

"Is it true that you took James Douglas to task last week?" Walpole asked Bennett.

"It is, yes. For all the good it did. I ran into him at the Garrick Club the very day the *Express* published that hateful stunt journalism."

John had never been to the prestigious private members' club. Its doors were determinedly barred to women.

Bennett continued, "What a malignant excuse for a human being Douglas is. The man's a fanatic, with an ego that brooks no criticism. It all got rather heated, I'm afraid, especially once Chartres Biron got involved."

"The lawyer?" Walpole said.

"Chief Magistrate these days. Biron should know better than to be defending the likes of Douglas. I gave him short shrift, too."

John had appreciated Bennett's championing of *The Well of Loneliness* in the *Standard* but hearing that he'd defended her to Douglas moved her almost to tears. "You can't imagine how grateful I am for your support."

"I believe you're aware of our plans for a petition against this unwarranted censorship of your work."

"Yes, Mr. Forster told me about it." It had been an awkward meeting. E. M. Forster had never been more than a passing acquaintance, their relationship limited to encounters at the PEN Club. John loved his writing, the man rather less so. He was one of the highfalutins, as Ida Wylie would have it, liable to look down his rather long nose at the efforts of others.

"I'd be happy to add my name," Walpole said. "And I'm sure I won't be the only one."

John thanked them before leaving the two men to their luncheon. She took her seat at a table for two, buoyed by the encounter. People wanted her book in print. Now she needed to make sure that Blanche Knopf was one of them. The diminutive American publisher spent the summers scouring Europe for interesting authors. In June, John had brought Blanche to the Savoy with the sole aim of wooing an American publishing deal out of her. She'd succeeded. Now she hoped lunch would help keep the contract in place. The *Express*'s attack and Cape's timorous response had given Blanche the jitters.

John lit a cigarette to calm her nerves. Now that *The Well of Loneliness* was notorious, America was clamouring for it. The Knopf edition was due out in five weeks. Success in America would seal her book's future. But the longer publication was delayed, the longer the forces who might oppose it would have to organise against it. The Knopf deal had to stick.

A few minutes later, Blanche arrived. John watched the younger woman make her way across the dining room. Petite, dark and unmistakably Jewish, she looked striking with her sleek bob and haute couture.

"Blanche." John got to her feet. "How good of you to come." They bumped cheeks in the French way before taking their seats. "How was Berlin? Uncovered anyone new?"

"It's been a productive trip. But I'm ready to get back to New York."

"I'm glad to have the chance to talk to you before your departure."

"Shall we order before we get down to business?"

After a quick scan of the menu, John decided on the sole à la meunière, Blanche the chicken salad. The business of ordering taken care of they turned their attention to *The Well of Loneliness*.

"Cape's put us in a real bind," Blanche said. "If he'd stuck to the original plan and we'd published together in the autumn, we wouldn't be in this mess. But no, he had to rush everything so he could publish in July ahead of Compton Mackenzie's nonsense of a book. All froth and bitchiness from what I hear."

The advance publicity for *Extraordinary Women*, Mackenzie's satire of Capri's lesbian colony, gleefully implied that one of the characters was based on the infamous Radclyffe Hall. It would be published at the weekend.

Blanche shrugged dismissively. "It's not a serious book. Cape shouldn't have treated it as a rival to *The Well of Loneliness*. Frankly, it's an insult to you to mention it in the same breath. But now we're stuck with trying to bring out a book in America that's been banned in its own country."

"It's not been banned," John said, hurriedly. "It's been withdrawn."

"At the request of a government minister. Let's not split hairs. By any account, it's been banned. What on earth made Cape roll over and show his belly to the Home Secretary? Alfred's furious, I don't mind telling you."

"Believe me, Blanche, I am very far from happy myself with Jonathan's response. I'm hoping that you will show the courage that he lacks."

"We've got religious lunatics every bit as extreme as Douglas and Jix in the US, working themselves into a froth over any book that has something interesting to say for itself. How are we supposed to defend your book when your own publisher in England won't? This could get expensive, John."

Both Cape and Knopf had tried to foist sole liability for any and all legal challenges onto John. Thank goodness Audrey had managed to negotiate them down to sharing legal costs. It could indeed get expensive.

Their food arrived. John picked up her knife and fork and wondered how to summon some charm. "It featured in the Wilde trial, the Savoy chicken salad," she said, lightly. "The judge was outraged that anyone would pay sixteen shillings for chicken and salad."

Blanche finished her first mouthful. "I must tell Alfred. He's a Wilde aficionado."

"He used to frequent the Savoy, Wilde, before the establishment destroyed him. Now Douglas and his ilk want to destroy me. We need people to stand up for the freedom to speak the truth. Inverts may be different, but we do not deserve to be persecuted."

"Your book makes that argument extremely persuasively. Movingly. Unfortunately, that doesn't alter the fact that Cape isn't standing up for it." Blanche returned her attention to her salad.

John set her knife and fork down. Her food remained untouched. "I've already been badly treated by one publisher, Blanche. I hope it won't be two."

Blanche could only avoid her eye for so long. John waited for the American to look up. "When you first read *The Well of Loneliness*, you said it was a perfect fit for the list you're building. It still is. Everything that has happened has only gone to show how much my book is needed. Cape's been inundated with requests from America. Americans want to read it. Please, give them that chance."

They stared at each other across the pristine tablecloth. John prayed for help as she watched Blanche's battle with herself play out in her dark, expressive eyes. At last Blanche nodded. "All right. We'll publish."

CHAPTER TWENTY

Another day, another sackful of mail. Hessian bags bulging with correspondence were taking over John's study. In the days since Douglas's diatribe, John had received hundreds upon hundreds of letters. Until they could find a new secretary, she was dealing with them herself. Try as she might, she couldn't keep pace with the gush of words.

She smoothed the latest letter out on her desk.

Dear Miss Hall,

I read your book after seeing Arnold Bennett's review in the Evening Standard. *I am an ordinary married woman and have never given much thought to the troubled world that* The Well of Loneliness *portrays. It has given me a great sympathy for the suffering that the normal world imposes upon the invert. The Home Secretary has no business banning it.*

Letters like this one proved that she'd been right to risk everything and tell the truth. John took a fresh piece of paper and quickly wrote what had become her stock reply.

Dear Mrs. Masters,

Thank you so much for taking the time to write to me. I am sorry that I am not able to respond to you more fully but please know how much I appreciate your support at this time.

Yours sincerely,
Radclyffe Hall

She addressed the envelope and placed her response in the pile for posting. The next two letters were variations on the Mrs. Masters one. John dispatched them with speed. The fourth letter had been written with such force that the paper was almost torn in places.

Miss Hall,
Hell awaits you. You will suffer torture for eternity. You deserve to be whipped and beaten. I would do it myself if I got the chance. I hope you die in pain. Leave normal women alone, you freak.
Yours,
A red-blooded Englishman

The first time she'd received a suffer-and-die letter it had been a punch in the face. Now she screwed the latest tedious little man into a ball and tossed him in the bin.

Dear Miss Hall,
It is no word of a lie to say that The Well of Loneliness *has changed my life. I'd been hating myself and thinking I was an abomination because I kissed another woman at a party. Now I know there is nothing wrong with feeling the way I do. Like you say, I have the right to my existence.*
Because of your book I was able to talk to my landlady and it turns out she's the same way, her and the woman she lives with. And they're happy. I'd never have been able to ask her if it wasn't for you. I don't feel so alone and I want to thank you from the bottom of my heart for that.
You are a hero to me and to many others, I'm sure. That man at the Sunday Express *is a good-for-nothing waster. So is the Home Secretary for banning your book. In the end courage beats hatred so you can hold your head up high and not listen to the likes of them.*

Courage beats hatred. Letters like this were worth more to John than silver and gold. Treasure letters, she called them. Inverts from across the country were writing in their droves, letter upon letter about what a difference her book had made to them. What more important work could she have put her life to than this?

The doorbell pulled her attention away. The servants had been granted leave to coincide with the now-aborted trip to France. Reluctantly she got up from her desk. A telegram boy was waiting on the doorstep.

Marguerite. You can't touch filth without getting filthy. Mother.

John read the telegram again. She took half a step back into her house. "I'm going out," she called in the general direction of The Drey. Without waiting for an answer she clattered the door shut behind her. Childhood memories burst through as she walked towards Phillimore Terrace. Her mother hurtling across rooms to slap and beat her, claw her face and pull her hair. *I hate you. You disgust me. You're no daughter of mine.* Years and years of snipes and sneers. *I never wanted you. I tried to get rid of you.* With every step her anger mounted. *Filthy.* How dare she?

Kensington High Street was thick with traffic. She had to rein herself in from dashing across in front of a heavy lorry. At last, a gap came and over she went and onto Allen Street. Almost there, red brick giving way to the white stucco of Phillimore Terrace. It was John who'd found the house for her mother and Visetti when they'd tired of their previous accommodation. It was John who'd renewed the lease when Visetti had allowed it to lapse, John who'd paid off the debts, John who'd found new servants when her mother's temper had driven the last ones away.

She mounted the steps to her mother's front door and pressed on the doorbell, keeping her finger hard against it. The housekeeper answered.

"Miss Hall. I'm afraid your mother asked—"

"Where is she?" She pushed past the housekeeper and into the hallway. "Mother!"

"She didn't want to be distur—"

The front parlour was empty but John found her quarry in the rear sitting room, reclining on a chaise longue. Her mother looked every day of her seventy-eight years, despite the pancake makeup and pencilled eyebrows. A side table next to her bore a glass, a teacup, a small plate of biscuits and reading glasses. Discarded magazines littered the floor.

"I tried—" the housekeeper began.

"Get out," her mother said. It could have been directed at either of them but the housekeeper took her chance to exit.

"So you do still know where I live." Her mother didn't get up from where she lay, nor did she invite John to sit down.

"What's the meaning of this?" John thrust the telegram into her mother's face.

Her mother batted the hand away. "Six weeks I've been widowed and not once have you visited."

"I asked what you meant by this telegram."

"What kind of child abandons her grieving mother?" She dabbed at her eyes.

"You can turn off the tear tap."

"You don't care about me. Or my poor Alberto. Publishing your filth two weeks after he died."

"My book is not filthy."

"Why else was it banned?" her mother snapped. "Dragging our name through the muck with your perversion."

"It's not perversion. I was born—"

"Filthy, like your father before you." Her mother sat up. "Having his way with the maid while I was giving birth to you. Oh, you're his child all right. There's not a drop of my blood in your veins."

"If only that were true."

"You ungrateful, spoilt—"

"Spoilt. Hardly. Without Granny Diehl I'd have perished for want of love."

Her mother grimaced. "You and her with your games and your cosiness. It made me sick. *My special little Tuggie*," she said in a fake voice. "*Oh, Granny, let me carry that for you.* What affection did either of you ever give to me?" Despite her age, she was on her feet remarkably quickly and John only just managed to block the blow she should have known was coming.

"Same as ever, mindless and violent."

"You're wicked." Flecks of maternal spit landed on John's cheek. "And unnatural. And now the whole world knows it. As if the photographs of you and that harpy weren't bad enough. Miss Hall and her companion at Crufts. Miss Hall and Lady Troubridge at the first night of this and the first night of that. Always, always wanting the limelight. Look at me, look at me. As if you are someone. You're nothing," she screamed. "Do you hear me? Nothing."

"Have you finished?"

"I may not have been the perfect mother—"

John started to laugh and her mother stumbled for a moment in her tirade.

"May not have been…But who could mother a freak like you? From the moment you were born, I knew there was something wrong with you."

John shook her head. "You call me unnatural?"

"Alberto always said the same. He knew there was something wrong with you, right from the start."

Words rushed out of John's mouth before she could think about what she was saying. "It was him there was something wrong with. Not me. Him. He forced himself…Did he tell you that? A grown man forcing himself…A child, a girl. His own stepdaughter. He forced—" A sob choked her, stopping the words.

Her mother stared at her. "You liar." She lunged forward, hands scrabbling, hitting and scratching before John managed to grab her by the wrists.

"Get off me." Her mother stamped and kicked at John's feet and legs. "Get off."

John pushed her mother hard onto the chaise longue, the table overturning, glass smashing, tea splattering over the rug.

"Liar." Her mother lay panting where she'd landed. "Liar."

John shook her head. "I'm not lying."

"Liar. Liar."

John looked down at the decrepit old woman. "I never want to hear from you again. Do you understand? If you contact me, I will cut off your allowance. You can rot for all I care." She turned towards the door.

"Run away, why don't you? Back to your filthy friend and your filthy life."

John carried on walking. She paused in the hallway long enough to fix her dishevelled tie and waistcoat, smooth down her hair. Back on Kensington High Street she felt eyes upon her. For years she'd ignored the stares and the whispers. If one wore the mark of Cain for all to see, they were to be expected. The *Express*'s attack had intensified the scrutiny. People knew who she was now. They saw not only an invert but Radclyffe Hall who wrote that book that's just been banned. She'd been mobbed at the theatre for her autograph. She didn't like the attention. She'd rather be left alone. At Hornton Street she left the prying eyes behind, glad to be almost home. She'd forgotten her key in her hasty departure. There was no option but to ring the doorbell and wait for Una to open it.

"Where on earth have you been?" Una hissed.

"Don't, Una."

"Where have you been?"

"To my…Phillimore Terrace."

"In heaven's name, why?"

"Let's not talk on the doorstep." John wanted to lie down somewhere cool and calm where Una could stroke her hair and tell her everything would be all right.

"E. M. Forster's here. I've been entertaining him in The Drey, pretending I knew you'd be back any minute."

John's head dropped. "I forgot all about…How long's he been here?"

"About fifteen minutes." Una looked at her properly. "You've been crying, haven't you? You shouldn't have gone to see that mad old witch."

"Is it obvious?"

"Only to me." She kissed John gently on the cheek. "I can hold the fort for a few minutes longer while you wash your face."

"Oh, please stay. I can't face him on my own."

"All right." She squeezed John's hand. "Now go and clean yourself up."

Morgan Forster jumped to his feet when John entered The Drey a few minutes later. His handshake was meagre and moist.

"Mr. Forster, I'm so sorry I was called away," John said. "Do have a seat." Forster resumed her favourite leather chair. It was a chair to occupy fully, its solid comfort embracing you. Forster perched on the edge like it might bite him.

"We've made good progress with the petition of protest." His voice was soft, with a hint of sibilance. "I've brought with me a draft..." He removed a folded sheet of paper from his inside pocket and handed it to her.

Sir,—We write to express our deep concern at the Home Secretary's unwarranted suppression of literature. Miss Hall's The Well of Loneliness *has been withdrawn on his order because its theme displeases him. No charge—*

"We've been canvassing support," he said, distracting her from the words on the page. "H. G. Wells, George Bernard Shaw, T. S. Eliot."

John returned her eyes to the draft petition.

No charge has been preferred against the book and no trial has been instigated. We query on what legal basis the Home Secretary has acted. We urge the public to protest. One man must not be allowed to maim and humble English literature.

"I was sure I'd brought..." Forster delved into his inside pocket but came up with nothing. "Lots of writers." As he spoke, he continued searching his pockets. "Laurence Housman's agreed, Hugh Walpole, Rose Macaulay. Ethel Smyth, the composer. Do you know her?" He didn't wait for a response. "James Agate at *The Sunday Times*. Upwards of thirty names, all well-known figures. I'll send the list on."

While he'd been flapping at himself John had managed to finish reading the petition. "May I ask who drafted this?" She tried to keep the edge out of her voice.

"Rather a joint effort. Mostly Leonard Woolf and me, but Virginia and Arnold also had a say."

She'd been grateful when Forster had mentioned the Woolfs' involvement the previous week but now she chided herself for her naiveté. Leonard Woolf had called her book a failure in his review for *The Nation & Athenaeum*. And his wife was hardly likely to want her name linked to a public defence of lesbianism, given the rumours about her love affair with Vita Sackville-West. "It's not the petition you led me to expect when you visited last week. I am the one being persecuted for my pioneering work but you scarcely refer to me. There is no mention of my honour, the quality of my writing or the moral integrity of my book."

"My dear Miss Hall, none of us dispute the integrity of your book, or its decency, but there is a greater principle at stake—to maintain the freedom of the creative mind."

"The *Express* has implied that I am morally derelict. A polluter of minds, corrupter of souls. I am no degenerate, Mr. Forster, and my book does not encourage depravity. Am I not to be defended against such accusations by my fellow writers?"

He avoided her eye. "Backdoor censorship has to be challenged."

"And cannot a letter defend the quality and decency of my book as well as challenge backdoor censorship?"

"Surely it strengthens the case for the public to know the quality of the book that has been banned," Una said. "This is not the scribblings of a tawdry hack, it's the work of a genius at the height of her powers."

"A letter that makes no mention of either the merits or the decency of my book compromises me in the eyes of the public," John said. "It suggests my fellow writers may think either I am immoral, or that my work is inferior. I resent both suggestions."

Forster sucked at his moustache. "I can assure you that there is no such suggestion."

"I tell you that is what people will believe. I am not prepared for it to go forward as it is."

"Miss Hall, time is of the essence. This ban poses a mortal threat to literature. We cannot allow the Home Secretary to set the boundaries of our imagination. It's almost a week since the announcement of the withdrawal. This letter needs to be published tomorrow."

"So you thought you'd bring me a draft and I would agree to it without a murmur? Can I remind you again, I am the one who has been attacked?"

"We're all under attack. Every writer in this country. There is no legal basis for what Jix has done. We cannot let it stand."

"And I'm just fodder in the greater fight?"

"You're being ridiculous."

"Ridiculous am I?"

"There is no need to shriek at me like a seagull."

"You sit in my home and insult me? At least I'm not hiding." She glared at Forster.

Crimson patches had blossomed on his cheeks, a sheen of sweat glistened on his forehead. He took a deep breath and let it out slowly. "Many writers, as I am sure you will be aware, will take up the cause of literature who may not be willing to attach their name…"

"Attach their name?"

"Do I need to spell it out?"

"You can tell them I am proud to have written in defence of the persecuted and reviled. I do not want the help of anyone who will not vouch for the decency of my work."

He paused. "If that is your wish, then I will communicate it to those who were willing to support you."

CHAPTER TWENTY-ONE

The house could be a sister of the one that I grew up in. Two-up two-down terrace, though the bricks here are brown not red. A woman is scrubbing the neighbouring doorstep, same as my Auntie Ruth used to do on a Saturday afternoon. She kept a clean house, inside and out. She'd've made someone a good wife if she hadn't been landed with rairing me.

A girl in a summer frock answers my knock. Before I've said a word, she hollers up the stairs, "Aunt Wilma."

"Send her up," Wilma calls down.

Mounting the stairs, Auntie Ruth is still in my head. I hope she's not looking down on me today. She'd think I was heading for damnation on account of me going out on the town tonight in search of adventure.

Wilma greets me on the tiny landing that separates the two bedrooms. She's looking especially dashing today in waistcoat and cravat.

"I brought you these." I thrust a tin of homemade ginger snaps at her.

"We'll have them later with a cup of tea. But business first."

I follow her into the back bedroom. A photograph adorns the wall above the single bed.

"Go ahead," she says, seeing me glance towards it.

A dozen women are arrayed around a bar. Wilma's near the front in a black dinner jacket, a pretty woman held close in her arms.

"Is this Scarlett?"

"No, that's…oh, what was she called?"

How many women does she have on the go?

"Alice, I think. Or Anna. Something with an A. That was my first trip to Paris." She beams. "This is Le Monocle, the bar I was telling you about. What a place. Dancing downstairs, rooms for hire upstairs. That's the owner, Lulu." She points to a woman with cropped hair in a dark suit and tie. "She set it up for women interested in meeting other women."

"Is the Cave of Harmony like this?"

"Who told you about it?"

"Janet."

Wilma tuts. "The Cave's nothing like Le Monocle. It's more of a cabaret night for arty types. They'll put up with women dancing together but it's not a lesbian club, not like Le Monocle. There's a few places for the boys in Soho but mostly women don't go in them."

"Will there be dancing tonight?"

"Hard to say. We're meeting Scarlett at the American Women's Club. It's a private member's place, the most glamorous in London, so I've heard. She'll sign us in."

"I'd love to learn to dance."

"I'll teach you the basics once we've got you kitted out."

A large wardrobe occupies the wall opposite the bed. She opens the door to reveal an abundance of shirts, skirts and trousers, waistcoats and jackets. A rail on the inside of the door is crowded with ties.

"Oh my word. Where did you get all these clothes?"

She grins. "Achille Serre. A lot of them, anyway. Things people put in to be cleaned and never bothered collecting. I know a few of the manageresses. You'll not believe the things you can get for nothing more than a friendly smile and a line of chat."

I got my worn skirt and plain blouse from the thrift shop in Euston Market. "I don't suppose I could…"

"Course. I'll take you with me next time I go. For now, let's see what you can borrow from my little stash. The trousers'll be too short for you, but you're welcome to try anything else."

I don't mind about the trousers. I've never worn a pair and I'm not sure I'm ready to start. Besides, Stephen Gordon wore skirts. So does Radclyffe Hall.

"I've a good few white," Wilma says, flicking through the shirts, "but I think a colour…" She picks out a pink one.

I turn my back on Wilma. My fingers fumble, undoing one set of buttons, doing up another.

"Done yet?" Wilma says.

"Yes." I turn towards her.

She steps forward, folding back my flapping cuffs and fastening them with cufflinks. Her fingers brush against the skin inside my wrists, tickling. "That's better. Bow tie or necktie? Or cravat?"

"Bow. But you'll have to tie it for me."

"Do it with me." She takes off her cravat, replaces it with a bow tie and begins to knot it. "Across, under, through, create the bow, fold back, pinch and tighten."

"They don't have this one on the firefighters' knot-tying sheet." I fidget the bow into place. "Is that right?"

"Pretty good." She straightens it for me, then hands me the waistcoat. The front is black twill, the back a silver silk paisley. "This is one of my favourites."

"Are you sure you don't mind me trying it?"

"Go ahead."

The waistcoat slides over the shirt. I button it: one, two, three, four.

"Ready for a look?"

We clatter down the wooden stairs to the front room. The mirror hangs above the fireplace. I gaze at my reflection. It's the best I've looked in my whole life, better even than in my firefighter uniform. I sweep my hair back from my face. I could be a young Radclyffe Hall.

The American Women's Club occupies a grand mansion on Grosvenor Street. You could house five families in the entrance hall alone. The ceiling above me is a lattice of elaborate wooden carvings, to my left an ornate staircase leads upwards past gold-framed paintings. I'm nearly scared to put my foot on the fancy rug. My hands are sweating. I pat them discreetly against my skirt. I don't want to be shaking Scarlett's hand with a slippery palm.

I follow Wilma towards the reception desk. Before we get there, a blond woman appears through one of the doors. "At last," she hisses at Wilma. "Some gruesome acquaintance of my mother has had me cornered for the last thirty goddamn minutes. She kept suggesting I meet her son." Her words are drawn out and slightly breathless. Noticing me for the first time she smiles sweetly. "You must be Maggie. Pleased to meet you. I'm Scarlett." She extends a hand, displaying bright red talons that match the lipstick on her rosebud lips. "Forgive my manners but I just can't be bothered with gold diggers wasting my time. Shall we go?"

"We only just arrived," Wilma says.

"Well I cannot possibly stay here."

"Course you can. It's a big place. We can find a different—"

"Honey, I'm not staying. But if you can find another member to sign you in…" She begins to walk towards the front door. We've little choice but to follow. From the tight look of Wilma's jaw I can see she's furious.

Out in the street, Scarlett smiles again. "Thank you for your consideration."

Wilma doesn't answer. I wonder if the evening's over before it's even begun.

"Don't be cross with me, honey." Scarlett leans forward trying to get Wilma's attention. I get an eyeful of cleavage. I retreat a few steps to give them a moment of privacy. There's some muttering between them that I close my ears to. I roll a stone back and forth under my shoe, hoping they can sort things out. I don't want to go home.

A few minutes later we're in a cab to Hertford Street. It's only a hop and skip away but Scarlett "couldn't possibly walk in these little bitty shoes." Her hand rests on Wilma's trousered thigh. I try not to look at it.

We exit onto a quiet Mayfair street. Scarlett knocks on the sombre black door of a tall Georgian house. A woman opens it. After a brief discussion we're admitted to wait in the reception. A large painting fills the wall above the desk—two women, faces turned towards each other, lips parted, about to kiss. I'm so busy gawking it's a moment before I realise my mouth's open. I shut it.

Scarlett summons a friend to sign us in.

"What is this place?" I ask Wilma.

"Scarlett says it's a private members version of Le Monocle. Very hush-hush."

Music and laughter and the ring of glass against glass filter down the curving staircase from the floor above. I hope Scarlett can get us in. I want to be up there, talking and laughing and clinking glasses.

"Scarlett, darling." I turn towards the voice. An olive-skinned woman in a white satin gown descends the staircase.

"Cleo." They half embrace, kissing air.

"I see you've brought company. I'm afraid the rules stipulate that I can sign in two guests only."

"I hadn't realized…" Scarlett says. "Couldn't you make an exception?"

"Rules are rules."

Her face is stern. It seems this night wasn't meant to be.

"I'll see you on Monday," I say to Wilma.

"Hold on." Wilma puts her hand on my arm. She glares at Scarlett.

"Rules are rules, honey."

"Well we'll have to—"

Cleo bursts out laughing. "Of course they're not. I'm the club president. If I feel like signing in three guests, I jolly well shall, rules be damned." She laughs again. "Oh, to see your face, like an unloved puppy. What's your name?"

"Maggie Dillon."

"First names are enough here. And you, the loyal friend?"

"Wilma."

"Welcome to Devoted."

The first-floor drawing room runs the length of the building with windows at both ends. Although it's still light outside, the curtains are closed and chandeliers illuminate the party. A black woman in a white dinner jacket sings the blues on a dais at the front of the room. All the musicians accompanying her are women, even the one playing double bass. Waiting staff, dressed in lavender shirts and black skirts, weave among the guests, serving cocktails, champagne and little bites of food.

Scarlett orders a bottle of champagne and three glasses.

"I don't…I've never drunk alcohol," I say.

"Why ever not?" Her tone doesn't invite an answer.

At least fifty women are present, most wearing evening gowns. I contemplate the beauty of bare necks and collarbones. A woman in a midnight-blue dress looks film-star good. She leans forward to whisper in the ear of her companion. From the way they touch I can't help but wonder what intimacies they've shared.

The champagne arrives. A slight froth builds in the neck of the bottle as the waitress eases the cork out. She pours out one, two, three glasses. Bubbles race to the top of my champagne flute, and race again, and race again. Scarlett and Wilma incline their glasses towards me.

"Bottoms up," Wilma says.

Our glasses clink together. "Bottoms up." I raise the flute to my lips. The fruitiness of the champagne fills my nostrils. I take a sip. Bubbles explode. I sip again, looking round the room. Scattered among the evening gowns are women who've affected the same skirt, shirt, tie look that I've adopted. A handful of others have gone the whole hog with gentlemen's evening wear. Wilma looks as good as any of them in her dinner jacket and black bow tie. Or almost any. A boy-woman in tails and white tie outshines the room. I force my eyes away from her but they keep drifting back. She's as graceful as a greyhound as she walks across the room. Despite their different colouring, she reminds me of Seven.

I'm giddy-headed before I've finished my first glass of champagne. "Is it time for dancing?"

"Soon," Wilma laughs.

"Have another glass of champagne," Scarlett says. I know I shouldn't because the first one's buzzing through my blood but I do. The band's moved on to a song I've heard Sibyl playing on the gramophone. I sing under my breath.

> *"I got the blues, the weary blues*
> *And I'm sad and lonely, won't somebody*
> *Come and take a chance with me?"*

I remind myself I'm not sad and lonely. I'm here with Wilma who didn't abandon me when it looked like we couldn't all get in. And I'm in a room full of women, beautiful women, women who are here because they like women and maybe someone will come and take a chance with me. I look for the woman in the tails. She's smoking in the corner. I wish I could go over and speak to her but my feet won't move.

Wilma's in conversation with Scarlett. While I'm waiting for a chance to interrupt and ask her advice, a woman in a flame-red satin gown approaches the woman in tails. They hug, then kiss on the lips, longer than a moment, enough for me to know they're together. I should have expected it. Why wouldn't a woman like her have somebody?

"Have another glass of champagne," Scarlett says. I know I shouldn't and so does Wilma who says I'm not used to it and orders me a Saint Clements. I'm sipping it when a woman comes over to where I'm standing. The room is full of bobs and crops but her hair is long and dark, falling round her pale shoulders.

"Haven't I seen you here before?" she says.

"Me? No."

"Really? You seem awfully familiar."

"You must be thinking of someone else."

"Are you enjoying yourself?"

"Yes, I am indeed."

There's a pause in the conversation and I should fill it with something but my mind's a blank. A waitress with a silver platter rescues me.

"What are they?" I ask.

"Smoked salmon blinis on the right, madam, crostini of crab and artichoke on the left."

The fish looks raw so I opt for the crab. I concentrate on getting it in my mouth without slippage and miss the woman's next line of chat.

"Pardon?"

"I was just wondering, you're not a member, are you?"

"No." Where would I have the money for a swanky place like this? "Are you?"

"Where are you from? That's not a London accent."

"Belfast, but I live here now, so I do."

"Did you come with anyone tonight?"

I turn to introduce Scarlett and Wilma but they're two feet further away than I remember them. We make our way over and I start the formalities but I don't know the woman's name.

"Lydia," she says.

The music changes and women start to dance.

"Excuse us." Wilma leads Scarlett to the dance floor.

I look at Lydia. She's older than me, early thirties maybe. I bet she's danced a lot in her time. I don't want to clobber her feet in their elegant silver sandals. But I want to feel her body next to mine, moving to the music. I hope Wilma's hour of tuition will be enough.

"Would you like to dance?"

I wrap my left hand round her right as if I've been waltzing with women all my life. My other hand finds its place on the soft skin of her bare shoulder, my little finger resting against the smooth silkiness of her fuchsia gown. I inhale the floral scent of her. One, two, three, one, two, three, one, two, three, we set off round the dance floor. Whatever the rhythm of the music I stick to the waltz. Lydia doesn't seem to mind. We hold each other close, and she looks into my eyes and I feel almost naked but I smile at her. One, two, three, one, two, three, one, two, three.

"Would you like to come home with me?"

"Pardon," I say, though I heard her perfectly clearly. I wasn't expecting it, and I don't know why not. Isn't that why I came here?

She looks away, thinking I don't want to, but I say, "Yes, I would."

Wilma's all smirks when I tell her I'm off. "Getting off, more like. Come find me on Monday."

Night has fallen. Lydia pulls her shawl close.

"Do you want my jacket?" I hope she knows I mean just for now because it's actually Wilma's and she'll be wanting it back.

"No, thank you. It's not far."

She stops outside a townhouse barely five minutes from the club. Carefully she slips her key into the lock, turning it slowly. It opens with barely a sound. She puts her finger to her lips. "Just give me a moment," she whispers. She disappears inside, leaving me like a fool on the doorstep. I shuffle my feet. *And that night they were not divided.* Could Radclyffe Hall not have given me a bit more detail than that? I'm losing my nerve but then Lydia returns. She takes me by the hand. "Come in."

I follow her into a room off the hallway. Even in the dim lamplight I can see it's far too grand for me with its buttoned sofas and portraits on the walls.

"Dance with me," she says. A gramophone sits in the corner but she doesn't put on any music. We sway together on the carpet to the sound of our beating hearts and then she kisses me, her lips warm against mine. Her tongue touching mine is almost too much, almost, and I feel I might explode.

"Lydia."

I drop kisses down her bare throat and across her shoulders and along her collarbone, and then below it, my lips edging closer to where bare skin ends and gown begins, closer and closer to the soft tops of her pale breasts.

She leads me to the nearest sofa and unties my tie and takes off my waistcoat and begins to unbutton the buttons of my shirt, one, two, three… She kisses me again and her hand eases into my brassiere and I think I really will explode as her fingers find my nipple. I let out a low moan and she stops kissing me and her other hand is in my brassiere and she has both of my breasts now, both of my nipples and I don't want her to take her hands away except I need her to because one of them has to do something about the ache building between my legs—

Light floods the room. A man stands in the doorway.

"Lydia, darling. I see you've got company."

CHAPTER TWENTY-TWO

"And he says, 'Lydia, darling. I see you've got company.'"

"You're joking." Wilma stops midstride.

I pause in our stroll through Victoria Park to let her see the pure honesty on my face.

"Who was he?"

"Only the husband."

"That's awkward. Oh!" She half-laughs. "That *is* awkward."

"Awkward? Honest to goodness, I near died."

"So what happened? Did he come after you with a poker?"

"No, nothing like that. 'I think introductions are in order,' says he." I put on his plummy voice, hamming it up for Wilma's benefit though it was far from funny at the time. "Cool as an icebox she says, 'Rupert, this is Maggie. Maggie, Rupert.'"

"Ooohhh." Wilma shakes her head.

"I start getting my jacket on," I say, which is something of a lie when all's said and done, because I was actually fumbling with the buttons of my shirt and scrambling on the floor for Wilma's tie and waistcoat and wondering if he'd seen Lydia's hands in my brassiere but I don't want to tell her that. "And he says, 'There's no need to go on my account. The opposite. Quite the opposite.' And he sits down in the armchair and asks if he can watch."

Wilma sucks in her breath. "Watch you and Lydia?"

"Aye. Can you imagine? He said he wouldn't be touching, only watching and what harm would it do, we were all adults. I ran for the door."

"At least you got out safe enough. You did, didn't you?"

"I did. I legged it down to Piccadilly and got the night bus home."

"All's well, as they say." She starts to chuckle. "And look at the story you got out of it. 'I see you've got company.'"

"And who but you do you think I'm going to be telling it to?"

"Fair point. Future lovers, maybe, if you stay with them long enough. And they're not the jealous type. And the right kind of friends. There's a few women I know would appreciate a story like that."

We carry on our walk in the early-evening sunshine. "Does that sort of thing happen a lot?" I ask.

"I wouldn't say a lot."

"But it does happen?"

"Not quite the way it happened to you. You do get men come looking for lesbians. Some get a thrill out of watching. Some are hoping for a threesome. Occasionally you'll get couples approach you together."

"At Gunter's?"

"No, not there. Not in my experience anyway. Sometimes in one of the boys' clubs, or at the Café Royal or one of those seedy places around Tottenham Court Road. I've even been stopped on the street. 'Are you interested in making a bit of money?' The first time I didn't know what he had in mind and was foolish enough to ask, 'Doing what?' Now I just say, no, thanks."

"Do you think Lydia knew he'd be there?"

"Probably. You do get women who like both."

"At the same time?" I know Angela Crossby had her husband and Roger Antrim on the go while she was leading Stephen a merry dance but she wasn't after them all in bed together or anybody watching.

"At the same time. At different times. At the same time and at different times. I stay away from them. There's always a husband lurking in the background and I don't want to be on anyone's divorce papers."

"I don't want that either."

"Don't worry. You'll find the right woman sooner or later. I'm having a party on Saturday week. Perhaps the woman of your dreams will be there waiting for you."

I leave Wilma at Grove Road and make my way home. I've come out of my way but it was worth it to be able to talk about Lydia. I couldn't tell Tilda or Sibyl. I didn't want them thinking I was some breed of hussy. And I certainly wasn't going to be talking about Devoted to anyone at work. Not that there's ever much time for chat. Drilling's been intense since we got back from holidays. Johnston's working us harder than ever to make up for any imagined slacking. My arms are near hanging off from hauling Charlie back and forth and my legs are still aching from two hours of ladder drills this afternoon.

Maybe I'll have a bath before tea, soak away the aches and pains. I trudge upstairs. An envelope rests against my bedroom door. Addressed to me. Since Granny Palmer passed away, I've no one who'd be bothered putting ink on paper for me. Besides which, nobody knows I'm here. I'm nearly scared to open it. But then I see the postmark. It's Kensington, not Belfast. I can hardly breathe as I open the envelope and pull out the letter inside. It's wrapped around a photograph. My eyes are in shock as I look at Radclyffe Hall. She's wearing a white dress shirt, ruffles foaming against her black jacket. Her face is in profile, staring soberly into the distance, mouth slightly downturned, head topped with a dark trilby. She's posed for an audience but an audience that seems entirely irrelevant to her. It's unsettling and captivating.

I turn it over. It takes me a moment to get to grips with the slanting flourish on the reverse. I trace the letters with my finger. *To Miss Dillon, 'Courage beats hatred.'* These are the very words I wrote to her, quoted back at me. She's signed her name below them. This photograph was in her hand. I'm touching something that she touched. A sacred object. I don't care if that's blasphemy.

I sit down on the bed and open out the letter, dark words on pale-blue paper.

My dear Miss Dillon,

Thank you for taking the trouble to write to me. I find myself humbled at the thought that my book may have played a role in helping you. It gladdens my heart to know that you feel less alone. I hope that you can find the strength to carry the burden of your inversion with dignity.

I am sorry that I am not able to answer more fully but please know that letters such as your own buoy me up in this sea of hostility.

Yours very truly,

Radclyffe Hall

An address is printed at the top of the page. 37 Holland Street, Kensington, W.8. Below it, PARK 7314. I won't go hanging about her door even though I thought about doing it before I had an address for her. Now it would be a betrayal of the trust she's shown me in sending a letter on her own headed paper. As for telephoning her—I've never used a telephone in my life and wouldn't know how, even if there was something coherent I wanted to say, which there isn't. I've got my letter and my signed photograph. It's more than enough.

When we sit down to eat, Sibyl asks if I got my correspondence.

"I did. Thank you."

I can tell she's dying to know who it's from but I'm not ready to be sharing my letter with anybody. It's my private comfort. Radclyffe Hall wrote to me. A secret link exists between us. *Courage beats hatred.* I will hold on to that message because she's said it to me even though it's my words in the first place but they're stronger coming from her. I'm not ready for anyone else to know them so I say, "Would you mind passing the green beans?"

Sibyl's too polite to press me. Tilda's not. "A secret admirer?"

"Maggie's entitled to her privacy."

"I've been invited to a party, so I have," I say to Tilda, because it's not lying so much as a hint of misleading. And what they don't know won't hurt them, so people say, but I don't know that they're right.

CHAPTER TWENTY-THREE

I arrive at Wilma's in time to help with the piano. Her brother is in charge of getting it off the cart and into the front room undamaged. There's plenty of *left a bit, right a bit, easy there*, but eventually we manage to shoehorn it into place at the window.

"Thanks, Georgie," Wilma says. "Do you have time for a cuppa?"

"Nah, I promised I'd have the cart back by six. Enjoy yourselves."

Wilma waves him off.

"What now?" I say.

"Now I think we'll have a bit of the cake you brought and a nice cup of tea."

We're sitting on her front step enjoying our refreshments when Seven comes strolling up the street, as languid as a lion. It's the first time I've seen her out of uniform. She wears a white shirt, dark skirt and leather brogues. At work she always has a cap or helmet on but today her dark curls are open to the September air.

"Perfect timing," Wilma says. "You've missed the hefting of the piano."

"Get it in all right?"

"George is good at that sort of thing. There's tea in the pot if you want a cup and Maggie's made us a Victoria sponge."

"I didn't know you could bake," Seven says.

I half-nod in acknowledgment.

She disappears inside.

"You didn't tell me Seven would be here," I whisper to Wilma. "Is she…?"

"Of course. Can you seriously imagine Seven on some bloke's arm?" She laughs at the thought.

Seven returns with a slice of cake. There's not enough room for the three of us on the step so she stands on the pavement.

"Don't you two look swish in your fancy waistcoats?" she says, between mouthfuls.

"Like it?" Wilma preens. Her black waistcoat is lined with ruby silk. "Departing gift from Scarlett."

"Did Scarlett choose the colour?" I say, remembering her red lips and talons.

"I chose it, she paid for it. Three-piece suit, no less, tailor-made on Jermyn Street."

Seven whistles. "Have you promised to be good?"

"I'm always good."

"And what about you?" Seven says to me. "Have you a secret sugar mummy buying you fancy clothes?"

I'm in the same outfit that I wore to Devoted. "This is Wilma's."

"It's yours now," Wilma says. "Suits you better than me."

"Really? But it's expensive."

"I told you before, it cost me nothing but a few minutes' charm. Have it."

I could nearly cry, I'm that grateful to her.

"Ah, here's Gert." Wilma gets to her feet.

The dark-haired pianist from the Finsbury Park party flounces towards us, heels clicking along the pavement. Her lipstick's thick and red and there's a beauty spot painted onto her cheek.

"Where have you been hiding yourself?" she says to Seven. "And who have we here?" She looks at me and starts to laugh. "My word, if it isn't young Rabbit."

"My name's Mag—"

"It's Rabbit, duckie. Anyone flees a party at the pace you did has gotta be a rabbit."

"Be nice, Gert," Wilma says.

"Janet's not that bad a kisser, is she, to make you run? Certainly not the way she tells it."

"I said, nice."

"Oh, do I have to? In that case you'd better show me the piano."

They disappear inside. I stand up, brushing the crumbs from my skirt. Rabbit. I wonder if it's just Gert's name for me, or whether it's what Janet calls me, too. I remember her whispering to that woman in the café and them looking at me and laughing. If there's a more ridiculous person in the world, may God help them. "I'm away home. Maybe you could tell—"

"Home? Because of Gert? Don't pay her any mind. She's caustic as soda but she plays a good tune."

In the background I hear the same note being played several times over.

"Flat as stale beer," Gert says on the other side of the glass.

"I can't..."

"Go on, stay. I've called you far worse than Rabbit. Maggot, for one."

"That's different."

"They're just words. Sticks and stones and all that."

"It's not true though, is it?"

"You have to make it true. D'you think I've never been called a name? And nothing as pleasant as Rabbit."

"Everyone will be whispering about me."

"You're worried about whispering?"

"Yes."

"People whisper about me every day. If I can manage, so can you."

Two hours later I'm shoulder to shoulder with the queerest bunch of creatures I've ever encountered. Men in dresses and women in trousers, women smoking pipes and men wearing lipstick, men dancing with men and men dancing with women and women dancing with men and women dancing with women. And noise and chat and music and laughter and singing and general hullabaloo. As well as Gert on the piano, there's a woman in a beaded dress playing a saxophone and a man in a toga on the clarinet. Wilma's been introducing me left and right. *"Meet Maggie. She's a firefighter,"* and people have smiled and made conversation till my head's nearly fit to burst with it. I didn't know parties were so exhausting.

How long do I have to stay to prove I'm not a rabbit? Another hour? Two? The whole night? I notice the bottom of the staircase and I think, Wilma won't mind if I go up to her room. Just for ten minutes, a bit of peace away from the throng.

I sneak up the stairs. It doesn't occur to me to knock on the bedroom door. I open it, and I let out a shriek and the woman on the bed with her clothes up round her ears lets out a shriek and the other one who's crouched between her legs turns round just as I shut the door and gallop downstairs.

I can't be running out of another party or I'll never shake the name Rabbit. I need a drink. I push my way through to the pantry and help myself to a glass of a punch.

"I don't think we know you." The speaker is a woman with rather a wide face, sporting a monocle. "I'm Lois, this is Anne," she says, introducing a brown-haired woman with a kiss curl on her forehead.

"Pleased to meet you."

"Quite the crowd. Wilma always did know how to throw a party."

"How do you know her?" I ask.

"Everyone knows Wilma," Anne says. "How do *you* know her?"

"I work at Achille Serre. I'm a firefighter."

"Another one. Do you mind working with the darkie?"

The word isn't whispered. Not shouted either. Just matter of fact like it's ordinary conversation. "Mind? I love working with her. She's the best firefighter we have."

"Well, some of them are very strong," Lois says. "As long as they don't have to think too much."

"She's not a donkey. Excuse me."

I push past people, looking for Wilma. She needs to know about these two women sullying her party. There's no sign of her in the pantry and she's not in the front room either. I try the pantry again but still no joy. I exit into the small rear yard in case she's come out for a breath of air. The music's not so loud here but I can make the tune out plain enough. Seven's dancing herself round the sixteen-foot square, hips swaying, feet tapping, shoulders shimmying.

"Dance?" she says, noticing me. I've no time to be saying ah, yes, nor no before she whirls me into motion. I try to make sure I don't tramp on her feet as she swings me close and away and close again. Delight takes over as she whirls me round the yard.

A toilet flushes nearby. The door to the outdoor lavatory opens. Wilma steps out and we stop dancing. "No need to stop on my account."

"Nature calls." Seven disappears behind the door, leaving me in the yard with Wilma.

"Enjoying yourself?" she says with one of her stock-in-trade smirks.

"I am but—"

"I love a good party."

"I was looking for you."

"And here I am."

"Two of the women…I don't think…" I drop my voice to a whisper. "They were saying nasty things about…" I point towards the lavatory door. "Seven."

"What things? Who?"

The toilet flushes.

"Lois and Anne. They called her a bad word and said she couldn't think."

"Are you sure? It's very loud in there."

"I know what was said."

"What are you two whispering about?" Seven says.

Without a moment's pause, Wilma says, "Maggie here was asking me for another dance lesson but I said to ask you."

"Me?"

"You're a far better dancer than I am."

"But you're a better teacher."

"You don't need to teach me," I say.

"Someone does," Wilma says. "The better you can dance, the more women notice you."

"In the problems of my life, being noticed has never been one of them," Seven says.

Wilma looks at her. "Well, no, I don't suppose it has."

A young man with bright eyes and fluttering hands joins us in the yard. "Wilma, darling. So this is where you're hiding. Oooh, I like your waistcoat." He fingers the silk. "Lovely. I always said you were the best-dressed tomcat in the whole of London."

Wilma introduces Seven and me.

"Firefighters. Oooh, how deliciously manly." He shivers in appreciation. "But enough chatter, I simply must use the facilities."

Before Wilma and Seven can resume their debate about which one of them should have the misfortune of trying to teach me to dance, I take myself back inside. Lois and Anne are in the pantry. I don't want to be hearing anything they've got to say so I push on through to the front room. The only people not dancing are the three musicians and even they are far from still. I see a woman that Wilma introduced me to earlier. She has a pronounced overbite and I'm worried she might eat me up, but I can't be standing in here on my own all night and I wonder can I get the nerve up to ask her to dance. I'm pulling all my courage together, ready to make a move, when I feel a tap on my shoulder. It's Seven. She leans in close so I can hear her above the music.

"When do you want your first lesson?"

CHAPTER TWENTY-FOUR

John slowed her pace as she reached the final paragraphs of the final story in Vere Hutchinson's short story collection, wanting every last drop of pleasure. As she let herself reach the end, she had the urge to clap. *Brava, Vere, brava!*

Carefully John closed the book and slid it into the leather satchel that nestled between her feet. She would have been proud to have written this collection of vivid, unsettling stories herself. For Vere to have conjured it out of the wasteland of psychosis and paralysis that had marked the last four years was nothing short of a miracle.

John lit a cigarette, inhaling the familiar pleasure. She must send Vere a gift. A bouquet of flowers, perhaps. Or a hamper. Yes, a congratulatory hamper packed with treats for Vere and Budge. She'd call Harrods in the morning.

Leaning back in her deckchair, John closed her eyes. September sun warmed her skin. It was another fine day, perfect for relaxing. On the beach below Folkestone promenade, the sea washed in and out. Hush wush, hush wush. The bustle of Calais lay only twenty miles away across the English Channel. Fields of wheat and barley, onions and potatoes for miles beyond the port. Grazing cattle. Onward and onward, rolling landscape punctuated by medieval towns, counting down to Paris.

Beloved Paris. She'd started *The Well of Loneliness* in the French capital, set the heart of the story there. Now Paris would save her book for England. The moulds for *The Well of Loneliness* had safely reached Pegasus Press. Order forms for the new edition were on their way to bookshops. Soon her book would be back in circulation.

John opened her eyes. Beside her, Una sat sketching. For a few minutes she watched her lover applying light and shade to the page. John's shadow fell across the sketchbook as she got to her feet.

Una looked up. "What's the matter, darling?"

"I fancy something sweet. Do you want anything?"

"What are you getting?"

"Whatever takes my fancy."

Una shut her book and bundled it into her bag.

"You don't need to come, Squig."

"I want to come. I want to be with you."

They walked arm in arm along the sea front, enjoying the glint of sun on sea and the endless murmuring of the waves. "Folkestone does have its charms. Maybe we should look for our bolthole here," John said.

"Let's enjoy a few days' holiday first."

John decided to drop it for now. Marsh & Sons caught her eye on the other side of the road, jewel sweets lighting its window. The bell clanged agreeably as they entered.

"Can I help?" The proprietor was the definition of a little old woman—less than four feet ten with a heavily lined face and a wavering voice. Shelves behind her held jar upon jar of sweets. After some debate, mint humbugs, fruit bonbons, butter toffee and Pontefract cakes made their way into Una's bag along with several bars of chocolate and a stick of rock.

They decided to take their swag back to their room. Music from afternoon tea in the Palm Court drifted towards them as they waited for the lift. Their suite at the Grand Hotel had been serviced while they were out. Fresh flowers filled a vase. Through the windows the sea sparkled. The Leas Promenade stretched away to the left and the right. John doubted there was a better-situated hotel in the whole of England.

Una came up behind John and slipped her arms around her. She kissed her softly on the neck. "Are you sure you want to go for a drive this afternoon?"

John turned so they were facing each other. "I thought it was you who wanted a drive."

Una shook her head. "I'd rather stay here with you." She kissed John on the lips.

The cold drop of ice that had lodged in John's heart since the *Express* attack melted. She led Una to the big soft bed.

* * *

It was the best September weather that John could remember. Lazy sunshine days of reading, gentle strolls, easy conversation and short trips to neighbouring villages. They breakfasted in their room each morning. On Thursday, two letters arrived on the tray along with their food. The first was a postcard of a ship. On the reverse Blanche Knopf had written *Full steam ahead.* Lunch at the Savoy had been a good investment. *The Well of Loneliness* would be out in America in a fortnight. She handed the card to Una and opened the second envelope. It was a letter from Audrey.

> *Dear John,*
> *I enclose an offer for publication of* The W of L *in Holland. The advance is low and I wouldn't normally recommend accepting it. However, I know how eager you are to reach readers beyond these shores so—*

"Eat, darling. It'll get cold," Una said but John carried on to the end of the paragraph.

> *—I feel duty bound to inform you of it. Please let me know how you wish to proceed.*

John set aside the letter and skimmed the proposal from the Dutch publisher.

"Anything important?" Una said.

"I've had an offer from Holland. Not much money but I'm inclined to take it if Audrey can squeeze a bit more out of them."

"Is there anyone we can trust to translate it into Dutch?"

"Hopefully Audrey will know someone."

John poured hollandaise sauce over her ham and eggs. Granny Diehl had introduced her to eggs Benedict the first time John had gone to Philadelphia as a young girl. It always reminded her of her granny.

"Coffee?" Una poured without waiting for an answer.

John helped herself to a few mouthfuls of breakfast before returning to Audrey's letter.

> *I spoke to John Holroyd-Reece at Pegasus yesterday. Orders are flooding in. He's engaged the bookseller Leopold Hill to handle distribution in Britain. Copies should start arriving by the end of next week.*
> *Looking forward to seeing you on your return.*
> *With love,*
> *Audrey*

John folded the letter. She approved the choice of distributor. Leopold Hill's shop on Langham Place was a treasure trove of exquisite leatherbound books. There was nothing he didn't know about the workings of the book trade.

"What time is Noël expecting us?" John said.

"About eleven."

"We should get dressed."

The words were simple. The task was not. Noël Coward was never less than elegant. John wanted to look just as dapper for her first visit to his country retreat. She stood in front of the wardrobe hating everything she owned. Or at least, everything she'd brought with her. "I've nothing to wear," she declared.

"I'm sure that's not true, darling."

"I've packed all the wrong things. Who would have expected the weather to be so fine?"

"What about one of your white shirts?"

"I want blue today."

Una picked out a dark blue. "How about this one?"

"It's too heavy for this heat."

John rifled through her wardrobe from left to right and then back again. Finally, she chose a pink shirt, navy necktie, navy skirt and crocodile-skin shoes. Standing in front of the mirror she disliked what she saw. She changed her mind, changed her skirt, changed her shirt, changed her tie, changed her cufflinks. Only the shoes survived.

"We really should get off, darling," Una said, as John smoothed her hair with water.

John turned to Una. "Do I look all right?"

"You look delicious."

John found a smile. "Shall we go?"

Noël's country retreat turned out to be a substantial timber-framed manor house set in extensive grounds.

"How can he afford this?" Una said, as John eased the Daimler through the front gates. "He's not even thirty yet and he doesn't come from money."

"No, but his plays are doing frightfully well." John didn't begrudge him his success. Talent will out. And she knew that he shared his good fortune with others, happily paying off the debts of struggling actors with whom he was barely acquainted. "Apparently he's got a Rolls-Royce."

"I prefer our Daimler," Una said stoutly.

"So do I, darling. So do I."

Their host emerged from his grand residence looking quite the dandy in slacks, an open necked shirt, cravat and trademark silk dressing gown. They'd become acquainted through mutual friends in the theatre. It was a friendship that once planted had soon flourished. John delighted in his quick wit and easy ability to make her laugh.

"Darlings, how lovely to see you." He kissed them in turn. "And this is Mother."

Although silver sprinkled her dark hair, and wrinkles edged her eyes, it was clear that Mrs. Coward had been quite the beauty in her time. She was tall, like her son, but not quite so thin. Her smile was warm as she greeted them.

"What a magnificent house," Una said. "I hadn't realised it was so large."

"It used to be a jumble of buildings," Noël said. "A farmhouse, an ill-judged extension, a few barns and a cottage. We've brought it all together to make one house. It's been gutted inside, all the ghastly wallpaper and tawdry tiles taken away to expose the original oak beams." He rolled his eyes at "ghastly" and John couldn't help but smile. Even off the stage he was inclined to theatrics.

"It was Jack's idea," Mrs. Coward said. "Jack Wilson. I assume you know him?"

John had met Noël's lover-cum-manager several times and didn't entirely like him. The handsome young American was rather too sure of himself and overly fond of a drink. But Noël was besotted with him so she'd kept her opinion to herself.

"Would you like a tour?" Noël offered.

They started at the recently finished barn conversion which was where Noël lived. It was impeccably decorated with antique oak and walnut furniture of the sort that John herself adored. A baby grand piano took pride of place in his sitting room.

"Is this where you work?" Una inquired.

"Sometimes," Noël said. "I work best in hotels or on ships. It'll often come out in a frenzy if I'm locked away for a few days. But I can't imagine a home without a piano."

"He's been listening to the piano since the day he was born. My husband sold them, and I've played since I was a girl," Mrs. Coward said. "Before Noël could even walk, he would sit up in his cot as soon as I sat down to play and beat his little fist to the rhythm. Once he was on his feet, he would dance around the room in time to the music."

"Mother raised me to be quite the show-off, didn't you dear? I was performing for her friends from the age of two."

"Only family, really. My husband's family are all musical, every last one. Noël was playing the piano himself before he was three, making up his own tunes and singing along to them."

John was touched by the pride in Mrs. Coward's voice. She asked what Noël was rehearsing at the moment.

"*This Year of Grace!*"

"We were at the first night in April," Una said.

"It was far and away the most entertaining show I've seen this year," John said. "I didn't know it was going to be on again."

"Not in London. We're taking it to Broadway. I've even written a couple of extra songs for it. Pop into rehearsals if you have the time. You too, Una."

They had reached the original part of the house. "This is Mother's wing."

"He exaggerates. My husband and my sister are here most weekends. They're moving in permanently at Christmas."

"Do you miss London?" Una asked her.

She shook her head. "I was raised in the country. I'm glad to be back in it. And I still go up to London as often as I want."

"Which isn't very often at all," Noël added.

"I've been glad to get out of London myself this past week," John said. "I don't seem to garner as much attention on the coast as I do under the microscope of Kensington."

"It's a very odd experience, isn't it, to have complete strangers staring at you, and then you see them nudge their friend and whisper and then the friend's staring too. It's one of the reasons I bought this place. It keeps me sane, somewhere to relax and enjoy myself in peace. And Jack thought it was wise to invest some of my money in bricks and mortar."

"Is he going with you to New York?"

"Oh, yes, he can't wait to get back to America. He's promised me a proper Thanksgiving dinner, whether I want one or not. I fear it will make me bilious." He reached into his pocket and removed an ornate cigarette holder and case. He offered a cigarette to John who took one readily. "Shall we smoke outside? Mother loathes the smell."

Whilst Una went with Mrs. Coward to the drawing room, John followed Noël out into the garden. After a pause to light their cigarettes, they strolled along the path beside the house.

"Folkestone's done wonders for you," he said. "You've lost that pinched look you had when I saw you last."

"It's been the most bloody few weeks."

"I'll say. You've taken on quite the task. I'm afraid that moral prejudice is deeply embedded in the Anglo-Saxon mind and it will take a great deal to uproot it."

"I have to try. People are looking to me."

"I know. But be careful, John. It's one thing for Stephen to be a martyr, quite another for you."

She turned to look at him. "So you've read it?"

"Of course I've read it. It's all anyone's talking about. You should be proud of yourself. It's a very brave book."

"Thank you."

He stopped to put his cigarette out. "I particularly liked that Brockett chap. Tall, witty, a wonderful playwright. I didn't even mind his feminine hands, being in possession of a rather similar pair myself."

John flushed. "I didn't deliberately draw on you, I swear. But aspects of you kept insinuating themselves into my writing. Do you mind awfully?"

"My dear, I'm rather delighted. Having no intention of writing anything significant myself, it's wonderful to feature in someone else's significant work. Besides, who else are we to draw on for our inspiration than the people we know? We write, as you say, with our eye pressed against the keyhole of other people's lives."

"But your plays are significant."

"Are they? I don't set out for them to be. My aim is to be entertaining. Though, I suppose, laughter is not insignificant."

They returned to the house for a luncheon of steak and kidney pie followed by sherry trifle. Afterwards they sat in the garden, Noël and his mother sipping dry martinis while Una and John opted for lemonade.

"I understand you're quite the experts on spiritualism," Mrs. Coward said. "I'm a believer myself."

Noël smiled wryly. "If it wasn't for powers beyond the grave, I might have ended up a bank clerk."

"Don't mock," his mother said. "You're outnumbered."

"What happened?" John asked.

"Have you ever been to one of the public seances?"

John was aware of the phenomenon, circus events, run by charlatans using hidden accomplices to dig up the secrets of members of the audience. That was the trouble with psychic powers, they were so open to abuse. However, she had taken a liking to Mrs. Coward. "No, I haven't, Mrs. Coward," she replied, diplomatically.

"Violet. Do please call me Violet. The one I attended was in the London Coliseum. 1911. Packed to the rafters. We were all asked to submit a question, along with a piece of clothing. Well, all I had with me was a pair of Noël's socks."

"A rather dull grey pair, darned at the heel," Noël interjected.

"He'd just got his first professional part and I was feeling rather guilty about him missing out on school and what would happen if he didn't make a career on the stage. So, I pinned my message to one of the socks. 'Do you advise me to keep my son on the stage?' I handed it to an usher. There were hundreds of other people doing the same thing, and all of us hoping, let her answer my question. She only does five or six. It was Miss Anna Eva Fay, have you heard of her? An American woman."

"She's been exposed as rather a fraud since she died," Noël said. "Houdini hated her."

"He was jealous. Miss Fay had the gift. You should have seen her. She came out onto the stage, hands all a-tremble, and her head was rolling around, and then she looked straight ahead and she asked for the owner of…a scarf, I think it was. Well anyway, that wasn't me. And then there was someone else after that. But the third time, she lifted up a sock and she said, 'Who owns this sock? Show yourself now, whoever owns this sock.'"

The line was delivered in the style of an American Lady Bracknell. Mrs. Coward raised her left hand, thumb and forefinger pinched together as if she held a sock.

"So I put up my hand. And now it was my hand that was shaking."

John watched with amusement as Mrs. Coward's right hand inched cautiously into the air and then began to tremble vigorously.

"And I said, 'That's mine.'

"'But who is the wearer of the sock?'

"'It belongs to my son, Noël.'

"And she held the sock up higher and said, 'I am getting such an energy from this sock. A tremendous energy. Mark my words, your son will flourish. He is going to be extraordinary.' I thanked her, but she was already moving on to the next one so I sat down. She only did a couple more after me before her head was rolling again, and she went deathly white and collapsed forward in a heap and had to be led from the stage. But I took her at her word and look how well it's turned out. Imagine, if I'd listened to my doubts back then. He might never have had the success he's achieved."

"Which would be rather a shame," Noël said. "I'm terribly fond of success. It comes with such pleasurable trappings."

He raised his glass towards John. "To success."

"To success."

CHAPTER TWENTY-FIVE

I don't know what to wear. My white blouse is dull and boring but maybe it's right to look everyday and not like I think this is a special occasion. Or maybe I should wear Wilma's pink shirt again. It's clean and fresh from being laundered and it's what I had on when Seven spun me round in Wilma's backyard so maybe she likes how I look in it. But if I wear that, will it seem like I'm trying too hard and that this means too much to me? Maybe all she wants is to teach me to dance. I need to decide one way or the other. I can't be standing in my brassiere all day. She'll be here any minute.

It's hard to know what to make of the week that's just passed. Seven's been the same as ever during drilling, calling me Maggot and Dobbin at every turn, but she's talking to me more on inspections and in break times. How is anyone supposed to know what another woman feels for her? I've consulted Radclyffe Hall for advice.

Mary said: 'All my life I've been waiting for something.'

'What was it, my dear?' Stephen asked her gently.

And Mary answered: 'I've been waiting for you, and it's seemed such a dreadful long time, Stephen.'

Have I been waiting for Seven all my life? I don't know. I've definitely been waiting for something, or someone, that would make me feel like I belong in this world and I don't think she does that but maybe nobody can and feeling excited to be in her company is enough. Mary knew in her heart that she loved Stephen and that Stephen loved her but *The Well of Loneliness* is a book, not real life, and I don't know if Seven is the answer for me and even less that I'm the answer for her and if I am, whether she wants the answer. Maybe she'd rather live her life full of questions.

I settle on the pink shirt, open at the neck, no tie, no waistcoat. The doorbell rings, Baby Girl barks and I clatter down the stairs. Go to your bed, I say, and she gives me a look of reproach before obeying. The nights are already drawing in and winter's only two steps away but today's an Indian summer day. Seven stands on my doorstep in the autumn sunshine. A song we used to sing at the mill comes into my head.

No maid I've seen
Like the brown colleen
That I met in the County Down

And the brown in the song is for hair not skin but the woman in front of me is surely as fine a colleen as ever lived in Bantry Bay or Derry Quay.

"Come on in." The words fill my mouth with happiness because this is the first time in my whole life I've ever had a friend visit me at home.

Baby Girl has to be stern voiced into keeping all four feet on the ground but Seven says, "I love dogs," and bends to stroke her and is offered the belly of delight.

"Would you like a cup of tea? Or there's ginger beer in the icebox."

"Maybe later." She looks round the room. "Nice place."

"I fell on my feet, so I did. It's got an indoor bathroom and everything, upstairs, next to my bedroom." The memory of the two women at Wilma's flashes into my mind. I wish it hadn't because it's wild hard to shift and I miss what she says as she crouches down to inspect the gramophone records stored in a cabinet on which the machine itself sits.

"Whose are these?" she says, flicking through them.

"Sibyl and Tilda's. They're my landladies. Well Sibyl is. Tilda's her…" I don't know what word to use. "Friend. Companion. Intimate… companion."

"They like their jazz and blues. Bessie Smith, Louis Armstrong and the Hot Five, Duke Ellington. Oh, Ma Rainey's new one. Can we put it on?"

A piece of paper flutters to the floor as I take the record out of its sleeve. Block capitals shout "PROVE IT ON ME BLUES" above a picture of a plump black woman in shirt, tie and waistcoat. She stands flirtatiously close to two skinny flappers, a policeman watching on from the shadows.

Seven stoops to pick the advertisement up. "Oh, I don't believe…If this is what I think…Put it on. Please." Her face glows, eyes bright as a robin's.

I crank up the gramophone. There's a hiss as I place the needle on the record. A muted trumpet and a jangly banjo play a short introduction but then Ma Rainey's voice takes over. It sounds like it's come up from the depths of the Earth through heat and rock and dust and gravel into sunshine and rain. The words she sings are even more extraordinary.

"I went out last night with a crowd of my friends
It must've been women, 'cause I don't like no men."

Seven clicks her fingers in time to the music, her eyes closed half the time. She's joining in the chorus by the end. "Sure got to prove it on me," she says when it's finished. "Oh, she's bold." She laughs. It's a truly wonderful sound, starting with a chuckle in her throat and expanding out like fireworks. I never noticed her laugh before. "That's one in the eye for the rozzers."

"What? Tell me."

She leans forward conspiratorially, though there's only me, her and the dog to hear. "The way I heard it, Ma Rainey was having a party a few years back for her friends. Women friends, if you get my meaning. Those gals were having a wild time by all accounts. Some say dancing, some say kissing, some say a full-scale orgy. Who should turn up in the middle of it all but the police?"

My hand goes to my mouth in horror. "They never!"

"Oh, yes. Arrested Ma Rainey and hauled her off to a police cell for running an indecent party."

"An indecent…Oooh. Imagine."

"It wasn't looking good for Ma, but luckily she has the best of friends. Who do you think goes to the cops to bail her out? None other than Bessie Smith herself, that's who. Made sure the charges got dropped for good measure. And now Ma Rainey's brought out a record to tell the world what she got away with. 'Sure got to prove it on me.'" She laughs again.

"How do you know all this?"

"I've met a couple of women who claim to have been at that party. Though by all accounts, half the women in Harlem not to mention a few hundred from Greenwich Village and the Bronx claim they were at that party which can't be true. Her house isn't that big."

"Have you been to her house?" I'm impressed.

"Not yet. But I'm going to go one day. Harlem. Someday I'm going to go there. Some day."

The laughter's gone and her face is sad so I say, "Shall I play it again?"

"You choose something this time. Something you love."

I search among the records. My first thought is Bessie Smith's "I Ain't Got Nobody" but I don't want her thinking I'm sad and lonely so I pull out Duke Ellington's "Creole Love Call." It's the perfect song to dance to.

She's smiling again and I'm glad because her sad was sadder than I knew how to manage. "Great choice," she says. As the music starts she takes my hand and places it on my heart. "It's not about steps. Listen to the music. Let yourself follow it." Briefly she presses her hand against mine before letting go.

The persistent *da-da, da-da, da-da, da-dum* of Adelaide Hall's countermelody has always captured me. Until now. Today I stand stiff and foolish, confused and exposed. I feel like I'm in one of those dreams where I'm out shopping or at church and everyone else is dressed and they're staring at me because somehow I've forgotten to put my clothes on.

"Don't be shy. There's only me here," Seven says. "I won't look if that helps." She closes her eyes but stays close by me, close enough that I can see the soft fuzz of the tiny hairs along the line of her jaw.

I close my eyes. *Da-da, da-da, da-da, da-dum.* No words, Adelaide's voice another instrument. *Da-da, da-da, da-da, da-dum.* The swoon of the clarinets, the blast of the trumpet, strings and piano at the back. *Da-da, da-da, da-da, da-dum.* Duke and Adelaide do their magic. The music reaches into me and I feel the plaintive hope of it and my body starts to sway and my feet begin to move. *Da-da, da-da, da-da, da-dum.*

"How was that?" Seven says softly as the song comes to an end.

I open my eyes. My lashes are wet but at least tears aren't spilling out. Her deep-brown eyes are looking at me and I nod and she smiles.

"Can we have it on again?" Seven says.

I do as she asks. She takes my right hand in her left, her other hand on my shoulder, mine on her arm. Our bodies touch in a gentle embrace that takes the breath from me. When I breathe in again my head fills with the smell of her. She smells like home. Not the dirt and grime of Belfast, a home I've never had and always yearned for.

"Same as before, don't worry about steps, feel the music."

I shut my eyes and listen and I seem to know she's going to step forward so I step back and she steps forward and to the side and I step back and to the side. And step and step and side and step and step and side as Adelaide croons love and the clarinets swoop and soar.

CHAPTER TWENTY-SIX

The study was a production line: Una in the armchair deciding which letters merited John's attention, John at her desk writing responses, the newly engaged Miss Webber in the corner applying stamps and filing correspondence. In the last five days, they'd dealt with more than a thousand letters. John put her pen down and gently rubbed the aching callus on her middle finger.

"Maybe you should take a break," Una said.

John dismissed the suggestion. She'd bought tickets for the farewell tour of *The Scarlet Pimpernel*, a thank-you present to Una. She was determined to get through the backlog before they set off for the matinée.

The next letter was from a Miss Hetherington of Northumberland, thanking John for the sense of connection to other inverts *The Well of Loneliness* had given her. There had been hundreds of letters like this one, isolated women all over the country reaching out to John in gratitude. She picked up her pen and began what had become her default response.

Thank you for taking the time to write to me. I am glad that my book—

"You need to read this," Una said, getting up from her chair and coming over to John's desk.

"In the pile." John gestured impatiently to her in-tray. Didn't Una know by now how much she hated to be interrupted?

"Knopf are pulling out."

John snatched the letter from Una's hand.

Dear Miss Hall,

I regret to inform you that we have decided that we cannot go ahead with publication. Preorders are slanted to the indecent end of the market. I am sorry to report that The Well of Loneliness *has gained a reputation as a dirty book.*

The coarseness of the phrase affronted John. Dirty book, as if she were a backstreet pornographer. She stood, her anger too great to be contained behind a desk.

"Oh, darling—"

John silenced Una with a gesture.

Events in England have skewed demand in America. A respected English publisher withdrew your book from circulation on the request of a Cabinet Minister. You acquiesced in this withdrawal.

A coward as well as a pornographer. So that's what Blanche Knopf thought of her. All the time John had spent pandering to Blanche's craving for personal attention, plumping up her greedy little ego, not knowing the traitor that lurked beneath the surface.

Defending your book in America when it has not been defended in its home country has proved a hopeless task. The market here has been irredeemably tainted. I advise you to focus your attention elsewhere.

From full steam ahead to rip out the engine in less than a fortnight. First Cape, now Knopf. Dastards and deserters both. Was there a decent publisher to be found anywhere in the English-speaking world? John tossed the letter on the desk. Her face was hot, her armpits damp. This wasn't happening. How could this be happening?

Una clucked sympathetically in the background. John didn't want sympathy. She wanted action. She picked up the telephone. The shrill of hysteria sharpened her voice as she told Audrey of Blanche's treachery. "What are we going to do?"

"I'm sure we can change her mind." Audrey was milk-calm.

"I'm done with her."

"It's nerves, John. I'll talk to her."

"I'm done with her, I tell you. Pulling out a week before publication. It's unforgivable."

"Let's not be hasty."

"I am not crawling to that woman."

"And I'm not asking you to. I said I'll talk to—"

"No. I won't have you crawling to her either."

"We need *The Well of Loneliness* out in America, sooner rather than later."

"Then find me a new American publisher."

"I know you're upset—"

"Upset? I'm a long way past upset. I cannot do business with a publisher that has called into question my integrity. You need to find me someone else. Pronto."

The pause was brief. "If you're sure, I'll talk to Carl."

John's snort was unintentional but unmistakably insulting. Carl Brandt, John's American agent, was another traitor. Either that or a useless fool. "I don't know why you have a reciprocal arrangement with him. If he'd done his job and found me an American publisher I wouldn't be in this mess."

"I know it's not been easy but let's not forget that it was Carl who secured such good deals for your previous American editions."

"He didn't secure one for *The Well of Loneliness*. Perhaps he doesn't care for the subject."

"I'm sure that's not the case."

"I want you in charge, Audrey. After all that's happened I need someone I can trust."

"But I'm not in America."

"Couldn't you go? Please, Audrey. I'll pay your fare, hotels, anything you need."

This time the pause at the other end of the line was long, stretching on and on, fraying John's nerves to a thread.

"Audrey?"

"All right, John. I'll take charge. But for now it'll have to be from London."

* * *

Heads turned towards John as she made her way to her seat in the King's Theatre. As soon as she sat down she hid from the attention behind the programme.

"More than two thousand performances," Una said, looking at her own programme. "It's about time *The Scarlet Pimpern*el had a farewell tour."

"I thought you were looking forward to it."

"I am. But twenty years with the same lead actors is more than enough. Can you imagine if they don't find another safe bet? 'Oh darling, do you think it's time for a revival tour of *The Scarlet Pimpernel?*'"

John's laughter was hollow. She should be at Audrey's making plans for finding a new American publisher instead of wasting the afternoon at a play Una didn't even want to see.

"Do you want to go home?" Una said.

"No." She meant yes, but how could she withdraw a thank-you present?

"Audrey will find you an American publisher."

John bit at her writing callus. "From London?"

"Yes, if she can. From New York if she has to." Una reached over and squeezed John's hand. "Let's try and enjoy ourselves now we're here."

The house lights went down and the curtain went up, transporting the audience to revolutionary France in all its gory glory. John went to America instead. The biggest English-speaking market in the world. *The Well of Loneliness* had to be published there.

America. The place where John had first experienced the physical love of another woman. She'd been young, restless, and newly wealthy when she'd set sail from Southampton in 1902. Her plan had been to spend a couple of months with her extended family. Falling in love has a way of changing plans. She'd stayed more than a year.

It wasn't the first time John had been in love. Her teenage years had revolved around her passion for Agnes Nicholl, her stepfather's soprano prodigy. John had willingly served as bag carrier and travel arranger, maker of soothing drinks and encourager in chief. More than willingly, ardently, troubling over every detail that might make Agnes's life a little better, that might help her become an operatic star. Nothing physical had ever happened between them, nothing beyond a peck on the cheek, a chaste meeting of their pursed lips. John hadn't minded. She was scared of sex in those days.

Jane Randolph was different. She was older for a start—thirty-five to John's twenty-one—and already widowed with three young children. She wasn't the prettiest of women. Her teeth were protuberant, her eyes a little pale, but her auburn hair was glorious, her figure trim. And she was vivacious and amusing and determined to enjoy life. Although they were cousins they'd only met once before, in London a few years earlier. It was in America that they got to know each other.

At the home of her Washington relatives, John had pondered how to get Jane to seduce her. She mustn't do the wrong thing and cause a scandal. A few weeks into her stay, they'd sat up late one night talking in Jane's bedroom. "No one's ever kissed me," John said. "I've often wondered what it's like."

Jane had leant over and kissed her, gently at first, but with growing passion. One kiss had led to two, to three, to twenty. And then they were pulling at each other's nightclothes, clamouring for more. But when Jane's hand had found its way into John's drawers, she had frozen.

"Do you want me to stop?"

John couldn't answer, couldn't find a single word to say. Yes, no, yes, maybe, I don't know. She'd kept her eyes closed, not able to look at Jane.

"We don't have to do anything," Jane said softly, "not if you don't want to."

But John did want to. She had to find a way to explain. If she kept her eyes closed, perhaps she could explain. "Something…happened."

The words were barely audible but Jane didn't need them any louder. "Oh, darling, did someone…has someone…interfered with you?"

Maybe that's why John had been attracted to an older woman. Maybe she'd known that perhaps Jane would understand the baseness of the world in a way that a younger woman might not. The story had come out in fits and starts, the years of abuse at the hands of her stepfather. All the time John had kept her eyes closed, her head down. When she was done, Jane told her it wasn't her fault. "You have to know it wasn't your fault." John had wept in her arms.

Over the days that had followed, Jane Randolph had vanquished the shame that had been planted in John. Suddenly she was free. While Jane's mother had looked after her children, they'd romanced their way across the southern states, smoking cigars, drinking champagne and making love. Over and over making love, till John's body and mind were healed and new.

She'd learned a lot about pleasure and laughter in those carefree days. Even now, America symbolised freedom and love and acceptance to her. Surely there was a publisher for her there. In the spring Carl Brandt had tried Doubleday (no), Houghton Mifflin (no), Harpers (no). John's chance encounter with Blanche Knopf in London had saved him the bother of looking any further. Now Knopf was another no.

Who else could she try? Harcourt Brace had published Virginia Woolf's *Mrs Dalloway*. Perhaps they could be persuaded to take on *The Well of Loneliness*. What other publishers had English authors on their books? She'd ask Audrey to check who'd picked up Forster. And Maugham, even Galsworthy. Maybe Lawrence, though she was wary of the association. And what about the quality American authors? They should find out who published Fitzgerald, Wharton, Ferber, Hemingway. Target the right publisher and surely she'd have a deal.

Applause rang out around John. The curtain edged downwards, signalling the interval. She was one of the first to the ladies' toilets, determined to avoid the perennial queue. It had started to form by the time she was washing her hands at the sink. She kept her head down, avoiding the stares, but the woman at the next sink said, "Miss Hall, please forgive the interruption. Would you mind signing my autograph book?" Via the mirror John glanced at the woman. She was wearing a frump of a dress paired with an ill-judged hat. Her damp hands were already rooting in her clutch bag.

"Of course," John said, because what else could she say?

"I always have it with me," the woman said, as John dried her hands and retrieved a pen from her inside pocket. "One never knows who one might meet on a trip to London."

The sight of John with a pen in her hand emboldened others and it was several minutes before she could escape the queue. She hurried back to her seat only to find a deputation waiting for her with praise for her book and her courage and condemnation for Jix and Cape and Douglas and would you mind signing this, that and the other. Gratifying as it was, it was also draining. She didn't know these people who seemed to think they knew her.

"Miss Hall, would you mind awfully signing my book?" The suit, shirt and bow tie of the latest arrival echoed John's own style. She held a copy of *The Well of Loneliness* in her strong, masculine hands.

Published in Paris by THE PEGASUS PRESS

Seven thrilling words printed along the bottom of the dust jacket. John felt a shiver of exhilaration. This was the first Pegasus edition she'd seen.

"A friend brought it from Paris this morning. I'm gripped already. There's so much…I had a Collins, a maid that I…Her name was Riley. I'm so grateful to you for writing it."

After signing the book on the flyleaf, John passed it back. The woman bowed before striding away. John settled back, ready for the second half of the play. The Blanche Knopfs and the James Douglases of the world could go to hell. Her book was making a difference. Audrey would find her an American publisher. She had to.

CHAPTER TWENTY-SEVEN

I'm on inspection duty with Seven on Friday morning. *Would you like to go out somewhere with me tomorrow night?* I can hardly concentrate on the hazards that might need addressing for all the practising that's going on in my head. *Would you like to go out somewhere with me tomorrow night?* For the six thousandth time. *Would you like to go out somewhere with me tomorrow night?* It's time to actually say the words.

What if she says no? I'll be beyond mortified. The face-burning shame of Janet in the Hungarian cafe with that other woman floods back. At least I was able to run away that day. I can't run away from work. I'll have to spend the rest of today and the Saturday morning shift tomorrow, with the "no" sitting between us, tripping me up when I hand her a length of hose or climb on the back of the motorcycle appliance behind her. A weekend of misery to follow, wondering how I could have been so foolhardy as to ask in the first place and what could I do to make my work bearable now I'd humiliated myself. It's no wonder it's been all practice and no words.

But what if she says yes? Laughing and talking over a picnic in the park. Hand in hand in the darkness of the cinema. Dancing cheek to cheek. Maybe even kissing. My body thrums at the thought.

Would you like to go out somewhere with me tomorrow night?

I sneak a glance at her as we emerge from the factory into the yard. Oh, but doesn't she look fine, with her dark eyes and her full lips and her determined chin?

"Would you—" Oh God, I've started speaking. "I was like, w-would you, somewhere, I was w-wondering do you have any, any plans, f-for tomorrow, the weekend?" I might die on the spot from embarrassment. Why do the wrong words always come out in a jumble when I'm nervous? I daren't look at her.

"Tomorrow? Nothing definite."

"I was wondering…Only if you're not busy, not too busy, I was wondering would you, would you like to go, to go with me, maybe, to the, to the cinema, or for a picnic, or or or to Gunter's, or maybe the C-Cave of Harmony?"

"Gunter's and the Cave of Harmony. You're quite the woman about town."

"I wouldn't say that, so I wouldn't. I've only been to Gunter's the once and I've not been to the Cave at all."

"It's overrated. How about a jazz club? There's a band from New Orleans playing in Soho tomorrow night."

I chance a look at her. She smiles and I grin as wide as a shipyard.

* * *

Sibyl's in the kitchen when I get home from work, doing something suspicious with nuts. I've taken to vegetarian food but I don't know about nuts for tea. I'm not a squirrel. I offer to peel potatoes so I can be sure there'll be something I can eat. I'm ravenous after another of Johnston's strenuous workouts.

English potatoes look fine raw but they don't cook up as well as the ones at home. There's no big floury spuds in London that just need a knob of butter to make a meal. Next to me, Sibyl is shaping the nut mixture into flat patties and laying them onto a greased baking sheet. I hope they taste better than they look. She opens the oven door and puts the tray in while I get the potatoes into water for cooking.

We sit down at the kitchen table. "How was your day?" I ask.

She makes a face. "One of those days where I wonder what on earth I'm doing with my life."

I don't know what to say.

"Don't look so worried. It's the lot of the artist to have doubts. That's what one of my teachers used to say. Nothing great can come without overcoming doubts."

I think that doubts might be the lot of the apprentice lesbian too. Wilma says it's a miracle that two women ever get together with all the uncertainty on both sides about feelings and attractions and the fear of saying the wrong thing to a girl who you think is the type that prefers girls but turns out not to be, or misjudging the situation with a girl who does prefer girls but doesn't prefer you. I told her relying on miracles wasn't exactly encouraging, but she said miracles happen all the time between women if only they're given the chance. In the short time I've known her she's juggled several women through her hands so I think maybe that's true for Wilma. But I'm not Wilma.

"Can I ask you something?" I say to Sibyl.

"Of course."

"How did you know that you had feelings for Tilda and that she had feelings for you?"

"Goodness me."

"Sorry. I…At work, there's this woman…"

"How exciting."

"Seven, her name is."

"The woman who gave you the dance lesson?"

"I'm seeing her tomorrow night but I don't know…How can I tell if she likes me?"

"If she's spending her Saturday night with you, I think it's safe to assume she likes you."

"Do you think so?"

"Definitely."

"But in what way? With Tilda, did you start off as friends or was it love at first sight?"

"Definitely not love at first sight. I don't think I even liked her for the first fortnight. She was rather standoffish in those days."

It comes into my head to say she can be pretty standoffish these days but I don't want to sound rude. I'm already being cheeky with these personal questions.

"She arrived at our ambulance unit in the midst of a bombardment. I'd been driving all night and most of the day before. When I got back to base I found her sitting in an armchair toasting a crumpet by the fire, casual as you like while the building shook around her. I remember thinking, who on earth are you?"

"I can just imagine it."

"She was ridiculously self-contained, of course, with a certain swagger that one couldn't help but notice. And then my co-driver lost half an arm to a lump of shrapnel and Tilda was assigned as her replacement." She shrugs in a "and that was that" sort of way.

"But how did you know that she liked you, as more than a friend?"

She shakes her head. "When the time came, somehow I just knew."

Somehow I just knew. It's not exactly much to go on. Nothing, in fact. Why does everybody else in the world know how to manage these things while I haven't a clue?

"It's not all make or break," Sibyl says. "Sometimes things take time to grow. Go out and enjoy yourself. If you do, I'm sure she will."

* * *

I stand in front of the wardrobe mirror. My new shirt is perfect, better even than the pink one. Wilma took me to the Hackney branch of Achille Serre after work and there it was, a pale-blue cotton, already laundered, waiting for me on the unclaimed rail. I bought myself a navy polka-dot tie to go with it in the haberdashers on Mare Street. It may be the only thing I get right tonight, but at least I have a good outfit. And I'm clean and I smell nice after a bath with Sibyl's lavender crystals. I've a few conversation starters prepared as well. When Tilda got home last night Sibyl recruited her into coaching me for my night out. It turns out she was quite the one in her suffragette days, breaking hearts all over Britain with her dashing looks and derring-do.

"Ask her about herself. What's her favourite song? Or book? Film? Hobby? What would her perfect day be? What was the happiest moment of her life? Anything to get her talking. And look at her when she answers and listen to what she says and nod and say uh-huh and that's interesting. Everyone loves to talk about themselves if only they can find someone who'll listen."

I'm going to start with music because I already know she's interested in it. I've listened to all the Ma Rainey records we have as preparation and Sibyl's told me everything she knows about New Orleans jazz.

I close my eyes and imagine the night ahead. I'll arrive at the bar and Seven will be waiting for me at a table for two. She'll smile when I enter and I'll smile back. We'll embrace and maybe electricity will jump back and forth between us like the kind of spark we have to avoid at Achille Serre on account of it causing explosions. The band will be playing and people will be dancing. It'll be the kind of place where they don't mind women dancing together and the tune will be perfect for the foxtrot and Seven will ask me to dance and I'll feel her close all down my body. I don't know what happens next but I know I won't run away from her if she kisses me.

I pull back my lips, checking there's nothing untoward caught in my teeth, then put my hand to my mouth and breathe out and in quickly to check it smells fresh. I'm giving my hair a final smooth down when I notice Baby Girl barking outside. Bark, bark, bark. Bark, bark, bark. You'd think we were being invaded by a horde of burglars from the racket she's making so I shut the wardrobe and go to the window. It takes a moment to register the problem, so unexpected here at home. I hurtle out of the room and down the stairs.

"Call the fire brigade. Clifden Road. Urgent," I shout at Sibyl as I pass the front room door. I sprint along the hallway and out to the back garden. Plumes of smoke shadow the sky above our back-door neighbours, darkening with every second. I grab a hammer from the shed and Sibyl's ratty gardening gloves and hurl myself at the back wall, scrambling up and over into our neighbour's garden.

A woman staggers out of the back door, her face streaked with dirt and tears. She coughs and gasps and at first I can't make out what she's saying. "Children," she rasps. "My children."

"How many?"

"My girl and my baby boy." She's half-sobbing. I don't have time for it.

"Where are they?"

She points upwards. Dark smoke gushes out of the first floor. Wisps of smoke are already seeping from the edge of the window on the floor above. It won't be long till the whole building's ablaze. There's no time to wait for the fire brigade.

"Where exactly?"

"Up there." She points again. "Top floor, back bedroom."

As she speaks I scan the building, sizing up my options. I've no ladder, no ropes, nothing.

"Anyone else home?"

"No."

"You're sure?"

"Yes." She dashes back towards the house but the flames have got a hold of the kitchen and she's beaten back.

Tilda has followed me over the back wall. "Get a blanket," I tell her. "And five or six neighbours to hold it. Quickly."

I tuck the hammer into the waistband of my skirt and dash to the drainpipe. It's firmly attached. I grasp it with both hands and begin to climb. Up through the smoke, hand over hand, feet roasting as I brace against the hot bricks, ears singeing, eyes watering. Up, up, counting as I go. Thirty steps should get me there. At eighteen, I reach the level of the first-floor room.

Twenty-four, twenty-fi—Boom! The first-floor window blows out. I turn my head away from the shower of hot shards. Toxic smoke spews into the air, thick and sour.

Twenty-eight, twenty-nine, thirty. Smoke shrouds me in darkness. Have I come far enough? Too far? I stretch out with my left hand but feel only scorching brick.

Thirty-one. A momentary change of wind. I glimpse the top-floor window above me to the left. Almost there.

Thirty-two, thirty-three. I hook my right arm behind the pipe and take the hammer out of my waistband with my left hand. Leaning towards the window, I swing the hammer. The glass gives way to my first blow. Again I smash, and again, trying to clear the edges as smoke swallows me, filling my mouth with greasy ash. I fight back a cough.

That will have to do. I tuck the hammer back into my waistband. I close my eyes, imagining in my mind how to pitch myself into the room. I've one chance to get this right. On three. One, two... I swing my feet over to the sill, through the window, letting go of the drainpipe at the last minute. Glass crunches as I dive feet-first into the smoke-filled room.

I crouch low where it's safer to breathe. "Hello!"

No answer.

The furnace hammers at the door and the floor and the ceiling. The room is putting up a fight but it can't hold back the fire for much longer. It's hot and dark in here, nothing to see but smoke. My biggest enemy.

I crawl along the wall, the back of my hand outstretched feeling for obstacles. Burning wood crashes down through the house, part of the stairwell giving way. Flames fizz and lick on every side. My hand hits something hard. I feel my way up the bed then run my hands over the mattress. Nothing. I crawl along the side of the bed towards the wall with the door. Something soft gives under my knee. I reach down. A hand. I pull the child from under the bed. My fingers search for a pulse. It's faint but the child's alive. I grab a sheet, loop it under her arms and tie her to me.

Where's the baby? I crawl along the floor, searching, my knees melting, my lungs burning for a clean breath. At last I find the cot, the baby inside. I don't know whether he's alive or dead and there's no time to check so I tuck him under my arm and crawl back to the window.

It's too hard to hold the baby and untie the semi-conscious child. I sweep the floor with my arm, clearing away the worst of the glass, and set the baby down. A loud crack behind me signals another bit of staircase gone. The door's hissing. It'll be flaming any moment. I lean out of the window. A huddle of people waits below me, staring upwards, blanket held between them.

"Ready to catch?" I shout.

"Ready."

The smoke moves back in and I lose sight of them. Please, God, let them be in the right place. "The first one's coming on three."

I lift the child out of the window as far as I can, holding her hands tightly in mine.

"One. Two. Three."

I let go.

Behind me the top of the door succumbs. Flames lick up the wall. The temperature soars. I'm running out of time. I pick up the baby.

"Ready?" I shout.

"Nearly."

"Hurry up." I daren't jump with him in case I crush him. Is there time for us both? A third of the door is ablaze. Poisonous black smoke hovers at the ceiling, thickening all the time. I can't see the drainpipe. Even if I could, it's not an option. The fire has too strong a grip below me.

"Ready," comes the call from below.

"On three. One, two, three." The baby follows the child into the void.

The cot catches light and I shrink away from it. I start coughing and can't stop.

"Ready," I croak.

There's no reply.

In the distance I can hear the bell of the fire engine. It will be too late for me.

I cough hard to clear my airways. "Ready?"

"Ready," someone shouts.

"One-two-three." I throw myself into the abyss, falling, falling through smoke and flame, a bad-dream descent. As I fall, I see again my father with blood on his hands. I was running pell-mell along North Queen Street, a riot at my back. He was up ahead, crouched over a policeman, trying to staunch the flow from a wound in the man's side. The sight of him brought me up short. I watched him try to stop the man's life bubbling away. I watched him fail. He shut the man's eyes. Then he drew his revolver and went on the hunt.

The blanket stretches and bucks as I land. For a moment I think the neighbours won't be able to hold me, but they do. They lower me to the ground. Tilda helps me up and Sibyl puts her arms around me.

"You brave woman." She pulls me close. I slump against her because it's been the most exhausting three minutes of my life but then the training kicks in. "We need to get clear. Are the children safe?" The coughing takes over again, and Tilda and Sibyl have to support me to the back of the garden. Some of our neighbours have gathered by the back wall, looking up at the brutal beauty of the blaze. The fire's in full flow now, the roof well alight, the windows black caverns spitting smoke and flame.

"You need to drink." Sibyl pours water from a pitcher into a glass.

I sip to start with, then gulp like a camel as it begins to soothe the parch at the back of my throat.

Tilda wets her handkerchief, wrings out the excess of moisture and holds it to my forehead.

"Where are the children?" I ask.

"On their way to hospital. The mother, too. Close your eyes." Tilda places the damp cloth against my eyelids.

"The baby…Is he…"

"He's alive. They're both alive, thanks to you." Sibyl gives me another glass of water to drink. "Take this one slowly."

A cheer reaches us from the front of the building as the fire brigade arrives. Within a minute, jets of water arc onto the blazing roof. They'll bring another hose round the back soon for a different angle of attack. Surround the fire and drown it. In any other circumstances I'd stay to watch the battle but as soon as I can clean myself up, I'm off to Soho.

"You should see a doctor," Sibyl says.

"I'll be—" A burst of coughing cuts me short.

Sibyl hands me her handkerchief. "Spit it out."

I can't be spitting nastiness into Sibyl's clean hankie.

"Your body wants rid of it," she says.

I take out my own hankie and spit. The mucus is streaked grey with smoke and soot.

"Let me see," Sibyl says.

I am utterly affronted at the idea of Sibyl looking at my spit-up.

"I'm trained in first aid. I saw a lot worse than a bit of sooty sputum during the war."

Reluctantly I turn the hankie towards her.

"At least it's not black. We need to get you indoors where the air's cleaner."

"Look at your knee," Tilda says. A spike of glass protrudes from my left knee, at the head of a trail of blood that runs to my shoe. "Stay still." She pulls the shard out.

"Ouch." I didn't notice it while it was there but now it's gone I can feel the throb of pain.

"And your arm." My shirt sleeve is flecked with blood where I swept away the glass.

"Where else does it hurt?" Sibyl says.

I don't want to think about where it hurts. I'm going to Soho. I'm going to see Seven. "I'm fine." I cling to the glass of water, trying to hold back the rising wave of nausea.

"Any dizziness? Nausea?"

"No. A quick wash and I'll be off."

"People can die from smoke inhalation. You must know that," Tilda says. "You can't go out tonight."

"I'm not leaving Seven sitting on her own thinking I didn't bother to turn up." The last few words are strangled by the cough I'm holding in. Some smoke-eater I am.

"She'll understand," Sibyl says. "You've just risked your life to save two children from an inferno."

I take a gulp of water. "She won't know that."

"We'll telephone the club," Sibyl says. "Let's get you home."

Back we go over the wall and into the house. Sibyl settles me on the sofa, Baby Girl at my feet.

"You really should see a doctor," Tilda says.

"I don't need—" A fresh wave of coughing interrupts my protest.

"I'll phone Margo," Sibyl says.

I neither know nor care who Margo is. When I regain the power of speech I say, "Seven, first."

"You need a doctor." Sibyl picks up the telephone receiver.

"Please. Seven."

"All right. But then Margo."

The operator puts Sibyl through to the club but the phone rings and rings and no one answers. That decides me. I get to my feet. "I'm going to the club."

"You can't go out."

"I'll be—" The coughing intrudes to betray me again.

"How will Seven feel if you end up collapsing, which is more than likely in a smoky jazz club?" Sibyl says.

Tilda joins in against me. "You could destroy your health if you push your lungs over the edge. You wouldn't be fit to work, to swim, to do anything. Is it worth the risk?"

I think it is and I start to cry because life's not fair and everything is going to be ruined with Seven.

"Sit down, Maggie. Please," Sibyl says.

"I can't leave her waiting on me, not knowing. I can't."

"I'll go," Tilda says.

"You'll go?" I say.

"Yes. I'll go to the club and find Seven and give her a message. Now will you sit down and let Sibyl phone the doctor."

I sit up in bed sipping a cup of hot honey, lemon and ginger. The coughing's subsided, and in truth I'm perfectly well enough to be downstairs. But I'm that disappointed at not being able to be with Seven that I'm staying in bed. Nothing ever works out for me. The doctor—Dr. Baker to me, Margo to Sybil—said I've to rest for at least twenty-four hours and Sibyl's to take me straight to hospital if the sputum turns black or I start vomiting or become breathless or confused. I'm not doing twenty-four hours. Thirteen or fourteen should be plenty. Tomorrow morning I'm going to see Wilma in the hope that she knows Seven's address and then I'm going to see Seven herself to explain in person what happened and why I couldn't come tonight. Maybe we can go for a Sunday afternoon walk in the park or a rake round the market which won't be as good as a New Orleans jazz band but better than nothing.

A sneeze comes upon me and I just get my handkerchief in place in time. I'm onto my fifth hankie between the coughing and the spitting and the sneezing out the soot and smoke that got in during the rescue. The firemen at London Fire Brigade have face masks and breathing tanks that let them go into even the darkest dirtiest smoke in search of the heart of the fire but Achille Serre hasn't got such innovations yet. Not that it would have helped me tonight seeing as I wasn't at work. For all its fury, the fire was out in forty minutes. Water always wins in the end. It's only a matter of how long it'll take and how much damage the fire gets to do first. The bricks are scorched all up the back of the house and the windows stare out black and empty. It'll be a wreck inside. I hope they've family who'll take them in till they get back on their feet.

I set my cup down on the bedside table. I'm nearly ready for sleep but I'm holding off till Tilda's back in case she has a message for me from Seven. I'm so grateful to her for going to Soho. Tilda and Sibyl are among the most decent people I've ever met in spite of them being English.

I wonder what Seven wore tonight. Tilda will know but I can't imagine asking her. In my mind I decide on the open-necked shirt she had on at Wilma's, cotton bright against her brown throat. I'm almost there, sitting next to Seven in the buzz of music and words, talking about Ma Rainey and Bessie Smith and New Orleans jazz, and finding out where she lives and who she lives with and if she has brothers and sisters and how she came to be working at Achille Serre.

A knock on my door interrupts me. "Come in," I say, eager for Tilda, and maybe a message. A lump as big as a pear forms in my throat and I can't swallow it down and a tidal flow of tears brims behind my eyes and I struggle to hold them back.

"Hello, hero." Seven smiles her lovely smile which would win first prize in the best smile in the world competition.

"I can't believe you're here," I whisper. I'm losing the battle against the tears which slide down my face and splish-splash into the crook at the bottom of my throat.

"Of course I'm here." She closes the door behind her and walks over to the bed, tall and elegant in a sapphire-blue shirt.

"I'm sorry I spoilt your evening."

"You didn't spoil anything." She sits down on my bed. I can feel her leg against mine through the blankets.

"You look beautiful," I say.

"So do you."

I'm still a bit teary so my laugh is gulpy like a drowning frog because I know I look anything but in my secondhand, old-lady nightgown and my hair tousled and my eyes rimmed red raw from the smoke. The laughing brings on a cough and I fumble for the cleanest of my hankies and spit the phlegm out as discreetly as I can.

"Shouldn't you be checking the colour?" She's right, of course, but I don't want to be studying my spit-up in front of her.

"I'll be back in a minute." I take the hankie with me to the privacy of the bathroom.

The sputum's not black and the bathroom trip allows me to curb my hair and brush my teeth. Tendrils of music filter up from the front room as I open the bathroom door. Seven's standing by the window of my bedroom looking out, even though night has already fallen. Lights are on in houses along the terrace but the one opposite is dark. She turns as I enter.

"Do you want to go down and listen to the music?" I ask.

"I'd rather stay up here with you." She pushes the door open wide. The record has stopped and we stand there like idiots for a moment but then the gramophone jumps into life and it's Marion Harris singing "It Had to Be You" and I look at Seven and she takes me in her arms and kisses me.

* * *

I wake up alone. Did I dream she was here? But I'm naked under the covers for the first time in my life so I know it wasn't a dream. I spent the evening with Seven kissing and dancing and a night together skin to skin. A dark curl clings to the pillow next to me. I twirl it between my fingers.

The toilet flushes, the sink gurgles. The bathroom door closes and the bedroom door opens. "I borrowed your nightgown," Seven says. "I didn't want to shock your landladies." She pulls the nightgown over her head, lighting a fire of want in me. But first I must pee and brush my teeth.

She's sitting up in bed when I return, her long arms folded outside the covers. I have no point of reference for the moment I now find myself in. There's a naked woman in my bed. A beautiful naked woman with chestnut skin, and brown eyes, and breasts small and perfect, and shoulders strong and wide, and a smile from heaven, and a collarbone I could kiss and kiss and kiss. She knows me now in a way no one has ever known me. Last night *we were not divided.* My solitary explorations had not prepared me for the extraordinary delights of fingers and thigh and tongue, the wonder of touch and friction and taut muscle able to go and go and go without tiring.

My flesh aches for hers. My manners intervene. She's been under my roof for more than ten hours and not a bare bite of food nor a mouthful of drink have I offered her. Granny Palmer would be appalled. "What would you like for breakfast?"

When she says, "You," I blush, shy but thrilled. She opens the covers. "Come back to bed."

And I do.

CHAPTER TWENTY-EIGHT

"Don't go falling in love with me."

That was the last thing Seven said before she left yesterday. As if it wasn't already too late for that before the night of non-division, let alone the *come back to bed* morning. Maybe I was looking a bit crestfallen because then she kissed me—a full-on, mouth-open, as-a-lover kiss that had my heart thudding and my bones melting and my head swirling.

What am I supposed to make of it?

My heart is full of so many feelings it's a wonder it doesn't burst open. Surely I can't have ruined everything already. She liked me enough to come over on Saturday evening. And to linger on Sunday morning. But then away she went, faster than a galloping horse. I shake my head. A horse and a rabbit. Has that any chance of a happy ending?

The factory is quiet, snoozing before the throng of workers arrives. I light the hot plate in the common room and put the kettle on to boil. Seven's usually first in but I've beaten her to it today. I'll be here when she arrives and I'll look at her face and maybe it'll tell me how things stand between us.

I watch the kettle not boiling and my Auntie Ruth's voice reminds me it never will. Under my breath I sing "Polly put the kettle on" to demonstrate my relaxed demeanour to anyone who happens to be arriving for work. Inside, my heart clamours. If she spurns me, how will I bear it? The kettle starts to whistle and I take it from the heat, singing "Kitty took it off again, Kitty took it off again." I fetch the teapot and make the tea, swirling the pot around, encouraging the draw. The door clicks open behind me but I don't turn so that it's clear I haven't heard it. The weekend was nothing. I'm not in love. I pour my first cup.

"Oh, hello," Seven says.

"Hello," I say, turning round. My eyes fill with the sight of her, so sleek and tall and beautiful, and I know it was foolhardy to have come here early and put myself in this tongue-tied, head-tied, heart-tied moment alone with her. Yesterday I held her naked warmth close to me, I kissed along her elegant collarbone, took her nipple in my mouth…

I turn back to my tea. I hope she doesn't notice the tremor in my voice when I ask if she wants a cup.

"I'll get it." She's close enough that our uniforms touch. As she reaches for a cup she brushes my arm.

"I'll get out of your way." I sit myself on the sofa, facing away from her but aware of every movement she makes—picking up the teapot, filling the cup, adding milk, sugar, stirring, first mouthful.

She brings her cup over and sits down next to me. "You're in early."

I don't say anything.

"How are you today?" she says.

I nod by way of reply.

"I didn't know if you'd be in. How are the lungs?"

"Fine."

"Good. That's good."

We lapse into silence but I feel her looking at me.

"What?"

"You're cross with me, aren't you?" she says.

"I'm not."

"You are. All stiff with no words. Look, I'm sorry I bolted yesterday. Old habit."

I don't know what to say. My teeth clamp the fleshy inside of my lower lip. I will not cry.

"Do you forgive me?" she says.

Is it supposed to be this confusing, falling in love, this terrifying? I chance a glance in her direction. Her face is earnest. My eyes close, my head moves forward in the smallest of nods.

"Good," she says softly. She lays her hand over mine. "I like you, Maggie."

I fold my fingers between hers. Her hand is warm, her fingers long and slender. "I like you too," I whisper.

"Perhaps we could do something together next—"

At a noise from the garage our hands spring apart.

"Do you want a top-up?" Seven stands. Johnston is in the door half a moment later shortly followed by Clarke with, "How was your weekend?"

"Maggie rescued two children from a burning building," Seven says.

"Did you really?" Clarke says.

"I did."

Clarke asks what happened and before I know it I'm giving an account of Saturday evening's fire.

"Lucky you," Clarke says. "Why does nothing exciting ever happen to me?"

"Not bad for someone who knew nothing a couple of months ago. To Maggot Dobbin, rescuer of small children." Seven raises her teacup towards me in a toast. The others follow suit, even Johnston who tells me she knew I had it in me from the very first morning of training.

The clock ticks on and soon it's time for work. It's my turn to be on equipment this morning with Johnston. I wish I was on inspection with Seven. She likes me. I slide under the sidecar on the wooden gurney and switch on my torch. Under my breath I hum "Creole Love Call." *Da-da, da-da, da-da, da-dum.* Seven likes me. Inch by inch I search for rust and damage. *Da-da, da-da, da-da, da-dum.* I wonder what she was going to say when we were interrupted. *Da-da, da-da—*

Someone taps my left foot.

"Excuse me." A man's voice.

I've barely had the chance to move when the tap comes again, three times, and more firmly than I consider necessary. I pull myself out at some pace, ready for a word with the overly firm tapper. A thin man with pitted skin stands above me. A man with a camera lurks behind him.

"Are you Miss Dillon, lives at Dunlace Road?" the thin one asks.

"Aye, I am."

"I'm George Goddard from the *Hackney Gazette*. And this is Will Marchant. Is there somewhere we could interview you?"

"Me?"

"You're the young woman that saved the children from the fire, aren't you?"

"Yes, but—"

"People will want to hear all about you. Lady Fireman Saves the Day."

"I'm on duty." I glance guiltily towards Johnston who's checking lengths of rope on the other sidecar.

He follows my gaze. "You don't mind if I do a quick interview, do you? Mr. Serre himself gave us the go-ahead."

"Don't be long."

I show them into the common room, wondering how not long will satisfy Johnston. The men settle themselves on one sofa, I sit on the other. I've never been interviewed by a journalist before. I've never done anything would make one want to interview me. He starts with my name, age and address and for some reason Lilliput Street comes out of my mouth.

"Sorry, I mean, 65 Dunlace Road. I used to…" I wonder what my father would think if he knew I'd saved the lives of two children. Would he still hate me?

"No need to be nervous. And the fire was at?"

"Clifden Road. I don't know what number. Their garden backs onto ours."

"I can find that out back at the office. And you're a fireman yourself. That was a bit of luck. I never knew there were lady firemen."

"Women can do anything men can given the chance and the training," I say, regurgitating Tilda.

He smirks. "Not quite anything, isn't that so, Will?"

I ignore the innuendo. "Any job. Given the chance and the training."

"She'll have us on the scrapheap in a moment, won't you, Miss Dillon?"

"All I mean is that women can fight fires every bit as well as men can."

"Though you didn't actually fight the fire on Saturday. It was London Fire Brigade that extinguished it, wasn't it?"

"I didn't have any equipment."

"What's a woman to do with no equipment?" Goddard smirks again, finding himself immensely entertaining.

I should have stayed on my gurney. At least I'd be doing something useful. "Do you see those trophies on the shelf? They were won by the Achille Serre Ladies' Fire Brigade for their skill in fighting fires."

"All right, love. Keep your hair on. Women can fight fires. You learn something every day, don't you Will? Why don't you tell us what happened on Saturday night, Miss Dillon?"

I start with the dog barking and looking out the window and seeing the smoke and out of the house and over the wall and up the drainpipe and the first-floor window blowing out with the heat and at last he's stopped smirking and he's writing down words as fast as I can speak them.

"So then I leapt out of the window and they caught me in the blanket, so they did." I stop, glad to have got to the end.

"You must have been scared, terrified even," he says.

"I didn't have time to be scared. All I could think about was how was I going to get those children out."

"Come now, Miss Dillon. Most people would be scared of going into a burning smoke-filled building, let alone a woman—"

He's really starting to annoy me. "I wasn't scared. Ask anyone that fights fires. Fear isn't what's on your mind. It's getting the job done, however you can."

He exchanges a sceptical look with his photographer. I've got nothing more to say to him. "If you don't mind, I need to get back to work." I stand up.

"Well I think we've got all we need. Except for a photograph."

"Of me?"

"No, of the Prime Minister." He leads the way out of the common room and over to Johnston, who's checking the wheeled fire escape. "We'll just get a photo and we'll be on our way."

The man with the camera speaks for the first time. "Where's your fire engine?"

Johnston indicates the two freshly polished motorcycle appliances.

"Don't you have a proper fire engine?"

Johnston's eyes narrow momentarily. "For your information, these two appliances do everything we need them to do. They're quick and manoeuvrable and they hold all the equipment we need. But if they're not up to your requirements, I suggest you find your own."

"This will be fine," Goddard says.

"On you get, love," the camera man says.

Usually I'm hanging on behind Seven but today I sit astride the motorcycle in her place.

"Cheese," Will says.

I don't want to smile. Fighting fires is a serious business.

"Go on, love," Goddard says, "give us a smile."

I think of Radclyffe Hall's sober expression in the photo in my bedroom. If she doesn't have to smile, neither do I. I stare defiantly into the distance.

CHAPTER TWENTY-NINE

Every inch of wall space in Audrey's cramped office was taken up with bookshelves and filing cabinets. The room was well organised but it was only a matter of time before the agency would need bigger premises. John had been part of its success, bringing the prestige of the Prix Femina prize, as well as the bravery of *The Well of Loneliness*. Audrey sat at her desk by the window, head bent, annotating a manuscript.

"A hit or a miss?" John asked.

"I haven't quite decided." Audrey put her pen down. "Nice to see you both. Do have a seat."

Una settled herself on one of the hard-backed chairs. Before sitting, John extracted a box of Harrods' chocolate brazils from her leather bag. She'd raided the food hall for treats after having her hair cut that morning. Harrods was one of her favourite places to shop. She'd treated Una to a new pair of gloves and herself to a necktie. She didn't care that she already possessed ninety-seven neckties. None of them were in the particularly pleasing shade of burgundy of her latest acquisition.

She handed the chocolates to Audrey. "These are for you."

"My favourites. You're too kind."

"We got these for Patience." John put a box of pralines on the empty desk in the corner. "Where is she today?"

"Collecting a box of your books from Leopold Hill. She should be back shortly."

"I signed my first Pegasus edition at the theatre last week."

"Everywhere she goes people are clamouring for autographs," Una said.

"I can imagine the attention is exhausting," Audrey said.

John shuffled in her seat but didn't answer. Her newfound notoriety was becoming a burden. Fellow inverts she understood, but how was she to manage the rest of the bold and the unmannered with their requests for autographs, the handful becoming a horde, until by the end she was a carcass picked clean?

"We're off to Rye tomorrow for a bit of peace," Una said. "We've signed a lease on a cottage. It needs a little work before we can move in but the Mermaid Inn will look after us till it's ready."

"Oh, that is good news," Audrey said.

"It's Anne Elsner's," John said. "The travel writer we stayed with in August. She thinks we need it more than she does. I tried to persuade the owner to sell it to me but I didn't quite manage to bring them round to my way of thinking." She smiled ruefully.

"But we'll be on the spot if something suitable does come up," Una said. "And John will get the rest she needs. Won't you, darling?"

"I've never been to Rye," Audrey said.

"It's remarkably picturesque," Una said.

"You'll have to come down for a weekend," John said. "We'll take you to the Mermaid Inn for lunch. It's somewhat down-at-heel but pleasing all the same. Walls of wattle and daub, great beams of Sussex oak, secret passages. There's something infinitely reassuring about old buildings, don't you think?"

"We've made a couple of chums already," Una said.

John laughed. "Una didn't like the look of them when Anne introduced us."

"Oh now, darling, that's unfair. It was you who called Dickie fat when I only suggested she was beefy."

"But it was you that said Wendy looked like a corpse who'd been dug up just before she turned rancid." John laughed.

Audrey rolled her eyes. "I dread to think what the two of you say behind my back."

"Only good things," John said. "Only ever good things. Anyway, you wanted to see me."

"I have news. Cape wants to take over the American rights from Knopf. He's offering very attractive terms."

"Cape? Jonathan Cape?"

"Yes."

"So he doesn't want to publish my books in Britain but he'll publish them in America?"

"Not directly, no. He's suggesting a sublicensing arrangement similar to the one with Pegasus."

"What do you think?" John said.

"My advice is to give him the rights. It's our best chance of getting *The Well of Loneliness* out in America soon. He's confident he can find the right American publisher fairly swiftly."

"Do you think he can?"

"I think *I* can. If you accept his offer, I'll go to New York, meet with the firms Jonathan has suggested and decide which one is best."

"You'll go to America?"

"I know how important this book is, John, and not just to you. I can sail next week. That's the soonest I can manage."

John let out a long breath. Slowly she nodded her head. "Thank you. It would be a relief to have a way forward."

"Excellent. I'll let Jonathan know."

Patience arrived soon after with a box of the Pegasus edition. As she set them down on the desk John noticed the amethyst ring on the younger woman's pinkie finger. She wondered if Patience knew that a ring worn on that particular finger was a lesbian code for those in the know. "What a pretty ring," she said, casually. "I don't think I've seen it before."

"Oh, yes," Patience said, her eyes brightening. "It was a present."

John suppressed a smile. Ever since she'd learned of the ring's secret meaning, she'd made a point of not only wearing one herself but of giving one to each of her lovers.

"Would you mind signing a copy for her?" Patience removed a book from the box. "Her name's Morny."

To Morny, With kind regards. John added her signature with a flourish. She handed the book back to Patience, who thanked her with a bashful grin.

"Can you do the whole box?" Audrey said. "I've a waiting list of people wanting copies."

"Of course," John said. She settled herself happily to the business of signing the rest of the box. Her book was back in the world and wherever she went people wanted to read it.

* * *

John stifled a yawn. Oh, for the packing to be over and done with and to be sitting in The Drey with a gin and tonic. Better still, to be already ensconced at Journey's End, a fire blazing in the hearth, and the redoubtable Mabel cooking up a delight in the kitchen.

"How many pairs of pyjamas do you think I should take?" John said.

"Two or three, I'd say." Una carried on winnowing clothes from her wardrobe, adding to the pile of dresses, blouses and skirts for the maid to pack.

John looked at the folded pyjamas in her chest of drawers. Should she take her favourites or ones that she always overlooked? When did she last wear the white crepe de chine? Her fingers closed against their cold slippiness. She laid them uncertainly on her side of the bed.

Una paused. "You look tired, darling."

"I don't seem to have the stamina for London at the moment."

"No wonder, with people hanging on you like leeches, demanding your attention," Una said. "I'll be glad to get you down to Rye. Let me see to your packing. You rest."

John felt a moment of guilt. Una was already doing so much, not least by agreeing to move to Rye. Una loved London. She'd spent almost her entire life in the capital. Even when she'd been married to the admiral, she'd often stayed in London rather than accompanying him to his latest posting. Yet she was moving to Rye without a moment's hesitation because John had set her heart on it.

"Thank you, Squiggie." John sank into the comfy chair in the corner of the bedroom. "And for being so agreeable about everything."

"No need to thank me, darling. You know I only ever want what's best for you." She picked up the pyjamas. "Wouldn't you rather have flannel? The hotel's mulishly draughty." The silk pyjamas were replaced by two pairs of thick striped cotton. Stockings, drawers and camis soon followed, then shirts and skirts, jackets and waistcoats, John's travel set of hairbrushes, an assortment of cufflinks, a selection of neckties. In no time Una had everything under control.

"I don't know how I'd manage without you."

"You don't need to, darling. You'll never need to."

* * *

John browsed the shelves of the bookcase in The Drey the next morning, looking for books to take with them.

"I should have done this last night," Una said.

"We've got plenty of time. It's not even nine yet." John pulled out the *Complete Works of Shakespeare*. "Should we take this?"

"No, leave it. We'll be able to pick up a secondhand copy if we need one."

"What about Rebecca West's new book?" She scanned the shelves without success. "I'll check the study."

"Can you get the Agatha Christie too?"

"Which one?"

"*The Mystery of…* The one I haven't read."

"*The Mystery of the Blue Train.*"

John made her way along the corridor towards her study. Una called after her, "And anything else that takes your fancy."

Miss Webber would be along shortly to carry on her filing and addressing of envelopes and dispatching of responses but for now the study was John's. The telephone interrupted her perusal of a pile of books she'd not yet read.

It was Jimmy from Cape's publicity department. "Thank God you haven't left yet."

"What's happened?"

"Customs have seized *The Well of Loneliness.*"

Back on Cape's turf, Jonathan pacing, Audrey waiting, Una worrying, John brooding. Six weeks ago they'd met in this very room and Cape had outwitted her. Blanche Knopf had been right about one thing—John's position was considerably weakened by Cape's failure to defend the book in Britain. She mustn't let him bamboozle her again. This time they were going to fight for her book, wriggle and squirm as he may.

"So what do we know?" Audrey said.

"Miss James, would you be so kind as to fill everybody in?" Cape said.

All eyes turned to Jimmy. When John had first met her, she'd wondered if Cape's head of publicity was an invert. The masculine nickname, the close-cropped hair, the athletic frame, the wilful independence. Alas for Jimmy, she was afflicted with a bohemian normality, her heart bruised by one disastrous man after another.

"I've spoken to Customs and Excise. A consignment of books was seized from a cargo boat at Dover Marine Station yesterday and has been transferred to the Customs House at Dover."

"They can't just destroy them, can they?" John said. "Customs? Can they?"

"We're seeking advice on that point," Cape said, midpace.

"The books have been detained under…" Jimmy glanced at her notes. "Section 42 of the Customs Consolidation Act 1876, which 'prohibits the importation of any obscene or indecent article.'"

"But no court has ruled *The Well of Loneliness* obscene," John said. "Surely a court has to decide?"

"According to the official, it's for the Board of Customs and Excise to decide if your book comes within the definition," Jimmy said.

"So what does that mean? They can burn my books without a hearing?" John said.

"We're seeking advice on that point," Cape said.

"And are you also seeking advice on whether you knew anything about leasing the rights to Pegasus?" John said, her temper igniting.

"I beg your pardon," Cape said, his reddening face betraying his discomfort.

"Oh yes, I already know about your statement to the press claiming that I arranged the Pegasus deal myself and that the import has nothing to do with your company." John glared at Cape.

"Who told you that?" Cape said.

"The *Daily Herald* when they interviewed me for tomorrow's front page."

"It's the *Daily Herald* that's got us into this mess," Cape said. "Blabbing about the imports—"

"I am not having it," John said, getting to her feet. "I am simply not having it. The *Herald* has done nothing but support *The Well of Loneliness* whereas you…You…" Words to express her fury escaped her.

"You will understand, Jonathan, the distress these events have caused my client," Audrey said. "First to hear that the books had been seized, then to discover that you'd disowned any involvement in their publication, now to find that Customs may be able to destroy *The Well of Loneliness* without a court hearing."

"We still don't know if that is the case. As I've already said, we're trying to understand the legal position ourselves," Cape said. "There is some suggestion that the seizure might result in prosecution—"

"Of John?" Una said.

"No, the publishers, I believe—"

"Can the British government prosecute a company based in France?" Audrey said.

"I don't know. We're seeking—"

"Advice on that point?" Audrey said, a full measure of derision poured into the four words. "I would rather have expected you to have obtained it before you encouraged my client to go along with your plan for foreign publication rather than fighting the Home Secretary's backdoor ban as she wished to in August."

Cape stopped pacing. "In hindsight…" he said, throwing up his hands.

"What does Holroyd-Reece say about the seizure?" John said.

Cape stood in the middle of the room like a ship becalmed. He didn't answer.

"You have spoken to him, I take it. He is the publisher."

Cape turned expectantly towards Jimmy, as if she should have been the one to contact Holroyd-Reece.

"Sorry, no," Jimmy said, her bright-blue eyes burning with chagrin.

"Phone him." John went over to Cape's desk and lifted the telephone receiver. She held it towards him.

"Now?"

"Yes, now. If, as it seems, he is the one that stands to be prosecuted, he's entitled to know what's happening."

"Now" was an elastic concept when it came to the vagaries of the international telephone system but eventually Cape's secretary managed to obtain a line through to John Holroyd-Reece in Paris. Cape sat at his desk, receiver in hand. Halfway across the room, John was sandwiched on the sofa between Una and Audrey, scarcely able to contain herself. Why on earth had she accepted Cape's plan? And then given him the American rights to boot.

"John, Jonathan here. I have with me Miss Hall, Lady Troubridge, Miss Heath and Miss James."

Strain her ears as she might John could hear nothing of Holroyd-Reece's response.

"Yes, quite the gathering. Listen, we've run into a spot of bother at this end. I don't know if you've heard."

John leant forward to no avail.

"Yes."

"I see."

"Yes, I understand."

Understand what? John could stand it no longer. She went over to Cape's desk. "Can I talk to him?"

Cape held one hand up towards her, still holding the phone with the other. "I see. Yes."

"Please," John said.

"I'm handing you over to Miss Hall."

John put the receiver to her ear. The line crackled and hissed. "Hello? Mr. Holroyd-Reece?"

"Miss Hall?"

"You've heard about Customs seizing the consignment, I believe."

"I have."

"I'm very anxious that we not let this attempt to suppress my book lie. We must challenge this action."

"My sentiments exactly. I've already engaged Harold Rubinstein. He's the best literary lawyer in London." The line crackled then cleared. "Let me assure you, Miss Hall, I am determined to fight the government to the last to ensure that your novel remains in circulation. You have my word."

CHAPTER THIRTY

Limehouse Town Hall thinks well of itself, arched windows looking proudly onto the busy thoroughfare of Commercial Road. I prefer the art deco building over the road, an unexpectedly glamorous sailors' hostel. A huddle of men stand on the pavement, kit bags on shoulders. Beyond them, Seven swaggers her way towards our meeting place.

I've been charmed by her walk since the day and hour I met her. They all have it, Seven and Johnston and even Clarke, a confident way of walking. But Seven takes it to an art form. She's a fine sight, stride long, head high, looking neither to the left nor the right, staying her course, unapologetic. Seeing me, she waves. A smile takes over my face that I couldn't hold back if I tried. I feel like someone from a fairytale whose luck has finally changed. Jack with the golden goose, Cinderella with the slipper. It's Saturday afternoon and we've the rest of the weekend ahead of us.

"You're here," she says.

"I'm here."

She's devastatingly attractive today, the open-necked shirt topped with a close-fitting jacket against the autumn chill. I want to touch her, to hold her against me, but it's impossible here. Instead I look at her and I wonder, how am I ever going to be good enough for you?

"What?" she says.

"What, what?"

"You were looking at me funny."

"That's just my face. So where are you taking me?"

"Have you been to Limehouse before?" Seven says.

I shake my head.

"Sailors, dockers, crooks and immigrants." She starts walking and I fall into step with her. Thirty paces bring us to an impressive church with a golden ball at the top of its flagpole. It's set back from the busyness of the road in a large churchyard. She holds the gate open for me and I go through. We walk down the path towards the church. She pauses near a twenty-foot-high pyramid, which seems like an odd thing to have in a churchyard. The words *The Wisdom of Solomon* are carved at the top, above a coat of arms featuring a unicorn.

"I came here last Sunday, after I left you," Seven says.

"Oh. I didn't…Are you religious?"

"I was brought up to be. Daily prayer, bible reading, church, Sunday school."

"Me too."

"But I don't go anymore."

"Me neither." I'm relieved. I've had enough of my own struggles with God without wanting to take on hers. "What made you come here?"

"This place was the beginning and end of me."

It's like one of those crossword puzzles that Sibyl and Tilda do that may as well be in a different language for all the sense they make to me.

"This is where I was found," she says.

"Found?"

"Mmm."

"Were you lost?"

"Was I lost? Perhaps. Or mislaid. Or stolen. Or discarded. I don't know. Nobody knows. But I was definitely found. In a pram. By the verger. Right here next to this pyramid. I had a hat and a coat but no note to say who I was or where I had come from."

"How old were you?"

"About two. Old enough to walk and talk, too young to remember."

"What happened to you?"

"I was sent to Dr. Barnardo's."

"Oh." Everyone knows what a great man Dr. Barnardo was, but at the end of the day, who wants to grow up in an orphanage? Even in my years of hoping my father wouldn't return from war, I had no wish to become a proper orphan. My dream was to carry on living in Lilliput Street with Auntie Ruth, not end up in an institution with no one belonging to me.

"Some of the girls hated the home. I didn't mind it. For a long time I thought I'd always been there. Until I was eight I thought I was made, not born."

"What do you mean?"

"I thought I'd never had any parents, that I'd been made out of the earth like Adam and placed under a bush in the garden at the Village Home for the housemother to find. That was why my skin was brown—because I'd been made from the earth." She closes her eyes and shakes her head. "They tell you that Dr. Barnardo's is your true family and you believe them but then an older girl explained how babies were made. She said everyone who lived on this Earth had had a mother and a father, even me. And she said at least one of my parents must have been coloured because I was just about light enough to be half-caste but just about dark enough to be full darkie." She looks at me. "I hate those words. I hate all the words that people like you use for people like me."

I don't want to be "people like you." A thin rain starts to fall, misting her hair and the shoulders of her jacket. She looks away from me, up to the sky. It spits in her face.

"I was named after this place." She looks back at me.

"Seven? Is it to do with…?" I can't imagine what it's to do with.

"Seven was my number. Everyone had a number. You had to chain stitch it into your clothes. But the name on my records is Anne Hawksmoor."

"Anne Hawksmoor." I try it out.

"Doesn't suit me, does it?"

I shake my head. "Not really."

"Dr. Barnardo's made it up. Anne from this church where I was found, Hawksmoor from the man who designed it."

"What's your real name?"

"Seven. It's the realest one I've got anyhow. I don't know what my parents named me. I used to make up stories about who they were and why they left me here, extravagant stories of being an African princess who'd been stolen away to England. Or maybe I was the daughter of students from far flung Caribbean islands who'd died in an accident. Or perhaps my father was an American musician who'd had a passionate affair with a white woman when he came to England on tour and was long gone before she even knew she was pregnant. The truth is, I've no idea why I was left in this churchyard. I probably never will."

Her face is sadder than a funeral. I wish I could comfort her.

"I don't know why I'm telling you all this except…" She pauses. "The past trips me up. You need to know that if…" She shrugs. "And sometimes I have to be on my own."

I wonder if I should tell her about my own problems with the past. But I wouldn't know where to begin, so I say, "That's all right. Sometimes, so do I."

She looks at me and nods, and suddenly, out of nowhere, she smiles. Her sadness dissipates in an instant. "We're getting wet."

"I don't care." I smile back at her.

"I could kiss you, Maggie Dillon."

"Then come home with me. Sibyl and Tilda are away for the weekend. We'll have the place to ourselves."

Rain jumps off the pavement as we run down Dunlace Road. I fumble with my keys, giddy with the thrill of the sprint from the bus. In the door at last, I hesitate for a moment, then shout, "It's me, Maggie."

"I thought they were away," Seven says.

"They are."

"So why are you shouting?"

"Habit."

Baby Girl is scrabbling at the door. She bolts past me when I open it and launches herself at Seven, squirming in and out of her legs, tail whipping back and forth like a weapon.

"Come on, you," I say. Baby Girl bids me no mind and I have to stern her with a second, "Come on."

"So masterful," Seven says and I don't know if she's impressed or taking the hand.

I lead the dog to the back door. She's not keen to go out. "Go on," I say, and she edges into the garden and begins her sniff for the right spot. I stay on the inside, waiting for her to finish. The burned-out house looks even more dismal in the rain. The windows and door have been boarded up. It'll be some time before anyone lives there again. Baby Girl trots back inside and makes a show of shaking off the rain even though she's only been out there a minute.

"She's so melodramatic," I say.

Seven bends down to stroke the dog's damp head.

"What do you want to do?" I say.

"What do *you* want to do?"

I shrug and smile.

"What does that mean?"

"Oh, I don't know. Just anything. Play records. Listen to the radio. Talk." Take you to bed, I don't say. I don't know how to say it. "I'll put the fire on. Come on through." Seven follows me into the front room, Baby Girl at her heels.

I laid the fire before I went out. The newspaper kindling is today's *Daily Herald*, all except for the front page. I kept it for the report on Customs seizing *The Well of Loneliness*. Bigwig writers like George Bernard Shaw and H. G. Wells have given Radclyffe Hall their support and the new publisher says he's going to fight the government all the way. I hope he wins. The bigots can't be let away with dictating what books people are allowed to read. As if it's not bad enough them screeching depraved-pervert-leper at anyone that's different to them. I look at Seven sitting on the sofa. She's not degenerate and neither am I and neither are Tilda nor Sibyl nor Wilma nor Ida nor Rachel. Maybe Lydia's husband qualifies.

I put a match to the scrunched-up paper. It catches, flame thin and weak at first, susceptible to going out, but then it strengthens and ignites the sticks. The coal will take soon enough. The light of the fire on Seven's face makes her more beautiful than ever. I sit down next to her and her arm comes round me and pulls me close.

"I've been wanting to hold you again for days," she says.

"Have you?"

"Sometimes at work my palms are practically itching to be touching you." She kisses the top of my head and I turn my face towards her.

My lips find hers. Passion rises.

"I love kissing you," I say to her, minutes later, when we pause for breath.

"I love kissing you too."

"Do you want…shall we go upstairs?" I say, but she suggests shutting the curtains so we can stay by the fire. Away go I like a brazen hussy to the window, pulling the drapes closed though it's only half past four. The dog's half-asleep but I relocate her to the dining room, not wanting her watching or interrupting us. Seven's standing in front of the fire when I return. She holds her hands out to me. I accept them, standing opposite her. Her eyes are gentle and I try to open to her, to let her see me, but it's terrifying and my eyes drop.

"Maggie." Her voice is tender.

I look again and she smiles and I bite my lip but hold her gaze. We stand looking at each other and the feeling between us grows, glowing rose, gold, red.

I lean forward and kiss her on the cheek. "I'm glad you're here."

"Me too."

I let go of her hands and take hold of her shirt, easing it up out of the waistband of her skirt. Slowly I undo the buttons. Beneath her shirt she's wearing white cami-knickers, edged with fraying lace. I lean forward and kiss the flesh where the cami stops and her skin begins. I go to unhook her skirt but she shakes her head.

"My turn," she says.

Deft fingers undo the buttons of my waistcoat. She folds it carefully and lays it on the sofa. Next she unknots my tie but leaves it draped around my neck. She undoes the top button of my shirt, looking at me as she does so. And the next button, and the next, still looking at me, working her way down by touch alone. When she gets to the waistband of my skirt, she pulls my shirt out and releases the final few buttons.

"That's better." She nuzzles into my neck. "I love the smell of you."

Her hands come around me and undo the fastenings of my skirt. It falls to the ground. I step out of it and kick it away. My shoes look strange with no skirt. I bend to untie them but she waves me back. She crouches down and unlaces them and I step out of the left and out of the right to stand in my stocking soles and my open shirt in front of her. She gathers up the shoes and moves them out of our way.

"My turn," I say. Her black leather shoes are worn at the heel. I set them aside and fold her skirt on the sofa next to my waistcoat. I kneel before her, gliding my fingers along each foot and slowly up her calves. Her legs are lion-strong, muscle and power. As I circle my fingertips along the inside of her thighs her breath quickens. So does mine. The cami-knickers extend below the top of her stockings, hiding her skin. I kiss her through them, inhaling the scent of her.

"I love the smell of you," I say, repeating her words.

The knickers are roomy and my fingers slip inside to find her dark curls and the swell of her lips. The buttons open easily and I have to hold myself back, no need to rush, better slow than too fast. The tip of my tongue savours the ocean taste of her, salty and alive.

"Oh," she moans, her hips rocking forward.

I give myself to her pleasure, tongue, lips and fingers finding their ways until her legs tremble and she gasps and cries out and pulls me close. The fire dances. We cling together.

* * *

I wake to the warmth of Seven's body against mine. A fierce joy surges through me, driving away any chance of me drifting off again.

The clocks went back last night. I wonder if I'll get to spend the extra hour with Seven or whether she'll take herself off again like last weekend. I mustn't make a fuss if she decides to go. I'm not her keeper.

She's still asleep, her breath soft and low. I lie next to her, revisiting yesterday night, watching it inside my head like my own private cinema. It was an evening of kissing and touching and melting and talking and laughing and dancing that has raised me up like water on a wilting plant. I forgot to mention eating. Loving gives you an appetite. I was grateful for Sibyl's cookery lessons. In no time I'd whipped up a cheese and mushroom omelette, which we ate in front of the fire, dressed only in our shirts. I wonder what she'd like for breakfast. How about pancakes? Or maybe straightforward toast with butter and jam? There is still so much I don't know about her, but I'm learning all the time, gathering up details like treasure.

I ran a bath for her last night, laced with lavender. I was mindful of her warning that sometimes she needs to be alone but then she invited me to share it. The delight of washing her body and her washing mine. We lay on my bed afterward, our bodies damp and relaxed, and it was just as Radclyffe Hall wrote—a feeling of happiness that I had never imagined could be mine, a glowing contentment of mind, body and soul. Of course, for Stephen and Mary that was in Orotava when times were good. It all fell apart for them in the end. The thought chills me. I don't want to lie here and worry about it so I ease my way out of bed. I think it should be porridge. Sibyl's special recipe with stewed blackberries. I'll have it ready for when Seven wakes up. I'm putting on my dressing gown when I hear her yawn and stretch. I turn to look at her.

"Morning." She stretches again, right to the tips of her fingers.

"Sleep well?"

"Perfect. Where are you off to?"

"Do you like porridge? Or I could do—"

"Porridge would be great. Do you want a hand?"

"You relax. I'll bring it up."

I find myself singing as I go about letting out the dog and making breakfast and a pot of tea. I'm still singing as I load the tray up and take it upstairs. Seven's sitting up in bed in my old nightgown.

"You sound happy," she says.

"I am."

"Me, too."

I hand her a bowl of porridge with a big dollop of stewed blackberries in the middle of it and get into bed beside her.

"This is the best porridge I've ever had," Seven says after her first mouthful, and I could hardly be more delighted.

"Grated lemon and a wee drop of vanilla essence. It makes all the difference."

"You're handy in the kitchen."

"Sibyl's given me lots of tips for adding flavour. Auntie Ruth's cooking was wild plain, God rest her."

"Who was Auntie Ruth?"

"My father's sister. She raired me after my mother died."

"What was she like?"

"Auntie Ruth? She was kind. The sort that wouldn't say a bad word against anyone." I put down my bowl and pull open the drawer of my bedside cabinet. Carefully I lift out Auntie Ruth's bible. Inside it there's a photograph, Auntie Ruth in her best dress, sitting on an ornate chair looking straight to camera, me standing next to her. I hand it to Seven. "This is her."

"Is that you beside her?"

"It is. Taken in Abernethy's in Bangor. 1915, I think."

"You were cute."

I look over her shoulder at my scrawny child self. "Puh."

"Do you have any others?"

I shake my head. "Just this one." The bible was the only thing I brought with me from Belfast. The photograph was Auntie Ruth's bookmark.

"The porridge'll be getting cold." I put away the bible but Auntie Ruth lingers. If she'd lived I wouldn't be here with Seven. I wish she wasn't dead but I'm glad to have escaped.

"Do you have other family?"

I shake my head. "There's only my father still living."

"What's he like?"

I don't know how to answer her. What is he like? To the minister he's a good Christian man who never misses a Sabbath. The men at the factory would say he's a hard worker who can always be relied upon. His comrades in the B-Specials and the UVF would call him a hero who fought for King and Country and the Protestant people. To my Auntie Ruth he was a man whose heart was broken by the loss of his wife, as if that excused his hatred and violence. Only Granny Palmer ever said anything against him.

"You don't have to tell me," Seven says.

I shake my head. "My granny used to say he was an ogre in the body of a man." Her voice comes back to me across the years. *Once upon a time in a land far and near there lived an ogre in the body of a man. He roamed the country, bent on destruction.* That was how she'd start her tale of a fearsome man calmed by the love of a gentle woman. A woman with the voice of a skylark. My songbird mother, who bled to death giving birth to me.

"An ogre in the body of a man." Seven says it slowly, pondering the words. "Was he?"

"Not to look at. And it's not like he ate babies for breakfast or anything like that. But he was a brute of a man, a tyrant." Brute. Tyrant. Did I really say those words aloud? "And a murderer."

"A murderer?"

Why am I telling her this? Will it put her off me? Guilt by association. But I can't seem to stop. "Two ordinary Catholics. At least two. Maybe more. Probably more."

"You're not joking, are you?" She shuffles herself round in the bed so she's better able to look at me.

"I'm not joking." I see my father, hands soaked with bright blood, crouched over the body of the policeman. I see him wipe his hands and draw his revolver. "A woman and her son. Unarmed. Shot them dead on Seaview Street."

"You saw him do it?"

"I saw him go up the street. I heard the shots. I'm sure it was him. It's the type of thing he would have done. He'd have done anything to make sure Northern Ireland survived." For God and Ulster. No surrender.

"Oh my God."

"He hated Catholics. And he hated me." I blurt it out, my emotions taking charge of my mouth. "The whole of my life he hated me."

I can't look at her. All my life I've tried to hide his hatred of me, terrified it would make other people hate me too. Now I've laid it all out in front of the one person I most want to care about me.

Seven reaches for my hands. "What's wrong?"

How can I say don't stop liking me? I don't want you to stop liking me.

"Look at me. Please."

I chance a glimpse, then another one, longer, letting her eyes calm the fear pulsing through me. "Do you still…"

"Do I still what?"

"Like me," I whisper.

"Of course I do. Why wouldn't I like you?"

"My father…"

"What do I care about him? I like you, Maggie. I more than like you."

She pulls me close, her hug like medicine. And I try to silence his voice that still mutters in my ear, *You came out wrong, you'll never be anything but wrong.*

CHAPTER THIRTY-ONE

John kept herself busy over the weekend following the Customs seizure, giving interviews to the press and praying for the safe deliverance of her book. It couldn't stop the gnawing fear that her books would burn. *The Well of Loneliness* was her child, made from her heart and soul and body and mind. How was she to bear it if it burned? She was brittle with anxiety by the time she and Una arrived at Messrs Rubinstein, Nash and Co. on Monday morning.

Harold Rubinstein welcomed them into his office, a large room overlooking the gardens of Gray's Inn. Despite his double chin and receding hairline there was something attractive about the lawyer's face. Perhaps it was the lopsided smile. He waited for John and Una to sit down before taking a seat on the other side of his orderly desk.

"Holroyd-Reece tells me you're the man to save my book," John began.

The solicitor inclined his head in a gesture of assent. "That is certainly my aim. I wrote to Customs on Friday seeking an explanation for their actions and giving formal notice that we will be opposing the seizure." He removed a letter from a buff folder and handed it to John. She rapidly scanned its contents before returning it.

Una retrieved a notebook and pen from her bag. She screwed her monocle into place. "You don't mind if I take notes? It helps keep us straight with the detail of this and the complication of that."

"Not at all," Rubinstein said. "On Saturday I engaged Counsel to act on behalf of Pegasus and Leopold Hill in challenging—"

"And on my behalf. I'm the one that stands accused of writing an obscene book." Her mother and the "filthy" telegram flittered to the front of John's mind. The old hag would be thrilled by the latest attack on John's work.

"A most undeserved slur, Miss Hall."

"And I'm paying half of the legal costs. Surely that makes me a party to any proceedings?"

"I'm afraid that in law only Pegasus, as the sender of the consignment, and Leopold Hill, as the recipient, can challenge this unwarranted interference."

John was used to money trumping all else. "So the author is nothing?"

"In this situation, legally, I'm afraid that rather sums it up."

How was it fair that she wasn't allowed to defend her own name? John closed her eyes, swallowing the injustice.

"I have every sympathy with your position, Miss Hall."

She looked at Rubinstein. "My book is neither obscene nor indecent."

He returned her gaze. "No, indeed. I found it a fine and sincere piece of writing. Our lead Counsel, Mr. James Melville, is of the same view."

"Is he the best? I want the best."

"Melville's the youngest King's Counsel ever appointed. An exceedingly able man, and one who is sympathetic to your cause. He thinks we have a strong case. There is nothing obscene about your book, unless one is to accept that the very subject of female inversion is, in and of itself, obscene." His resonant voice was beginning to soothe John's fractured nerves like camomile lotion on burned skin.

"Which it is not," John said. "It is a fact of nature."

"There was a fellow when I was at Oxford, a friend. He killed himself when someone threatened to expose his relationship with another man." Rubinstein's features were wreathed in sudden gloom. "The waste of that young man's life, that was true obscenity."

"So many lives wasted. It's one of the reasons I wrote this book. Now they want to burn it." The image that had haunted her all weekend returned—an anonymous man beside an incinerator, reducing her novels to ash. "They can't, can they? Burn it without a hearing?"

Rubinstein assured her due process had to be followed. "The Customs and Excise Board must review your book before coming to a decision. We'll put evidence before the Board to ensure they reach the right one—your book's social significance, the absence of anything explicit, its literary merit and the overwhelmingly positive reviews it has garnered, the *Express* aside."

"Do you have copies of the reviews?" Una said. "I've kept every single one."

"If you could send a list through, that would be helpful."

"Jix will try to stitch it up," John said. "He'll tell Customs to ban it."

"The Board's chairman is a rather independent-minded man. Sir Francis Floud. Do you know him?"

John didn't.

"Trained as a lawyer, originally, before the civil service. He has a keen appreciation of literature. Floud isn't Jix's puppet."

"I pray to God that you're right." John fingered the Saint Anthony medal in her pocket.

"As well as our legal strategy, I plan to keep the seizure and backdoor censorship in the public eye. I'm issuing a statement to the press today. Anything you can do in terms of interviews yourself, Miss Hall, or getting literary friends to publicly protest would be all to the good."

"Yes, of course. I'll do whatever I can," John said.

"Is there anything else either of you would like to ask?"

"I don't think so. But you will please keep me informed, won't you, of any developments?"

"Of course. And rest assured, Miss Hall, I will do everything in my power to make sure that we win."

* * *

After breakfast the following Tuesday, John telephoned Harold from her study. He'd been elevated from Mr. Rubinstein at some point during their endless calls of the previous seven days.

"Any news?" she said, as she said to him every morning.

"No, I'm afraid not." Harold's usual answer.

She shook her head for the benefit of Una, who lurked nearby awaiting an update.

"When are they ever going to make a decision?" In August, Jix had taken less than forty-eight hours to decide her book was obscene. It seemed the Customs Board was in no rush to reach the opposite conclusion.

"Melville's made an excellent submission. We're keeping the issue in the public eye. I'm sure it won't be much longer."

"Call me as soon as you hear anything."

"I will. Of course, I will."

John rested her head against the heel of her hand, eyes closed, fingers splayed in her hair. How many more days in limbo?

Una put her hand on John's shoulder. "You need a break. Let's go to Noël's rehearsal. It's the last one before he sails for New York."

John resisted at first but Una was right. She did need a break.

On opening nights at the London Pavilion, the foyer thronged with people wanting to see and be seen. Today it was deserted, the ticket office closed. John had never been inside a theatre outside of a performance. It was almost eerily quiet.

"Hello," John called. No one responded.

They made their way to door B, one of the entrances to the stalls. John was already regretting coming. What if there were news? She'd let Harold know where she was going before they left home, but how was he to contact her in an unstaffed theatre?

Cautiously, Una pushed the door open. John was half-hoping the theatre would be dark and they could go home, but the curtain was up, the stage lit. "This looks promising." Una led the way towards the front.

A man called out to them, "Excuse me. Sorry. The theatre's closed today." The voice was polite, but firm.

"Mr. Coward invited us to attend the rehearsal," Una replied.

"Oh, he did, did he? Well, I suppose you'd better take a seat. We'll be starting soon." He returned his attention to his notepad.

Una and John continued towards the front. They'd reached the third row when the man looked up again. He got to his feet. "Miss Hall, Lady Troubridge. Please accept my apologies. I didn't realise it was you."

"Mr. Cochran." John's previous encounters with the theatre impresario had been limited to opening night parties. His greying hair was aggressively parted down the middle but his face wore a smile of welcome.

"I'm delighted you're here. The whole of theatre is rooting for you in this dreadful business with the censors."

John thanked him for his support. He returned to his seat in the front row and picked up the notepad and pen. "Don't mind me. I've still a few things to sort out before we depart for New York."

John and Una settled in the third row. A few minutes later, members of the orchestra took their seats in the pit. Even in the empty theatre, John felt a pang of anticipation as they began their warm-up.

The first sketch was set in an underground railway station. A high-society lady looked around the booking office in bewilderment. John had never had a need to use the underground. She wondered would she be so inept at buying a ticket. At first, she was shy to laugh aloud, but as the high-society lady pushed more and more pennies into the ticket machine, obtaining ever more tickets, she found she couldn't resist. Noël had a gift for laughter. It would be rude not to enjoy it.

In the middle of the third sketch, John heard a gravelly laugh from a few rows behind her, a laugh she recognised. She chanced a glance over her shoulder. Tallulah Bankhead. When had she arrived? Tallulah caught John's glance and winked at her. With a smile, John turned back to the show.

At the end of the first act, Cochran announced a one-hour break for lunch. John turned to greet Tallulah. The American was already on her way along the aisle towards them, looking glamorous in a velvet chiffon coat. But then, when did Tallulah not look glamorous? The woman accompanying her was vaguely familiar, but John couldn't quite place her.

"Darlings," the actress said, the word drawn out in her Southern drawl. She embraced first Una then John.

Almost against her will, John's heart started to beat a little bit faster. She'd developed rather a schoolgirl crush on Tallulah Bankhead when they'd first met four years earlier. The attraction was mutual. They'd dined together in London's best restaurants, danced in jazz clubs till the early hours. It was enjoyable while it lasted, but they both knew it would be a mistake to take things further. The flirtation had ebbed, though not entirely died.

Tallulah stroked John's cheek with a slender hand. "You look worn out."

A lump rose in John's throat. She'd barely slept since her books had been seized, and when she did, she was tormented by nightmares. "Just a little tired."

Tallulah's companion had been waiting in the background. Now she stepped forward to shake hands. "I'm Mrs. McPherson. You might know me better as Sister Aimée."

John had read in the press about the American evangelist. Opponents had tried to persuade the Home Secretary to block her entry to England, objecting to her crowd-pleasing theatrics and accusing her of scandalous behaviour in her homeland. Even in the shadow of Tallulah's beauty, the hot gospeller was striking, with high cheekbones and sensual lips. She was fashionably dressed, her golden hair tucked into a cloche hat, a fox-fur stole draped round her neck. Appearance aside, she seemed an unlikely companion for Tallulah Bankhead. Sister Aimée denounced dancing, nightclubs, gambling and wine. Tallulah lived for them.

"How are you enjoying the rehearsal?" John said.

"It's a feast of a show," Tallulah said. "Quick, clever, witty. What more could an audience want? And as for the songs…"

"I thought 'Dance, Dance, Little Lady' was especially good," Sister Aimée offered. "A warning of the dangers of letting present-day pleasures distract you from what matters. I make the same point in my sermons."

"I hear your Royal Albert Hall shows have been going very well." Una was always polite.

"Indeed they are. More than fifty thousand people heard me preach last week."

"How very impressive," Una said.

"I'm here to save every soul that I can. I'm off on a tour of Britain from tomorrow but I'll be back at the Royal Albert Hall on the fourteenth and fifteenth of November. I'd be thrilled if you and Miss Hall could attend."

John forced a smile. "We'll consult our diary." Really, the woman was much too forward.

"Miss Hall and Lady Troubridge are already spoken for by his Holiness in Rome," Tallulah said.

Noël joined them from the stage. "Mrs. McPherson, if I'm not mistaken. I hear you've come to save London from sin. I'm afraid you're out of luck with me. I am a devoted agnostic."

"I'm having a day off preaching, Mr. Coward. But beware, Jesus is coming soon. Be sure to be ready."

"I'll bear that in mind. For now, I'm more concerned about luncheon."

The evangelist was silent as they made their way to a nearby tearoom. Once they'd placed their order she inquired if Noël had ever been to Los Angeles.

"Not so far, but I'm hoping Hollywood will call, sooner rather than later."

"Back home, I use Hollywood set-builders to stage my sermons. The old ways are losing their power. Entertainment is the way to save people from hell."

"The old ways have lasted almost two millennia," John said.

"That may be true, but they're failing in our modern world."

"If you don't mind, I'd rather not discuss religion over luncheon," Noël said. "It's bound to give me indigestion and I've got the rest of the rehearsal to get through."

As they walked back to the Pavilion, John fell into step with Noël and Tallulah, leaving poor Una behind with the evangelist.

"Thank you for coming today," Noël said, "and for applauding with such conviction. It's terribly vulgar and common of me, but I do love applause."

"You're going to be a great hit in New York," Tallulah said.

"I do hope so. I'm looking forward to being back there. It's so wonderfully alive."

"When I first moved to New York, my father warned me to stay away from alcohol and men." She paused. "He never mentioned cocaine and women." The three of them laughed.

They'd reached the door of the theatre. "Cochran will have endless notes when we finish. This is the last I'll see of you till after New York."

"Break a leg," Tallulah said.

"Good luck," John added.

"And to you," Noël said, briefly squeezing her hands. "Don't let them wear you down, darling. I'll be thinking of you."

* * *

Next morning, John telephoned Harold as usual. "Any news?"

"Not from Customs, no," Harold said. "But Jix was posturing last night. He told a meeting of church leaders that he should take on the role of dealing with 'disgusting books' himself."

"He's threatening Customs, isn't he? Uphold the ban, or I'll do the job for you."

"It seems there is no end to the powers our Home Secretary wants for himself. The sole arbiter of the nation's morals and literary tastes."

"We've no chance now, do we?" John said.

"Of course we have a chance. Sir Francis Floud is not a man easily bullied. Don't give up hope."

Despite his positive words, John slumped with her head in her hands for some minutes after the telephone call. The trip to Noël's rehearsal had lifted her spirits, but back here in Holland Street she felt oppressed. She rubbed at her left eye, where a stye had erupted overnight.

"Let's go to Rye this weekend," she said suddenly, "whether Customs have made a decision or not."

The cottage wasn't quite ready but John managed to reserve the Queen Elizabeth room at the Mermaid Inn. It would be good to get away.

John went to early Mass the next morning, staying on after the other worshippers had departed to pray to Saint Anthony for deliverance. The stye scraped at her eye. She embraced the discomfort, offering it up to God. Perhaps this small penance would help free her book.

There was no news from Harold when she called him later that morning. On Thursday morning there was still nothing. At four o'clock on Thursday afternoon the telephone rang. It was Harold. "The consignment's been released."

It took a moment for the words to sink in.

"Did you hear me, John?"

"Released? You mean…"

"The Board of Customs and Excise has confirmed what we already knew—*The Well of Loneliness* is not obscene. Your books are free to circulate."

"Yes," she said, on her feet now, joy coursing through her like sunlight. "Yes." She clenched her fist in triumph. "Yes."

"What is it?" Una said.

Holding the phone with one hand she grasped Una's hand with the other. "We did it," she said, laughing. "We did it."

"We did." She could hear the smile in Harold's voice.

"Thank you for your support."

"It's been a privilege."

"Does Holroyd-Reece know? And Cape?"

"Not yet. I called you first."

John was touched by his consideration.

"Leave the others to me," Harold said.

John pulled Una close, holding her tight, eyes closed, thanking God for answering her prayers.

"Congratulations, darling," Una said.

John held Una for another moment, then let go. Her address book was on her desk. She looked up the number for Arnold Dawson of the *Daily Herald*. She'd been a Conservative all her life but the left-wing *Herald* had become her newspaper of choice. A lot had changed in the last two months. Why should she support a Tory Party whose Home Secretary was persecuting her book? The *Daily Herald* had been her staunchest backer. She was lucky to have it. No newspaper in England had defended Wilde. After a couple of rings, Arnold answered.

"Radclyffe Hall here. Customs have ruled that *The Well of Loneliness* is not obscene. I thought you might want to be first to get the author's reaction."

CHAPTER THIRTY-TWO

I turn the key in the lock and step into the hallway out of the rain. Seven follows me through. "Hello, you." She pulls me close. I've barely a moment to enjoy her arms around me before Baby Girl barrels into the middle of our hug. Seven stoops to give her the affection she demands.

"It's only us," I call. Us. I can't keep the smile off my face. So much happiness in such a small word.

"Come on through," Sibyl replies.

In the few weeks that we've been courting, Seven's barely spent a minute with my landladies. Between weekends away and art exhibitions and trips to the theatre and suffragette-fellowship meetings and stop-vivisection meetings and commemorate-Mrs-Pankhurst meetings they've always something on the go. But tonight the four of us are having tea together, which Sibyl still insists on calling dinner even though she's outnumbered. I'm excited, but I'm nervous too. What if they don't like each other?

Sibyl leads the welcome as we enter the kitchen, asking how we are and if it's still raining.

Tilda pauses from doing the washing up to look in our direction. "Good to see you again, Seven." She even smiles which is more than I ever get.

"Do you need a hand with anything?" Seven offers.

"I think we've got it all under control," Sibyl says. She returns to grating lemons at the table.

"Have we time to get changed?" I've not managed to dry out after Charlie drill in the pouring rain. Handling that misshapen dummy is hard enough at the best of times without him being soaked through. Typical Johnston. No weak links!

Seven and I take ourselves off to my room. It's a chance for a cuddle and a kiss. And another kiss. And another. This is heading for bed and how can we be doing that with Tilda and Sibyl downstairs waiting and wondering what's keeping us and getting quick enough to the answer? I break away from her. "I should get you some dry clothes."

We're not dissimilar in build, except for Seven being a few inches taller. She starts to unbutton her tunic while I root in the wardrobe for shirts and skirts. She's down to her cami and stockings when I turn to place the dry clothes on the bed.

"You are the most magnificent woman I've ever seen," I say.

"I didn't quite hear you." She cups her hand to her ear, beckoning me to her. "Say it again."

I lean my face close to hers. "You're gorgeous."

How can I not kiss her? And kiss her again. And again. And the bed's just there. But then the bathroom door next to my room closes with a firm click and we leap apart. Seven starts to laugh and so do I. I've laughed more in the past few weeks than I have in the last five years. I never knew there was so much laughter waiting inside me to come out.

Tilda's emerging from the bathroom as we make our way from my bedroom downstairs. "Perfect timing." She smiles again. That's twice in ten minutes.

We usually eat at the kitchen table but tonight we're feasting in the dining room. The table's been set with the fancy patterned china that Sibyl saves for guests. A silver candelabra takes centre stage, lit candles reflecting off the gleaming mahogany.

"Sibyl's pushed the boat out," Tilda says. "I hope you're ready for five courses." She returns to the kitchen to help Sibyl.

"Five courses!" Seven says.

"Sibyl loves to cook," I say, oddly defensive.

"I've never had five courses before."

"Me neither. I'll be glad of it. I could eat the table I'm that hungry."

She grins. "I'm changing your name to Maggot Five-Course."

Sibyl hasn't served me a bad meal yet so I'm not surprised when the first course of devilled eggs tastes divine. Seven declares the French onion soup that follows to be the best soup she's ever had. She's even more delighted with the mushroom risotto. And by the time we're onto the lemon tart she's suggesting that Sibyl should open a restaurant.

"I considered it," Sibyl admits. "I was full of ideas after our grand tour—"

"I never called it that," Tilda says. "As far as I was concerned, it was Sibyl's postwar holiday plans getting out of hand."

"Don't believe a word of it," Sibyl says. "She was as eager as I was to go travelling."

"Note she said travelling, not grand tour." It's an affectionate jibe.

"Where did you go?" I ask.

"Paris, first," Sibyl says. "Then on to Italy. Venice, Florence, Rome."

"Sardinia. I'd love to go there again. Rock pools big enough to swim in." Tilda closes her eyes for a moment, remembering.

"It sounds wonderful," I say. I think, I'll never get the chance to go anywhere like that. No sun-soaked honeymoon for me and Seven. Not that we're near the honeymoon stage yet. I've not dared mention the love word for fear of scaring her off. Could I ask her to go away with me without it seeming a major declaration? A romantic night or two, somewhere by the sea.

My Granny Palmer's cottage comes unbidden to my mind, sitting on the hill above Portmuck, looking out to sea. I'll never go there again, never climb the track to the red front door. I'll never go back to Ireland, never show Seven the places that shaped me, the land that I loved. It's my father's country and can never be mine, as far out of reach as the other side of the world.

"Spain," Tilda says. "Seville. Granada."

I had to let my homeland go the day I left Belfast. I let it go again.

"Oh, to see the glory of the Alhambra. I went five days in a row. It was extraordinary," Sibyl says.

The newspapers are full of advertisements for guesthouses along the coast near London. I wonder what Southend's like. Or Ramsgate or St. Leonard's.

"And on to Portugal," Tilda says. "Lisbon. Somewhere else I'd love to go back to. Then a few of the Atlantic islands. Madeira. Las Palmas. Teneriffe."

My dreaming's cut short. "You've been to Teneriffe?" It's an accusation.

"Just for a couple of nights," Sibyl says.

"Where?" Envy flares. Did they honeymoon among the cypress trees on a headland above the port?

"Hotel…oh, what was it called?" Sybil says. "Monopol. Hotel Monopol."

"Was it at Orotava?"

"I think it was, yes. Port Orotava."

I feel a ridiculous sense of betrayal. As if they've deliberately kept from me knowledge of a place they don't even know I hold special.

"Where's Orotava?" Seven says.

"It's in *The Well of Loneliness*," I say. "It's the place where Stephen and Mary are happiest, where they first make love."

"You haven't read it?" Tilda asks Seven.

Seven pulls a face. She told me she wasn't wasting her time reading about posh white women, even if they fall in love with other posh white women.

"You're not missing anything," Tilda says. "Unless you enjoy a doom-laden ending for women like us. Radclyffe Hall is living happily ever after with Una Troubridge but she offers no hope to women at war with themselves."

Why does she keep making this argument? I still don't know how to answer it. *I don't care* is all that I have.

Seven turns to look at me. "She gave you hope, didn't she?"

"Why do you love it so much?" Tilda says, her head cocked like a curious bird.

I turn the question around in my mind. "It gave me a way to see myself, I suppose."

"You don't believe in all that sexology invert claptrap, do you?"

"There's more than the lens of sexology—" Sibyl starts, but I want to finish my own thought.

"I don't care about the theories. What mattered was reading about women who let themselves love other women. Even if it didn't end happily, they followed their feelings. It sort of gave me permission to follow mine."

"Well I can't argue with that," Tilda says.

The tension in the room has gone. Seven slips her hand over mine. It rests there for a minute, the warmth from it tingling up my arm. She stood up for me.

I start to clear the plates. Sibyl objects, saying she's the hostess but I object back. "You can't be doing everything." In the end, we all help take the dishes to the kitchen. Seven washes and Sibyl and I dry and put away and Tilda takes Baby Girl for a quick walk.

We settle ourselves in the living room for the final course—a selection of fancy wee tarts and biscuits that must have taken half the day to make. Sibyl says they'd be served with coffee in France but we have them with tea so as not to be awake half the night. Tilda winds up the gramophone. She starts out mellow but then she puts on "Sugar Foot Strut." It's the song I caught her and Sibyl dancing to all those weeks ago when I barely knew them and everything about them fascinated me. Up they get, swinging each other back and forth and Seven pulls me to my feet and we're doing the same. Sibyl chooses "Blue Skies" next and we foxtrot round the front room.

I feel like blue skies really are smiling at me as I dance and laugh with my lover and my friends for the next two hours. We finish with Ma Rainey's "Prove It On Me Blues," raucously singing along with the risqué lyrics.

It's late when we get to bed. Too late to make love with work in the morning. But neither of us can resist once we're lying down next to each other, skin to skin. Afterwards, Seven falls swiftly to sleep. It's not so easy for me. Happiness fills me. Too full. How can I be living this life? This laughing, singing, dancing, kissing, loving life, this bliss of caring for someone who cares for me. Me, Maggie Dillon, unwanted mother-killer. I feel almost dizzy, vertigo of the heart. It's only a matter of time before I come crashing down.

CHAPTER THIRTY-THREE

Rye reached out her arms and welcomed John and Una back, offering them a rainbow as they drove into town. Journey's End would be ready the following weekend. Till then, the Mermaid Inn would take care of them. Their new life was beginning and not a moment too soon. In Rye, John would restore herself. Here she would tune herself back to life's rhythm, listen again to the heartbeat of the Earth. Here she would be able to write again.

"Lady Troubridge, Miss Hall. How wonderful to have you back with us." The hotel manager was an Irish woman whose smile cracked lines in her aging face.

"The pleasure, Miss Breem, is all ours," John said.

"Would you like to relax in the lounge while we finish getting your room ready? Or you can go through to the bar if you'd rather."

The carpet in the hallway leading to the bar was worn and faded. "Why do I like this place so much?" Una asked John. "It really is quite the shabbiest hotel I've ever stayed in."

"That's part of its charm."

The bar was deserted but a fire blazed in the huge fireplace that stretched along one side of the room. They took a seat nearby. John lit a cigarette.

"Do you think someone will come?" Una said, after a minute.

John was on the verge of going back to reception when Miss Breem entered.

"Now, ladies, what can I be getting you?"

John ordered potted mackerel and a glass of stout, Una a game pie and a pot of tea. The drinks arrived swiftly. "You're sitting right where the leaders of the Hawkhurst gang used to sit, loaded pistols on the table," Miss Breem said. "Started out heroes, ended up villains."

"We've heard this was quite the place for smuggling," Una said.

"A secret passageway runs from here to the Olde Bell Inn. If the Excise was after them, the gang used it to make a quick getaway. And did you know we have a priest hole? In this very chimney. You're of the Catholic faith yourselves, I believe."

"Yes, we are." John wondered how Miss Breem knew.

"And you've met Father Bonaventura?"

"He gave me this." John showed Miss Breem her St. Anthony's medal.

"Oh, now, wasn't that kind? He'd have been a wanted man, of course, if he'd been here in the sixteenth century. Imagine a priest hole in the same inn that Queen Elizabeth herself stayed in, with her the very woman that was the cause of needing to have a priest hole. Oh what an awful persecutor of the Roman Catholic faith she was. Worse even than her head-chopping father. Thanks be to God we're in better days. But listen, I should stop gassing and get you ladies your lunches." She departed the bar, leaving them in peace.

John sipped her stout. "It's a relief to be here." She lit another cigarette.

"You already look a better colour," Una said.

"Thank you for allowing me Rye. Do you think you'll miss London dreadfully?"

"If I do, I'll go up to town. It's not as if we've turned our backs on London forever. We've still got the house. We've still got the servants. As far as I can see, we can have the best of both worlds."

Their food arrived soon after. John spread a thick layer of mackerel on the crusty bread and topped it with a smear of cranberry jelly. "Delicious," she pronounced. The sharp sweet of the cranberry was perfect against the rich smoky fish.

"The pie's excellent," Una said, between mouthfuls.

After they'd eaten, John sat back, satisfied, and lit another cigarette.

"What do you want to do with the rest of the day?" Una said. "It's not really the weather for a walk but we could go for a drive."

"Perhaps tomorrow. What I'd really like is to lie in bed and have you read to me."

They raided the sweet shop first, then hurried back along the cobbled streets as the rain turned heavy. Elated and breathless at their escape from the deluge, they mounted the stairs to the Elizabethan bedchamber. Over the years the lattice windows had shrunk away from their frames, allowing in cold draughts. Una stuffed her stockings into the cracks and pulled the red velvet curtains shut. Outside the rain strummed against the glass. A log fire blazed in the grate.

There was something decadent about putting on pyjamas during the day. John climbed onto the four-poster bed and wriggled under the covers. "Pass the sweets, darling."

Una rifled in her handbag and deposited more than half a dozen bags on the bed. John rustled through bag after bag until eventually she found the butter toffees. She popped one in her mouth. "Mmmm," she sighed contentedly.

"What do you want me to read?" Una said.

"Something new, something interesting."

Una scanned the pile of books they'd brought with them. "How about this?"

"Why not?" John kissed Una on the cheek as she settled into bed beside her. "Isn't this cosy?"

"*Orlando: A Biography* by Virginia Woolf." Una turned to the dedication page. "'To Vita Sackville-West.'"

"I wonder what Mr. Woolf thinks of that." Did he pretend not to notice his wife's affair with another woman? That was how it had been with Ladye's husband, George. He was considerably older than Ladye, his pep long gone. He accepted John as a fait accompli. So long as Ladye was discreet and so long as she didn't leave him, he was prepared to turn the blind eye.

"Chapter One. 'He—for there could be no doubt of his sex, though the fashion of the time did something to disguise it—was in the act of slicing at the head of a Moor which swung from the rafters. It was the colour of an old football, and more or less the shape of one, save for the sunken cheeks and a strand or two of coarse, dry hair, like the hair on a cocoanut.'"

What a strangely unsettling image. That was the thing with having one's own publishing house, you could start a book in whatever peculiar fashion you had a fancy to and still get it published. John's own life would certainly have been easier these last months if she'd published *The Well of Loneliness* herself. No time wasted looking for a publisher, no sending it to the Home Secretary at the first sign of trouble from Douglas, no voluntary withdrawal, no behind the hand deal with Pegasus. The fight for her book would have been in her own hands. Still, she wouldn't have wanted to be her own publisher. It smacked too much of vanity publishing, no stamp of approval from people who knew about the business. Virginia Woolf didn't seem to mind that.

A knock on the door.

What kind of hotel interrupted its guests with unwanted knocks in the middle of the afternoon?

"Miss Hall?" Miss Breem's voice from the hallway.

The knock again.

"Miss Hall?"

A third time.

"Miss Hall?"

John snatched up her dressing gown and stomped over to the door. She glared at Miss Breem.

"I'm sorry to disturb you," Miss Breem said.

"And I am very sorry to have been disturbed."

"He insisted. He said I had to come and tell you to call him immediately."

"Who did?"

"Mr. Rubinstein."

From irritation to panic in two words. "When did he call?"

"Just now. I came straight up."

"I'll be down in a minute." She shut the door in Miss Breem's face.

John almost tripped in her hurry to remove her pyjama bottoms. She dragged on her skirt.

"Shall I come with you?" Una said.

"You'll take too long." She flung off her pyjama top in favour of a shirt. Frantically she began to do up the buttons.

"It might not be something bad," Una said.

"It's hardly going to be good news, is it?" John snapped. "No one ever interrupts your life with good news."

With mounting dread, John descended the stairs. Miss Breem let her use the telephone in the office.

"Tell me," John said, when the call connected.

"The police have raided Jonathan Cape and Leopold Hill. They've seized all the copies of your book they could find."

"But the Customs Board cleared it." She heard the whine in her voice, a child complaining *it's not fair.*

"The Home Secretary clearly didn't like the decision."

"It's a vendetta. My book is not obscene." She felt the taint of the constant denial, the exhaustion of having to say over and over that her book was not obscene. Yesterday she'd thought she was free at last only for the bogeyman to jump out of the bushes and grab her by the throat today. Except Jix was no imaginary monster. He was a flesh-and-blood bully. And she wasn't a child, she was a grown woman of means. "Can we take him to court?"

"The Home Secretary?"

"Yes. Sue him. For libel. Or slander, is it? Something." Let Jix be the one to squirm.

"I'm sorry, John. We've no case against him. It's your book that will be on trial. Cape and Hill will have to show in court why *The Well of Loneliness* should not be destroyed."

She'd been expecting banned. She could have managed banned. Destroyed was too real, too dangerous.

"Destroyed." Her voice sounded strange and distant in her ears. A nightmare surfaced, the furnace door open, Visetti flinging her books into the fire, a manic glee lighting his face. He turned to grab John's arm, dragging her towards the flames.

"John? Are you still there?" Harold's voice pulling her away from the furnace.

"We have to win, Harold. Whatever it costs we have to win."

CHAPTER THIRTY-FOUR

Seven's lounging on the sofa when I arrive at work on Saturday morning. She looks up from the *Daily Herald* when she sees me. "I see your friend's book is in trouble again." That's what she calls Radclyffe Hall—my friend—on account of the letter and the signed photograph and my love of *The Well*. She hands me the newspaper.

I don't need to go searching to find the story. *Summons To Follow Banned Book Seizure* dominates the front page. I hate the Home Secretary, persecuting Radclyffe Hall for no good reason, persecuting her book. I hand the newspaper back. "She's going to fight them all the way, so she is."

"She's wasting her time," Seven says, flatly.

"No, she's not."

"The system's all about stitching things up for the men in power."

"But there's nothing…obscene." I whisper the last word. "Surely that must give her a chance." I don't know why I'm arguing that the system is fair coming from where I come from, knowing that people like my father can get away with murder if the victim's a Catholic, get away with it as if it's nothing.

Before Seven can reply, Johnston arrives. I pour myself a cup of tea and sit down on the other sofa, away from Seven. We keep a distance from each other at work, unless the task at hand requires us to be close. Johnston and Clarke haven't a clue what's between us. Neither have the factory workers we pass each day, except Wilma who thinks it was all her idea. I wonder if women are secretly having affairs all over the world, hiding their goings-on from the people around them. Maybe even in the linen mills of Belfast, doffers and spinners secretly in love. The thought comforts me.

My workday starts on equipment with Clarke. There's something soothing about checking the motorcycle appliance inch by inch, removing any dirt, polishing the metal to a shine. We're making sure that all the ropes are in the right place, when Seven and Johnston return from inspection. I'm expecting one of Johnston's drills to follow. Instead she announces that the morning will be dedicated to RAT boards. I wonder what RAT stands for.

"My friend in Fulham had an invasion," Clarke says. "Big as cats they were, stealing her underwear for a nest in the cupboard under the stairs. I got her a tin of Liverpool Virus. That stuff works like magic—killed the lot of them."

"You mean rodent rat?"

"We're the Savoy Hotel to rats," Seven says. "Clothes for making nests and plenty of fresh water on hand."

"I thought we sealed every hole last time," Clarke says.

"Mr. Serre saw an article in *Power Laundry* magazine about installing boards below the gutters and now he wants them putting in place." Johnston doesn't give away what she thinks of this instruction.

I can't stand rats. The scuttling feet and baldy tails. "Isn't that a maintenance job?"

"It's a ladder job. And who knows better than us how to use ladders?" Seven says.

We work in pairs, me with Seven, Johnston with Clarke. Up the ladder I go with a hammer and nails, Seven behind me. At the top Seven reaches the board she's been carrying up to me and I hammer it into place. There's no way a rat could swarm up here. A six-foot wall maybe, but not a six-storey building. Down we go, move the ladder along, back up, hammer another bit of board in place. And down, and up, and down, and up, till my thighs are burning.

"See you Monday," Seven says, at the end of our shift.

"See you Monday," Clarke and Johnston reply.

I say it too. "See you Monday." But it's a lie because I'll be seeing Seven in a few hours. I'm going to her house for the first time. I wonder should I take flowers.

Seven's street is narrow and dirty. Water lies in the middle of the passageway that separates one tottering terrace from the other. I half expect rats to swarm around my feet. It's like a scene from Dickens but this is 1928. The smell of grubby clothes and unwashed bodies fills my nostrils as I pass a clump of children. I carry on up the street to number 31. Paint peels off the door and a big crack runs down the building from the edge of the sagging roof.

Seven answers my knock. "Welcome to the Stepney Palace." As soon as we've the door closed, we're in each other's arms. My body purrs in response to hers.

After the thrill of our hallway embrace, the ascent to her room on the second floor is depressing. The staircase is barely holding itself together, some steps rotten and broken, others sloping away at an angle. There's a gap in the wall halfway up you could stick your arm through and part of the ceiling's given way in the top landing. She shouldn't be living in this sodden squalor. It's not fit.

She shows me into a cramped room that's damper than Billingsgate Fish Market. "It's a bit of a comedown from your place."

I don't want to be rude so I pretend I don't notice the broken-down state of the house. "You've got such interesting things," I say, looking around me. Brightly coloured cloth covers Seven's narrow bed and boldly patterned raffia mats adorn the mildewed walls. A small bookcase houses carved wooden figurines. My favourite's a cheetah, about eight inches long, front paws stretching forward, back legs tall.

"Go ahead. Pick it up."

Carefully I take it in my hands. It's exquisitely painted, down to the dark lines on the slender face and the banding on the end of the tail. "I love this."

"I bought it from a man selling them out of a bag on Cable Street. I got this from him, too." She picks up a kneeling female figure, with a roughly hewn face and breasts so pointy they could take your eye out. "Osun, fertility goddess of the Yoruba people."

"A fertility goddess. Sibyl would love it. You should see her Sheela na Gig carvings, everything out—"

"I don't want you to tell Sibyl about Osun."

"Oh." I set the cheetah back in place.

"You mind, don't you?"

I thought she'd enjoyed our dinner with Sibyl and Tilda. "Do you not like her?"

She shakes her head. "It's not about liking."

"What is it about?"

She puffs out air—puhhhh—and shakes her head again and sighs. "I don't know. She seems nice enough. But she's posh. You scratch a posh person and you'll find someone whose family has stolen from Africa, someone whose money is soaked in the blood of black people."

I don't know where to start with thinking about what she's saying. I know nothing about Sibyl's family or their money. All I know is that she's been good to me.

"I'm sorry," I say.

"Why are you sorry? You're not posh and you're not English. I don't mean you," she says, but the anger hasn't left her voice.

I chew the inside of my cheek, wondering what to say. Nothing comes to me.

Her sigh is heavy. "Let's go out. I'm hungry and I've nothing in. You can't store food in this dump without vermin getting at it."

She puts on her jacket and stamps out the door. I follow. She slams it behind us and I can't help but flinch. We take our lives in our hands again, descending the stairs. She does this every day. We walk through the streets of Stepney without a word between us. I don't know how to fix things. With every step, the silence deepens.

I stop walking. After a few paces she realises I'm no longer alongside her. She turns back. "What?"

"I can't stand this."

"Not here, Maggie."

"Yes, here."

"It's the middle of the street," she hisses.

Around us people are going about their business, women with shopping bags trailing children behind them, men strutting around hands in pockets, or standing on corners gossiping like fishwives.

"I don't care," I say, though I do make the effort to lower my voice. "If you're done with me, I'd rather get it over with."

"Is that what you want?"

"No." I look up to the sky, trying to keep the tears in my eyes.

She touches me briefly on the arm. "Me neither." Her voice is soft. "Now will you come, please, we're not safe here." Her eyes swivel in the direction of two men, twenty feet away, lounging against a wall, watching us. As we walk past them, one of them tells Seven to clear off back to the jungle. The other spits out a racial slur in case she didn't get the message. I don't know what to do. I look to Seven. She doesn't respond so neither do I. We carry on walking through streets I don't know, a left here, a right there until we reach Cable Street.

More and more of the people that we pass are coloured. Two Arab-looking men ahead of us go into a café on the right but we carry on another fifty yards until at last we stop outside a place called Mama Afrika. Seven holds the door open for me. Vibrant zigzags and triangles of red, gold, green and black cover the walls. A large wooden gorilla surveys the scene from a corner. Most of the diners are black men but there's a smattering of white women too. Several of them look like what my Auntie Ruth would have called women of ill repute, a term I didn't understand as a child but knew it went beyond not keeping a clean house.

We find a table for two. Seven reaches for my hand. "I didn't mean to upset you."

"Me neither. I promise I won't say anything to Sibyl about Osun. About anything."

I'm all serious but she laughs. "I think you'll have to say something to her about something, if you're going to carry on living in her house."

"I mean about anything to do with you. Or anything that matters to you."

"You matter to me." She looks straight into my eyes.

I can't hold her gaze. "I thought you were sick of me. Before."

"I was. But not in a let's end it sort of way. More in a stop annoying me sort of way." She strokes the back of my hand with her long fingers. It's ticklish but I like it. I look at her. Her eyes are soft.

"Can I interrupt you lovebirds to take your order?" The waiter is a handsome man with strong cheekbones and full lips.

Seven withdraws her hand from mine. "Sin, this is Maggie. Maggie, Sin."

Sin. That's a name would surely have you worrying about the fate of your soul.

"Nice to meet you," he says. "So you managed to drag yourselves away from the charms of the Stepney Palace?"

"She thinks it's a dump," Seven says.

"I never said—"

"It is a dump. But better than the streets. Now what would you like to order?"

"I'll have goat curry," Seven says. "And chai tea."

"Erm," I say. I haven't a clue what this place serves.

"The menu's on the blackboard," Seven says. "Behind you."

Maharagwe
Rice and Goat Curry
Kenkey with Turkey Tail
Jerk Chicken with Plantain

Red Bean Stew

I'm barely any the wiser. Sibyl's made curry a couple of times but not with goat in it. I'm too embarrassed to ask what maharagwe is so I opt for the bean stew and hope for the best. Sin departs with our order.

"So he knows about us?"

"He's a good friend. He lives at Stepney Palace too."

"Is that why you stay there?"

She looks at me like I've lost my mind. "I'm fond of Sin, but not fond enough to live in a cesspit for him."

"So why are you living there?"

She shakes her head. "Short version—the woman I was with took a fancy to someone else and chucked me out of her flat. The Palace was all I could get at short notice. I thought it wouldn't be for long but there's twenty people looking at every decent place that comes free and most landlords want white tenants."

I feel guilty about my lucky break with Dunlace Road. She's told me before about the name-calling and the staring and being spat at and jostled in the street but I hadn't really thought about the rest of it, like not being able to get somewhere decent to live.

The food arrives. I try a mouthful of Seven's curry, avoiding the meat, and she tries my red bean stew which is spicy and warm and full of flavour. Our argument is long forgotten and we've the rest of the weekend waiting for us. Her house may be squalid and her bed narrow, but all that matters is being with her.

We're halfway through our meal when a woman in a sharp trouser suit arrives. She comes straight over to our table. "Well look who it is." She grins at Seven, perfect teeth bright against ebony skin.

Seven gets to her feet to embrace her. "Irie! I thought you were in Paris."

"Did you not get my letter? I'm back in London for a couple of months. But guess where I'm going after that?"

"Where?"

"Guess." If she grins any harder her face will split open.

"Not New York?"

Irie's laughing now and so is Seven. "Right in one. Irie Taylor is off to Harlem." She shimmies on the spot.

"Harlem." I hear the yearning in Seven's voice. If Irie does, she ignores it.

"Performing at a new club on 133rd Street right in the heart of the action. It's my big chance. Columbia are on the lookout for new singers. Maybe I'll finally make a record."

"I bet you will. You're as good as any of them." The yearning's gone, replaced by excitement. "Maybe you'll get to go to one of Ma Rainey's parties."

"If I'm lucky I might even get to sing on the same bill as her."

"Or Bessie Smith," Seven suggests. "When do you go?"

"Six weeks. Till then I'm performing at the Sunset Club."

"On Dean Street?"

"The very one. But Mama's lent us upstairs for a rehearsal if you want to sit in. Unless you and your lady friend have other plans." She directs a curt nod towards me.

I was brought up to be invisible, at least when my father was around. I used to be used to watching from the sidelines. Belatedly Seven makes the introductions. "What do you think?" she says to me. "Shall we go to the rehearsal?"

I think, the two of you have been lovers. I can feel it. And if Irie had her way you'd be lovers again. But Seven's put me on the spot so I say, "If you're sure we won't be in the way."

Irie leaves us to finish up our food.

"What a stroke of luck," Seven says. "She's an amazing performer. If she was American, she'd have records in the shops already."

"How do you know her?" I say, trying for casual.

"I met her at one of Mama's parties." She chortles at a memory she doesn't share with me, then loads her fork with curry and carries on eating.

I pick up my own fork then put it down again. I've lost the urge to eat. How am I ever to compete with a woman like Irie? Gorgeous. Talented. And black. I'm rice pudding bland in comparison.

Seven finishes her curry. "Your stew's getting cold."

I take a couple of mouthfuls for form's sake.

"I thought you liked it."

"I think I've had enough." I push the plate away. "Where's this rehearsal then?"

She leads the way upstairs to a room that runs the length of the first floor. Walls, ceiling and floor have been painted black. Irie sits at an upright piano on a low stage, practising scales. A small bar occupies the opposite corner. A handful of tables are scattered between, all empty.

"Is this a club?" I ask.

"Not officially," Seven says. "Mama puts on entertainment and parties when the urge takes her. I've had some wild nights here."

Was the night she met Irie one of them? We take a seat in the centre of the room. Warmups finished, Irie's ready for business. She starts with "Downhearted Blues." Her voice caresses the words, filling them with heartache.

"Good, isn't she?" Seven whispers.

She is. I'm glad she's going to America. It can't be soon enough.

"What time do you call this?" Irie says at the end of her first song.

The door behind us closes. A man with skin the colour of caramel crosses to the stage.

"Don't grind your gears. We've got plenty of time." He opens his instrument case and takes out a saxophone.

"Ladies, this idler is Snake Waterson," Irie says.

Snake acknowledges us with a nod of the head, then carries on attaching a neck strap to his instrument. He takes a deep breath and blows out a long, low note. And again. A slow scale follows and then a flurry of fast notes up and down. And the long, low note again.

Seven rests her arm along the back of my chair. "I love the sax."

I try to let her nearness reassure me. She's with me not Irie. "Me too."

Snake concludes his preparations. He looks at Irie.

"Ready?" she says.

The opening riff on the saxophone is slow and haunting, the piano follows in and then Irie's voice rises above both and we go with her on a blues journey of sadness and sorrow. After a brief pause they ease into the "St. Louis Blues." Seven asks if I want to dance. Soon she's holding me heartbeat close as we waltz in the space between the tables and the stage. The next number's upbeat. My fears recede as we lindy hop to the faster tempo.

More people have joined us upstairs. A dozen black men sit at tables and several others are on the floor dancing with white women. The bar opens and I buy us ginger beer. A black woman in a swanky dress arrives on the arm of a sweet-faced white woman. "That's Mama Afrika," Seven tells me, "and her wife, Betsy."

"They're married?"

"In every way that matters."

Seven catches Mama's eye and she and Betsy make their way over to our table.

"Who's this girl didn't eat my stew?" Mama says.

Seven laughs while I die of embarrassment. "This is Maggie."

"You should have had the goat curry," Mama says.

"She doesn't eat meat," Seven tells her, which is hardly helpful. I could crawl under the table. I'm glad that they don't sit down with us.

"What did you tell her that for?" I say to Seven.

"It was only a bit of fun. I bet you'll finish your plate next time."

Sin enters the room with a bearded man. They begin to dance, an intimate cheek-to-cheek sway, shocking and beautiful.

"That's Ismail. They look good together, don't they?" Seven says.

"They do."

She offers me her arm and we return to the dance floor. We only get one dance in before Irie announces that the next song will be her last. Her voice powers through the first verse. My feet can't seem to find the right steps, my mind too distracted to take proper charge of them. The last song—and then what? Will Irie come and sit with us, spend the evening flirting with Seven while I disappear into the background?

Snake moves into a saxophone solo. Suddenly Irie's on the dance floor beside me. "You don't mind if I cut in."

Irie and Seven dance away from me. I'm left standing in the middle of the floor, in the way. I exit to the table, my heart gripped with fear. Irie can really dance, far better than I can. They look so handsome together, Seven tall and strong, Irie smaller, but just as dazzling. She has what it takes to become a star—the talent, the looks, the personality. She'll be a hit in Harlem.

Harlem. The black metropolis, full of artists and writers and people trying to change the world. Seven has always wanted to go there. In Harlem, maybe she wouldn't have to face the jibes and hostilities of a world that doesn't want her. I think of the men earlier, their insults and their spite. I don't know what it is to live with that. I'll never know. Irie does.

I chew on my finger as I sit watching them, trying to hold my panic at bay. I don't want Seven to go to Harlem with Irie. Is that selfish? I love her. And I think perhaps she's beginning to love me. She's told me she more than likes me. What is more than liking if not the beginning of love? Is it selfish that I want her to stay here and love me?

I don't want to be like Stephen Gordon in *The Well of Loneliness*, sacrificing her own happiness to give Mary a better life with Martin. I don't want to break my own heart. And what guarantee was there that Mary was better off with dull-as-mud Martin Hallam? What guarantee that Seven would be happier in Harlem with full-of-herself Irie Taylor?

I make my way across the dance floor. Suddenly I'm next to Irie. "You don't mind if I cut in."

Seven takes me in her arms with a smile. Irie's forced to retreat to the stage. She holds out a hand, acknowledging Snake. The audience whoops and claps its appreciation. Taking her seat at the piano, Irie leads us into a frenetic final chorus of the song. The last chords vibrate in the air at the end of the performance to be replaced by whistles and cheers and shouts for more, more!

As the racket dies down, Seven leans over and kisses me on the lips. "Let's go home."

It's dark and foggy outside. We walk side by side, not quite touching. The last few hours ripple through my mind. I haven't seen off Irie, not by a long shot. I wish she was going to New York tomorrow. No time for her to turn Seven's head. I'd go and wave her off myself. Seven's quiet. Perhaps she's thinking about Irie too, about Harlem.

Three men appear from the shadows, blocking our path. "Well, well, well, what have we here?" one of them says.

Another one leers at me. "Look at this one." He blows cigarette smoke into my face. "Thinks she's what's her name that wrote that filthy book." I try to step back, away from him, but the third man has circled behind me. Seven is next to me. We exchange a quick glance.

"You off home to do something pervy?" the first man says. "You know what you need?" He grabs my hand and pulls it towards his groin. I go with his weight and forward roll out of his grip. I'm quick to my feet, into the stance, left foot forward, right foot behind, knees flexed, balance centred, arms raised. Next to me, Seven assumes a boxer's pose.

"We don't want any trouble," I say.

"They don't want any trouble," one of them says. He flicks his burning cigarette at my face. As I duck, he swings his fist towards me. I'm late seeing it and he catches me on the left cheekbone.

Seven hits him and his lip spurts blood and he roars and the three of them are on us. But Tilda's been teaching me jujutsu and I've the strength and speed of a firefighter and so has Seven. I throw one of them to the ground, using his weight to defeat him. He lands heavily on the cobbles and lies there moaning. Another one grabs me round the throat from behind, but I duck down and arm lock him hard till he screams for submission. And Seven's giving the third man one-two combinations to the body and face and he's too busy swinging and missing to protect himself and a left hook to the jaw sends him staggering and he half tramples over the one I put on the ground earlier. That's when they realise that the better part of valour is discretion, not that they have any valour, and away they stagger, shouting insults over their shoulders.

Seven and I leg it in the other direction. I tell her she was amazing and she says what about you, where did you learn to fight like that and I say that's one of the perks of living with a suffragette.

CHAPTER THIRTY-FIVE

John spent the weekend following the police seizures quietly gathering her strength. She walked on the marsh, went to Mass, prayed to Saint Anthony and rested. On Monday she returned to London to prepare for the fight of her life. Jix was Goliath, the power of the Philistine army behind him. John would be David. Who better to be than David? David who had slain a giant. David who had loved Jonathan as his own soul.

On Monday evening, the housekeeper showed Harold Rubinstein into The Drey. He settled himself on the sofa. "As expected, Cape and Hill have been summonsed to appear before court. The trial will be on Friday the ninth of November at Bow Street Magistrates' Court."

Bow Street. Poor Oscar had appeared there, charged with gross indecency, after the collapse of the disastrous libel case against his lover's father. Now the fate of John's book would be decided in the same court.

"It will be before Sir Chartres Biron," Harold continued.

"Chartres Biron. I'm sure I've heard that name," John said, an uneasy feeling gathering in her stomach.

"He published a memoir a couple of years ago. He's a member at the Garrick."

The Garrick, Biron, Douglas—the conversation with Arnold Bennett came back sharp and clear. "Oh no, we can't possibly have him. He's already made up his mind against my book."

"What makes you say that?"

"Arnold Bennett told me he confronted Douglas at the Garrick following his attack on my work. Biron intervened—to defend Douglas." She spat the final name, bitterness in her mouth.

Harold paused long enough for a breath in and out. "That is unfortunate."

The understatement was maddening. Spilling a cup of tea was unfortunate. Getting caught in the rain without an umbrella was unfortunate. A bigot judging the fate of one's life's work was more than unfortunate. Calamitous came to mind. "We'll have to ask for someone else."

"I'm afraid that's impossible."

"Surely we can point out that Biron is already prejudiced against my book." John's voice was rising in tandem with her fear.

"All that will do is alienate Biron. He's the Chief Magistrate. They're not going to appoint someone else."

John closed her eyes. Was this British justice, famed as the fairest system in the world, her book to be judged by a man in league with the enemy?

"It's absolutely disgraceful," Una said. "Unfair and disgraceful and—"

"Do you think there's any chance we can win?" John looked at Harold.

His face wore its customary calm expression. "Biron believes in the law. We know your book isn't obscene. We need to persuade him of that fact."

"But is he persuadable?" The enormity of the question filled the room, pushing out the air. John waited, breathless, for the answer.

"I think so, yes. But our case must be compelling. We need to make it impossible for Biron to rule against us."

The air rushed back in, fuelling breath and words. "I intend to take the stand. I must be allowed to defend myself." And all who live as I do.

"I've been working on a strategy. Firstly, we need another legal team."

"Get rid of Melville?" John had been impressed by their lead counsel's command of the details and his assured submission to the Board of Customs and Excise.

"Sorry, what I should have said is we need an additional legal team. Until now the legal process has been limited to Pegasus as the publisher and Leopold Hill as their distributor in Britain. One team was enough. That changed on Friday with the police raid on the offices of Jonathan Cape. Cape will need separate representation."

"I presume he's agreeable."

"He is. I don't wish to be indelicate but a second team will significantly increase costs."

"Don't worry about costs."

"It could be as much as eight or nine thousand pounds, John. Maybe more if we get a top KC, which I think we should all things considered. A star who'll light up the court. I'm aware you're liable for half. I wanted to be clear with you—"

"I appreciate that, Harold. As I've told you before, I'm not losing this case for a lack of money." The only issue was where the money was coming from. She pushed the thought away for now.

He nodded, satisfied that he'd done his duty. "Cases like this are all about the weight of evidence. The more weight on our side, the more compelling our case. I plan to find as many people as possible who are willing to testify in court that your novel is not obscene."

"Who do you have in mind?" Una said.

"People of standing from every facet of life that the issue of inversion touches. Authors, doctors, scientists, clergymen, social workers—scores of eminent witnesses, nailing their colours to *The Well of Loneliness*'s mast. Think of it, witness after witness, taking the stand, each one explaining the importance of your book, each one testifying that it is not obscene." His voice, usually so calm, was filled with passion.

"Brilliant," John said, catching Harold's enthusiasm. "What a brilliant idea."

"We'll need to be prepared to reimburse the costs of travel and hotels for those who don't live in London. But the big problem is time. We've only got two weeks to find our witnesses. If you're sure about the costs, I propose bringing in an additional member of staff to help."

"I'm sure," John said.

Thank God for Harold. Harold knew what he was doing. So did Melville. So would the new barrister, the star to dazzle Biron. After Cape's mishandling of almost everything it was a relief to have competent men in charge of defending her book. Cape wouldn't be able to bungle it.

Over dinner they began compiling the list of witnesses. John offered Hugh Walpole, E. M. Forster and Virginia Woolf. Una added Havelock

Ellis and Storm Jameson, Harold suggested George Bernard Shaw and H. G. Wells.

"We should try John Galsworthy," John said.

"I did enjoy his *Forsyte Saga*," Harold said. "Do you know him?"

"He presented the Prix de Femina to John when she won it two years ago," Una said.

"More importantly, he's chairman of the PEN Club, the international writers' organisation. Defending literary freedom is part of the organisation's raison d'être."

"Yes, that's the kind of weight we need." He added Galsworthy to the list. "What about Sir William Beveridge?"

"Beveridge? I don't think I know him," John said.

"Vice-chancellor of the University of London. He was the brains behind the introduction of national insurance and the labour exchange system."

Worthy as this might be John didn't see what it had to do with her book.

"He'll bring gravitas if we can get him on board," Harold said. "It's all about the weight of evidence."

By the time they'd finished the main course the list stretched to more than fifty. Una suggested contacting all those who had positively reviewed the novel.

"And any journalists who've objected to Douglas's attack," Harold added.

They worked their way through Una's scrapbook of press coverage. Una had addresses for almost half of the reviewers. Harold assured them that he'd chase down the others.

The list continued to grow but as the evening wore on John contributed fewer and fewer names. Her mind turned to the issue of money. *Don't worry about cost.* Easy to say. Pegasus and Cape were paying half the costs between them. John had to find the other half on her own. How was she going to lay her hands on that much cash? Her savings had been depleted by the refurbishment of The Drey and the cost of Visetti's lavish Westminster Cathedral funeral. Her inheritance was tied up in investments—stocks and shares, paintings, antiques. How quickly could she turn any of them into cash? And how much time and energy would it take—time and energy that she needed to prepare for the court case?

John's heart contracted as the obvious answer occurred to her. Her house. Of all her assets, the Holland Street house was the easiest to sell quickly for a significant sum.

Why did this have to be the answer—to save her book, she had to lose her home? Her wonderful home. It had taken years to find it. When she first set up home with Una, they'd ended up in one unsatisfactory property after another. Datchet was too small, Chip Chase too far out, North Street the victim of a rat infestation… Five different properties in six years. All had failed to make the grade.

And then they'd found 37 Holland Street. On paper it was everything John had been looking for—a substantial residence with spacious rooms and a garden on a quiet street in the heart of Kensington. But estate agent descriptions had often disappointed in reality. Not with Holland Street. It had an atmosphere that was hard to put into words, somewhere between calm and possibility that both soothed and stimulated her. She'd felt it as soon as she crossed the threshold. In that moment she'd known that she was destined to live here, that in this house she would achieve greatness.

She'd spent time creating the perfect study—a new parquet floor, a Persian rug, an American rolltop desk, oak bookcases. The room was well-proportioned, plenty of space for her to pace back and forth, back and forth, unlocking the words and ideas that she needed. She'd written her most important work at Holland Street. And she'd been happy. Now she had to leave it.

"He's at 127 Harley Street, W.1.," Una read from her address book.

Not only John's home. She bowed her head. Una her stalwart, her constant support. Selling Holland Street would break Una's heart even more than it would John's. She thought of Cape and his cowardice in August, cowardice that was adding thousands to the cost of the legal fight. Cape wasn't selling his home. Neither was Holroyd-Reece.

"I fear I've worn you out," Harold said, breaking into John's contemplation.

"No, not at all." John forced a smile.

Harold had the good manners to take his leave. His departure left her alone with Una. How was she to tell Una about the house? She sucked at her bottom lip, wondering how to begin.

"It's so unfair about Biron." Una provided the opening.

"It's going to cost a lot to persuade him." John paused, feeling for the words. "I think we're going to have to sell the house." *I think* to soften the blow. Let Una get used to the possibility before making it definite.

Una stared at John, eyes widening.

"It's the only way, Squig."

"No." And again, more forcefully. "No."

"I know you love it here—"

"We both love it."

There was no point denying it. "How else am I to raise the money?"

"You told Harold money wasn't a problem."

"And I meant it."

"In what world is selling our house not a problem?"

"I don't have the kind of cash I need lying around in the bank."

"This is our home."

"We'll find another."

"We've only just finished The Drey."

"I know, Squiggie. I know."

"Don't you have other investments? Stocks and shares you could sell?"

"Not enough. Nowhere near enough."

"You never said anything about losing our home." There was anger in Una's grey eyes, her sharp voice.

"I never expected…But what am I to do? Let Jix win?"

"There must be some other way."

"We'll find somewhere smaller, a flat for now, until the court cases are out of the way."

"Cases?"

"Given the trouble we've had here, I suspect we may run into problems in America. I need money to fight."

"There has to be another way. There has to be." Una stood, arms folded. For a small woman she looked remarkably fierce.

"This isn't just about us. If we lose…You know what it says if we lose. It would mean the idea of two women loving each other is condemned as obscene. We have to fight."

Una looked at John for a long moment. Then she turned and walked out of the room.

The lights were out in the bedroom when John came upstairs. She paused on the threshold, letting her eyes adjust to the gloom. Una was huddled up in bed, her back to the door. John edged over to her own side of the bed. She groped for her pyjamas. Where were they? The maid was under instruction to lay them out every evening. How could she have forgotten? John would have words with her in the morning.

A different culprit suddenly came to mind. John imagined Una tossing the pyjamas aside, signalling her wish to sleep alone tonight. She didn't have John's quick-as-a-flash temper but once roused Una was a formidable foe, stubborn and implacable.

"You can put the light on," Una said.

"I didn't want to disturb you."

"It's too late for that."

John hesitated, then switched her bedside lamp on. The pyjamas were waiting on the pillow. She stared at them, framed against Una's unrelenting back. How had they evaded her? She switched the light off. It showed too clearly Una turned away from her. John couldn't face getting undressed. "Do you want me to sleep in the spare room?"

"Do you want to?"

John didn't know the answer. The spare room would confirm the rift with Una. Was sleeping next to her hostile body any better? Attempting to sleep. Sleep would not come while Una hated her. These past weeks when all the world had seemed against her, Una's faith had kept her going. Una's belief in her. *It's a great book. You're a hero. You're changing the world.* How was she to manage without Una on her side?

"Are you coming to bed?"

"I don't know." Perhaps she should go to the spare room. She couldn't stand here all night.

"Come to bed, John."

"You don't want me there." The words jagged her heart. *You don't want me.* The feeling familiar since her earliest days.

Una sat up and switched on her light. "I don't want you to sell the house. It's hardly the same thing."

John blinked against the light but didn't respond.

"This is our home, John. Our home."

"Are you saying you want me to give up without a fight? Accept them calling us obscene?"

"No. I'm not saying that."

"Then what are you saying?"

Una paused. When she spoke, her voice was small. "Is there really no other way to raise the money?"

John pressed her fingertips against her forehead, trying to think. She'd spent time going through her finances before coming to bed. Had she missed something? Was there really no other way? None that she could think of. "I'm afraid not," she said at last.

Una crumpled into herself, her head bent low, sobbing. John watched on helplessly, wishing there was some comfort she could offer, knowing there was nothing she could say or do that would make any difference. All she could do was wait for the tide of Una's pain to turn.

CHAPTER THIRTY-SIX

Neither of them slept well that night but by morning Una had found her brave face. Over breakfast she listed a variety of faults the house possessed—the lack of sunlight in the best rooms, the early morning noise of the nearby bakery, the neighbour's cat—faults she'd never mentioned before.

John reached over and squeezed Una's hand. "Thank you." How lucky she was to have Una. John couldn't have put up with herself, her temper and dark moods, her endless insecurity.

"We'll find somewhere even better in the future, once you've won your cases."

* * *

London detained them for the rest of the week. John was determined that her own evidence would have the weight that Harold required. She met with experts on sexology, psychology and women's health. She reread the books on inversion that she'd used when drafting *The Well of Loneliness*. On Friday morning she went into town to scour the bookshelves of H. K. Lewis, the specialist medical and scientific bookshop. She purchased a summary of the proceedings of the First International Congress of

Sexology, the anonymously authored *The Invert and His Social Adjustment* and a collection of essays on inversion by an American physician.

Satisfied that she had acquired everything she needed, John caught a taxicab to Piccadilly. It was precisely one o'clock when she entered the lobby of the Berkeley Grill.

"Buon pomeriggio, Filippo. Come sta?" She'd known the Italian manager since his time at the Savoy a decade earlier.

"Molto bene, grazie. Welcome back, Miss Hall."

Harold was waiting for her in the anteroom. They followed their waiter to a table in the corner away from the windows. The restaurant was crowded as always, alive with chatter. Even here, supposedly a place of fine breeding, John felt eyes upon her. She wouldn't have thought it possible, but public interest had grown even more intense since her books were seized. Everywhere she went people pointed and stared and nudged and talked. She had newfound sympathy for the animals in the zoo.

Ignoring the interest, she took her seat. After the briefest perusal of the menu, she gave the waiter her order. Harold defaulted to steak.

"Any news on securing our star barrister?" John said.

"Nothing definite, yet. I'm trying for Norman Birkett."

"From the Pace case?" John said, eagerly.

Harold beamed. "Indeed."

The murder trial had been the sensation of the early summer. Beatrice Pace had looked to be heading for the gallows for murdering her husband. Means, opportunity, and motive were sewn up. She had access to arsenic, she'd prepared her husband's meals, and his violence and cruelty made her life a torment. John had avidly followed proceedings in the newspapers, convinced of Mrs. Pace's guilt throughout the first three days of the trial. But that was before Norman Birkett had shredded the police's evidence in cross-examination. The judge had instructed the jury to return a verdict of not guilty.

"One of the greatest legal brains to emerge since the war," Harold said.

John's heart quickened. If Birkett could save Mrs. Pace, surely he could save her book. "Is he interested? It's not a criminal trial."

"Birkett works across all aspects of the law—big-name divorces, libel cases, public inquiries. There's nothing he loves more than getting stuck into a significant case."

"Ours is certainly that."

"He's agreed to read your book this weekend. It'll be a coup if we get him."

John offered up a quick prayer to Saint Anthony. Let Birkett say yes. "Have you a plan B?" The trial was only a fortnight away.

"And C and D," Harold replied. "But I'd like Birkett."

Their food arrived. Harold had barely swallowed a mouthful before he resumed their conversation. "Our other task is making the bullets for our barristers to fire. I'm sorry to say that the hunt for witnesses is not going as well as I had anticipated."

"Do you need more help in tracking down addresses?"

"That's not the problem. We've contacted ninety-seven potential witnesses. So far, thirty-one have replied. Only eight have said yes."

Eight. Only eight people willing to stand up for her. And most potential witnesses hadn't even bothered to reply. Didn't they like her? Didn't they like her book? Shame ambushed John.

"I'd expected a few noes, but not this many. We need to find more names. I was thinking church leaders—" Harold continued to talk but John's own thoughts drowned him out. Untalented. Unwanted. Unloved. Lessons learned with her first breath. She'd tried to unlearn them. Here they were, back again. People didn't care about her or her book. Forever the outsider. Disliked. A freak.

She couldn't look at Harold. He'd see her pain, her shame.

"John?"

"Pardon?" She pushed the poison-thoughts away. That was the past. Focus on Harold, on the fight.

"Perhaps we should come back to this after we've eaten." Harold cut a piece of steak and popped it into his mouth.

John had lost her appetite. Eight. "Who said no?"

Harold set aside his knife and fork to rummage in his briefcase. He handed her a typed sheet headed "Noes." The first name was a shock.

"George Bernard Shaw said no?"

"I'm afraid so," Harold said.

"But he defended me in the press."

"I know. I was banking on him being a yes."

"Did he say why?"

"He's of the view that he's too immoral a character to be of any use in court."

"Have you told him we need him?"

"Of course."

John scanned the list of rejections. H. G. Wells, Arthur Conan-Doyle, writers that she'd known for years, turning their back on her. Even her friend May Sinclair who'd celebrated the prize-winning success of *Adam's Breed* in John's own home only eighteen months earlier.

And John Galsworthy. Anger swept away shame. As President of PEN, Galsworthy was honour-bound to defend literature and uphold free speech. "What was Galsworthy's excuse?"

"You will scarcely believe it. He said the government's actions posed no threat to literary freedom."

"No threat?" John exploded, drawing glances towards them. She lowered her voice. "How are efforts to suppress and vilify a work of literature not a threat?"

"Quite. We could really have done with him. The weight of an international writers' organisation would have been very helpful."

"Yes, I'm aware of that," John snapped. Even as the words came out she regretted them. This wasn't Harold's fault. "Try Hermon Ould," she said, her tone more measured. "He's PEN's general secretary." And an invert himself. "You might find him more sympathetic."

"I will, thank you. We do at least have a yes from E. M. Forster. I attended one of his lectures last year. He'll make an outstanding witness. And several other writers have come through—Hugh Walpole, Storm Jameson, Vera Brittain—plus three medical practitioners, and Professor Huxley, the zoologist from Kings College."

"It's not enough," John said.

"Not as it is, no."

"What about Virginia Woolf? Havelock Ellis?"

"No word yet. We'll chase up those who haven't responded next week. Assuming a quarter of them say yes, that would take us to around twenty-five. We can just about work with twenty-five. Not the overwhelming support I'd hoped for but if they're of the right quality, still difficult to dismiss. But twenty-five now seems a big assumption. Surely those most likely to say yes would have done so promptly? Less than twenty-five, well, let's not go there yet. In short, I'd like to approach another fifty or sixty potential witnesses. It'll give us a much better chance of a decent list."

After lunch, John sought the comfort of Fortnum & Mason's food hall and the small indulgences of sugared almonds and marrons glacés. A box of chocolate brazils caught her eye. Audrey's favourite. How she longed to talk to Audrey. Her agent's trip to New York had been essential. An American publisher had to be found. But John could have done with her here in London too. She missed her quiet calm, her ability to take a step back and see the right thing to do.

And Audrey was supremely well-connected. With her spider's web of contacts, finding another fifty or sixty names would have been just another day's work. She'd be back from New York in time for the trial but of no help before then. John would have to make do with her assistant. She added contacting Patience Ross to her mental list of things to do. It was growing ever longer—the house to sell, furniture to be put in storage, a flat in London to be found. None of this could be allowed to crowd out her most important task—her own statement. It was her chance to explain and persuade. She would give Birkett the bullets he needed. Her statement had to be perfect.

* * *

The gloom of approaching evening was gathering by the time John parked the Daimler in Church Square. The repairs on Journey's End had finally been completed. Their new home was waiting for them. They lugged their luggage through the archway into Hucksteps Row. It was almost dark when they reached the kink in the laneway where the view to the marshes opened up. A last hint of the setting sun invited them forward.

"Come in, ladies." Mabel welcomed them across the threshold. After closing the door she hung an old grey blanket in front of it to keep out the draught.

"Something smells good," Una said.

"Bully base," Mabel said.

"Bully base?" Una said.

"French, I think. Fish stew with tomatoes."

"Ah, bouillabaisse," Una said. "Excellent."

While John and Una sat down to eat in the dining room, Mabel hauled their suitcases upstairs and unpacked their clothes. After dinner, they retired to the sitting room, settling on the faded sofa opposite the fire, watching the flames. A knock on the door interrupted their reverie. It was only Mabel letting them know she was off home. They were left to themselves.

"I ought to do some work," John said. "The speech isn't going to write itself."

"Oh, darling, you look so tired. It will wait till tomorrow."

John didn't have it in her to argue. "Tomorrow."

* * *

They attended Mass at Saint Anthony's the next morning. John had always found the Latin words soothing, the ritual of the service a balm. She was part of God's creation. He would look after her.

In the afternoon, they walked across the marshes, late autumn sunlight glinting on the water. But when they returned, John knew it was time to start work. During the day, the study gave glorious views out across the marsh. Now, in the darkness of evening, the lights of unknown cottages and the rhythmic sweep of the lighthouse beam offered her comfort. She was not alone.

A desk had come as part of the furnishings. It didn't have the beauty of her American rolltop, but it was perfectly functional. John placed a photograph of Una on one side, one of Ladye on the other. Dear Ladye. How she would hate the uproar and fury surrounding John's book. Una wasn't so easily daunted. She looked again at the photo of her lover. It was one of her favourites, Una holding Mitsou in her arms, triumphant after a successful day at Crufts. How lucky John was to have her.

You'll lose everything. That had been Ladye's warning. It wasn't true. Una would stick by her no matter what, shoulder to shoulder, every step of the way, in victory or defeat. John was determined it would be victory. She'd win the court case, restore her reputation, gain millions of readers, earn the money for a new Kensington residence, a new quiet street, the perfect house for herself and Una. She offered a prayer to Saint Anthony, holding the medal in her hand.

It was time to get to work. She'd been writing notes all week, ideas from the books she'd read and the experts she'd consulted. Quickly she skimmed through them. She took up her pen and a fresh piece of paper. At the top she wrote, "Statement for *The Well of Loneliness* Trial."

When she began her novels, the first few words were often the most difficult to get out. Once she'd put pen to paper, however, the ideas would usually flow. Tonight she didn't know where to start. She stared at the pen in her hand, willing it to write. Nothing came. She added a colon and "Key Points" after "Trial." Still nothing came. She underlined the heading, then moved the pen to the start of a new line. A few words emerged onto the page.

- *Inversion—part of Nature*

Yes. Of that she was certain.

- *Social problem*
- *Ruined lives. Suicide*
- *Pressure to lie. Conspiracy of silence*

She paused again. What was it she wanted to say? The words that would change Biron's mind. This wouldn't be a jury trial. It all came down to the opinion of one man, a man who was already prejudiced against her book. How was she to persuade him? She took a fresh piece of paper.

Sir Chartres Biron
- Eton
- Cambridge
- Barrister
- Memoirist
- Previously active in the Liberal Party
- Unmarried

Unmarried. There were all sorts of reasons why men chose not to marry. Among them, most certainly, was that they preferred their own sex. What if Biron was an invert? Did it help to think of Biron as a potential invert? She wasn't sure it did.

This was hopeless. She lit a cigarette. What if she couldn't find the words? Some of the most vicious enemies of the inverted were inverts themselves, terrified that their own secret attractions would be discovered. What would persuade someone like that to let her book stand? The explanations of science? The promise of God's love? Maybe both. She had needed both—to know that she was part of nature and part of God's plan. These were the ideas to put at the heart of her defence.

It was only after lengthy consideration,

She scored out "lengthy."

It was only after ~~lengthy~~ the most profound consideration, and the ~~sincerest~~ deepest study of the subject of inversion, that I decided to write The Well of Loneliness. *I wrote it out of a sense of duty to tell the truth about this grave social problem. Being myself ~~an invert,~~ a congenital sexual invert, I have an understanding of the subject from the inside as well as from ~~scientific~~ medical and psychological textbooks. I felt that no one was better qualified to write the subject in fiction than ~~a novelist~~ an ~~expirenced~~ experienced novelist who was actually one of the people about whom she was writing, and was thus in a position to understand their ~~battle~~ unceasing battle against a ~~world~~ cruel world which seeks to label a fact in Nature as "unnatural."*

Late into the night she worked, long after Una had retired to bed, formulating and reformulating, searching for the words that would save her book.

After breakfast the next morning she read the statement aloud to Una, stumbling at times as she tried to make sense of the crossings out and insertions, the scribbles in the margin. As John read, Una typed, occasionally suggesting amendments. Then John rewrote it, and Una typed it up again. And so it went on all week and into the week after, rewriting and retyping, polishing and repolishing, until her statement shone with truth and beauty. Surely even Biron would be persuaded.

CHAPTER THIRTY-SEVEN

"One more time," Tilda says.

I get to my feet and take my position opposite Seven.

"Attack."

I throw a punch. Quickly Seven blocks, steps across me, gets a hold of my arm, drops her body and throws me to the ground. I land with a dull thud on the cushions littering the front room floor.

"Excellent. You've really got the hang of that now," Tilda says.

This is Seven's fourth lesson since our escape from the bullyboys. Boxing's all very well but nothing beats jujutsu. If the thugs and abusers thought they might end up thrown on their backs, they mightn't be so quick to harass women.

"I think that'll do us for today."

Seven smiles as she helps me up. I stash it with the ones I've stored up already. Every one of her smiles is precious, even more so now they might run out. Ever since we encountered Irie at Mama Afrika's a fortnight ago, Seven's never done talking about Harlem. It's been Irie's going to do this in Harlem and Irie's going to do that, imagine if Irie gets to meet Ma Rainey, imagine if Irie gets to sing with Bessie Smith. She hasn't said she wants to go too, not yet…

I'm doing everything I can to make Seven stay—helping with jujutsu training, having her over for dinner, playing her favourite records, dancing with her, baking her shortbread and making love to her as best as I know how. I don't know if being useful and fun is enough against the temptations of Irie and Harlem, but what else have I got?

We gather up the cushions and put them back where they belong. Sibyl joins us, already dressed in a hat, coat and scarf. "I don't want to be late," she says to Tilda.

While Tilda goes to fetch her own outdoor things, Sibyl asks if I've heard about the National Union of Railwaymen issuing a statement in support of *The Well of Loneliness*. "The miners are supporting her too."

The news is heartening. I'd never have expected ordinary working men to stick up for a novel about lesbians.

"She'll still lose," Seven says.

"We don't know that," I say.

She raises her eyebrows as if to say *Don't we?*, which I decide to ignore.

"Shall we go?" Tilda says. They're off to a meeting of the Suffragette Fellowship. It sounds a bit serious for a Saturday night out. I prefer my plans. Scarlett's back in town. She's signing us into the American Women's Club for a drink and then on to Devoted. All week I've been imagining dancing cheek to cheek with Seven on a proper dance floor instead of in Sibyl's front room, knowing I can touch and kiss her without anyone turning a hair. She'll feel the love I have for her, even though I still don't dare say the words, and maybe she'll think I'm worth staying for.

I go and run a bath. When it's ready, Seven suggests we bathe together to save time which it doesn't on account of the pleasure of our mutual nakedness. We kiss, our faces wet from the washing and when we stop I look at her and she looks at me and I'm sure I can feel love traveling between us, from my eyes to hers and back again. Maybe she won't go to Harlem. Maybe she'll stay.

There's only time for a quick cheese on toast in our dressing gowns and then into our finery and off to get the bus into town. Wilma's waiting for us at Piccadilly Circus. She looks dapper in a grey overcoat, homburg hat and red scarf.

"Love the coat," Seven says.

"My latest bargain. I got it for next to nothing at Petticoat Lane. Dark stains all down the front. But my old chemistry set took care of them. Good as new, innit?" She grins. "Look at the three of us. It's not about what it costs, it's about how you wear it."

We make our way up Bond Street towards Scarlett's hotel. Was my Stephen Gordon pilgrimage only three months ago? I'm not listening to Seven. Radclyffe Hall's going to win. She has to.

"Off to the American Women's Club at last," Wilma says. "Me and Maggie only got as far as reception last time on account of Scarlett having the hump. But it was like Buckingham Palace. Plushy carpets, paintings everywhere. Wasn't it, Maggie?"

"It was," I say. Not that I've seen inside Buckingham Palace to compare.

"And that was only the entrance hall. Scarlett says the social rooms are even better."

I expect Wilma to go in to collect Scarlett from her hotel but we carry on past it.

"She'll have taken a taxi," Wilma says.

"But it's just round the corner," Seven says.

"That's Scarlett for you. She's allergic to rain."

It's barely spitting, a rain so light it hardly justifies the word rain. I remember Scarlett's "little bitty shoes" from last time. Maybe she just doesn't like walking.

Five minutes later we're at the club. Big arched windows glow invitingly. Up the steps and into the entrance hall where chandeliers glitter and sparkle. Wilma takes off her hat and goes over to the reception desk. Seven and I follow behind, taking in the glamour of the place as we go.

The receptionist looks up. Her face sours. "No negroes."

"What?" Wilma says.

"This club is for whites only." She speaks directly to Seven. "Please leave."

"Stuff your club." Seven turns on her heel.

"Wait," Wilma says, but in a few quick strides Seven's across the hall and out the front door.

For a moment I'm caught in Wilma's indecision, hardly able to take in what's just happened, but then I'm off after Seven, leaving Wilma to decide whether to follow or stay with Scarlett in this foul place.

Seven's already twenty yards ahead of me, barging through anyone in her path.

"Seven," I shout. "Seven." If she hears me, it doesn't halt her. I break into a run. "Seven."

I'm only a yard behind her now and she must hear me but she storms on. I run faster till I'm close enough to grab her arm. "Wait."

"Leave me alone." She shrugs me off and carries on walking.

I grab her again.

"What?"

I can think of nothing to say but, "I'm sorry."

"Go back to your friends."

I drop my hold on her.

"You've been talking all week about this great night out. You don't want to miss your *wonderful* American Women's Club."

"You think I could go back there after what that woman said to you?"

"Do what you like."

"Where are you going?"

She doesn't answer.

I see it all in front of me. Irie's dressing room in the Sunset Club on Dean Street. Seven's bitterness and hurt, Irie's sympathy and understanding. *Come with me, come to Harlem, away from all this.*

I see myself, lost without Seven, broken like Stephen Gordon, no love, no hope.

"Please don't go to Harlem," I say.

"What?"

"Harlem. With Irie. Don't go."

"Harlem?"

"I know you were lovers."

"Me and Irie?"

"I know she wants you back. But I want you to stay. Please stay."

"Back with Irie?"

She's stuck in questions when I want answers. I need an answer. "You were lovers, weren't you?"

There's a pause before she replies. "I'm not sure one drunken night counts."

"One night?"

"Actually, the next morning too, just to be sure. We didn't fit, not in that way."

They didn't fit. They didn't fit. "So you don't want...I've been worrying...Do you not want to get back with Irie?"

"No! Great friends, bad lovers." She lowers her voice. "The sex, it wasn't...it was all bread and no butter. Not like with you."

Seven reaches her hand towards me. I take it.

CHAPTER THIRTY-EIGHT

Every day, John fell in love with Rye a little bit more. The Tudor buildings, the cobbled streets. The big skies, the river, the distant sea. The quiet, the calm. She took long walks with Una or ventured out to the quaint shops. If people recognised her, they kept it to themselves.

She rang Harold every few days from the public telephone at the Mermaid Inn. Each time he had news of more witnesses secured. Twenty-seven confirmed. Thirty-four confirmed. Forty-five confirmed. Counsel would have the bullets they needed. There was, however, no firm news of a star barrister.

"Don't worry," Harold told John, a week before the trial. "It's not unusual for counsel to be confirmed in the final four or five days before court."

"If Birkett doesn't want the case shouldn't we try someone else?"

"Oh, he wants it. He's confident he can successfully defend your book. The problem is a potential diary clash with another case. We'll know by Monday."

John prayed to Saint Anthony with renewed vigour over the weekend. She was still praying when she phoned Harold on Monday morning.

"It's good news, John."

"Do you mean Birkett's said yes?"

"He's said yes."

John exclaimed in delight, drawing stares from a couple passing on their way to breakfast.

"I'm sending the witness statements to Birkett and Melville this afternoon. Would you like copies?"

"Yes, send them to Holland Street, please."

"Final briefing with counsel will take place on Thursday afternoon at my office."

John confirmed that she would attend. She held the receiver to her heart after Harold had rung off. They had Birkett. They had Melville. They had the weight of evidence. They were ready.

John returned to London the following day, not merely refreshed but buoyant. After lunch she ventured into the study where Miss Webber was working her way through the latest sack of correspondence. Half a dozen stationery boxes were neatly stacked on John's desk. The first one contained letters from personal friends. The second, from members of the public.

"I thought you might want to look at these yourself," Miss Webber explained. "I've sent standard responses to almost three hundred others."

"And these?" John indicated four boxes set on top of each other.

"They're all donations."

"To me?" John had made no call for donations.

"For your legal costs. One thousand and eleven pounds, six shillings and four pence at last count."

"One thousand!"

"Small donations on the whole, from individual supporters. But there are a few large ones from trade unions. I've made a list."

All her adult life John had been suspicious of trade unions. It was her Tory heritage. Suspicion had turned to outright hostility during the general strike two years earlier. Now the unions that she'd opposed were supporting her against a Tory Home Secretary. John opened the topmost donations box and removed the elastic band holding together the first ten envelopes. Most contained postal orders for sums between ten shillings and two pounds. A couple contained pound notes. She scanned the accompanying letters, offering their sympathy, thanking her for her courage, castigating Jix.

She couldn't keep the money. Of course she couldn't keep it, given all her assets. The routine luxuries of John's life would be forever out of reach to most of her donors—the nurses and housewives, factory workers and miners who'd offered their support. But they'd given her something just as valuable. Their kindness, their compassion. Their solidarity, she thought with a wry smile. A trade union word if ever she'd heard one.

She thought of Galsworthy's refusal to back her, Shaw and his spurious excuse. To hell with them and the other cowards who'd said no. It was the yeses that mattered. Inverts saying yes to themselves. Ordinary people saying yes to the freedom to make up their own minds, yes to accepting those who were different. They wanted her to win.

* * *

Audrey called in after work that evening. The housekeeper showed her into The Drey where John was practising her statement. She set it aside to embrace her friend. It was almost four weeks since Audrey had left for New York.

"It's good to have you back," John said.

"You're looking well," Audrey said.

John's hair had been freshly barbered at Harrods that afternoon. Love Rye as she did, she hadn't wanted to risk a provincial hairdresser in advance of her court appearance. "How was New York?"

"Productive. I think I've found you a publisher. Covici-Friede."

John hadn't heard of them.

"They're new. Thoroughly progressive. An American version of Pegasus Press, if you will. They'll be perfect for *The Well of Loneliness*."

"Will it be out before Christmas?"

Audrey nodded. "Yes. Second week of December."

"You really are the best agent any writer could hope to have."

With a brief nod, Audrey accepted the compliment. "Just doing my job."

After dinner, Una and Audrey listened to John rehearsing her statement, helping her find the right weight to place on the right words. Audrey offered her advice for the witness box—focus on the question, think before answering, stay calm.

"And don't lose your temper," Una added.

Focus. Think. Calm. Temper. John turned it into a mantra that would help her do her best in court.

* * *

The trial was fast approaching but first there was the matter of finding the money to pay for it. On Thursday morning, she and Una attended an appointment at Chesterton's estate agency. The agent had no doubt the house would sell quickly. Substantial properties with gardens were always in demand in Kensington.

"We're also in the market for a two-bedroomed flat," John said.

The agent took them to see half a dozen, none of them outstanding. Not dreadful either but lacking the style and atmosphere of Holland Street. They settled on a stopgap flat in Hornton Street. Pleasant enough, if not what they were used to, and no room for a study for John. Rye would have to be her place to write for now.

* * *

After lunch, the chauffeur dropped John off at the offices of Rubinstein, Nash and Co. Jonathan Cape, John Holroyd-Reece and Leopold Hill were getting out of a taxicab a little further down the street. She waited for them on the pavement. Holroyd-Reece had the glamour of a resident of Paris with his scarlet cravat and glass-topped cane. Next to him, Cape and Hill looked decidedly dull.

"When did you arrive from France?" John said.

"This morning," Holroyd-Reece said. "Dreadful crossing."

"The Channel can be mulish at this time of year," John said.

She hadn't seen Hill since he'd agreed to be Pegasus's distributor and representative in Britain. His face was drawn. Hill's passion was crafting beautifully bound books. Now he was caught up in the biggest censorship fight for years. It was taking its toll.

The legal team awaited them in a large, well-lit boardroom. John recognised Norman Birkett immediately from the press coverage of the Pace case. Tall and red-haired, he was imposing if not entirely attractive. His voice, however, had an appealing timbre. "Pleased to meet you, Miss Hall. Mr. Cape. Mr. Holroyd-Reece." He shook each of them by hand.

Further rounds of handshakes followed with James Melville, who'd been working on the case since the Customs' seizure, and the supporting barristers, Walter Frampton and Herbert Metcalfe. When all were seated, Harold called them to order.

Melville spoke first. "We'll want a strong opening." He was a dark-haired man with perceptive blue eyes. John took an immediate liking to him. As he flicked through his bundle of witness statements, she noticed notes in pencil in the margins, phrases underlined in the text. "Sir Michael Sadler stood out for me with his praise for the novel's literary quality. 'A masterpiece in the same category as Rousseau's *Confessions*.'"

John enjoyed the comparison but refrained from saying so.

"I'd be inclined to start with Professor Huxley," Birkett said. "Get the scientific angle into play from the start."

"The literary merit of the novel is crucial," Melville countered. "We need to emphasise that this is not a pornographic work."

As the barristers debated the pros and cons of different witnesses, John's confidence blossomed. Whatever order they appeared in, the witnesses provided support across many spheres—literature, science, religion, social work, psychology, education... Harold had achieved what he had intended.

"At what point will I be called?" John asked.

"Actually, I don't plan to call you at all, Miss Hall," Birkett said.

"I'm afraid, neither do I," Melville added.

"I beg your pardon?" John said.

"Mr. Rubinstein has made it clear that you wish to take the stand but—" Birkett said.

"I insist on taking the stand. If you've read my statement, you'll understand—"

"I have read it," Birkett replied.

"Then you will know why it is important that I speak."

"There is much to commend in your statement," Melville said, "but I fear that you would be more likely to alienate Biron than endear yourself to him."

"Precisely," Birkett said. "He's a man of very traditional views, particularly when it comes to women."

"Meaning?" Though she knew exactly what he meant. Her cropped hair, her masculine attire, her well-known relationship with Una. In other words, her inversion.

Birkett didn't answer.

"I know you must be disappointed—" Harold began, his tone placatory.

"May I remind you all that I am the one on trial," John said.

"No, Miss Hall," Birkett said. "Your publishers are on trial. I have been retained to represent Jonathan Cape Ltd. and I intend to win this case for my client."

"I'm your client," John said, angrily. "I'm paying half your fees."

"I wasn't aware..." Birkett began. "But it doesn't change the argument. You will better serve your book by not appearing."

John looked at the eight men assembled round the boardroom table. Every single one of them married. They had never faced the ignominy of being labelled unnatural, depraved, perverted. It was not their lives and their work that were being dishonoured.

"Have any of you read Frank Harris's biography of Oscar Wilde?" John said. "Wilde was determined to make his trial memorable. My statement was written with the same intent. I resent being deprived of the opportunity."

"And did Mr. Wilde win?" Birkett looked at her across the table.

"That's not the point," John said.

"I would suggest, Miss Hall, that it is exactly the point."

John had no ready answer. She subsided into silence, twisting her ring round and round in agitation.

"I don't plan to call you either, Mr. Cape," Birkett said. "Whatever your motives in deciding to withdraw the book and lease the rights to Pegasus, the prosecution would undoubtedly make you look duplicitous."

It was no comfort to John that Cape was also seen as a liability. If anything, it made it worse.

"If I am not to take the stand, I want the court to be clear that my book is about *inversion*, not *perversion*. Inverts are a fact of nature and of God's creation. That's very important."

"Yes, of course," Melville said.

"And when we win tomorrow, the reading public will once again have the chance to discover that for themselves," Birkett said.

CHAPTER THIRTY-NINE

Battledress. Dark suit, Spanish trilby, leather motor-coat, freshly cropped hair. John intended to be at her masculine best, standing out, not fitting in. *I am exactly what you say I am.*

She'd been fourteen and in the first flush of love when Oscar Wilde had plummeted from the heights of literary success to incarceration in Reading Gaol. Agnes Nicholls, the object of John's adoration, was seventeen and already on her way to stardom. The first time John had heard the soprano rehearsing in her stepfather's garden studio, she'd been transfixed, the exquisite voice elevating her spirit from the baseness of her daily life to a world of thrilling beauty. She'd become the singer's acolyte, seeing to her every need.

At the time she hadn't connected her tender feelings for Agnes with the lurid scandal of indecency with young men that had ruined Wilde. How had he felt facing his trial, she wondered now? He must have known he was going to be found guilty after all that had emerged in the ill-judged libel case. The foolishness of love. Five years later he was dead and buried. Was she to be the new martyr? She had dared to speak for "the love that dare not speak its name" and she was being persecuted for it. Whatever Birkett said, John *was* on trial.

She dabbed Chypre on her wrists and throat. The woody citrus scent brought back Paris, the place where she'd first discovered it. She set the bottle back down on the dressing table where Una sat, slathering on makeup. John couldn't blame her. She was on trial every bit as much as John herself.

At last Una stood. "Do I look all right?" she said, unusually nervous.

The mauve dress was fussy, the makeup excessive. John kissed the top of Una's head. "You look lovely, darling."

On the way to court, they collected Harold from his house on Ladbroke Terrace. "How are you this morning?" he asked, settling alongside them in the rear of the Daimler.

"I'd be much happier if I were going to take the stand," John said.

"I know, John, but I think it's for the best. Biron might dismiss you as self-interested but how can he dismiss fifty of the most eminent minds in Britain?"

"As long as none of them sell me short." Bad enough the friends and colleagues who'd refused to help her. She didn't want to hear any of those who were willing to step forward give their support conditionally. *I didn't care for the book but I defend her right to write it.*

"What do you think our chances are?" Una said.

"I'm quietly confident. The weight of evidence is on our side."

The chauffeur set them down on Bow Street. The pale edifice of the Magistrates' Court loomed above John. She thought again of Wilde. His first night behind bars was in one of the police cells in the bowels of this building. Poor Oscar. Whatever happened, she mustn't let her opponents destroy her.

The lobby was alive with people crowding round the listings of the day's business. She was here with the aiders and abetters, the minor motor offenders, the unlawful aliens, the drunkards and the prostitutes. Her book was adrift on the tide of London's flotsam and jetsam.

"Court Two," Harold said. "This way."

The slender figure of Virginia Woolf walked ahead of them. John made a point of catching her up.

Mrs. Woolf greeted them, her voice low and melodious.

Harold responded with a short bow. "Mrs. Woolf."

"We adored *Orlando*," Una said. "I read it aloud to John while the wind whistled round us in Rye."

John had enjoyed the novel almost against her will, so different in style to her own work.

"Thank you," Mrs. Woolf said.

"I appreciate your support," John said. "You wouldn't believe the excuses that some so-called defenders of literature have given for not being here today."

"It's been a season of unprecedented family crises and last-minute trips abroad for rather more of our colleagues than one might have hoped."

"Quite so," John said.

"I've never given evidence before, but I'm happy to do what I can. The government must not be allowed to tether the imagination."

"If we lose today, I intend to keep on fighting the censors, no matter what the cost."

"We're close to five figures already and John's liable for half. We're selling the house, don't you know?" Una said.

"Oh, that's unspeakably unfair," Mrs. Woolf said. "I'll talk to Leonard about launching an appeal fund."

"Thank you, but that won't be necessary," John said, not wishing her financial affairs to be the gossip of Bloomsbury. Really, sometimes Una should learn when to keep her mouth closed.

There was an awkward silence until Harold intervened. "My niece tells me you had the students of Girton College checking behind curtains in search of Sir Chartres Biron."

Mrs. Woolf smiled. "Did she indeed?"

"And all about Shakespeare's sister. What an inspired idea."

"Shakespeare's sister?" John said.

"Judith Shakespeare, the genius sister who never got a chance," Harold said. "Mrs. Woolf invented her for a recent lecture on women and fiction."

"It may interest you to know that I'm actually descended from Shakespeare," John said. "Through his daughter Susannah who married Dr. John Hall in Stratford-upon-Avon." She wondered if she should add it wasn't a direct line, for fear of being thought to over claim.

Before she'd made up her mind, Mrs. Woolf turned to face her. "Oh yes, Miss Hall. I was indeed very aware of that fact." The look was long and meaningful. "And I did have the students checking behind curtains for Biron. These past months have shown, have they not, how powerful men seek to control women's words, especially when those words are about women's relationships with each other."

John felt a rush of gratitude. The Bloomsbury darling was a curious woman, shy as a mole half the time, and frighteningly clever. But Mrs. Woolf also had an unexpected store of courage. She was a welcome ally against the forces that were out to destroy John and her work.

Harold held open the door to Court Two. The courtroom was noisy, the public gallery packed.

"Good luck," Mrs. Woolf said. She made her way to a seat next to Forster in the well of the court. The biologist, Julian Huxley, was seated in the row in front of them. Birkett had won the debate with Melville. Huxley would be the first witness called for the defence.

John and Una followed Harold to the solicitors' table, nodding to witnesses on the way. These were the people who stood between John's book and the government's furnace. The sound of her own blood pumping filled John's ears. The eyes of the world were upon her. She would not let them see her fear. Head high, she took a seat next to Harold.

The prosecution team entered the courtroom and took their places in the seats reserved for counsel. Persecution team, John thought. Harold informed her that the bulbous-nosed man farthest from them was none other than Sir Archibald Bodkin, Director of Public Prosecutions.

"He was responsible for banning Joyce's *Ulysses*."

"Pray God we deny him the same pleasure today," John said.

"He won't be leading the prosecution. It'll be the man next to him. Eustace Fulton. A very able counsel."

Fulton looked as dour as Bodkin, with his downturned mouth and cemetery expression.

The defence barristers arrived soon after, Melville leading the way. He walked with a pronounced limp, the result of war injuries according to Harold. He was followed by the two juniors, Frampton and Metcalfe. Birkett was nowhere to be seen.

"I'm sure he'll be along shortly," Harold said.

He wasn't. When the door at the top of the court opened at half past ten to admit the Chief Magistrate, Birkett was still missing.

"All rise," the Clerk said.

Sir Chartres Biron made his way to the bench. His appearance was austere—snow-white hair, alabaster skin, thin lips, black suit, black tie, white shirt. At the sight of him, John's spirits fell. This cold, stark man would judge whether her book would live or die.

A young policeman called the names of Jonathan Cape and Leopold Hill. The two men were escorted to seats in front of John, facing the magistrate. The trial was starting but still no sign of Birkett. Where the devil was he?

Fulton, her grim-faced persecutor, got to his feet. "Sir, the Crown case is that *The Well of Loneliness* by Miss Radclyffe Hall is an obscene libel," he began. "It was voluntarily withdrawn by Jonathan Cape Ltd. in August of this year—"

"Should we ask for a delay?" John whispered to Harold.

"It wouldn't be granted. Metcalfe will step in." He put his finger to his lips, silencing her.

The first witness was Chief Inspector Prothero of Scotland Yard, a man with bristling eyebrows above narrow eyes. His evidence began with the seizures at Leopold Hill and Jonathan Cape Ltd. on the nineteenth of October.

Fulton turned to a marked page in his copy of *The Well of Loneliness*. "Chief Inspector, I wish to read you a quotation. Stephen is about to be parted from Mary. These are her thoughts:

> *'In this world there is only toleration for the so-called normal. And when you come to me for protection, I shall say, I cannot protect you, Mary, the world has deprived me of my right to protect; I am utterly helpless, I can only love you.*

"Does that passage convey a normal or a lesbian passion?"

John was startled to hear the word lesbian. Outside the world of the invert, it was rarer than rubies.

"It conveys a lesbian and physical passion," Prothero said.

Fulton shut the book decisively. "Thank you. I have no further questions."

It was time for the defence. Birkett was renowned for his skill in cross-examination. But their star barrister still hadn't arrived. Metcalfe, forty-five years old and not yet a King's Counsel, began.

"Prior to the book being seized, had you read *The Well of Loneliness*?"

"I had."

"You knew, did you not, that the *Sunday Express* had run a campaign against it?"

"I knew the *Sunday Express* had criticised it."

"Were you aware that the more important literary journals had reviewed the book favourably? *The Times Literary Supplement* described it as 'sincere, courageous, high-minded, and often beautiful.' Do you agree?"

"I do not," Prothero said. "It is an objectionable book."

"What do you find objectionable about it?"

"It deals with a repulsive subject—unnatural physical passion between women—which should be dealt with only by medical men and scientists."

"Medical and scientific experts will give evidence that *The Well of Loneliness* is not obscene. What say you to that?"

Before the Chief Inspector could answer the Magistrate interrupted. "The opinion of this witness is of no great importance." Biron's manner verged on downright rudeness. John exchanged a worried glance with Una.

Metcalfe concluded his questions. As Prothero stood down from the witness box, Norman Birkett finally arrived.

"I have no other witnesses," Fulton said.

No other witnesses? John's spirits rose again. Where was the prosecution's weight of evidence? All they had was the ill-informed opinion of a policeman.

Fulton addressed Biron. "As I have demonstrated, the theme of this book is unnatural physical and sexual relations between lesbian women. Since the theme is obscene, the book itself cannot help but be obscene."

The prosecutor was lying by omission. Compton Mackenzie's *Extraordinary Women* had the same theme. No one was trying to ban it. Mackenzie's spiteful little satire was far more explicit than anything John had written, yet it had escaped censure while her book had been hounded. But then Mackenzie was a married man and John was an invert. Mackenzie had mocked inversion, John had pleaded for understanding.

Fulton continued, "Sir, the test of obscenity is anything whose tendency is to deprave and corrupt those whose minds are open to such immoral influences, and into whose hands a publication of this sort might fall. I submit that this book meets that test. It is an obscene libel and should be destroyed."

Biron picked up a quill pen, dipped it in ink, and scratched out a few lines of notes as Fulton resumed his seat.

It was time for the defence. John rubbed her thumb against the Saint Anthony's medal in her pocket. *Oh, Saint Anthony, hear my prayer. Please, please, please save my book.*

When Biron finished writing, Birkett finally got to his feet. Even from behind there was something impressive about him standing tall and straight before the court, waiting for complete silence.

"Sir, it is a misuse of the word for the prosecution to call this book obscene. It is a misuse of the legislation to have initiated these proceedings. *The Well of Loneliness* is not the disgusting material of Shaftesbury Avenue. To act against a book of character is to strike a blow against both literature and the public good."

Una muttered "hear, hear" under her breath.

"There has been a grave misconception in this case. The book is not in any way connected with perversion, but with what has been tabulated by medical science as *inversion*."

Inversion not perversion. John was relieved that the point had been made. Her relief lasted only a moment.

"Stephen's relationships with women are not physical," Birkett went on. "They are purely of an intellectual character. Sentimental and romantic, yes, but not physical."

Not physical. John couldn't believe what she was hearing. Not physical? She'd taken care to avoid titillating sexual details, but it was surely impossible to read of Stephen and Mary's honeymoon love in Orotava and be under any illusion that their relationship was not physical. What else did ardent fulfilment imply, what else the turbulent river beyond which lay the placid harbour? She clenched her fists, nails digging into her palms. How could he be lying like this?

Biron sat forward. "Do you say that the book does not deal with unnatural offences at all?"

"I say not. This book is a sincere effort by a distinguished novelist to help those who bear a tragic affliction for which they are not responsible." He held *The Well of Loneliness* aloft. "This book does not contain an obscene word or a lascivious passage."

Biron interrupted, "There are certain passages which appear to my mind to contain lurid descriptions of unnatural vice. Are you able to explain them?"

John had only Birkett's back to look at, the black gown, the edge of ginger hair under his yellowing wig. His neck was flushed but his voice was calm as he sidestepped the question. "This book is a work of art."

"A book may be a work of art and yet be obscene. I must consider whether it has a tendency to corrupt."

"I have here in court distinguished people from every walk of life, experts in literature, science and medicine, who will testify that this book is not obscene."

Biron sipped from a glass of water. Carefully he set it back down. "I shall not admit that sort of evidence. The question of obscenity is for me alone to determine."

There was a stir in the Court, mutters from those seated behind John. If the expert witnesses were refused, the case was surely lost.

"Can he do that?" John whispered to Harold. He gave the briefest of nods.

"Sir, I must protest," Birkett said. "Expert witnesses are at the heart of our defence."

"You may call your first witness but I will decide if his evidence is admissible."

Birkett called Professor Julian Huxley. He did not come forward.

"Professor Huxley," Birkett said again. There was no response. John turned to look at the gallery. The seat in front of Forster and Woolf was empty. Huxley had deserted.

Birkett moved on to Mr. Desmond MacCarthy. This time the call was answered. MacCarthy, a literary critic for more than a decade, settled his bulk in the witness box.

"Having read *The Well of Loneliness*," Birkett said, "in your view is it obscene?"

Before MacCarthy could answer, Biron intervened. "No, I won't allow that. It is only an expression of opinion."

"Sir, the whole question here is whether, in the opinion of a reasonable man, the book tends to deprave," Birkett said.

"Opinion is not evidence," Biron replied.

"With all respect, if expert evidence is to be excluded, it would mean that through an individual magistrate, the law could impose censorship of the whole field of literature."

"I may be a very competent or a very incompetent magistrate, but the responsibility is mine and I am going to shoulder it," Biron said.

"It is not for the magistrate to act on his own personal view, but upon the views of reasonable people generally," Birkett countered, his neck now a hot red. "Authors of distinction are willing to testify that the book does not tend to deprave or corrupt anyone who reads it."

"Oh no. That could not be evidence under any circumstance," Biron said scornfully. "It is for me to consider whether the weak-minded would be incited to unnatural practices by this book. Such practices involve acts of the most horrible and disgusting obscenity. That is a fact which no one could deny."

I deny it, thought John. Most vehemently I deny it. I am not unnatural. I am not disgusting. I am as God made me.

"Well, I tender the evidence," Birkett said, his voice raised. "I have booksellers who will testify that *The Well of Loneliness* is not obscene. I have social workers who wish to testify that this book is not obscene. I have biologists, medical doctors and even a magistrate who will testify that this book is not obscene."

"And I reject it all."

The Waldorf Grill was only a few minutes away from Court. John walked with Una in silence, bitterness lodged in her throat. The wind was cold and they huddled together against it. Biron's contempt for the witnesses was sickening, Birkett's deliberate betrayal, devastating.

A waiter showed them to a table in the corner of the busy restaurant. They sat next to each other. John needed Una close. "I'm not sure how that could have gone any worse," John said.

"No," Una replied. "That was one of the most dispiriting mornings of my entire life. They really do despise us."

John buried her head in her hands. Even Una had lost hope. Her books were going to burn, and without a proper defence having been made to save them. She was selling their home for this nonsense of a trial.

Una's hand on her arm brought her back to the restaurant. "Darling, the others have arrived."

John sat up, folding her arms over her chest. Across the restaurant, a waiter was guiding Harold, Holroyd-Reece, Cape and Birkett to their table. At the sight of the latter fury flashed to the surface.

"How dare you undermine the purpose of my book?" John said to Birkett, as he took a seat at the table. "I am paying you to defend it with conviction, not to lie about its intention and meaning." She didn't want to cry but anger was pushing tears out of her eyes.

"Miss Hall," Birkett said, "I had a strategy—"

"You opened the defence of my book with a barefaced lie. It's no wonder you didn't want me on the stand."

She turned to Harold. "You promised me he would not sell inverts short. You promised."

Hot tears flowed. She wiped them away furiously.

The waiter arrived to take their orders.

"A few minutes," Cape said, waving him away.

"I was unaware that Mr. Birkett was going to run that line," Harold said, softly.

"Were you behind it?" John said to Cape.

"No, John. No," Cape said.

"I would have objected vociferously if you had laid out this strategy at yesterday's meeting, Mr. Birkett," Holroyd-Reece said.

"With respect, none of you are barristers," Birkett said. "I have been engaged to win this case. I considered that—"

"I don't care what you considered," John said, her voice flashing anger, sharp as a knife. "Lives are destroyed through the lack of proper understanding of inversion. Destroyed, I tell you. My book set out to change the minds of the thinking public. And you chose to lie about it."

"I did not dispute—"

John raised her voice over Birkett's. "The physical aspect is a natural part of the invert as it is a natural part of the heterosexual. How dare you deny it?" Her armpits were sweating beneath her jacket. She knew her face must be flushed.

"I see that you are overwrought, madam—" Birkett began, as if she were a hysterical woman.

"I have every right to my anger. You are selling me short."

"I am trying to win."

"With lies? I would rather lose the case on the truth than win it on a lie. I demand that you retract your denial of the physical aspect of inversion in *The Well of Loneliness*. And if you don't, I'll stand up in Court and tell Biron the truth."

Biron entered Court at precisely two o'clock. He settled himself as before with *The Well of Loneliness* in front of him, a glass of water to his left. Birkett got to his feet. John hoped he could feel her eyes upon him.

"Sir, your refusal to admit expert testimony has hampered the defence's ability to advance its case. May I begin by requesting that you state the legal basis for your ruling."

Birkett was supposed to start with the retraction. John wondered how long she should give him.

"I am not minded to do so."

"Most irregular," Birkett muttered, loud enough to carry. He fussed with his papers for a moment.

Biron looked at him disdainfully but did not speak.

"In the light of your decision, I do not think any useful purpose would be served by my calling Mr. Cape to give evidence," Birkett said.

The witnesses behind her muttered and murmured in response. Writers had been astounded by Cape's capitulation to the Home Secretary, his secret deal with Pegasus. They wanted an explanation.

Biron made a note on the pad in front of him. "Silence, please," he said, quelling the crowd.

John stared harder than ever at Birkett's back. *Retract.*

"Sir, with regard to this morning's evidence, I do not wish to have made any false impression on your mind," Birkett said. "I am not in a position further to contend that the book does not refer to physical relationships between women."

A flash of glee momentarily brightened Biron's eyes.

"My client is most anxious—as is the authoress—that it should not be thought by anybody that there is any desire to evade the true issue."

At least they had returned to a place of honesty.

"In conclusion, the contention for the defence is that this book could not possibly offend against the law. It deals with what is undoubtedly a fact of life, in a manner which the critics have praised. It singularly accords with good taste and high artistic and literary merit." Birkett fell silent. The pause extended. After a few moments he sat down, apparently having run out of anything else to say.

Slowly, James Melville got to his feet, his stance not quite erect. "Sir, your role today is to decide on the basis of the evidence whether *The Well of Loneliness* is a book that glorifies indecent practices, or whether it is a work of literature with a serious intention. The book accepts inversion as a fact of life, as a fact of nature, as a fact of God's own creation. I submit to you, Sir, that this book treats the problem that arises from that fact with great care and reverence."

His quiet voice was almost confessional, yet it was utterly captivating. He spoke to Biron directly, as if no one else was in the Court. "Your mind is quite open at this stage, I know."

Biron's mind had been as closed as a clam thus far. Perhaps Melville could shame him into fairness.

"I intend to deal in detail with the book, in order to make plain that it is not obscene."

Hope flickered in John's heart. When it came to detail, there was not a single word that could be viewed as obscene.

"I know that I address a Magistrate who will have taken the greatest care to acquaint himself with the contents of this book." Melville flicked to a marked page in his copy of *The Well of Loneliness*. "Page 222. After the heroine, Stephen, is betrayed by Angela, it says:

> *'[Stephen] did not know the meaning of herself. But she loved, and loving groped for the God who had fashioned her, even unto this bitter loving.*

"I would refer you to another passage of that type at page 244."

He waited while Biron skipped through to the right page. "Here Stephen's former governess tells her that 'we're all a part of Nature.'

"And on page 474, *'How long would God sit still and endure this insult offered to His creation?'*"

"That is referring to the two characters, Barbara and Jamie, and the fact that they were ostracised?" Biron said.

"Yes, Sir."

"You do not dispute that those two characters are living for the purpose of indulging in unnatural practices, and that the supposed insult is that they are not tolerated by normal people?"

"The point that is being made is that these two women are God's creatures."

Melville was a practising Catholic. He understood about God.

"Every person is God's creature, though he may be a criminal." Biron's brow puckered. John wondered whether he regarded female inverts as criminals in all but name.

"You may be aware of Mr. George Moore's view that real literature describes life and thoughts about life rather than sexual acts. Pornographic writing is the opposite." Melville paused to look at Biron. "I believe this definition may assist you in your deliberations."

Melville was scoring point after point. He was their star, not Birkett.

"As you will know, Sir, a relationship grows up between Stephen and Mary at Orotava."

"A physical relationship, you mean," Biron said.

"Yes. And how does it end? The character Martin, a friend of the heroine from her youth, comes to Paris and is obviously attracted to Mary. Being a deeply religious woman, Stephen decides not only to give up Mary, but to ensure that she develops a normal affection for Martin. If you will kindly turn to page 503, you will see how it is put:

> *'And now [Stephen] must pay very dearly indeed for that inherent respect for the normal which nothing had ever been able to destroy, not even the long years of persecution… Never before had she seen so clearly—'*

"And is this, Sir, obscene?

> *'—all that was lacking to Mary Llewellyn, all that would pass from her faltering grasp, perhaps never to return, with the passing of Martin—children, a home that the world would respect, ties of affection that the world would hold sacred, the blessed security and the peace of being released from the world's persecution.'"*

John felt almost tearful, hearing her words quoted and explained.

Melville closed *The Well of Loneliness* and set it down. He looked up at Biron. "Sir, you are a man of principle. This book is not written in a manner that is calculated to excite lustful thoughts. I implore you not to suppress a fine literary work by a distinguished writer. If you read this book in its true light, I believe you will find it impossible to ban it as an indecent publication."

CHAPTER FORTY

The hallway light is on. I shout my customary, "It's me, Maggie." No answer. I fling off my coat and go in search of Sibyl. The living room's dark. I switch on the light to make sure she isn't in there. She's not in the dining room or the kitchen either. I should get the lentil pie in the oven while I'm here, but I need to find Sibyl first. Surely she's home by now?

Up the stairs to her bedroom. I knock on the door.

"Sibyl?"

Still no reply.

"Sibyl?" My voice is loud enough to waken the dead.

"Up here," she calls, at last.

I climb the stairs to her studio. She's sitting at her desk, newspaper photos of Radclyffe Hall scattered around her. Her pencil's working furiously, like nothing exists in the world but her and the page in front of her. I shouldn't intrude but I have to know what happened today. I clear my throat which doesn't need clearing. It sounds fake to my ears. I'm about to launch into my question but Sibyl waves me in the direction of the comfy chair in the corner of the room. "I'll just be a minute."

I sit down, awkward as a donkey, still none the wiser. If I'd any sense I would've stopped for a copy of the *Evening Standard* on the way home, instead of waiting to ask Sibyl what happened at the trial. But I couldn't face finding out the verdict from dry words on a page. If *The Well* has been banned, I need to hear it from someone who feels the blow of being judged obscene. And if it's free, I need to celebrate with someone who knows how much it matters that our lives are not hidden away as too shameful to exist.

I chew at the side of my nail, waiting. At last Sibyl puts her pencil down and turns towards me. "Sorry. I wanted to get her down while she was still clear in my head."

She holds up the sketch. Dark Spanish hat, aquiline nose, sensitive mouth—Radclyffe Hall brought to life. I register the eyes, looking out from the page with an expression somewhere between pain and defiance. Her gaze is a wound to the heart.

"Did she lose?"

Sibyl shakes her head. "It was adjourned. Biron will give his verdict next Friday."

* * *

I'm supposed to be at work. I'd intended to go. I got up and dressed this morning, same as usual, but when it came to it I couldn't push my feet out the door. Today is judgment day. I have to hear for myself whether *The Well of Loneliness* is reprieved or condemned.

The hearing's not till two o'clock. I'm in my bedroom trying to read. I can barely get through two sentences before my mind whirls away in terror at the fact that I haven't gone to work. Since I first started at Jennymount Mill more than seven years ago, I've only missed two days of work—one for my Auntie Ruth's funeral, a second for my escape to London. I don't suppose taking today off makes me a skiver, but I feel like I'm half-criminal nonetheless. I do twenty press-ups to ease my conscience.

Sibyl knocks on my bedroom door just before eleven o'clock. "We should be getting off."

Now it comes to leaving the house, fear gets me in a head lock and starts squeezing. What if someone sees me? I might get the sack. How would I ever get such a good job again? And how would I stand not being with Seven all day?

"You don't need to come," Sibyl says.

"But then what was the point in staying off work?"

She lends me a hat with a veil to help disguise me. A storm's brewing, wind howling, rain lashing. I turn the collar of my winter coat up and step outside. I keep my head low as we battle our way towards the bus stop. The hat nearly lifts off in the wind but I manage to cram it back down in time. I keep my hand on it till we're on the bus. I glance furtively around me but there's no one on board I recognise. We take a seat on the upper deck, Sibyl on the window side to hide me from outside view. At least we're not going anywhere near Hackney Wick.

Rain beats against the bus. "You wouldn't put a fox out of a henhouse on a day like that." It's what Auntie Ruth used to say when the weather was bad.

"The Irish seem to have found ways of using the language that the English never thought of."

"I suppose so."

"Do you miss Ireland?"

I hesitate before answering. "What I miss most was already gone when I left. My granny, my Auntie Ruth. Only my father's living and if I ever speak to him again it'll be a day too soon."

"My parents haven't spoken to me for ten years."

"What happened?"

"In a word, Tilda. A lower-class, female ex-prisoner was not who they saw their youngest daughter settling down with."

"Going to prison for being a suffragette shouldn't count."

"That's not how my parents saw it. Especially given…"

I peer at her through the veil. "Especially given what?"

She doesn't answer immediately and I wonder if she's going to tell me or not. But then she says, "She burnt down a church."

I can't stop my gasp of surprise. I knew about mansions and train stations but a place of worship?

"I know, it's rather shocking," Sibyl says.

Even if you weren't a believer, surely part of you would be worried about being struck down by the hand of God. I imagine a big finger pointing down from the sky and firing off a bolt of lightning. I begin to laugh.

"No wonder Ida found it funny that I was training to be a firefighter. I suppose she was an arsonist too." I say it louder than I mean to. Sibyl puts her finger to her lips. I glance around the bus again but the few bedraggled passengers aren't looking in our direction.

"I don't think so," she says quietly. "Though Rachel was convicted of conspiracy to cause explosions—"

"She never was."

Sibyl nods. "Oh, yes. Though the evidence against her was mostly trumped up."

"But in Tilda's case she actually did it?"

"She actually did it."

"Why a church?"

"The Church of England rather sided with the government regarding the vote."

"I never knew that."

"Not all ministers, of course, but the men at the top."

The men at the top are the problem again. As the bus trundles on towards the centre of town, I ask Sibyl whether she thinks Radclyffe Hall has got a chance of winning. It's the question we've been pondering all week.

"Melville was very persuasive," she says.

He didn't get much of a mention in the newspaper coverage of the trial. I bought a stack of papers on Saturday, wanting to be sure I'd extracted every detail there was to be had. Most of them focused on the clash between Birkett and Biron over the witnesses. Only the good old *Daily Herald* paid attention to Melville.

"And Radclyffe Hall was pleased with what he said?" I know she was. Sibyl has told me so a dozen times. No harm in hearing it again.

"It looked that way. After Biron adjourned she shook Melville's hand and talked to him in the most animated manner."

"She must think he got it right."

"I thought he did. Now it's down to what Biron thinks."

We get off at Tottenham Court Road and hurry down to Bow Street Magistrates' Court. A dozen women are already queuing for admission to the public gallery, rain streaming off their jostling brollies. Rachel and Ida turn up soon after us and by the time the doors open for the afternoon session, there are a couple of hundred hopefuls waiting in the rain. It's a scramble for seats but I gallop forward and bagsy four in the second row. I'm sandwiched between Sibyl and Rachel. I'm living with an arsonist and sitting next to a convicted conspirator.

The Court is full to bursting with well-heeled women, ones that don't have to go out and work for a living. A few sport the monocles and pinkie rings which I've learned are secret lesbian codes. I'm going to get one myself in the future. Not a monocle, but a pinkie ring, and wear it with pride.

Here comes the woman herself, Radclyffe Hall. I keep a tight hold of myself for fear of blurting out the excitement I feel at the sight of her walking into court. I'd imagined her tall like Stephen Gordon but she can't be more than five foot two. It's impossible to tell the colour of her hair in photographs but now that she's only thirty feet away I see that it's a dark ash-blond. She's wearing the leather coat with the Astrakhan collar that the newspapers mentioned in reports of last week's trial. A sprig of white heather is tucked into the band of her Spanish hat for luck. I hope it works.

For the next hour or two, I will be breathing in the air that she's breathed out. She nods to Rachel and Ida and several others before sitting down and it's nearly like she looked at me. Her eyes are the grey-blue of the sea on an overcast day. A woman wearing enough makeup to paint the ceiling sits down next to her.

"Is that Una?" I whisper to Rachel.

"It is."

"The man is Harold Rubinstein, their solicitor," Ida says. "His wife was a suffragette. And his mother-in-law was tried here for stone throwing after Black Friday."

"Nearly every woman arrested in London appeared here," Rachel says, looking at me. "Hundreds and hundreds of them. It's part of suffragette history."

"Did you?"

She nods. "My pre-trial hearing was here. Archibald Bodkin was prosecuting. That's him at the prosecution table, the miserable-looking one. The gallery was packed with suffragettes. I was glad of the support." She looks around. "It'll help John today, having us all here."

A male voice calls out, "All rise."

I get to my feet. A funereal man, vampire-pale, takes his seat at the front of the Court. He places a copy of *The Well*, a notebook and a quill pen with a black feather in front of him. Who writes with a quill these days? Does he not know it's 1928?

We're allowed to sit. Biron waits for silence. "Firstly, I want to make one thing clear—there is no question here of censorship." Tight lips form the words. "The only question for me to decide is whether this book is an obscene libel and should be destroyed."

If it's destroyed, surely that is censorship. Isn't it?

"I was amazed when my learned friend Mr. Birkett suggested that this book did not relate to unnatural offences between women."

Unnatural. Offences.

He's talking about how I love.

"Mr. Melville insisted that this book would not induce women to indulge in these horrible practices, acts which between men would be a criminal offence."

Horrible. Practices.

I think of Seven, my fingers inside her, my thumb on her velvet, her breath quickening, and she looks into my eyes and I am there with her in the to and fro of finding the right pressure and the right pace, and the wave gathers and gathers and gathers and I dance her to that perfect moment where the wave breaks, carrying her to the farthest point of pleasure.

Is that a horrible practice?

"In arriving at a decision I must be guided by the test of an obscene book as laid down by Chief Justice Cockburn in 1868: whether the tendency of the matter charged as obscenity is to corrupt and deprave those whose minds are open to such immoral influences, and into whose hands a publication of this sort may fall."

It didn't so much fall into my hands as they reached out and grabbed it. It didn't deprave me. It saved me.

"The fact that this book has some literary merit can be no answer to these proceedings. The better an obscene book is written, the greater the public to whom it is likely to appeal. The more palatable the poison, the more insidious."

I wonder did James Douglas help write the judgment. It's clear which way it's going to fall.

Biron looks up for a moment. "I'm afraid I must speak rather plainly. The subject of this book is unnatural offences between women, involving acts which are undeniably horrible, disgusting and obscene."

I look around the courtroom at the women with the monocles, the women with the pinkie rings, the women with the cropped hair, the women with the long hair, the women with the frilly frocks, the women with the shirts and ties. Are they unnatural? Are they horrible, disgusting, obscene? Am I?

I try to close my ears against this withered man who would rob me of my delight in Seven, who would take me back to a half-life. His words are the poison, airborne poison seeping into my mind.

He tells us that the theme itself would be permissible so long as the author presented women fighting against this "horrible vice." It would be permissible if the author condemned them if they failed in such a fight. What was not permissible was to plead for toleration and recognition of people who should not be tolerated and not recognised by decent society.

And I wonder what decent society is. How can a society that includes men like Biron and Douglas and Jix but excludes women like Wilma and Sibyl and Seven be decent?

"According to the writer of this book, a number of women who were engaged in driving ambulances at the front were addicted to this vice."

Next to me Sibyl shakes her head, her face pale.

"I protest." Radclyffe Hall's voice is crisply English, sharp and clear. "I protest emphatically."

Biron doesn't look up. "I must ask people not to interrupt the Court."

"But I am the author of the book and what you say is shameful."

"If you cannot behave yourself, I shall have you ordered out of the Court."

"Shame. It is a shame." She shakes her head, still agitated.

A police sergeant approaches her and I wonder if she's going to be removed. He bends down and whispers something to her, then returns to his place. She stays where she is, silent now. She might be better off out of here than listening to this venom.

Biron continues mercilessly, accusing Stephen of debauching Mary, and on to Orotava where he says they were living in filthy sin. A sob is trapped in my throat as he slanders a story that has given me hope and strength.

At last he stops speaking. I think he's done and I can get away but it's only a pause for effect. "This book seeks to persuade decent people to tolerate unnatural practices between women which should be condemned," he says, condemning me as well as *The Well.* "Its publication is an offence against public decency. I have no hesitation whatever in saying that it is an obscene libel that would tend to corrupt those into whose hands it should fall." His tight lips widen in a grimace of a smile. "I order it to be destroyed."

It's *all rise* again for Biron's departure. Finally, it's over. The colour's drained from Sibyl's face. Her head droops forward, her eyes closed. Seeing her shaken, shakes me even more.

The crowd surges round Radclyffe Hall.

"We should go and offer our commiserations," Ida says.

I don't want to go into the busy huddle, the babble of noise, the flashing monocles semaphoring messages I can't decipher. And what words of consolation could I offer? What is there to say? She lost. We all lost.

CHAPTER FORTY-ONE

I push my way out of the court and onto Bow Street. Disgusting. My feet take me to the end of Russell Street. Corrupt. I walk along it as far as the Presbyterian Church. Unnatural. Obscene. I stand looking at the church as the old fears bubble and boil inside me.

You'll never be anything but wrong.

Biron's words run down tracks gouged deep in my soul. I'm sick to my stomach, sick at myself, my weakness. How easily Biron has brought me down. I should never have gone to the hearing. I don't have the strength for people like him.

What am I doing here? I think back to that Sunday after I'd kissed Janet, sitting in this church, shamed and appalled at what I'd done. And secretly thrilled and delighted. Have I learned nothing over these last few months?

A few minutes' walk takes me to Waterloo Bridge. The river is brown and sullen today. I write words on a page in my mind—disgusting, unnatural, corrupt, obscene. Across them I scrawl, *You'll never be anything but wrong.* I float the page off down the Thames.

People hurry past me, wanting out of the rain. I turn and open my arms to it. Let it wash away the last of the shame, the poison, the pain.

Is this how it feels to be born again?

* * *

Tomorrow I will lie to Johnston and to Clarke about how I spent today, a tale of gastric calamity that had me in its grip for twenty-four hours. I cannot lie to Seven. I stand in her doorway waiting for her to come home.

I must look a state with my sodden coat and the ridiculous veiled hat that I daren't ditch till I'm safely inside. There's no shelter to be had on this grim street. The rain has stopped but the wind is cold. I sing to take my mind off it, the nonwords of Adelaide Hall, a burst of Bessie Smith, an unexpected chorus of "All Things Bright and Beautiful" dredged up from Sunday School, "Black Velvet Band" from the mill.

I'm starting to shiver. I cup my hands and blow hard, warming the right-hand fingers, swap hands, blow and warm the left-hand fingers, swap and blow, swap and blow. I need another song.

It had to be you, It had to be you.

The perfect song, the one that was playing the first time Seven kissed me.

*I wandered around and finally found
Somebody who—*

When I see her turn into the street, I want to run towards her. Wanting becomes doing. I run along the wet cobbles, hoping she'll run to me. She doesn't. Maybe she doesn't recognise me in the veil. I throw it back. She quickens her pace, striding towards me on her fine long legs.

"What's happened? Are you all right?" Her brow furrows with concern. Her hand reaches for mine. "You're freezing."

"I'm fine. A bit cold."

She unlocks the door. "Come in out of the wind."

The hallway's only a fraction warmer. If anything, I feel more shivery. A woman in a shawl with a babe in arms and a toddler hanging round her feet opens the door to our left. She squeezes past us and out the front door.

"Let's get you upstairs," Seven says.

I follow her up the ramshackle staircase to her cold damp room. She lights the fire already laid in the grate. "Come and get warmed."

I take a seat on one of the stools in front of the fire, though it's all smoke and hissing coal for now. Seven perches on the other stool. She takes my hands between hers, rubbing them to warm them.

"What's wrong? Why weren't you at work?"

"I went to the hearing. *The Well of—*"

"You didn't come to work so you could go to hear that book be banned?" Her eyebrows knit together in anger. She drops my hands. "Do you know how much more dangerous it is when there's only three of us?"

She's every right to be angry.

"I'm sorry." As if that's going to be enough.

"You could have told me you were going instead of leaving me worrying about you all day."

"I didn't know myself till this morning. Until the moment it came to leaving the house, I was planning to go to work."

"So you just made a spur-of-the-moment decision to put your colleagues in danger?" Her tone is harsh. But I'm the one in the wrong so I don't complain.

"I really am sorry. I just had to be in that court. I had to be."

"But you knew it was going to get banned. I've been telling you so for weeks."

"I needed to hear the judgment firsthand, whatever way it fell, not filtered through someone else's eyes. But listening to Biron, I wished I hadn't gone." The sadness that I thought I'd left behind at Waterloo Bridge wells up in me. I'll never get to have my own copy of *The Well of Loneliness*. The story that's meant so much to me has been taken out of the world. "He said terrible things about women like us. He'd ban us if he could."

Seven shrugs. "They've already banned the men. It hasn't stopped them falling in love with each other. It wouldn't stop me." Her face is lit by the dancing flames. She has never looked more beautiful.

"I love you." The words come out easily.

A hint of a smile plays on her handsome face. "When I get round to forgiving you for skiving, maybe I'll tell you I love you too."

I slide my hand towards hers. She takes it.

"Your hands are still cold. I'll make you a cup of tea."

She hangs the kettle on a chimney crane over the fire, the same way my granny used to make tea. I smile, remembering the evenings by her fire in Portmuck, listening to her tales.

"My Granny Palmer had the best stories. Princess Pearl was my favourite. She was a mermaid who went on wild adventures. My granny invented her for me. Pearl. It's what my name means. Margaret means pearl. She used to say I was a mermaid in the body of a girl."

"A mermaid in the body of a girl. I like that. Mermaids are one of my favourite things in the world."

"My granny believed that stories were as important as food and drink."

Seven nods. "I needed the stories I made up about who my parents were to get me through my childhood. Look, I'm not saying I agree with you skipping work, but I suppose I do understand it." Her hand strokes my face. "There'll be other stories, you know. The men in charge can ban books, but they can't stop women making up their own stories."

CHAPTER FORTY-TWO

On Wednesday morning, John lay in bed, eyes closed. If she didn't look at the day, maybe it would go away. A new day. What a lie those words were. There was nothing new about her days, only the endless tedium of meetings and letters and letters and meetings. And now packing up the house to add to her burdens. And searching for a new flat after the one they'd made an offer on fell through. The very thought exhausted her.

She'd gone through the days following the judgment like an actor playing the part of Radclyffe Hall. A not very good actor, stiff and graceless. Even the promise of an appeal couldn't elevate her.

"It won't be down to one narrow-minded man," Harold had explained on Monday. "The appeal will be heard by a bench of magistrates."

It was reason for hope but she couldn't feel it.

She'd spent Tuesday in bed at Una's suggestion. "You're tired, darling. A rest will do you good."

It hadn't. If anything it had made it worse. Now she couldn't hide from the weariness she felt in every cell, the leaden dreariness that smothered her soul. She should get up. There was so much to do. Holland Street had been snapped up by the first people to view it. The Laskeys wanted to be in by Christmas. Una had talked them round to the eleventh of January. Less than eight weeks to pack up a whole house, a whole life. A literary life at that. So many papers to sort, books to wrap.

And then there was the furniture. It didn't take a mathematician to work out that the furniture of a five-storey house wasn't going to fit into a two-bedroom flat, a flat they hadn't even found yet. And the paintings, the vases, the figurines and sculptures, where were they to go? Not to mention the clothes.

Was the only feeling she was permitted anxiety?

Next to her Una eased her careful way out of bed, not wanting to wake John. John knew she should say something. *It's all right, I'm awake.* But then Una would fuss and cluck. *How are you today, darling? Feeling any better?* John didn't have the strength for it. She kept her eyes resolutely closed.

She must have drifted off. The next time John awoke, Una was sitting at the table in the corner of the room, sipping a cup of tea and scribbling notes on a pad of paper.

"What time is it?"

"Nine thirty."

John sat up in bed. "You should have woken me."

"I was glad to see you resting. How are you feeling today? Any better?"

John answered with a cryptic mumble.

"Do you want a cup of tea? Breakfast?"

"Just tea for now." John put on her dressing gown and went over to the table. A couple of packages were waiting on her chair. She moved them onto the table and sat down. "What are these?"

"Books, by the feel of them. I rescued them from the deluge of post."

Carefully John unwrapped the first one. *Thy Dark Freight* by Vere Hutchinson, emblazoned above a striking image of a dark-haired woman on a blue-and-yellow background.

"I didn't know Vere had a new book out," Una said, looking up from her list-making.

"Neither did I."

Two books in six months. Even the most lost of causes could see an unexpected upturn. If only John could remember that on her bleaker days. She offered a brief prayer, thanking God for the improvement in her friend's fortunes.

A short letter accompanied the book.

Dearest Johnnie,
Please find enclosed a copy of my latest novel. Hasn't Budge done a brilliant job with the cover?
We were outraged at Biron's handling of The Well of Loneliness *hearing. What a nasty little man he is. I can only imagine how awful it was for you to have to listen to him. We'll be rooting for you with the appeal. Let justice be done!*
Love to you and Una,
Vere

John slipped the letter inside *Thy Dark Freight* and set the book down on the table. If it was half as good as Vere's short story collection she was in for a treat.

The second book was slim, its cover plain apart from the words *The Sink of Solitude*, printed in scarlet across the front. There was no accompanying note. She opened it up. The dedication read: *To Mr. Compton Mackenzie's Extraordinary Women.* What did that mean? Warily she turned the page over. The Preface introduced an anonymous lampoon and drawings by a Beresford Egan inspired by "the fuss over Miss Radclyffe Hall's novel, *The Well of Loneliness.*"

Fuss. A dismissive word for the persecution of these past months, the death sentence hanging over her novel. John turned the page.

The Drawings

And turned again.

St. Stephen

The words stood alone on the left-hand page. Her hand went to her mouth as her eyes took in the image on the right—John nailed to a crucifix, a naked woman cavorting across her midriff while Jix looked on askance.

"No," she moaned. "No." It was blasphemy. She pulled her dressing gown closer, wanting protection. She'd been raised on meanness and spite but the cruelty of people still sometimes shocked her. Who was this Beresford Egan with his vicious, depraved drawings?

"What is it?" Una picked up the book, still open at the image of St. Stephen. "Oh no. My poor darling." She stalked over to the wastepaper bin and threw the book inside. "Vile trash."

Out of sight was not enough. John could feel the evil coming from the book, poisoning the air around her. "Get rid of it. Please, get rid of it."

Luncheon at the Ritz was usually restorative. When she'd arranged to meet Audrey there John had hoped a bit of glamour might lift her spirits. Beresford Egan had put paid to that. To have been used to offend God—what could be worse? Had she brought this on herself by naming Stephen after the first martyr?

These thoughts distracted her from perusing the menu. When the waiter came, Audrey, decisive as always, opted for partridge with piquante sauce. Lacking the energy to choose for herself, John ordered the same.

"I have good news from Arrowsmith. They intend to reprint *The Forge* and *A Saturday Life* in time for Christmas. And Jonathan Cape wants the American rights for *The Unlit Lamp* and *Adam's Breed*."

A weak "Excellent," was all John could muster. She should shake herself out of this fug. The prospect of extra income was good news. Birkett's bill had been even higher than John had anticipated. It was a shame that lawyers weren't paid like writers—an initial advance with the rest based on results. It would have saved her thousands. At least no more money would be wasted on their "star barrister." His services had been dispensed with for the appeal.

She buttered a bread roll. If her mouth was full she wouldn't have to talk. She tried to focus on what Audrey was saying, but her mind kept drifting back to the scarlet letters on the plain cover, the disgusting drawing inside. It took several moments for her to notice the lapse in conversation. She looked up to meet Audrey's concerned gaze.

"Are you all right?"

"Yes, of course."

"Are you sure?"

John nodded. "You were saying?"

"Holroyd-Reece says Paris is in a frenzy for *The Well of Loneliness*. As fast as he can print it, it's going out of stock. Apparently lots of English visitors are smuggling copies home."

John chewed slowly.

"You'll be one of the best-selling novelists of the year. And once you win the appeal—"

"If I win."

"We've an excellent chance of overturning Biron's ruling."

It was what Harold said. And Melville and Cape. Even Una. Now Audrey.

"I know the judgment was bloody, but I'm thrilled that new audiences will get to discover your back catalogue. Everyone wants to be reading Radclyffe Hall."

John blinked, trying to dislodge the image of the crucifix, the naked cavorting woman. It was too dreadful to discuss, even with Audrey. She wondered if she could tell a priest. Perhaps she should go to confession on the way home.

A savage pain shot through the left side of her face. She dropped her fork as her hand went to her cheek. Fingertips sharp as hot knives. Instead of comfort, their touch intensified the agony.

"What's the matter?" Audrey said.

A minute passed before John could answer. "Neuralgia," she whispered. She'd had it once before and had hoped to never have it again. "I have to go."

Shards of pain stabbed her face as she journeyed home. She staggered from the taxi to the front door. Una helped her back to bed, dosed her with painkillers and sat with her till the attack eased. John drifted into a restless sleep.

* * *

The neuralgia receded overnight. She was well enough to attend Bow Street Police Court to act as surety for the appeal. The Woolfs were waiting in the lobby with Harold when she arrived.

"Miss Hall." Leonard Woolf's nod was curt.

Although John appreciated him taking a public stand in support of her book, she'd never taken to him. Too tall and thin to be trusted. Mrs. Woolf's smile, however, was warm.

"Thank you for coming," John said.

"Not at all," she replied. "I'm very sorry about the judgment. And your house."

John ducked her head, not trusting her voice.

"We've got a date," Harold said. "Friday the fourteenth of December at the London Sessions Court."

"Let us hope that justice is served then," Mrs. Woolf said.

The formalities were over in ten minutes. After the Woolfs had departed, Harold updated John on the latest developments.

"I've written to the Director of Public Prosecutions asking him to release copies of *The Well of Loneliness* to the magistrates in plenty of time. And we've got another seven witnesses."

"I didn't know you were recruiting new witnesses."

"Not actively. After Biron's behaviour, some of the on-the-fencers have come down on our side."

"And will they be allowed to speak this time?"

"The decision to bar expert witnesses had no legal underpinning. I doubt it will happen again."

"Have we a chance?" John said it in spite of herself. That was the thing about a little bit of hope. It wormed its way in against your best intentions.

He squeezed her hands. "Yes, John, a good chance. If I didn't think you could win, I'd advise you not to appeal."

* * *

The following day John and Una made an offer on a bright, airy flat that had just come on the market. "I'm glad the other one fell through," John said that evening as they talked about what needed to be done before they moved out of Holland Street.

"We need to plan where the furniture's going to go. What are we going to keep, what are we going to store, what are we going to sell."

"Sell?" John was taken aback. Storage yes, but she'd never said anything about selling.

"There are pieces that you yourself no longer like."

"There are not."

"Are too. You've told me at least three times that the Jacobean hutch is the wrong shape and size."

"Yes, but it looks so interesting."

"And we both know that the Henry the Eighth box stool is the most uncomfortable seat anyone ever devised."

"It's Henry the Eighth. Think of the history."

"Think of the numbed posterior. For the flat to be a haven, we need to pare back. You know it yourself. Isn't this the exact argument that Hilary and Susan have in *The Forge?*"

John smiled. "Well, yes, I suppose it is."

"And think of the fun you'll have finding new pieces when we're properly settled again."

* * *

Holland Street's new owners came to pick over their furnishings on Saturday morning. Una subtly directed them towards the pieces of furniture that she and John had agreed to get rid of. By the end of the visit two redundant refectory tables, the bed and wardrobe in the spare room, half the carpets, all the curtains, a tallboy, two sofas, an armchair and the Jacobean hutch had been acquired by the Laskeys.

"You're quite brilliant," John said after the new owners had departed.

Una smiled in response. "I have my moments."

The suggestion of a trip to Rye had been another of Una's moments, a week's rest before setting their shoulders to the task of packing. They arrived in Rye to a grey afternoon, threatening rain. John didn't care. She breathed in the fresh air, listened to the cries of the gulls. How had she stood the years in London without a bolthole?

The cottage on Hucksteps Row was more than a bolthole now, of course. It was home. They would have the Kensington flat when they needed to be in London. The flat wasn't perfect—still no study for John—but good enough for now. She was glad they'd found it before coming away. One less thing to worry about. She wasn't here to worry. She was here to relax.

They'd planned for a week of early nights and restful days, nothing more taxing than a walk on the marsh, a trip to the beach, afternoon tea at the Mermaid Inn. The first few days unfolded as they'd hoped. John slept long and woke a little more refreshed each morning. In the afternoons she lounged on the sofa while Una read to her aloud.

On Tuesday after breakfast, they were contemplating a walk to Camber Castle when their peace was ruptured. A telegram from Harold. *Urgent developments. Please contact me.* Within a few hours they were back in London.

Harold's secretary showed John into the boardroom. Harold, James Melville, Jonathan Cape and Leopold Hill were waiting. John took a seat.

"I'm sorry to have had to drag you back like this," Harold said.

Part of John hadn't wanted to return, hadn't wanted to be ripped from her sanctuary. But the book was still her baby. It wasn't dead yet. If there were decisions to be made, she wanted to be the one making them. She wasn't leaving it to Cape.

"What's happened?" John asked.

"This morning, I received a letter from Archibald Bodkin, the Director of Public Prosecutions. He's decided not to release copies of *The Well of Loneliness* to the magistrates hearing the appeal."

"Not to?" John wondered if she'd misheard.

"Not to," Harold repeated.

"But how are they supposed to come to a decision without reading my book?"

"How indeed?"

"It doesn't make any sense. How could that be considered fair?" John said.

"I don't think Bodkin's got much interest in being fair, certainly not in this case."

"This is outrageous," Cape said.

"You haven't heard the half of it yet." Harold's voice was clipped, his anger unmistakeable. "In making his decision he consulted with Sir Robert Wallace. Sir Robert concurs."

"Who's Sir Robert Wallace?" Cape asked.

"The man who will chair the appeal. The man to whom the bench will look in making its decision. It rather begs the question of whether Sir Robert has already made up his mind. Or had it made up for him."

"But this is…It's immoral…unethic…outrageous," Cape blustered.

"Why don't we supply the magistrates ourselves?" John said. "Surely we have enough copies between us."

"As it stands, your book is banned," Melville said. "It would be unlawful to proceed as you suggest for anyone other than Bodkin."

Panic twisted in John's guts. "This isn't fair." She was on her feet now, staring at Harold, then Melville.

"No," Melville said. "And I'm afraid the release of books isn't the only problem. The prosecution will be conducted not by Eustace Fulton—"

"But by Bodkin himself." John slumped back into her seat.

"I'm afraid it's worse. It will be the attorney general, Sir Thomas Inskip."

"Why is that worse?" Cape said.

"Firstly, the attorney general is far and away the most expensive lawyer in England. If we lose, the costs will be even higher. Secondly, the attorney general is afforded a privilege no other prosecutor in the country has. He gets not only the first word, but the last word. It stacks the odds entirely against the defence."

There was no point carping about fairness again. It wasn't one hand tied behind the back, it was both, and a leg iron to boot. "A good chance," Harold had said. Only a few days ago. A good chance. John shouldn't have asked that question. She shouldn't have listened to the answer. He'd said the same before the trial. And look how that had turned out.

"We must lodge a complaint," Cape said.

"To whom?" Harold said. "Wallace reports to Bodkin, Bodkin reports to Inskip. And Inskip's the most senior lawyer in England."

Cape looked as defeated as John felt.

Hill had been quiet until now. "What are our options?"

Harold sighed. "We go ahead with the appeal, in spite of the difficulties, or we—"

"We're not withdrawing, if that's what you were about to suggest," John said.

"What's the point in continuing if there's no chance of winning?" Cape said. "It's good money after bad."

"Not quite no chance," Melville said. "No verdict's a certainty till it's made. The bench could rebel, refuse to be complicit in enacting injustice."

"That hardly seems likely," Cape replied.

"It doesn't matter whether or not it's likely," John said. "We have to see it through. For the sake of everyone looking to us, we must defend the artist from the tyranny of the censors, and we must defend the invert from the slur of perversion."

* * *

A crowd of cheering supporters greeted John and Una's arrival at London Sessions Court for the appeal. John smiled and waved as people called her name. Their allegiance was an invisible layer of protection. She carried it with her into the packed courtroom.

She was under no illusion about her chances of justice. The government's top lawyer had not come to Newington Causeway to see John's book reprieved. The men of power were out to get her. Melville was an excellent lawyer. He would do his best. But when the game was rigged, his best would never be good enough to win.

The court was crackling with anticipation. Marie Stopes and Stella Churchill, campaigners for sexual reform, sat together near the front. Vita Sackville-West, Virginia Woolf's lover and inspiration for *Orlando*, lounged with aristocratic languor in the middle of the court. John felt an almost childish sense of disappointment that Mrs. Woolf herself was nowhere to be seen. But Hugh Walpole was there, and Ida Wylie and Rachel Barrett, and Arnold Bennett and Norman Haire.

People of reputation had turned out in force, even though none were to appear as witnesses. Melville had cancelled their star-studded list in return for the prosecution cancelling their own frantically recruited "experts." Bad enough the costs of the defence witnesses without being shackled with the expenses of those appearing for the prosecution. Most of them had been dull public servants, or medical men for hire from Harley Street. Rudyard Kipling had been the only literary name of note willing to speak against her. A traitor to literature, as far as John was concerned.

"All rise."

Silence fell over the court as the magistrates entered. Ten men, two women, led by the bespectacled Sir Robert Wallace. John had a clear view of the prosecution bench to her right, her opponents standing until the magistrates had settled into their places. Bodkin was here again today. So too Eustace Fulton. But when proceedings started, Inskip led the attack.

"*The Well of Loneliness* is the most demoralising, corrosive, and corruptive book ever written."

John wondered was there a secret competition for the most gratuitously offensive hyperbolic insult to her book.

Inskip had unusually large hands that he flung around as he spoke. "It is without doubt obscene. Being so, it is your duty to uphold the ban imposed by Sir Chartres Biron..."

John had heard it all before from Douglas and Jix and Fulton and Biron. She tuned Inskip out. Eleven days till Christmas. She'd already found an exquisitely bound edition of *Clark's Guide and History Of Rye* for Una, but she wanted something else. Something special. A new ring perhaps. Or a gold watch. Maybe they could fit in a trip to Bond Street before they went back to Rye. There was the last of the packing to finish first. The biggest job left was the books. She'd finished about half of them but the rest needed to be done, ready for the removers to place in the packing cases.

John insisted on wrapping the books herself—tissue paper for the most valuable, newspaper for the rest. She didn't want some dirty-fingered removal man causing damage. *Books are precious, Tuggie. Make sure to look after them.* That's what Granny Diehl used to say. She'd loved books, too.

Next week, John would be carefully wrapping books, while some government lackey burned *The Well of Loneliness*. Where would they do it? Was there an official state furnace? She mustn't think about it. Not here in court, among her enemies. She didn't want to give them the satisfaction of seeing how much pain they were causing her.

Yes, a gold watch, a stylish gold watch. Each time Una checked the time she'd be reminded that John loved her. Should she choose it herself or invite Una to do the choosing?

A pause in Inskip's oration drew her attention back to court. With elaborate care he removed two copies of *The Well of Loneliness* from a briefcase. Holding them at arm's length, as if his life would be endangered if they came any closer, he carried them over to the magistrates. "I've marked the offending passages."

When it was finally his turn, Melville revisited the same arguments he'd made to Biron five weeks earlier. A true work of literature. Positively received by renowned critics. Explores a human problem. Nothing offensive or pornographic. "The book asks for no approbation of unnatural practices—"

Even her own barrister was using the term. It's not unnatural, not for Stephen, not for me, not for women like me.

"—but for understanding of the invert and Christian charity for those whose misfortune it is to be differently constituted from their fellows."

Inskip began his closing statement in the same tone of priggish hysteria that he'd opened with. Beyond him, members of the press eagerly recorded his words. John would have her chance to speak to them after this nonsense of an appeal was over. Silently, she rehearsed her statement.

I do not consider that either myself as a serious-minded writer, or my book as a very serious work of fiction, have received justice at the hands of the law. I would fight on, but I am assured by counsel that there is no further appeal possible.

How naïve she'd been. She remembered the morning she'd started writing *The Well of Loneliness*. Paris, late summer. The desk by the window of their hotel room, the thrill as the first words made the page. The birth pangs of social change were always painful. She'd been prepared for controversy, condemnation even. But banned as obscene? It had never crossed her mind. How could it be that her book had been made a crime, when the crime should be burning books?

At twenty-five past two, the magistrates retired to consider their verdict. Less than ten minutes later they were back.

"The view to which I am giving expression now, I say at once, is the unanimous view of the court." A trace of his Irish roots remained in the voice of Sir Robert Wallace. The abashed faces of several of the magistrates gave a lie to his words.

Wallace was known as The Merciful Judge but it was soon clear that his compassion would not extend to John and her book. It was a remarkably long speech to have been agreed in such a short adjournment. But heaven forfend any suggestion that the case had been prejudged and English justice was anything but fair.

John kept her face neutral but she could feel her jaw tightening. How she hated these men. They made her sick, literally. She'd had another attack of neuralgia after Bodkin's letter had torpedoed any hope of winning the appeal, a night of vomiting the following week. Only Rye gave her respite. Without it, she might have broken altogether.

"The view of this Court is that this is a disgusting book when properly read. It is an obscene book, prejudicial to the morals of the community. In our view, the order made by Sir Chartres Biron was a perfectly correct one and the appeal must be dismissed with costs."

It was at an end, the death sentence confirmed. Una gripped her hand as they left the court. John's supporters crowded in around her, filling the air with *I'm sorry* and *It's a disgrace*. Many had brought *The Well of Loneliness* with them. She stood outside the court, signing copies of her banned book and listening to women telling her how much it meant to them.

"Good luck with it in America," someone said. The Covici-Friede edition would be published tomorrow. She prayed it would fare better in the land of the free.

CHAPTER FORTY-THREE

A fire was blazing in the dining room hearth when John came down to breakfast. They'd arrived at Journey's End the previous evening. It was a relief to be back in Rye. Her back ached. Another stye had erupted. And at random moments, her mind would ambush her with images of her books on fire, pages blackening, words destroyed. Would it ever be published in England again?

Andrea sat at the dining table, a book open in front of her. She'd arrived back from school a few days earlier for the Christmas holidays, but John had managed to avoid spending time alone with her until now.

"Ah, you're up already," John said, falsely jovial. "Did you sleep well?"

"Yes, thank you."

"Good. Good. Have you had breakfast yet?"

"Mabel made me porridge, thank you."

On cue, Mabel emerged from the kitchen, her sleeves rolled up to the elbow, exposing powerful forearms. "Miss Hall, I thought I could hear voices. What can I get you? There's porridge in the pot or I could cook you up sausage, bacon, and eggs, if you'd rather, or a kipper."

"Porridge would be fine, thank you, Mabel. And a pot of tea."

John sat down opposite Andrea. "How's school? Your mother tells me you had an excellent report this term."

Andrea nodded. She had Una's oval face but her eyes were blue like her father's.

"And still planning on Oxford next year?"

"Yes. If I get in."

"I'm sure you're working hard for the entrance exam."

"I've a few books home with me."

"Good. Good."

John couldn't think of anything else to ask. Luckily her porridge arrived, relieving her of the burden of conversation. Una joined them downstairs soon after, full of easy chat about how they might spend the forthcoming days. John had invited Audrey and Patience for Christmas, a thank-you for their support. Audrey was due to arrive that evening. Patience was coming tomorrow, and bringing her "special friend," Morny, with her. It would be a full house.

After breakfast, they spent an unexpectedly pleasant morning shopping for supplies—a turbot for dinner, a bounty of vegetables, dried fruit, nuts and cheeses. They ordered a goose and a cooked ham to be delivered, found presents for Mabel and their guests. For a small town, Rye was blessed with an array of shops. Finally they chose a tree and hauled it back to Hucksteps Row.

While Una and John manoeuvred the tree into place in the corner of the sitting room, Andrea fetched the box of decorations that they'd brought from Holland Street. Most of them dated back to 1917, the first Christmas the three of them had spent together. In the years at Holland Street and Chip Chase before it, they'd always decorated the tree together and so it was today. Andrea took out the snow globe which John had bought for her more than a decade earlier. She shook it up then watched as the snow settled, as captivated as the young child she'd been when it had first been hers. Carefully she wound up the key on the back, not too tight, as John had taught her.

"Silent night, holy night," Andrea sang along to the music, her voice sweet and clear. She shook the globe one more time before placing it on the windowsill near the front door.

"How about 'O Come, All Ye Faithful'?" Una said, when Andrea returned to the sitting room.

Andrea began the old favourite with a pretence of trumpets, as if they were in a great cathedral. Soon Una joined in with her off-key soprano, and even John began to hum as she found the perfect places for the little drummer boy and the white reindeer and the blue glass angel.

"I love decorating the tree," Andrea said when they'd finished. She hugged her mother and even gave John a brief squeeze. "Happy Christmas."

John felt a surge of love for the girl and wished she wasn't always so hard on her. She vowed to herself to do better.

* * *

"I thought I'd meet Audrey off the train," John said. "Do either of you want to come?"

Una and Andrea were installed on the sitting room sofa, opposite the fire, reading their books and spoiling their appetites with sugared almonds and peppermint creams. They both passed on the opportunity.

John put on her overcoat and hat against the chill. Darkness had fallen. A sharp half-moon shone brightly. Her breath steamed the cold air as she made her way past the shops and houses along West Street and Market Road and down towards the station. As she stood on the platform waiting, she lit a cigarette.

The train chugged in a couple of minutes late and Audrey emerged, carrying a small case. John stepped forward and took it from her. "Thanks for coming down."

"I'm only sorry I can't stay for Christmas Day but I must go to Mother. She's expecting me on Christmas Eve."

"We'll make the most of the next few days. How was the journey?"

"Pleasant. I finished writing the last of my cards. Do we pass a post box?"

"Several," John said.

They stopped at the one closest to the station. Audrey opened her bag and removed a host of envelopes. She posted them into the box in batches.

"Don't you check they've all got stamps?" John said.

"No. Do you?"

John didn't answer for fear of seeming neurotic. She was neurotic but there was no need for everyone to know it.

"How are you holding up?" Audrey said, as they resumed the climb to the Citadel.

"Better now I'm here. I can't bear London at the moment. I'd go abroad if I could."

"Why don't you? Take a long holiday. It would do you the world of good. Not to mention making it a lot easier to handle the translations. It's such a nuisance that we can't get proofs sent into this country."

"I can't leave now. Everyone would call me a coward who'd turned tail and run."

"Do you care?"

"Yes, I do. Inverts are looking to me for a lead. I can't let them down. There must be a way round the proofs problem. I want *The Well of Loneliness* out across Europe by spring, now that we've got the American edition out of the way. Would you believe I got a Christmas card from Blanche Knopf? I didn't send her one, I can assure you."

Audrey didn't respond for a moment. "I got a call from the American publishers today," she said, finally. "It looks like we might be heading for a legal challenge there too."

"Already? It's not even been out a week."

"The New York Society for the Suppression of Vice has started a campaign against it. It's not reached the court stage yet, but Donald Friede expects the worst."

* * *

John sat in the study gazing out the window across the marsh. She had taken herself in here after an early breakfast, supposedly to deal with the backlog of correspondence that had come with her from London. She'd managed to read one letter in the previous half an hour, a request for a private meeting from a woman who vowed they had so much in common it would be almost a sin if their paths failed to cross. John's involvement with Una was hardly a secret, but that didn't stop other women pursuing her. She wished they wouldn't.

From the sitting room came a shriek followed by peals of laughter. John was beginning to regret inviting Patience and Morny, who'd arrived the previous day. Patience was always so sensible at work but Morny brought out a different side. They were only a few years older than Andrea and the three of them had hit it off rather too well. Another four days of this. John would go mad.

A tentative knock at her door. Go away, she thought. The door creaked open.

"Only me," Una said, coming in. "How are you getting on?"

John sighed. "I'm not."

"May I?" Una picked up the letter on the desk. She skimmed the contents. "You should pass ones like this on to me. I shall write back in red capitals, 'KEEP YOUR HANDS OFF MY JOHN.' Honestly, it's not worth you wasting your precious time on this."

"In truth, I've been sitting watching the tall ships on the Rother and the changing light on the marsh. I haven't answered a single letter."

"I'm glad to hear it. Sometimes you need to give your brain a holiday."

"There's so much to do but I can't seem to make myself do it. And now another trial."

"We don't know that for certain yet."

John made a face. "Yes, we do. The man from this American vice society is from the same cloth as Douglas and Jix. If we lose in America, the whole of the English-speaking world will turn its back on me. And what will happen in the European countries where we plan to publish? It could be trial upon trial upon trial until my book is hounded out of existence."

"We will just have to deal with them as they come."

John looked at Una. "Do you ever wish you'd said no? When I came and asked if I could write this book?"

"No." Una shook her head. "No, I don't wish that."

"But?"

"There isn't a but. Not really. I only wish it wasn't so bloody for you. You're worn out." She kissed the top of John's head. "You've made a difference. You know that? A huge difference."

"We lost the fight."

"You lost a court case. That's all. It was rigged against you."

"America will be the same. We'll lose there too."

"America isn't England. And whatever happens, they can't take away from you the fact that it's a great book, a brave book."

"You still think so?"

"Of course I do."

"Even if it's my last." John started to cry.

"It won't be, darling." Una put her arms round John and held her while she sobbed.

"I can't write anymore."

"Of course you can."

"I can't."

"You're just tired, darling." Una stroked John's hair, bringing comfort. "There, there."

The sobbing subsided to a trickle of tears. "What if it's gone for good?" John said, looking up at Una through brimming eyes. "What if I never write again?"

"You will, darling. A good long rest and you'll be writing again. You were born to write."

"Do you think so?" John said, her voice doubtful.

"I know so."

The bells of the church were chiming, calling the congregation to prayer.

"Perhaps you should skip Mass today. Stay home and rest," Una said.

John dried her eyes on her handkerchief. "I can't hide in here saying bah humbug to myself for the rest of the holidays."

"I've never met anyone less like Ebenezer Scrooge than you." Una smiled.

"Thank you for always being on my side."

"I always will be."

Saint Anthony of Padua was only a few hundred yards from their front doorstep. John, Una, and Andrea blessed themselves when they entered. The other three women, not being of the faith, lowered their heads respectfully. They claimed a pew together near the front. The church had been freshly decorated with holly and ivy. A white-and-gold cloth lay across the altar. John closed her eyes, breathing in the calm. Father Bony entered in his purple advent robes, lavishly decorated in gold and black, and the congregation rose for the first hymn.

"He doesn't look very bony to me," Morny whispered to Patience as they sat back down.

Fat he may be, but the priest's luxuriant voice was perfect for the Mass. John let his words wash through her, cleansing and comforting her. When it was time to receive Holy Communion, she made her way slowly up the aisle, hands held together, and kneeled at Father Bony's feet to receive the host.

"Who wants to go to Camber Sands?" John said, as they walked back down Watchbell Street.

Everyone, it turned out. Audrey, Andrea, Patience and Morny climbed into the back of the Daimler, Una into the front. John was getting rid of it in the new year, another economy for the forthcoming legal battles. The drive to the beach took a little over ten minutes. The three younger women set off at a pace, talking and laughing as they scrambled over the dunes and onto the expanse of sand. John followed at a more sedate pace, Una on one arm, Audrey on the other. The sun was shining but the wind off the sea was brisk. She could feel her cheeks rosing. Overhead a gull called, voice raucous. She remembered Forster calling her a seagull a lifetime ago and laughed.

"What?" Audrey said.

"Nothing." John squeezed their arms against her. "Thank you, both of you, for all you've done for me this year."

"You've exposed the nonsense of normality," Audrey said. "The genie's out of the bottle now."

"I could never have got through without you."

"Isn't that what friends are for?" Audrey said.

"Do you think there will be a trial in America?" Una said.

"It looks that way," Audrey said, "though I doubt anything will happen immediately."

"We have to win this time," John said. "We need experts on censorship to represent us in court. I don't want another generalist like Birkett. And we need them to start work now, so we're ready when the attack comes."

"Donald Friede will want to win as much as you do. He's more like Holroyd-Reece than Cape. He'll fight for you. I'll call him this evening."

"Thank you," John said.

They walked on in silence, parallel to the slaty sea, the wind hitting the side of their faces. In the distance John could just about make out the figures of Andrea, Patience and Morny.

"Oh, it's cold." Audrey shivered. "I wish I'd brought a scarf and gloves."

"I think I'm ready to go home," Una said.

"You two go ahead," John said. "I'd like to stay a while longer."

"Are you sure, darling? You don't want to trigger your neuralgia."

"I'll be fine. Honestly."

John watched them walking back towards the dunes. She turned and made her way right to the lip of the sea. The tide was going out. She walked along its wet edge, salty air filling her nostrils, the wind biting at her cheeks. Above her the gulls soared and glided. White froth at her feet, the endless hush wush, hush wush of the sea. Each breaking wave made up of millions and millions and millions of drops of water, all coming together, moving, separating, reuniting. She paused, looking out to sea, feeling its vastness, her insignificance. At last she turned away, heading for home.

CHAPTER FORTY-FOUR

No one tells you that *I love you* is really *Abracadabra* or *Open Sesame* or any of those other magic words. First I said it, and then Seven said it, and it's like a ladder fell down from the sky that's taken us to a whole new level of being with each other. So I suppose it's actually, *I love you* squared that's the serious magic.

I still want a honeymoon, or at least a few nights away together, but that will have to wait for next year. After what happened at the American Women's Club, I'm not risking booking somewhere until I know that Seven will be welcome there. Or at least not actively unwelcome. In the meantime, we've got Dunlace Road to ourselves over Christmas. Tilda and Sibyl have gone to Tilda's family in Bristol. It'll be like having a holiday at home.

I take off my helmet and axe and put them in my locker. Seven's doing the same on one side, Johnston on the other. Clarke's nearly out the door, eager to catch the train home to her family.

"You've a mark on your face." Seven reaches towards me but notices Johnston watching. "There, on your cheek." She leaves me to rub it off myself.

"Happy Christmas!" Clarke says. "See you on Thursday."

"Happy Christmas!"

I go into the WC and wash my hands and face. Seven's gone by the time I come out. Johnston's walking round the apparatus bay, checking everything's in place.

"Do you want a hand?" I ask.

"No, I'm nearly done. You get off." I wonder how she's going to be spending the next two days. I hope she won't be on her own.

"Happy Christmas!" I say.

The light is fading as I leave the fire station. Work finished an hour early today, seeing as it's Christmas Eve. And we got a bonus in our pay packet. I haven't decided what I'm spending mine on yet. Maybe a camera, so I can take pictures of Seven. There's a Brownie for eight and six in a shop on Mare Street.

Seven's waiting for me on White Post Lane. She's in conversation with Wilma and the sight of them puts a smile on my heart. We walk down the street together.

"What are you doing for Christmas?" Seven asks Wilma.

"My brother and his lot are coming over tomorrow, big family do. But I'm taking it easy on the eating 'cos I've been invited for dinner for two tomorrow evening. In Knightsbridge, if you don't mind."

"I take it you've got a new lady friend," Seven says.

"Indeed I have. Met her at Gunter's weekend before last. Lovely, she is. An heiress."

"Another one?" I hope she's got better morals than Scarlett. Wilma gave her the elbow after she tried to make out that the trouble at the American Women's Club was all Wilma's fault for being stupid enough to bring a black woman there in the first place. Quite the row, by all accounts, conducted at full volume in reception.

"You'll like this one. She's funny. And smart. Tabitha De Vere. Doesn't that sound classy? You want to see the place she has—billiard room, wine cellar, big windows everywhere. She's picking me up at five o'clock tomorrow in her chauffeur driven Rolls-Royce, no less. I'll be sipping champagne cocktails by six."

"You're a lothario, do you know that?" Seven says. "A lesbian lothario."

"I prefer Valentino. Or should that be Valentina? Either way, I don't take advantage of no one. Can I help it if the ladies find me irresistible?"

We pause on the corner of Cassland Road.

"I hear you've got this one as a house guest for Christmas," Wilma says.

"I have. And we're going to Mama Afrika's for a party tomorrow." I've never been anywhere but church on a Christmas Day. A party sounds a lot more fun.

"Seems like you two will be enjoying yourselves as well," Wilma says. "Well don't do anything I wouldn't do."

"There's nothing you wouldn't do," Seven says, laughing, and Wilma laughs too.

"Happy Christmas!"

"Happy Christmas!"

Wilma heads off home and Seven and I carry on towards Clapton. Men are hanging around outside the pubs, waiting for them to open at half past five. I keep my eyes out for anyone that might mean us harm. Not that we couldn't give most men a run for their money but I'd rather not have to tonight. Usually Seven's the focus of insults but they come my way too with all the fuss in the papers about *The Well*, and with me having a look of Radclyffe Hall, if she was twenty-five years younger. I knew she'd lose the appeal. I sent her a Christmas card wishing her all the best in America. She deserves a bit of luck.

"Do you fancy fish and chips?" Seven says, as we pass the chippie on Chatsworth Road. "My treat."

It isn't meat and Sibyl isn't home. We eat it from the wrappers with our fingers on the front room sofa, still in our coats while we wait for the fire to take a hold.

"I can't believe you're here," I say to Seven. "And that we've got three whole nights and two whole days together."

She grins. "It's good, isn't it?"

We burn the chip papers in the fire. The flames are getting a hold now, warming the room and we're able to take off our coats. The Christmas tree takes up half the window and I can only pull the curtains part way. It's cosy all the same.

"Do you want a cup of tea?" I say and she does, so away I go into the kitchen where I find a note on the table from Sibyl.

> *Dear Maggie and Seven,*
> *I made almond biscuits and mince pies this morning. They're in the larder. Help yourselves.*
> *Tilda's wangled a couple of extra days off work. We'll not be back until Sunday evening.*
> *Happy Christmas!*
> *Love Sibyl*

I forget about putting on the kettle and dash back to the front room to tell Seven and she's as excited as me about the extra days and nights and we hold hands and jump up and down like two children, beaming at each other till our faces are nearly aching.

"Time for music?" Seven says.

On goes the first record, "Creole Love Call," chosen by Seven for me, and then I put on Ma Rainey's "Deep Moaning Blues" for her. All our favourites follow, one after the other after the other, and we dance and sing and laugh until we're tired. We sit on the sofa, watching the flames until they die.

It's time for bed. Up we go to my room. Seven brought a bag of her things round yesterday and her pyjamas are already waiting for her under the pillow. I let her have the bathroom first and then it's my turn. When I get back with teeth brushed and hands washed, she's sitting up in bed, a small parcel in her lap. It's wrapped in brown paper and tied with a red ribbon.

"Happy Christmas." She holds it towards me.

I'm shy at the sight of it, unaccustomed as I am to receiving gifts.

"Aren't you going to open it?"

"It's not Christmas yet," I say.

"Close enough. Go on, open it."

I get into bed and pick up the parcel and carefully untie the ribbon to reveal a small leather box. I open it up. Inside is a silver garnet ring. My eyes mist.

"It's a pinkie ring. I know you've been wanting one," Seven says.

The least encouragement would have me crying. It is the most wonderful thing I've been given in my entire life. "You shouldn't have," I say, because I feel guilty at her spending her hard-earned money on me. What I should be saying is thank you, thank you, thank you.

"I know it's not gold—"

"I prefer silver."

"And your birthstone's ruby not garnet..."

"It's beautiful."

"Really. Do you like it? Try it on."

I slip it onto the little finger of my left hand. It fits perfectly.

"It suits you."

"I love it." I hold the ring to my lips and kiss it.

"So long as you like it." Her smile's bashful, but I know she's pleased with herself. So she should be. A lesbian pinkie ring from my own sweet love.

Now it's my turn. I get out of bed and put my hand to the back corner of my wardrobe. The shoe box is wrapped in red tissue paper and tied up with silver ribbon. "This is for you." My heart is pounding loud as thunder as I hand it over. What if she doesn't like it?

She turns the parcel over in her hands and then lifts it to her ear and shakes it. It makes a dull thudding sound. "What can it be?"

I smile but don't give anything away. I stand watching her but then she says, "Get back in bed before you freeze your arse off," so I do.

I've made the knot too tight on the ribbon. It takes her a minute to get it loose and then she's unwrapping layer upon layer of tissue paper till finally the last sheet falls away.

"It's not shoes," I say, thinking maybe she'd rather have had a new pair than what I've got her and wanting the disappointment over quickly. "The box is just for protection."

Seven takes off the lid. She stares at the carving inside. The figure's naked torso is smooth polished wood, her fish tail is carved red-brown scales. In her right hand she holds the tail of a snake. It writhes across her shoulders, its head emerging between her breasts. Her left hand holds a tiny mirror. There's a dangerous smile on her face.

"It's a mermaid." She picks it up, studying it closely.

"A water spirit, the man said. From Nigeria. Mami Wata."

"Where did you find her?"

I can't tell yet whether she likes it or not. "Cable Street. I thought maybe I'd find someone selling animal carvings and I nearly bought a lioness but then the man brought this out and…"

"I can't believe you got me this. An African mermaid."

"I didn't show it to Sibyl. Nobody's seen it but me and the man selling it."

She puts the carving down and pulls me close. I can feel her crying and I cry too. We hold each other till the tears subside.

"I don't know where that came from." She wipes her nose on the back of her hand which I would find disgusting in anyone else but in her it's endearing. I hop out of bed again and fetch her a hankie.

"Look at the state you have me in, Maggie Dillon. I'm not used to presents. And this one…Do you believe in coincidence? Or something that's more even than coincidence?"

I think about how I ended up here with Sibyl and Tilda, who were the perfect people for me to come and live with, and how I found Seven and Wilma at Achille Serre. I feel like I belong to these women. I find myself nodding. "Yes, I think I do."

"It just so happens that I have another present for you. It's not wrapped up, unless you count me as the wrapping." I think she's going to kiss me, but instead she says, "Get yourself comfortable."

I snuggle down in the bed next to her, wondering what's coming.

"Ready? Then I'll begin. Once upon a time, many years ago there lived a pirate queen by the name of Captain Septima. She sailed the oceans on the crest of a wave, stealing from the rich and giving to the people. She was legend made flesh.

"Septima's ship was called the Mermaid's Purse and no finer ship ever sailed the seas. One day a great storm blew up. The wind was stronger than a thousand demons, the waves bigger than the tallest mountains. The ship bucked and dived and Septima was lost to the sea.

"Hours passed. The sea calmed. Septima woke to find herself on a sandy beach. A sleeping mermaid lay next to her. The mermaid's skin was soft and pale, her hair was a dark auburn, her tail a shimmer of abalone. Her eyes, when she opened them, were as blue as the sky above them. She smiled at Septima.

"'Did you save me?' Septima said.

"'I did.' The words sounded like the rush of a wave but Septima understood them.

"'How can I repay you?'

"The mermaid leaned over and kissed Septima on the lips. She smelt of the ocean, a woman's smell. The missing hours hurtled back to Septima. Her body burned with hope and fear. The mermaid turned away.

"'Don't go,' Septima said.

"'I must. But I will return, and when I do you will have a decision to make.'

"For three weeks Septima lived alone on the island, growing fat on fish and fruit. One morning, while she sat thinking of her lost mermaid love, a gush of wetness soaked Septima's strong brown thighs. A great ache spread from below her belly button, tightening and tightening, radiating out and down until with one astounding push she birthed a mermaid's tail, the colour of dark rum spotted with pale gold.

"From the sea she heard the voice of her mermaid lover. 'My name is Pearl. You—'"

I lean up on my elbow, looking at Seven. "Pearl? Like Princess Pearl, the mermaid in my Granny Palmer's stories?"

And she half shrugs and smiles and I settle down next to her, my hand on her belly, my head on her chest.

Seven carries on with her story. "'You can be a mermaid, if you want, and swim the oceans with me,' Pearl said.

"Septima hesitated. All her life, she'd been a human.

"'If you don't like it, you wouldn't have to stay. All you'd need to do is come to the shore, and turn round three times, and you'd have a human body again.'

"So Septima pulled the tail over her legs and immediately became a mermaid. She wriggled down the beach and into the sea where Pearl was waiting. The sun shone and sparkled on the water and when they kissed, Septima's whole body was filled with a joy greater than any woman had ever felt. The loneliness that had followed her all her life was banished from her heart.

"For a year and a day Pearl and Septima swam the oceans of the world, singing with whales, and playing with dolphins, and racing against seals. But then a restlessness grew inside Septima, a restlessness for the land that she'd sometimes felt when she was a pirate queen.

"'You can become human again,' Pearl said. 'You can get your legs back anytime you want.'

"'What's the point of having legs if I don't have you?'

"'If you really need the land, dearest love, then some of the time I'll have to have legs too.'

"So they swam to the island where Septima had built a home in her pirate-queen days, and she turned round three times and suddenly she felt the sand beneath her feet. Her tail floated to the surface of the water and she lifted it in her arms. And then Pearl turned round three times and a moment later she too had legs. They carried their tails up to Septima's house, which stood on a headland overlooking the sea. And when they arrived, Pearl chose one of Septima's pirate treasure chests, which was lined with ruby velvet, and placed her tail inside it. Septima chose a different treasure chest, lined with blue silk, and placed her tail inside it. Each chest had a lock and a key. Septima kept the shiny silver key that unlocked her chest, and Pearl kept the cast iron key that unlocked hers, because neither of them wanted to own the other.

"And whenever they wanted they could return to the sea and they often did. And whether they were on the land or on the sea, their lives were full of love and they lived happily ever after."

I hear the beating of Seven's heart and the echo of her voice and I think, maybe we can live happily ever after too.

Author's note

This novel is fiction grounded in historical fact. In 1926, Radclyffe Hall won the two most celebrated literary prizes of her day—the Prix Femina and the James Tait Black Memorial Prize—for her fourth novel, *Adam's Breed*. She felt she was well enough established to write a novel aimed at breaking the public silence on lesbianism. Within four weeks of its publication, under pressure from the right-wing press and the Home Secretary, her publishers had withdrawn *The Well of Loneliness* from sale. Three months later it was banned. Lesbianism itself had been put on trial and judged to be obscene.

This was one of the starting points for *As a Lover*. The other was a series of photographs of the Achille Serre Ladies Fire Brigade that I came across on social media (included among vintage photos of women firefighters at https://www.vintag.es/2015/04/23-stunning-vintage-photographs-of.html#google_vignette). I was intrigued by an image of four young women sitting on a motorcycle sidecar firefighting appliance. Three of them look at the camera. The fourth one gazes instead at the woman sitting in front of her, an affectionate smile warming her face.

The photo delighted me. Not just women firefighters, but possibly lesbian firefighters from the late 1920s when *The Well of Loneliness* was banned in Britain. I wondered who these women were and what impact the furore surrounding the novel had on them.

If I were a historian, I'd have very little to tell you. We know nothing about the identities of the Achille Serre firefighters. They're not named in the photographs or in the Achille Serre archives. Their lives are not part of the public record. I can't tell you who the real women were, but I can imagine Maggie Dillon and tell you her story. Historical fiction allows us to fill history's gaps and silences to reclaim a lesbian past.

Unlike the Achille Serre women, Radclyffe Hall's life is part of the public record. She is the subject of several biographies. Her books are still available. Her literary achievements, as well as the controversy surrounding the publication of *The Well of Loneliness*, are reported in newspapers of the day. Documents relating to the court case are available in the UK National Archives. The Harry Ransom Center in Austin, Texas holds many of her personal papers. The diaries of her lover, Una Troubridge, can be accessed at the National Archives of Canada.

My fictional depiction was informed by these and other sources but has gone beyond them to imagine what it might have been like to be at the centre of a very public controversy about lesbianism and censorship.

Through John and Maggie, *As a Lover* brings to life the lesbian past. But my novel is also about the present. Misogyny, racism, male violence, homophobia and restrictive gendered expectations still damage women's lives. Differences in class, wealth and race still impact on the opportunities and living conditions of diverse groups of women who love women. And a new era of censorship is well underway, with speech and literature about and by lesbians particularly under attack.

In the face of present-day oppression and repression we can look to the past for inspiration. Radclyffe Hall defeated the censors in America. *The Well of Loneliness* was one of the best-selling lesbian books of the twentieth century. The fight is not yet won. Our struggle for liberation continues.

Bringing the Past to Life

In writing this novel, I have tried as far as possible to stick to the facts about the publication and subsequent censorship of *The Well of Loneliness*. The majority of events took place on the dates stated. All of the newspaper reviews and articles mentioned or quoted are real and can be accessed at the British Newspaper Library. The words spoken by the lawyers, witnesses and magistrates at the obscenity trial and subsequent appeal adhere closely to public records: newspaper accounts, a note on James Melville's defence (the Lovat Dickson bequest at the National Archives of Canada), Sir Chartres Biron's judgment (UK National Archives), and Sir Robert Wallace's judgment (newspaper accounts). Likewise, Blanche Knopf's letter to John informing her that Knopf had decided not to publish is close to the original (the Lovat Dickson bequest at the National Archives of Canada).

John's speech at the Holland Street party on the day *The Well of Loneliness* is released is informed by her letter of April 1928 to Newman Flower explaining why she had written the novel. The conversation between John and Una regarding John's decision to write a novel about "sexual inversion" is informed by an account in Una Troubridge's hagiography of John, *The Life And Death Of Radclyffe Hall* (Hammond Hammond, 1961). Cape's letter to the Home Secretary is informed by his letter to the *Daily Express* about James Douglas's attacks on *The Well of Loneliness*, published on 20 August 1928. The petition that E. M. Forster presents to John is informed by the letter that he and Virginia Woolf wrote to the editor of *The Nation and Athenaeum* (published on 8 September 1928). Tallulah Bankhead's reference to her father's warning about men and alcohol draws from a quote attributed to her. The statement John prepares in advance of the obscenity trial is informed by her 1934 account, "Why Did I Write *The Well of Loneliness*," available in *American Queer*, ed by David Shneer and Caryn Aviv (Paradigm Publishers, 2006). The statement she rehearses during the appeal hearing is based on newspaper accounts published following the hearing.

Diana Souhami's *The Trials of Radclyffe Hall* (Weidenfeld & Nicholson, 1998) includes a quote from John's mother, Marie Visetti, when the controversy about *The Well of Loneliness* erupted: "You can't touch filth without getting filthy." I used these words for the telegram that triggers John's confrontation with her mother about her stepfather.

Historical figures

The following real people appear in *As a Lover*. Birth and death years included where known.

Tallulah Bankhead (1902–1968). American actress living in London from 1923 to 1931. Had relationships with both men and women. Personal friend of Radclyffe Hall.

Rachel Barrett (1874–1953). Former militant suffragette. Met the author Ida Wylie in 1913 while out of prison on licence having been convicted of conspiracy to commit arson. Their relationship lasted until the late 1920s.

Mabel (Ladye) Batten (1856–1916). Accomplished singer and pianist. She'd been married to George Batten for more than thirty years when she met Radclyffe Hall in 1907. Gave her the name John. Introduced her to Catholicism. After Ladye's husband died in 1910, she and John lived together. Their final year together was fraught after John began an affair with Ladye's cousin, Una Troubridge. Died of a stroke in 1916.

Arnold Bennett (1867–1941). Author, journalist and influential reviewer for the *Evening Standard*.

Norman Birkett (1883–1962). Methodist, former Liberal MP (1923–24). Rose to legal prominence in 1925 and much in demand. Represented Jonathan Cape at *The Well of Loneliness* obscenity trial in November 1928.

Sir Chartres Biron (1863–1940). Barrister who became Chief Magistrate of the Metropolitan Police Courts in 1920. Presided over *The Well of Loneliness* obscenity trial.

Sir Archibald Bodkin (1862–1957). Barrister who was appointed Director of Public Prosecution in 1920. Responsible for banning James Joyce's *Ulysses* in 1922. Refused to release copies of *The Well of Loneliness* to the magistrates hearing the appeal against it being banned.

Father Bonaventure Priest at Saint Anthony of Padua Roman Catholic Church on Watchbell Street, Rye.

Dorothy (Budge) Burroughes (1883–1963). Successful artist, illustrator and children's author. Met her partner, Vere Hutchinson, in the militant suffragette movement. Became friends with John and Una in 1922.

Jonathan Cape (1879–1960). Established the Jonathan Cape Ltd. publishing house in 1921. Published *The Well of Loneliness* in July 1928.

Noël Coward (1899–1973). Celebrated playwright, actor, composer and performer. Close friend of John's who inspired the character Jonathan Brockett in *The Well of Loneliness*. John and Una's interest in spiritualism is believed to have inspired, in part, Coward's 1941 play, *Blithe Spirit*.

Granny (Sarah) Diehl (?–1910). Radclyffe Hall's American maternal grandmother who she visited in Philadelphia as a young child. Moved to England during Radclyffe Hall's childhood and lived with the Visettis. After Radclyffe Hall left the Visetti household on coming of age, Granny Diehl lived with her.

James Douglas (1867–1940). Right-wing journalist and exponent of "Muscular Christianity." Editor of the *Daily Express* and *Sunday Express*. Called for *The Well of Loneliness* to be banned in August 1928.

Beresford Egan (1905–1984). Artist, illustrator and author. Illustrated *The Sink of Solitude*, a satire on the censorship of *The Well of Loneliness* that greatly upset Radclyffe Hall.

Anne Elsner Travel writer. Invited John and Una to stay in Rye in August 1928 and subsequently allowed them to take over her rented cottage as a refuge.

Sir Francis Floud (1875–1965). British civil servant. Chairman of the Board of Customs and Excise from 1927 to 1930.

E. M. (Edward Morgan) Forster (1879–1970). Celebrated novelist. *Maurice*, his novel of gay love, was completed in 1914 but not published until a year after his death. Friend of Leonard and Virginia Woolf. Outspoken about the threat to literature posed by censorship.

John Galsworthy (1867–1933). Novelist and playwright best known for *The Forsyte Saga*. Played a key role in establishing the PEN (Poets, Essayists, Novelists) Club in 1921 and was its first president.

John Radclyffe Hall (1880–1943). Born in Bournemouth. Traumatic childhood: abandoned by her father, physically and emotionally abused by her mother, sexually abused by her stepfather. Began her writing career as a poet, publishing under her birth name Marguerite Radclyffe Hall, before turning to fiction with the encouragement of her lover, Ladye (Mabel Batten). Her fifth novel, *The Well of Loneliness*, is widely regarded as the first overtly lesbian novel written in English. She published two further novels and a collection of short stories. Died in 1943 from cancer. Buried in Highgate cemetery with Mabel Batten.

Audrey Heath (1888–1957). Radclyffe Hall's literary agent. Cambridge graduate. Established the agency, A.M. Heath Ltd., with her friend and colleague, Alice May Foreman, in 1920.

Leopold B. Hill Publisher and bookseller. Appointed as distributor for the Pegasus Press edition of *The Well of Loneliness*.

John Holroyd-Reece (1897–1967). Translator and publisher. Established Pegasus Press in Paris in the 1920s. Republished *The Well of Loneliness* in September 1928 after it was withdrawn from sale by Jonathan Cape Ltd. the previous month.

Vere Hutchinson (1891–1932). Writer and former militant suffragette. Lived with her partner, Dorothy (Budge) Burroughes, for nineteen years. Budge cared for her after she became ill in 1924. Paralysed for the latter part of her life. She continued writing up until her death.

Sir Thomas Inskip (1876–1947). Conservative politician. Appointed attorney general in 1928. Led the prosecution case after Jonathan Cape Ltd. and Pegasus Press appealed against the ban on *The Well of Loneliness*.

Norah (Jimmy) James (1896–1979). Publicity manager for Jonathan Cape Ltd. Her first novel, *Sleeveless Errand*, was banned for obscenity in 1929.

Sir William (Jix) Joynson-Hicks (1865–1932). Conservative politician. Appointed Home Secretary in 1924. Threatened to prosecute Jonathan Cape Ltd. unless *The Well on Loneliness* was withdrawn. Ensured the Pegasus edition was seized leading to the obscenity trial.

Blanche Knopf (1894–1966). Co-founded American publisher Alfred A. Knopf Inc. with her husband. Reneged on a deal to publish *The Well of Loneliness* in America.

Gladys Leonard (1882–1968). Well-known English psychic who claimed to navigate the spiritual world through Feda, an Indian ancestor. Radclyffe Hall consulted her following Mabel Batten's death and attended sessions with her for many years.

Toupie Lowther (1874–1944). Close friend of Radclyffe Hall. Former tennis and fencing champion. Established the Hackett-Lowther Ambulance Unit with Norah Desmond Hackett, an all-female unit which operated close to the front line in France in World War I.

James Melville (1885–1931). Eminent barrister who represented Leopold Hill at *The Well of Loneliness* obscenity trial. Elected as a Labour Member of Parliament in 1929 and was appointed solicitor general.

Patience Ross (1906–?). Poet and literary agent at A.M. Heath Ltd.

Harold Rubenstein (1891–1975). Solicitor and playwright. Acted on behalf of Pegasus, Leopold Hill and Jonathan Cape Ltd. from the time that the consignment of the Pegasus edition of *The Well of Loneliness* was seized by Customs and Excise and throughout the obscenity trial.

Andrea Troubridge (1910–1966). Una's daughter. Attended Oxford University. Worked in the entertainment industry.

Una (Squiggie) Vincenzo, Lady Troubridge (1887–1963). Translator and sculptor. Married Ernest Troubridge, 25 years her senior, in 1907. Contracted syphilis from him. Left Troubridge for John during World War I. Dedicated to John and her career. Survived John by twenty years. She was buried in Italy as her wish to be buried with John in Highgate Cemetery was not known.

Alberto Visetti (1846–1928). Radclyffe Hall's mercurial and abusive stepfather. A well-known music teacher at the Royal College of Music. Died 10 July 1928. Buried 13 July 1928, two weeks before the publication of *The Well of Loneliness*.

Marie Visetti (1854(?)–1945). Radclyffe Hall's mother. Born Mary Jane Diehl in Philadelphia. Married at 17, widowed by 23. Married again to Radclyffe Radclyffe-Hall (known as "Rat," Radclyffe Hall's father) and had two daughters. The elder died when Radclyffe Hall was a few months old. Divorced Rat, citing his cruelty and violence. Married Alberto Visetti when John was nine years old.

Sir Robert Wallace (1850(?)–1939). Barrister who was Chair of the London Sessions courts from 1907 to 1931. Presided over the appeal against the banning of *The Well of Loneliness* in December 1928.

Leonard Woolf (1880–1969). British political theorist and author. Co-founder of Hogarth Press with his wife, Virginia. Concerned about the impact of the censorship of *The Well of Loneliness* on literature. Along with Virginia, stood surety in the appeal against the banning of *The Well of Loneliness*.

Virginia Woolf (1882–1941). Celebrated modernist author. Her relationship with Vita Sackville-West inspired her to write *Orlando*, published in October 1928. Her lectures at the University of Cambridge, which formed the basis of her nonfiction book, *A Room of One's Own*, took place during the furore surrounding *The Well of Loneliness*. Despite disliking the novel, she agreed to appear as a witness at the obscenity trial.

Ida (I.A.R.) (Uncle) Wylie (1885–1949). Successful writer. Suffragette. Met Rachel Barrett at "Mouse Castle," a suffragette safe house. They were lovers until the late 1920s. Reviewed *The Well of Loneliness* for *The Sunday Times*. Supported John and Una during the attacks on the novel. Her memoir, *My Life with George: An Unconventional Autobiography* (Random House, 1940), discusses her involvement in the suffragette movement.

Places and Organisations

The following real places and organisations appear in *As a Lover*.

Achille Serre Factory – the Achille Serre dry cleaning company was established in Dalston in the 1870s by a French couple, Achille and Eugenie Serre. By the 1920s it had four factories in the Hackney Wick area. The company subsequently relocated to one site in Walthamstow. It had both a women's and a men's fire brigade. The company ran a scheme enabling donations to Barnardo's to be directly deducted from employees' wages.

American Women's Club – a private club in a mansion in Grosvenor Street.

The Cave of Harmony – a cabaret and jazz club in the Seven Dials area of Covent Garden, frequented by writers, artists and actors.

Gunter's – a fashionable eatery in Berkeley Square. Barbara Bell describes it as a venue for the beginning of lesbian encounters in her memoir, *Just Take Your Frock Off: A Lesbian Life* (Ourstory Books, 1999).

37 Holland Street, Kensington, W.8 – Radclyffe Hall and Una Troubridge moved there in 1924. In 1992, English Heritage erected a blue plaque at the house to commemorate Radclyffe Hall.

Journey's End, Hucksteps Row, Rye – Anne Elsner's rented Tudor cottage. Radclyffe Hall took over the lease in October 1928 and lived between there and Holland Street until the latter was sold. She subsequently bought a house on the High Street in Rye, which also bears a blue plaque, before eventually purchasing Journey's End as a gift for Una.

Le Monocle – legendary Parisienne lesbian bar, located on Boulevard Edgar-Quinet.

Mermaid Inn – a Grade II listed inn on Mermaid Street, Rye, which Radclyffe Hall and Una Troubridge stayed in on several occasions and where they dined frequently after their move to Rye.

PEN (Poets, Essayists and Novelists) Club – the writers' organisation founded in 1921, with John Galsworthy as its first president. It held regular dinners for members. Radclyffe Hall joined in 1922. Now known as PEN International.

Glossary

The following Irish idioms are used in the novel:

Broonies – household spirits that perform chores at night.
Dander – stroll or wander.
Elf-stones – unusual stones used by fairies.
From I was no age – since I was a young child.
Raired – an equivalent to the English term "reared," meaning to raise a child to maturity.
Taking the hand – mocking or making a joke about someone.
Wee-folk – leprechauns.
Your man – that man.

Abbreviations

B-Specials – unpaid, armed, reserve police force, established during the Irish War of Independence to support the creation of Northern Ireland. Notoriously sectarian.

UVF – Ulster Volunteer Force. A unionist paramilitary organisation that opposed Home Rule in Ireland. Formed in 1913 from the Ulster Volunteers which had been established the previous year.

Bella Books
Happy Endings Live Here
P.O. Box 10543
Tallahassee, FL 32302
Phone: (800) 729-4992
BellaBooks.com

More Titles from Bella Books

Jones – Gerri Hill
978-1-64247-598-2 | 260 pages | Mystery
One weekend getaway, six friends, and a deadly secret that will wash away everything they thought they knew.

Merry Weihnachten – E. J. Noyes
978-1-64247-610-1 | 292 pages | Romance
Christmas traditions aren't the only things getting mixed up when these two hearts collide beneath the mistletoe.

Sweet Home Alabarden Park – TJ O'Shea
978-1-64247-570-8 | 362 pages | Romance
She came to restore a royal estate—she never expected to rebuild her heart.

Dr. Margaret Morgan – Christy Hadfield
978-1-64247-628-6 | 286 pages | Romance
Facing the professor on campus everyone hates is terrifying—but falling for her might be even worse.

Overtime – Tracey Richardson
978-1-64247-630-9 | 278 pages | Romance
A charming romance about second chances, found family, and scoring the goal that matters most.

The Big Guilt – Renée J. Lukas
978-1-64247-657-6 | 206 pages | Romance
What if the one who got away became the one you can't have?